THE
PURPLE
SCAR
ARCHIVES

THE THRILLING LIBRARY:

The Best of Thrilling Adventures

The Black Bat Archives, Volume 1

The Black Bat Archives, Volume 2

The Black Bat Archives, Volume 3

The Black Bat Archives, Volume 4

The Black Bat Archives, Volume 5

The Black Bat Archives, Volume 6

The Crimson Mask Archives, Volume 1

The Crimson Mask Archives, Volume 2

Diamondstone Archives

Dr. Zeng Archives

The Eagle Archives

George Chance—The Ghost Archives, Volume 1

The Masked Detective Archives, Volume 1

The Purple Scar Archives

THE PURPLE SCAR ARCHIVES

BY

JOHN S. ENDICOTT

INTRODUCTION BY

WILL MURRAY

THRILLING PUBLICATIONS

2017

TABLE OF

CONTENTS

INTRODUCTION i

I   MEDALS OF MURDER. I

II   THE NIGHT OF MURDER 83

III   MURDER IN GOLD 147

IV   THE CHAIN OF MURDERS 217

WILL MURRAY

N O MORE obscure pulp crimebuster ever existed than John S. Endicott's Purple Scar, the star of *Exciting Detective* in 1941–43.

Patterned after Thrilling Group's other super-detectives, The Phantom, The Black Bat, and the Crimson Mask, he was part of that wave of pulp heroes that flooded newsstands after the Black Bat took *Black Book Detective* by storm. And like the Black Bat, his roots can be found in a previous story published by the Thrilling Group.

"The Sign of the Scar" was the lead novel in *The Phantom Detective*, September, 1936. The villain, an extortionist calling himself the Scar, wore a false head—a rubbery gray thing of featureless scar tissue-that made him look like a walking corpse. Crimson contact lenses gave him eyes like burning coals. He spoke in a cadaver's sepulcheral voice.

But the Purple Scar probably owed as much to the Norman Daniels' Black Bat. When D.A. Tony Quinn is blinded by acid, he loses his sight and decides to fight crime as the Black Bat, wearing a black hood over his head to hide the acid scars around his eyes. He takes on two assistants, a former confidence man named Kirby "Silk" Norton and a girl, Carol Baldwin.

For the Purple Scar series, this formula is repeated. The hero dons a scarred mask to conceal his true identity, while his main male assistant is a former pickpocket. That old standby, a mastery of disguise, is lifted from the pages of *The Phantom Detective*, but of course it goes back to Nick Carter.

One twist is that the nominal police presence is not antagonistic to the hero's alter ego, but is a silent but staunch supporter.

As with Thrilling's other hero series, they were solid plot-driven formula pulp stories.

"They were completely interchangeable," editor Mort Weisinger recalled. "It's like saying, do you want ham or bacon and eggs? One day

I'm on Black Bat and the other I'm on Phantoms. Many of them were rewritten in the office by myself and some of the other editors to get them in shape. But they were damn good plots."

The prolific ghostwriter of both series. Norman A. Daniels, assessed them this way: "They were kid stuff—just an offshoot of the old magazines they used to read behind the corncrib. Those things were just unsophisticated. They had a place, that's all."

The nominal author, John S. Endicott, was a Thrilling house name, most often employed to conceal the in-house writers of the filler short-short stories written around the covers. Originally, it was J.S. Endicott. For the Purple Scar series, the non-existent writer was granted a first name. During Puritan days, John Endicott was the zealot who tore down the maypole at Merrymount, Massachusetts.

Who this particular John S. Endicott was remains a mystery.

It's easier to say who didn't write the Purple Scar than did. It wasn't either Norman A. Daniels or G.T. Fleming-Roberts, who kept complete records of their pulp sales. Stylistically, it's not Laurence Donovan. He was too busy with the Phantom at that time.

Ray Cummings, Joe Archibald, maybe one of the new generation of writers like Don Tracy or Samuel Merwin Jr. are likely suspects.

Anatole France Feldman can be considered a strong suspect. Also known as Tony Field, Feldman broke into the gangster pulps in 1929, made a big splash with his Chicago hoodlum-hero "Big Nose" Serrano, then moved over to the Thrilling Group after Repeal killed the romantic myth of the Prohibition gangster.

He started ghosting episodes of The Phantom Detective early in that series' long run, some in collaboration with series originator D.L. Champion. Over the years, he scripted *Crime Photographer* on radio, edited a slew of crime and confession magazines, and briefly edited comic books around 1940.

But my money's on George A. McDonald, another veteran of the *Phantom Detective* series, who apparently wrote "The Sign of the Scar." A newspaperman and U.S. Army veteran McDonald was one of Thrilling's most prolific scribes. He began ghosting *The Phantom Detective* in 1934, and between 1935–38, he was the writer behind the Lynn Vickers novels in Dell's *Public Enemy* and *Federal Agent*, where his byline was Bryan James Kelly. Under his own name, he wrote the "Killer Czar" stories for Thrilling's *Popular Detective*.

In his regular life, McDonald broke into that field writing for the *Lynn Daily Item* in Massachusetts. Like Feldman, his first significant pulp sale was to *Underworld*. In 1934, he joined the staff of the *New*

York Sun, later becoming railroad and public utilities editor. At the time of his death in 1962, McDonald was working as a financial writer for the *New York World-Telegram,* which he joined in 1957. He served his army hitch on the Mexican border during the period when Uncle Sam was chasing Pancho Villa, and then went over to France to fight in the First World War.

The chief problem with identifying Thrilling's house-name authors was the huge amount of rewriting done by editors and other writers. "The Sign of the Scar" for example, shows signs of both Feldman and McDonald's stylistics. It would not surprise me if the Purple Scar was some sort of collaboration. In fact, whoever wrote the first two may not be the same scribe who finished out the series. This was a period when the pulp magazine field was fast losing writers to the draft, or enlistment after the attack at Pearl Harbor.

Here and there, this unknown called his weird hero The Purple Mask. A slip of the typewriter? Or was this an editorial lapse? It's conceivable that the Scar originally was known as The Purple Mask and the Thrilling editors changed him to the Scar, sometimes missing a stray noun. For this edition, we've corrected those mistakes.

The first cover was the work of Newton H. "Newt" Alfred. Primarily known as an interior artist, Alfred was simultaneously illustrating the interior pages to Street and Smith's *The Whisperer* in 1940-42.

The Purple Scar ran in three consecutive issues of *Exciting Detective,* then skipped three. Plans to have him become the lead feature a la the Black Bat in *Black Book Detective* evidently hit some sort of snag. His fourth adventure was his final one.

After the Scar was phased out of *Exciting Detective* in favor of Laurence Donovan's "Wildcat" Martin, McDonald shifted over to *Private Detective.* His Cupid "Killer" Cain stories appeared in 1943-44. Cain was noteworthy as the first pulp detective to pack a .357 Magnum revolver.

The Purple Scar was just gearing up when Pearl Harbor happened. Between enlistments and the draft, the pulp magazine field began losing writers, artists and editors. Writers were in great demand, and therefore consequently in short supply around a middling pulp house like the Thrilling chain. It may be that the loss of a steady ghostwriter more than any other factor led to the abandonment of the series. The Purple Scar might have been a paper casualty of World War II.

For a series that has passed under the radar of most pulp magazine collectors, the Purple Scar is an unsuspected treasure.

The stories come from that pulp period when the "bang-bang" style of writing—action-for-action's sake—was being phased out in favor of character-driven stories. You can see it in the grisly motivation of Dr. Miles Murdock as fate forces him into a frightening new role.

So here they are—the full quartet all in one volume. Turn the page and learn the fatal secret of the unforgettable Purple Scar.

I

MEDALS OF
MURDER

CHAPTER I

MAN IN
THE MORGUE

JOHN MURDOCK walked slowly in the darkness of midnight. His lips were clamped tightly on his cigarette. Abstractedly his eyes stared straight ahead.

The streets, so busy and crowded during the day, were now deserted. The tall office buildings stared across at each other like black, silent sentinels in the bleak gloom.

John Murdock did not see the limousine that came out of the alley not half a block behind him, a deadly spider crawling from its lair. If he had seen it, his hands would not have remained so deep and snug in his coat pockets. They would have flashed for the Police Positive holstered beneath his left armpit.

John Murdock had been wearing the blue too many years not to recognize rats and the way they acted when ready to strike, but he was engrossed in his own thoughts.

He was on his way to perform a disagreeable duty. He had to arrest someone tonight for murder, the climax to a case on which he and the entire Department had worked diligently for months. It was his good fortune to have tracked down the evidence he needed to convict this killer. It might mean a promotion, yet John Murdock did not like the task.

Rolling slowly, silently, keeping close to the curb, the car crept nearer. The man on the sidewalk didn't even suspect he was being followed. And then, without warning, an automatic that poked through the window belched flame, lead, sudden death.

Six shots, sharp, staccato, rattled through the inky hollowness between the tall buildings. The sound bounced back and forth across the deep, dark chasm, magnified and distorted.

The six slugs found their mark in John Murdock's spine. With a groan he fell against the brick wall of the building and collapsed to the ground with a sickening *thud*. He was dead before his head touched the sidewalk.

ONE OF the killers leaped out of the car. He was a big, burly fellow with gorilla-like arms. He swept up the dead body of the detective like a sack of flour and dumped it into the back seat of the automobile, then piled in beside it.

The car streaked away with a nerve-shattering grind of gears. At the corner it turned right, at the next corner left, right again. Then it headed straight for the river.

It was a gloomy spot where they halted and snapped out the lights. Few people ventured this particular section at night. To one side rose a row of low-built, dilapidated warehouses. The other side, black and silent, vanished into the river. The only sound was the occasional *toot* of a tugboat groping through the night, the hushed *lap-lap* of the waves washing against the side of the bulwark.

The burly hood hopped out of the limousine and peered cautiously up and down the street. His short and ugly companion slid out the far side and came around.

"This sure is a creepy spot," the second said uneasily, twisting his narrow, haunched shoulders under his topcoat.

"Then stop gassin'," Burly Guy rumbled. "Gimme a hand with this stiff and we'll beat it out of here."

They reached inside the car, dragged the body of the man they had just murdered to the water's edge and proceeded to strip off his clothing. They took every stitch off him, even down to his socks and shorts. He had a signet ring on his right pinky, a green gold band with an Old English "J" set in black onyx. They slid that off, too.

Then Short-and-Ugly took a small bottle out of his inside pocket. The label couldn't be read in the dark, but it bore a skull-and-crossbones and said:

POISON!
Sulphuric Acid

"I ain't got the stomach for this stuff," Short-and-Ugly declined.

Burly Guy snatched the bottle, yanked out the cork with his teeth and poured the contents over the nude corpse's face, hands and the soles of his feet.

Short-and-Ugly retched, but Burly Guy was unmoved about the whole business. He calmly tossed the empty vial into the water. He took a last look at the dead detective, made certain they hadn't left any marks of identification on him, then nudged the body into the river with his blunt toe.

Making a neat bundle of the dead man's clothes, he tucked them under his arm and started back to the car. Short-and-Ugly was already behind the wheel, waiting.

Burly Guy suddenly remembered the murder gun. He withdrew it from his hip pocket, held it in the flat of his hand and pitched it far out into the blackness of the river.

"Okay, Weak Stomach," he sneered at the thug at the wheel as he climbed in. "Let's go!"

Short-and-Ugly needed no engraved invitation. He threw the car into gear and gunned it on its way as if the dead man's ghost were after them.

ON THE flood tide, two days later, the mutilated body of John Murdock came to the surface. One of the riders on the foredeck of the ferry that plied between the city of Akelton and Red Point spotted it floating just beneath the waves. The Harbor Police fished it out.

Six-thirty that same night, Dan Griffin stood in the autopsy room at the city morgue. Dan Griffin was captain of detectives of Akelton City's police.

In the big room were a dozen or more operating tables, each under its own brilliant, individual domelight. On the white-topped table before him was sprawled the grisly remains of the man fished from the river.

Griffin's face was rock-hard and lined with deep concern as he turned to the tall, white-haired man beside him.

"Been in the water two days, you say, Doctor Andrews?"

The chief medical examiner nodded in a slow affirmative.

"And he was dead before he even hit the water. Six bullets in his back."

Griffin tried to study the mutilated face of the cadaver.

"Fish eat him away like that?" he asked.

"Sulphuric acid."

Griffin rubbed his square jaw reflectively. His mouth formed a grim slash under square-shaped nostrils. His graying hairline was straight, separating flat temples and thereby forming another square. The square motif was broken only by round, snapping black eyes, but it was picked up again by his square shoulders and body. Griffin's character matched his physique. He was an all-around square man.

"Any idea who it might be?" the medical examiner wanted to know.

Griffin lifted his eyes slowly from the almost inhuman face lying before him. There was unconcealed moisture in his eyes.

"Yes, Doc," he said in a broken voice. "A very good idea."

Griffin was sure that in life this mutilated corpse had been his best friend. True, there wasn't a mark of identification on the body. The face was little more than a grotesque outline. But when a man works side by side with someone for more than fifteen years joking, fighting and philosophizing, there are some things that even sulphuric acid cannot wipe out.

"Don't put him away," Griffin said in a hollow voice. "I'll be back."

Gray-faced, he lumbered across the room and out the door. He had performed many painful acts during his career on the Force, but what he had to do now was the toughest of all.

When he clumped down the stairs, he had no usual joke for the keeper who sat behind the desk. He unwillingly took up the phone, dialed a number and waited.

IN HIS comfortable studio on the top floor of the huge Swank Street mansion which housed his office and white-walled laboratory, Doctor Miles Murdock was busy modeling

Six bullets found their mark.

the skull of a man in fresh wet clay. This was no idle hobby. Sculpturing kept Doc Murdock's fingers supple and quick for the delicate lifework he had chosen.

He was exactly six feet tall, trim and powerful as a young oak. In addition, he had a profile which dowagers and sweet young debs found much to their liking. He had black, wavy hair which never needed combing, because it looked good just the way nature had grown it. Burning genius looked out of his jet eyes.

The phone on the taboret behind him purred softly. He wiped his big, sensitive hands on the towel hanging beside his latest "creation" and picked up the transceiver.

A feminine voice, low, sweet, young, came to him. It was Dale Jordan, his efficient chief nurse in the downstairs office.

"Detective Captain Griffin on the wire, Doctor."

Griffin! Every muscle in Doc Murdock's big body stiffened. Tiny nerves of fear tugged at his brain. Since two days ago, when his brother John had mysteriously disappeared, the doctor had received a dozen calls from Griffin. Each brought the same answer—nothing yet.

Miles Murdock had lived in dread anticipation for these past forty-eight hours, waiting for the call that would tell him they had found his brother. He knew in his heart how they would find him. Miles had a sixth sense about things like that. His brother John always used to say that Miles could scent bad news and danger five miles away.

Dr. Murdock stiffened his jaw.

"Put him on." There was a faint metallic click as Dale Jordan plugged in the connection.

"I think we've found your brother," said Griffin heavily.

Miles could feel the blood leaving his face. He waited.

"Will you come to the morgue right way?"

"Yes," Miles answered lifelessly and hung up.

He stood there quite still, feet spread wide apart, as if to brace himself. Only his heart seemed to go on battering his ribs hollowly.

John was dead—John, to whom he owed his grand start in life, his brilliant career.

John had been fifteen years older than he. When their parents died, Miles was only eight, so John took on the responsibilities of managing this small family of two. He worked hard to see that his brother got an education. Miles could remember the day John was appointed to the police force. How proud and happy he was!

Miles had yearned to follow in his footsteps, but John insisted that he finish college. It was then that the great talent which was his came to the fore. Miles might have gone far in medicine, for he had heard himself praised by some of the most renowned professors as having a truly great medical mind. But he chose plastic surgery in which to specialize.

SOME CLAIMED he was the most brilliant man of his time in this field. Surely the miracles he had performed substantiated this praise. Rebuilding the entire left side of screen starlet Ann Carlow's face, after it had been ravished by fire and threatened her bright career, had made part of plastic surgery history.

Success had come more swiftly to this young plastic surgeon than to most men. His prowess was worldwide. His patients listed people from all walks of life. Pillars of society. Greats of the stage and screen who must be kept young and beautiful for the critical, exacting glare of the spotlight. Luminaries of the sports world.

And then, too, there were those unfortunates who came, not out of vanity, but because nature or mishap had decreed deformity or mutilation to their faces and bodies.

For all this grand success, John had been in no small part responsible. And now he was gone!

Tearing the earthen-colored smock off his big frame, Doc Murdock slipped into his jacket and topcoat, walked with hunched shoulders through the door.

John was dead....

CHAPTER II

WHO KILLED JOHN MURDOCK?

DAN GRIFFIN was waiting for Doc Murdock in the office at the morgue. The men exchanged an almost inaudible greeting. The detective-captain laid his hand sympathetically on the young surgeon's shoulder.

"It isn't very pretty, Doc," he warned. "Was fished out of the river and there's no mark of identification to prove it's really him—not even fingerprints—"

"Upstairs?" Doc Murdock interrupted tonelessly.

Griffin nodded. They climbed the stairs to the autopsy room. Miles knew the white-coated crew busy at work dissecting bodies. No one spoke. They had learned who the corpse was.

Murdock halted before the table upon which the body lay. Griffin hesitated a moment, his square-fingered hand gripping the top of the white sheet that had been thrown over the cadaver. He shot Miles a warning glance to steel himself against what he was about to witness. Then grimly the detective-captain threw back the covering.

Miles stood and looked down, loose-kneed, swaying, everything dead in him but pain. Yet his face did not change. Only his eyes narrowed a little. His right eyebrow and the lines of his brow shadowing it twitched to form an oddly shaped spade.

That spade was the result of an injury sustained during his college football days. It was not actually a scar, but a slight paralysis of certain muscles over his right eye. He could have had it straightened out, but it in no way impaired his vision, nor did it alter his appearance—except when rage gripped him. Then, and only then, did that black spade appear, a warning of danger for someone.

"Sulphuric acid," Miles repeated, studying the obliterated features of the figure on the white-topped table.

"But he was dead before it was thrown on him," a voice said.

Miles looked around with a frown.

"Shot," the medical examiner continued. "Six bullets lodged in the spine. Sulphuric acid was added later, possibly in an attempt to make identification impossible."

"There's no proof it's him, Doc," Griffin put in hopefully. "It's only my guess."

"We'll soon see," Miles replied almost in a whisper.

He turned to Medical Examiner Andrews again, asked for several materials and a set of surgical tools. Griffin gulped, wide-eyed.

"Doc! You don't mean you're going to—"

"Restore his face," Miles finished stonily.

In a moment he had the necessary materials and instruments that he would need for the operation spread out before him on an adjoining white table. Then he studied the structure of the skull carefully, to ascertain the width and depth of the mutilated features.

"Convex-concave profile, cheekbones high, nose aquiline, jawbone wide," he muttered. "Fortunately there are no bones broken or missing." To Griffin he said: "You've got pictures?"

"Taken from every angle," Griffin answered, "for the Department files. I hope some day they become Exhibit A."

DOC TOOK one long, last look at that awful face before him on the table and then thoroughly cleansed the area he intended rebuilding. Taking several clumps of plastic surgery wax, he rolled them between the palms of his hands to gain an even texture.  Then he skillfully applied it to the skull before him.

It was no simple task, working from a foundation that was little more than a skeleton. The belief that this was his brother made it no easier.

Gradually, under his expert hand, the grotesque, hollow-eyed skull began to take form and show some indication of features. Dan Griffin, Medical Examiner Andrews and the other doctors in the big, white room, who were grouped around to watch this master at work, stared wide-eyed.

When at last Doc Murdock had put the finishing touches to his work, he stepped back to examine it, not proudly, but with deep hurt in his heart. A noticeable quiver showed in his usually steady hands. Emotion choked up in his throat.

The face that stared back at him from the table—the face he had just rebuilt—was that of his brother, John Murdock!

Inside, he had known all along who it was. Like every other human being in a similar situation, he had tried to make himself believe he was mistaken. Now it was impossible to doubt. This was his brother, dead—murdered!

Doctor Miles Murdock

It took all the self-control Miles could command to keep from going wild then. Teeth clenched together, fists tight granite balls, he snatched up his hat and coat, pivoted and went through the door.

Dan Griffin was at his heels, followed him down the stairs and into the street.

Parked at the curb was Doc Murdock's flashy roadster. They walked to it and climbed inside. The detective-captain was amazed at the rapidity with which Doc Murdock had mastered his emotions. That brief walk down the stone steps of the morgue was all the plastic surgeon had needed to restore him to normal.

"Griff," he said bitterly, "who killed my brother? Why was it done?"

Griffin's black brows came together in a dark frown.

"I wish I knew, Doc."

"We've got to find out."

"Cop-killers don't brag about it."

Miles put his foot on the starter and shot the roadster into traffic. He drove, hands tight on the wheel, eyes glued straight ahead, lips a cold line.

"Stripped him, didn't they?" he asked. "Took everything?"

Griffin nodded slowly.

"John had a ring," Miles said.

Griffin remembered. "An onyx with a 'J' in it!"

"It was worth a lot more than it looked. I don't think the one who took it would hold onto it very long."

"No. You're right about that. If they were picked up with that black baby on their person, it would call for an awful lot of tall and fancy explaining. But no fence or stoolie is going to sing a piece about that, no matter how much pressure you put on 'em."

Miles continued to stare straight ahead through the windshield.

"Maybe I know one who doesn't need sweating."

LEAVING DAN GRIFFIN on the sidewalk in front of Police Headquarters, Doc Murdock swung his roadster into the narrow, dark corridor that was Mullen Street. Sullen, gray tenements walled in each side, housing noise, dirt and poverty. This was where Doc Murdock had learned life in the raw.

After graduating from medical college, he had served his internship in the city hospital, located in the worst and filthiest section of the slums. Here he gained the vast storehouse of knowledge that had proved so valuable to him in his work.

When success came to him, and moved him over to the more prosperous part of the city to tend the fashionable sick, he did not go with an eye to personal wealth, or to fire an overzealous ambition. There was no greater glory in his mind than making the sick well again, whether they be rich or poor. But most of the poor who so badly needed him could not afford to pay, and money was essential for him to carry on.

Even in the slums a doctor needs supplies with which to work, people to assist him. That costs money. It was a case then of making the right hand pay for the left hand. The rich he could charge big fees, which they would never miss. These fees would buy those things which the poor needed.

On Down Street, in the very heart of the slums, Doctor Miles Murdock had built himself a clinic. A white-faced building, it stood out like a beacon of mercy in contrast to the surrounding gloom. It was free, yet those who came received the same expert attention for which the swells on the other side of town paid dearly.

This work had brought Doc Murdock many friends here in the slum section—true friends, people he could call upon whenever he needed them. He was on his way to visit one of these friends now.

He shoved down the brake pedal in front of a bleak seven-story tenement house, one in a row of several. A rusted fire-escape crawled up the sheer face of the building like a tangle of heavy, black vine. Dull yellow squares, which were the shadeless windows, looked out.

Doc went up the four steps of the front stoop. He studied the bells. The party he sought lived on the sixth floor.

He was reaching for the doorknob when it turned and the door opened. A man came out. Doc Murdock knew him even in the dim light.

"Hello, Wisply," he said.

Arnold Wisply was a tall, fat man. Lard bulged unpleasantly beneath his black clothes. The lowest of his triple chins almost hid from view his soiled, wrinkled, white collar. His eyes had deep bluish satchels beneath them and his mouth was a weak, wet gash beneath dilated nostrils.

Wisply was the close-fisted owner of a great percentage of these slum tenements. A vulture who preyed on the poor, he charged as much as he could squeeze out for these fire-traps.

It was no great surprise that Doc should meet this man here. One was forever meeting him everywhere in the slums, mainly because he was a penny-pinching skinflint, too cheap to hire an agent. He worked night and day, collecting his own rents and answering incessant complaints.

CHAPTER III

SEARCH FOR A RING

MURDOCK AND the miserly landlord were not entirely strangers. Doc had conducted an open, unending war to clean up the slums, but the fight had been in vain. Wisply not only had money, but the unfortunates who lived in his buildings seemed to fear him. Moreover, they were so resigned to their unsightly surroundings that they offered no support to Doc in his fight.

Wisply squinted his beady eyes. When he saw who it was standing before him in the gloomy vestibule, he sniffled insultingly and went past. Doc Murdock watched him until he went down the stoop. Then he turned around and opened the door.

He went up the stairs briskly. While at school, he had taken time out from studies to gather in four letters—football, boxing, swimming, and rifle. If he had come to college solely to collect letters, he might have added several more to the list, but those four were plenty to earn him a scholarship.

He hadn't permitted himself to soften since. On the top floor of his Swank Street mansion, adjoining his studio, was a completely outfitted gymnasium. There he managed a daily workout to keep his reflexes quick, his muscles firm and to prevent fat from thickening his lean middle.

Reaching the sixth floor landing, he walked toward a little door in the rear. A conglomeration of smells and sounds filled the ill-lighted hallway. Knotting his fist into a big ball, Miles banged it against the door.

Nimble, hurried footsteps scampered over the bare floor inside. The door opened. A little girl stood on the threshold before him.

"Doctor Murdock!" she cried.

"Hello, Janie."

She jumped into his arms and he caught her, as if it were something they were both quite accustomed to doing. She hugged him and planted a big kiss on his cheek as he carried her across the threshold into the poorly furnished room.

"Daddy," she cried out, "look who's here!"

A thin little man with sparse hair pushed his chair back from the table, came forward hurriedly. He had a skinny face, furtive eyes, but his smile was as warm and sincere as the little girl's.

"Doc, what the devil're you doin' here?"

He grabbed the young surgeon's hand and shook it vigorously.

"I came to ask you a favor, Tommy."

"A favor? *You* askin' me a favor?"

The man's face was a question mark. It seemed impossible to him. Doc set the little girl down.

"Janie, suppose you run into the front room for a minute. I'd like to talk to your Daddy."

SHE GAVE him exactly ten million dollars' worth of dimpled smile and then danced away through the railroad flat.

Tommy pulled over a chair, dusting it off with the sleeve of his gray shirt. He offered it to the plastic surgeon. Doc dropped into it wearily.

"You look down in the dumps, Doc," said Tommy. "Anything wrong?"

Miles told him briefly about his brother. Tommy sprang up and swore explosively.

"You name the guys that did it, Doc!" he growled, his green eyes narrow with fury. "You just name 'em and—"

"No, Tommy. All I want you to do is locate a black onyx ring."

Miles described it.

"I'll find it," Tommy vowed with savage fury. "If it's been turned in, I'll find it. I'll scratch every fence there is, pump every stoolie alive. You gave my Janie a new face after that car mangled it. I told you I'd never forget, that I'd go straight. I got a job tendin' furnaces for a row of apartments, but I ain't lost touch with the boys. I'll find that ring for you, Doc!"

Tommy left Janie with one of the neighbors. Then he and Doc started the search for the missing ring. Tommy didn't exaggerate. He knew the haunts, every likely place where a rat would come to turn hot gold into cool green.

The first place they visited was Uncle Sylvester's, a cheap little pawn shop located in a none too prosperous section on the other side of town. The former Sticky-fingered Kid had done a lot of business with Uncle in the past, and Uncle had reaped handsome profits from the Kid's pickings. He was indeed sorry to hear that Tommy had found a narrow hole in the fence and crawled through to the legal side.

"I'm lookin' for a ring that was lifted from my pal here," Tommy told him. "He's an okay guy and he's willin' to cough up twice what you paid for it."

Uncle's shifty eyes settled briefly on Tommy's gaunt face. He shrugged his narrow, hunched shoulders sadly.

"I ain't even seen it," he grunted.

Tommy knew Uncle Sylvester wouldn't swim against a tide of greenbacks, which meant he hadn't seen the ring.

Tommy wandered away with Doc, but he had a fresh idea.

"That clears some of the smoke outa my eyes," he said. "The guy who blew them lead periods at your brother—or at least the guy who swiped his ring—ain't local talent. If he was, he'd have paid Uncle Sylvester a call right off the bat. Every light-fingered gent operating in the city knows Uncle pays top prices and ain't scared to take chances.

"He'd fence the Empire State Building, if anybody brought it to him. The trigger guy we're bloodhoundin' is from outa town, so it looks like we'll just have to keep tryin'."

HE TOOK Doc Murdock to every pawn shop, every fence in the city, but it was the same answer at each they visited.

"We'd be glad to turn it over for an old pal like you, but we ain't seen it."

It was almost dawn when the two of them sank down on a pair of stools in the Greek's coffee house, just around the corner from Doc's slum clinic. They were foot-weary from climbing up and down stairs. Tommy was thoroughly dejected because he had failed in his promise to deliver the ring. He ordered coffee and sinkers. While waiting to be served, he said to Doc Murdock:

"There's just one place we ain't tried where he mighta fenced it. And if it ain't there, then the guy's either blown town with it, or he's bucking the form-sheet and holding onto it."

"And this last place?" Doc asked.

"The Web," Tommy replied with a none too enthusiastic expression on his skinny face. "One of the few places in this city where I ain't welcome. I was never sorry about it before. It's a hotel, if you want to call it that They ain't careful about who signs the register. It's usually the first place a 'visitor' holes up when he's got cops on his tail.

"I just never got along with 'Spider' Kelly, the rat who owns it. If he thought I was lookin' for the ring, and he had it, he'd sooner swallow it than give it to me."

Doc looked with sharp eyes at Tommy.

"Why can't I see him?"

"You?" Tommy's eyes came around and met Doc's. "Why, you wouldn't last any longer in that place than an icicle in the devil's back pocket! They're tough monkeys over there. They'd be all over you before you got your head halfway through the door."

"Maybe not. Maybe with your help I'd be very nicely received."

"With *my* help?"

Doc waited until the Greek had served them.

"When somebody from out of town comes to visit a place like the Web," he asked, "doesn't he usually have a letter of introduction?"

"Yeah, but where'll you get one?"

Doc smiled gently. "Not meaning to reflect anything—but wasn't one of your past accomplishments forgery?"

Tommy put three heaping spoons of sugar into his cup, then answered coyly.

"Well, I wasn't the best, but wasn't so bad, either."

"Do you know anybody out of town who might send a customer to Spider Kelly?"

Tommy dunked his doughnut, considered a moment.

"A couple of guys." He took a bite. " 'Bugs' Lattimer, out in Chi, for one...."

"Swell. Write a letter to Spider, from Lattimer, introducing 'Rings' Jackson. I've got a little idea to go with that name."

Tommy turned and frowned darkly.

"I wish you wouldn't tackle it, Doc. You don't know this Spider. He's bad medicine, worse than a Black Widow."

Doc lifted his cup, sipped with the appreciation of a connoisseur, then remarked briefly:

"The Greek makes swell coffee."

Tommy shook his head worriedly and finished his doughnut.

CHAPTER IV

MISTER RAT CRAWLS IN

HOW SPIDER ever picked up a fine old Irish name like Kelly was one for Ripley to decipher, but "Spider" fit him to a crooked T. He was black and creepy-looking, his face and hands covered with coarse, wiry, black hair. He was big, too, with the beef and shoulders to go with it.

He glared darkly at the unkempt stranger who handed him a smudged, wrinkled letter.

Doctor Miles Murdock's society friends would have been shocked to see him now—if indeed any of them could have recognized him as the famous plastic surgeon.

This was Doc's first attempt at disguise, but he had made an extensive study of make-up in connection with his work in plastic surgery. His knowledge of physiognomy was unsurpassed. He knew each plane and its relation to the other, each tiny nerve and muscle, and what caused each light and shadow in the human features.

The masterpiece he had accomplished on his own face for this dangerous mission was a tribute to his genius. He used no trick wigs or whiskers, no mechanical devices to alter the contours.

A clever ointment paled his skin. He had raised his brows and lowered his hairline. A grease which he rubbed into his hair temporarily removed the wave, besides changing it almost to gray. Bits of surgical wax, fastened to his gums, heightened his cheekbones, and an artful blending of lights and shadows made his nose look long and tapering. A cheap, frayed gray suit completed his remarkable characterization.

Spider Kelly read the letter twice with due care. Then, raising his pigeyes, he studied the stranger.

"So Lattimer sent you, eh?" he asked in a raspy voice. "What's he doin' these days?"

"Makin' book."

Tommy had told that to Doc. In fact, Tommy had primed him for all the questions Spider was likely to throw at him. Tommy hadn't guessed far wrong. The keeper of the dilapidated hotel fired them all at Doc, but he parried each query neatly.

"What're you runnin' away from?" Spider finally asked.

"Bank stick-up."

Spider's dark face glowed greedily.

"That must've left you pretty well greased."

Doc nodded. "But I can't touch the big lump till the heat cools. Marked dough. Don't worry though. I can pay my freight."

As he spoke, Doc kept rubbing the rings on his right hand against the lapel of his coat. Spider grinned.

A grin didn't become his evil face at all.

"I'll fix you up with a nice, quiet room—private, or any way you want it."

"Swell. I'll be around only a few days. I got a tip there's a harvest ready to be cut up around Boston. But while I'm around, if you get wind of any jobs that call for fast thinkin', don't forget my room number."

He rubbed the rings on his coat again, studied them critically.

"Them's some rings you got there," Spider commented.

"Yeah," Doc replied. "I make a hobby of collectin' them. They're my weakness. That's how come I got my monicker, Rings Jackson."

He pulled out a worn leather wallet, crowded with greenbacks. He knew he was gambling his life by flashing a roll like this, but it was part of his plan.

"What's the bad news, pal?" he asked. "I know you'll want it in advance."

The Spider's small eyes were glued on that wallet.

"No hurry, Rings, no hurry," he said oilily, licking his puffy lips like a cat contemplating a canary. He gestured Doc to lean across the desk and said in a hushed voice: "You wouldn't wanna see a little collection of sparklers I got, I don't suppose."

DOC'S HEART pounded fast and furious. The fish had grabbed at his bait. He could scarcely curb his eagerness to yank him in, but he knew if he played him too fast, there was the danger of losing his quarry. He forced a frown, which wasn't easy.

"I don't know," he drawled. "I ain't got many fingers left."

"I got some that'll knock your eye out. Real class and cheap!"

Doc shrugged. "It ain't the price. A good ring's always worth dough. But—"

"I'll show 'em to you," Spider interrupted insistently. "Come on up to my room."

He punched a tinny bell with the heel of his thick hand. A filthy old man shuffled forward lazily.

"Watch out nobody don't run off with the desk, Pop," Spider said with a weak attempt at levity.

He led Doc up the rickety stairs, past unsightly rooms, some of which possessed no doors. The beds were unmade and gray with dirt. Doc shivered inwardly at the thought of having to spend a night here.

They entered a sparsely furnished room with an unmade brass bed, a table, two chairs and a couple of pictured nudes adorning the walls. There were a bottle of whisky and two glasses on the table.

"Help yourself, Rings," Spider invited.

Doc took one look at the dirt streaks on the glasses and declined. He wasn't sure whether, if he had taken a drink, he would have left this place alive.

SPIDER CLOSED the door and turned the key.

He walked over to Doc and frisked him. Doc frowned.

"What's the idea?" he demanded.

Spider smiled. "No offense, pal. Just can't be too careful with a guy you never met before."

Finding Doc had no weapon, he walked to the larger of the two pictures on the wall. He brushed it aside with his hand and revealed a wall safe.

"This ain't no tin can, either," he bragged. "I've had some of the smartest safe-crackers try to open it. They didn't even make an impression."

He ordered Doc to turn his back so he couldn't follow the combination, then spun the tumblers. When Doc turned to face him again, Spider had the safe open and was removing a big boxful of rings, cuff links, studs, bracelets, necklaces, earrings. He upset the box on the table.

Doc went over them carefully. His heart sank.

The ring he sought was not among them!

Spider couldn't help but note the look of disappointment on Doc's face. He frowned his resentment.

"What's the matter? That's the neatest collection of jewelry in the city."

Doc managed a spiritless grin.

"Sure, they're oke, but they're not exactly what I want. I've had all them kind. If I'm gonna buy something, I want something different."

Spider rubbed his jaw and studied Doc carefully.

"Wait a minute," he said finally. "Your name's Jackson, ain't it? I got somethin' maybe you'll go for, only it's hot—plenty hot. I wouldn't even let you look at it if you was gonna stick around town very long."

Doc's heart took up that rapid thumping again.

"If it's what I want, I'll keep it off until after I've blown."

Spider considered. "That's fair enough, but remember you didn't get it from me. I'll call you a liar if you say you did."

He went back to the safe, dug his black, hairy hand into the darkest corner and came out with a small package wrapped in tissue paper. He tore it open with blunt, sweaty fingers.

Doc watched in breathless silence as the contents of the package rolled out onto the table.

It was his brother's ring!

His bony jaw stiffened. That black spade appeared even through the make-up. He snatched up the ring almost tenderly, read the inscription inside the band:

To John from Dad

Spider miscon-strued it all. He gri-maced gleefully and rubbed his big hands together. Doc whirled to face him angrily.

"Where did you get this ring?"

Spider's grin spread and he held up his big paw.

"I never remem-ber names, Pal."

"You'll remember this one!"

The grin washed from Spider's face, was replaced by a glower.

"Gimme back my ring," he snarled. "I don't take no guff from nobody!"

Dale Jordan

He made a quick grab for the ring in Doc's hand. Doc straight-armed him back against the wall. Instantly Spider's hand flew to his hip pocket. Doc expected to see a gun come out. Instead the hotel owner yanked out a clasp knife. He touched a spring and a stout, deadly-looking blade sprang out. With a curse he pushed forward.

Doc set his weight on the balls of his feet, knotted his fists and waited for the lunge. It came. Doc took one short step to the side, grabbed the knife-wrist as it whizzed past. He knew every hidden, sensitive nerve center in the wrist. He found one and pressed his thumb hard against it.

The knife dropped to the ground and Spider went to his knees, groveling, yelling with pain. Doc snatched the knife and pressed the point of it against Spider's throbbing jugular vein. The knife was sharp, as Spider realized. It brought big beads of perspiration to his wrinkled brow.

"From whom did you buy this ring?" Doc demanded.

"I don't know!"

There was a banging of fists on the door, voices wanting to know what was the matter.

"Tell them it's nothing," Doc ordered. "Tell them to go away."

"You won't get away with this," Spider gritted. The knife blade pricked his neck. He howled: "Beat it! There ain't nothing wrong."

The mob in the corridor went away, muttering.

"Now," Doc snapped, "from whom did you get this ring?"

Spider swallowed. Doc knew he had figured his chances and realized they were all bad.

"Okay, okay, I'll spill," mumbled Spider. "Lemme up."

"From whom did you get this ring?" repeated Doc inexorably.

"A lug named 'Punchy' Gus Martin. Come from outa town. Did a job for somebody here in the city and swiped the ring off the corpse. I paid fifty bucks for it."

"You didn't cheat yourself, did you? This ring is worth every penny of three hundred dollars."

"I hadda hold onto it till it cooled, didn't I? It was an investment."

"Where does this Martin live now?"

"I don't know."

"Don't lie!"

One more jab and the blade would draw blood.

"Okay! Okay! He gimme an address. Be careful with that knife!"

He rattled off the address.

"Sorry I've got to do this to you, Spider," Doc said with mock regret. "I don't want you yelling until after I'm gone."

He struck a quick, painless blow at the base of Spider's hard skull. Doc knew the exact spot where it would do no real damage.

Spider folded like a collapsible camp chair and lay stretched out on the floor, slumbering like a babe. Doc went to the window, opened it and dropped the short distance to the ground.

When he reached home, he put through a call to Police Headquarters, got Detective-Captain Dan Griffin on the wire. He explained that he had the ring, where and how he got it, and where Punchy Gus Martin could be picked up.

"Nice work, Doc," Griffin complimented. Then, with impatience to get started, he added: "I'll take care of Mister Martin right away. I'll give it my own personal attention."

CHAPTER V

TRIAL AT LAST

GRIFFIN SWUNG into quick action. Upstairs to Rogue's Gallery he chased, had one of the clerks look up the data on Punchy Gus Martin. There was none. The man had no local record.

Griffin got on the teletype, ticked out his question to every constabulary around the country. The information he sought came clicking back from Chicago.

Punchy Gus Martin had a record that included everything from vagrancy and purse-snatching to assault and battery. There were a couple of murders mixed in, but they never stuck.

The reply said he was always spoiling for a fight.

"Let him try it," muttered Griffin.

He took a couple of strapping bluecoats with him, piled into a police car and shot over to the place where the hotel owner had told Doc Murdock Gus Martin lived.

Griffin and the bulls crashed Martin's quarters and found him propped up in a brass bed, thumbing a magazine. He put up an argument about their breaking in on him like this, but he didn't show a spark of fight.

Maybe it was the presence of the two heavy-fisted lads Griffin had brought with him that convinced Martin a scrap wouldn't be so wise. Somehow Griffin's gray matter told him that wasn't the answer.

One look at this human ox and it was plain as black on white that he was built for fighting. He was six-feet-six of bone and muscle, solid, hard rock. His great chopping-block arms hung at his sides. His small, mean eyes glared out of his pockmarked face with a savage glint.

The bluecoat frisked the giant, poked through all his belongings. They stripped the bed, the mattress, searched behind pictures, under the rug, looking for the murder gun. But Martin was as clean as a baby's mind.

"Okay," Griffin finally growled, disappointed. "Get on your coat and hat. You're goin' to Headquarters."

The giant looked down at the squat detective-captain with eyes filled with contempt.

"I don't suppose it's none of my business what you're taking me in for," he said with biting sarcasm.

"You'll find out when you get there."

"Okay, sad eyes, but you're makin' a bad mistake."

"Maybe you're the baby who made that bad mistake," Griffin snapped back. "Get movin' and keep your trap shut!"

When they reached HQ, Punchy Gus Martin was booked at the desk. Then Griffin and several other detectives took him downstairs to the subcellar, into a little room they aptly labeled the "steam room."

THEY SAT the burly thug on a straight-backed chair in the middle of the cement floor. Out of the darkness, they poured the blinding ray of a cone-shaped light at him. Then they began firing questions from all sides of the echo-chamber.

They started out with routine questions. What was his name? Where did he come from? How many times had he been arrested? Convicted? What for?

Then they worked around to the ring. He didn't deny for a minute that he sold the ring to the fence. He admitted it the first time they shot it at him. But he told them he found it on Marion Street the night before last.

The lot of them were willing to bet their badges he was lying. They made up their minds they'd keep him down in that sweat-box until he cracked.

They were just about getting warmed up when the door of the room opened. A harness bull poked his big head inside, caught Griffin's eye and beckoned.

"What's up?" the detective-captain asked.

The cop flickered his eyes for caution.

"Mister Chris Korpuli to see the prisoner, Captain."

Storm clouds gathered in Dan Griffin's square-jawed face, but there was no cloudiness in his brain. He could see quite clearly why Punchy Gus Martin was so self-confident, why he hadn't put up a fight when they came to nab him. Martin had evidently been told beforehand if the pinch came, to clam up and he'd have nothing to worry about. But start mentioning names and he'd fry in his own fat.

The detective-captain met the man who stepped into the room with a scowl that showed his obvious distaste. He was a wizen-faced, expensively dressed little man with a shiny leather briefcase gripped under his right arm. He had an eagle's beak for a nose and an eagle's cold, watery eyes set in his coconut head.

Chris Korpuli was one of the most brilliant criminal lawyers in the city, with an astounding brain for fashioning strange escapes from the

Spider Kelly

law. He knew all the answers and wrote most of the questions. No cop on the force, from the top to the bottom, liked to see him in the corner of a man they had brought in. Chris Korpuli had a way of making even the cleverest of them sweat up there in the witness box.

"You got here kind of quick this time," Griffin said sarcastically.

"I don't like insinuations," Korpuli retorted acidly. "A man like you should know better. Another job wouldn't be easy to find at your age."

The square-built captain could feel the anger seething inside. The lawyer brushed past, impudently close. He walked arrogantly to the prisoner seated in the middle of the room. Martin grinned from ear to ear the minute he saw him.

"Put on those lights!" Korpuli barked. The lights came up.

"They pull any rough stuff on you?"

"Naw." Gus Martin stood up and stretched his gorilla-like arms. "Lucky for them they didn't."

"Very lucky!" the eagle-beaked attorney asserted.

That was just about all Dan Griffin could stomach. He knew they'd never make Punchy Gus Martin talk, with slim Chris Korpuli back of him.

Griffin snorted, turned, stomped through the door and slammed it emphatically behind him.

PUNCHY GUS MARTIN'S trial was a short and decisive one. Korpuli cleverly guided the cross-examination. The district attorney, with nothing to go on except the ring angle, had his hands tied. The papers said the State was foolish to bring the case to trial on such scant evidence. But against anyone except Chris Korpuli it probably would have sufficed.

Korpuli turned the proceedings into a shambles, made the district attorney look like a graduate trying his first case.

Miles Murdock sat in the courtroom beside Dan Griffin as the jury filed in. The foreman arose and proclaimed:

"We find the defendant not guilty!"

Griffin laid his hand on the plastic surgeon's forearm. He could feel the muscles tighten in Miles' powerful arm, see that spade form over his right eye.

"He's guilty," Miles said through clenched teeth. "That man killed my brother."

Griffin nodded dejectedly. "The law just wasn't strong enough to hold him, I guess. There's not a thing we can do about it, now that he's exonerated."

Miles sat with his eyes glued on the smirking face of the burly giant who, with his wily lawyer, was receiving wild congratulations from the crowd.

"There's something I can do about it!" Miles ground out.

There was no bravado in his words. Griffin knew that, for he had watched Miles Murdock grow from a kid into the great surgeon he was now. He knew Miles was not given to idle boasting. A wild thrill surged through the detective-captain's being because this man wanted to take up his dead brother's fight, yet at the same time it made him afraid.

"I wouldn't do anything rash, Doc," he cautioned.

"It won't be anything rash, Griff. It will be something quite sane." He turned and sternly looked at his friend. "Don't think I'm blaming you or the law because Martin got away. You aren't at fault. Things unfortunately turn out that way sometimes. But my brother was murdered without a chance to fight back or defend himself. I let the law have its chance and the law muffed. Now I'm going to have my crack!"

"I wouldn't, Miles," the detective-captain advised worriedly. "I know how you feel, but—"

"I don't intend breaking any laws," Miles assured him, "at least not intentionally. But rats have to be treated like rats. They can't be allowed even one small hole, or they'll slip through it. During these past few days, sitting here in this courtroom, I've been doing a lot of figuring, piecing things together. Gus Martin killed my brother. Maybe the jury couldn't see that, but I could. Every minute he was in the witness box, I watched him. He did it, all right."

"I know, but you can't take the law into your own hands. He had his trial. He happened to beat the rap."

Miles either didn't hear Griffin, or didn't want to hear him.

"Martin did the actual killing, but it wasn't his idea," he went on. "Somebody ordered that murder, then pulled Korpuli into the case to spring Martin. Gus Martin never saw the kind of money Korpuli asks, and I don't believe Korpuli knew Martin even existed until the day he took over. Somebody hired both of them. I'm going to find out who that somebody is and why my brother was killed. And when I do, we'll have a new trial that will end a lot differently from this one!"

CHAPTER VI

NO ESCAPE FROM JUDGMENT

A FRAIL HAND came down on Doc Murdock's big shoulder as he sat in the courtroom. Doc twisted, looked up into the long, sad, colorless face of Peter de Gaul.

Peter de Gaul was a soft, smallish man who liked to be called "the wise man of Down Street" and spoke always of the slum people as *his* people. He ran the Mission House, a dingy little hall a few doors down the block from Doc's clinic. He offered bingo and checkers as main attractions to draw people into the hall so he could preach to them.

Just what he was preaching, or what his doctrine amounted to, few people understood. But to those who believed in him, he was sort of a one-man domestic relations board, community mail-box, advisor. For the illiterate he read and wrote letters and documents. He had a "sardine can" safe in his office in which he would store their "valuables."

He charged for these services always, no matter how trivial the task. With the pennies and small donations he could wheedle out of susceptible social workers, he ran his haven for the "downtrodden."

"I'm sorry, Doctor Murdock," de Gaul said in a slow, solemn, sermon-preaching voice. "I've sat here in this courtroom and watched this great injustice done to your brother. Believe me when I say that I have suffered with you in this crisis, for your brother was not only a protector of *my* people, he was one of us."

"Thanks," Miles said.

He had known de Gaul since the days when he had been an intern in the city hospital. He wasn't overly impressed with the little man, but he tolerated him. De Gaul seemed harmless enough. Since every slum appeared to have one of these characters, Miles supposed that de Gaul was no better or worse than the average.

De Gaul was always dropping in and out of the clinic with his people. Doc recalled that just a few weeks ago he had come in with "Crazy George," one of the derelicts who flopped in the foul cellar of the Mission House and paid for his food and bed by working as handy man around the hall.

Crazy George had burned both his hands badly. Doc Murdock found it necessary to graft flesh from other parts of the body. During this episode Peter de Gaul really displayed the brotherly love he preached. Out of his own pocket he paid for the costly medicants that Doc needed and didn't have in the clinic to patch the man's hands. So, Doc conceded, maybe underneath it all Peter de Gaul wasn't a half-bad sort.

It was natural that this odd little character of the slums should be in the courtroom today. Doc Murdock was an important cog in the workings of the slum section. Besides, John Murdock, as de Gaul intimated, had once patrolled that part of town as his beat.

People would want to know firsthand just what had happened at the trial. They would come to the mission head, as they always did about such matters, and ask questions. He wanted to be able to give them eyewitness details, for there was a certain inflation of ego that went with his being known as a "wise man."

KORPULI AND Punchy Gus Martin were getting ready to leave the courtroom. On his way out, the giant stepped over to taunt Dan Griffin.

"You shoulda took my advice, sad eyes," he jeered out of the corner of his mouth. "I told ya that you was makin' a bad mistake."

Miles laid a restraining hand on the detective-captain's square shoulder. This was neither the time nor the place to settle scores. Peter de Gaul elbowed through and waved a horny finger in the big thug's face.

"You can't escape the day of judgment!"

"Shut up, screwball!" Punchy Gus Martin growled.

With one sweep of his hamlike hand, he brushed the little man back into the row of seats. Then, with a smirk, he rejoined his mouthpiece.

As he assisted de Gaul to his feet, Miles stared after the human ox. Miles' face was a mask for his true feelings. Only the spade over his right eye revealed the fury in his heart.

Later, on their way from the courthouse in his roadster, Miles asked Captain Griffin:

"What cases was John working on when he was killed?"

"Nothing officially. I've gone through his reports with a fine-tooth comb, hoping for the very thing you're thinking—that maybe I could twist it back to the motivation for this murder. His files gave me nothing to work on. I just can't figure it. I keep askin' myself, why would anybody want to kill a swell guy like John Murdock?"

"How about the murder of Mrs. Small?" Doc brought out. "Wasn't John sort of persistent about that?"

The Small case was one of the unsolved mysteries of the slums. Mrs. Small, an old Italian woman, had lived with her aged husband in one of Arnold Wisply's tenements. Just two weeks before she was found dead, her husband passed away. Old age and a heart that had been strained by the shock of extreme poverty thrust upon them had caused his death.

There was a great deal more mystery and horror attached to the death of his wife. She was found in the squalor of her two-room flat, the victim of a fiendish explosion. There wasn't a trace of a clue for the police to follow, not the semblance of a lead. They worked doggedly on the case, but the riddle of what had caused the explosion and why anyone would want to kill a destitute old lady went into the records unsolved.

"Not a chance of its having anything to do with the Small case," replied Griffin to Miles' question. "Why, the best brains in the Department couldn't find anything! Not that John wasn't just as capable. He was one of the best cops that ever lived, but—well, it just isn't plausible."

Miles didn't argue. On the other hand, he wasn't wholly convinced.

Detective-Captain Dan Griffin

He was still worrying the thought when he pulled up in front of the station house and deposited his square-shouldered friend on the sidewalk. Griffin leaned in through the open window of the car and worriedly said:

"If I were you, Doc, I'd forget that wild idea you had in the courtroom. Korpuli and Gus Martin don't play the game the way you do. You start mussin' around with them and you'll wind up in the river, too. Screwy as it sounds, they've got the law on their side. Martin was cleared. Take a piece of advice from somebody older than you are. Mark that idea on the ice. Like Peter de Gaul says: 'It'll wash out in the rain.'"

Doc smiled, but the smile was forced. He slammed into first and quickly spurted away from the curb. It was about three o'clock in the afternoon when he got to his Swank Street quarters. Dale Jordan met him as he came in. She advanced slowly, looking up at him with emerald green eyes which were deep with concern.

Dale was tall and gracefully slender, with long, reddish-brown hair framing a cornflower face. Even in her spotless, stiffly starched uniform, men looked at her and grew wistful.

She had heard of the jury's unjust verdict.

In a hushed voice, she said sympathetically:

"I'm sorry."

Doc looked down at her with hollow, troubled eyes.

"Come upstairs, please."

Without comment she followed him up to the studio. The rest of the staff was busy in the downstairs laboratories, or tending patients. Doc locked the door behind him, laid his hat on the table and hung his coat on the rack.

Dale looked down at his hands. The flesh was drawn white across his knuckles. That spade over his right eye seemed destined to stay there permanently now. Though she had been with Doctor Murdock almost since he first took over this big house, she had never seen him in such a dark mood before. He told her to lay out materials on the table beside the workbench he used for modeling. He turned and went into the adjoining bedroom. Dale prepared the table for him to work upon. He returned to the studio in his earthen-colored smock, sleeves rolled to the elbows. In his right hand was a photograph.

Dale craned to see. It was the morgue picture of John Murdock after he had been fished from the river, a three-way study of the hideously scarred face before Doc had rebuilt it. Miles had obtained this duplicate picture from the police files for his own records, he had said.

He placed the picture on the desk.

His eyes were narrow and sultry, his mouth firm with determination.

"Your materials are ready, Doctor," Dale said, perplexity added to the concern in her eyes.

"Thanks. You can go now."

She did not move. He turned to face her.

"I said you can go," he repeated.

She came forward with hesitant steps.

"I want to help you," she pleaded.

He frowned. "Help me? Help me do what?"

"I don't know. But I believe you're going to try to find the people who murdered your brother."

HE LOOKED at her stonily. Had it been anyone else, he would have followed through his pretense, but Dale was more than just another nurse, or even a good friend. In fact, Doc had come to wonder just how much she really did mean to him. Was it only her resourcefulness, her efficiency that seemed to bring them so closely together?

"I'd rather you didn't help, Dale," he said. "I don't know for sure just where it's all going to lead."

"I'm not afraid," she declared.

"But you don't realize what you'll be letting yourself in for. These people are ruthless murderers."

"All the more reason why you'll need someone to help you and work with you."

Doc was still looking down into her pretty, oval-shaped face. He knew it would be useless to try to dissuade her.

Besides this, he wasn't quite sure whether he wanted to. He would need someone to assist him in this dangerous work besides Tommy Pedlar, who was at work for Doc on the outside.

He could think of no one he would rather have working with him than Dale.

"Set up enough clay for a life-sized head," he said.

CHAPTER VII

BIRTH OF THE PURPLE SCAR

F IRST DOC made a full-size head of his dead brother out of clay, following the mutilated face in the picture, which he had tacked up on the wall before him. Every scar, every torn line, every mangled tissue he followed until he had an exact duplicate of the face. It was so perfect in detail that it was positively blood-chilling.

He hardened the clay face with a specially-prepared drier. Then from it he made a plaster of paris cast. This he also prematurely set with the drier. Next he prepared a solution of melted gum elastic, coloring it with a faint purple dye.

Into the finished mold he poured the sticky, hot elastic. It set instantly. When he removed it from the mold, he had a perfect reproduction of his brother's scarred face in the purple pliable rubber mask, which he fitted over his own face.

It drew a shudder of repulsion from Dale. Anyone entering the room at that moment would have thought it was John Murdock, returned from his river grave. The acid-destroyed face had been so skillfully copied that the dullest, least sensitive eye would recoil at seeing it. It was the face of a corpse!

"I don't intend it to be merely a horrifying sight," Doc explained as he peeled it off. "I won't hide behind it to intimidate people, either. When possible, I'll work in ordinary disguise, using the mask only when I need its protection, or when I want it known that the Purple Scar is on the trail."

"The Purple Scar?" repeated Dale in an awed whisper.

"It's a name that the underworld will find easy to remember," said Miles grimly. "And if they have any trouble with their memories, the exploits of the Purple Scar, as well as the sight of him, will jolt their minds into remembering."

"But why did you choose purple?" she asked.

"Principally because I wanted to imitate my brother's features as closely as possible for this case. Flesh that has been eaten by acid and submerged in water turns a dark purple, as—as John's was. But there's also a practical reason. Purple becomes black at night, which will make my face invisible, instead of a betraying pale glow in the darkness."

He sat down before a mirror. From the bottom drawer of his desk he had taken a make-up kit. He opened it and set to work. When he was finished Dale's gleaming blond hair swung from side to side as she shook her head in admiration.

"I'd never know you in a million years!" she exclaimed.

Doc Murdock had assumed a character similar to the one who had visited Spider Kelly's hotel. A sharp-nosed, sallow-faced individual who seemed none too bright, he was dressed a little better than before in a discarded suit with all marks of identification removed. Deliberately he had made himself the type of man who would attract little attention wherever he roamed. Under his coat he stowed a revolver in a hip holster.

"I hope I never have to use old Betsy," he said, "but it's going to be comforting to know she's right there if I need her."

"And what about me?" asked Dale. "When do I help?"

"I have to relieve Tommy Pedlar on a job I assigned him to," Doc replied. "After I learn how he's made out, I promise to call if I need you."

"I'll be at my apartment," she said.

He nodded, placed the purple mask in a carefully concealed pocket in his coat. It made not the slightest bulge. He clipped a small pencil flash to his vest.

Dale put her slim fingers on his forearm. There was a slight catch in her voice as she said:

"Please be careful."

HE PUT his hands on her slender shoulders and looked deep into her lovely eyes. Forcing off the impulse to kiss those tremulous red, inviting lips was almost beyond his strength, but he knew that was not for him now. Until he had avenged his brother's ghastly death and smashed the wave of crime that threatened to engulf the city in a river of blood, he could not dare to fall in love. That must wait until the end of his mission.

Resolutely he turned and went through the rear door, which led into an alley that ended a block away. The builders of this house, a famous family that preferred privacy to the publicity that constantly overwhelmed them, had constructed the alley as an escape from hounding reporters. In the past, Miles had also used it for the same purpose, when insistent visitors refused to stop annoying him. But now it would enable him to come and go in secret, giving the enemy no chance to identify Doc Murdock and the Purple Scar as the same man.

It was seven P.M. and dark. Tommy Pedlar, huddled in a dark, vacant doorway only a few blocks from the tenement in which he lived, saw a man walking slowly up the street. He paid no heed. People had gone past him all afternoon and evening. But this one ducked into the darkness in which Tommy was hiding and asked abruptly:

"Do you have a match, Mr. Pedlar?"

For an instant Tommy was frightened. Then, when he realized, he blurted in amazement:

"Doc, it can't be you! How the devil did you do it—with mirrors?"

"Only one mirror," the Scar corrected. "What happened?"

Tommy indicated the rooming house directly across the way.

"Martin's still camped in there. I've been on his tail ever since he left the courtroom, just like you told me to, in case the jury brought in the wrong verdict. He came straight home. I don't know whether he got any calls or not, but he ain't left the house since he went in."

"Thanks, Tommy. I won't forget what you've done for me. By the way, you're not going to tend furnaces any longer. You'll be working for me. And Janie'll get away from these slums for good."

Tommy grinned sheepishly.

"Forget it, Doc. You done more for me and Janie than we'll ever be able to pay back."

"We won't argue now. I'll take over. If I'm here all night, be back first thing in the morning. Sooner or later he's coming out. When he does, he's going to march to the party or parties who hired him and we're going to be right behind him. At least one of us is."

"Okay, Doc," Tommy agreed.

Pulling the brim of his hat down almost to his eyes, he slipped from the shadowy doorway and sauntered away.

For almost two solid hours, Doc hid in the narrow doorway, waiting for Punchy Gus Martin to show. A cop came along and it was only through a bit of super-salesmanship that he convinced the bluecoat he was waiting for his wife.

By nine-thirty, it looked as if this vigil were to be in vain. Punchy Gus Martin seemed determined to stay in the house for the remainder of the night.

DOC WOULD have relished going in and trying to beat the right answers out of the slap-happy one. After watching him in the courtroom, though, Doc had more than a halfway hunch that Martin wouldn't talk, no matter how much drubbing he took. The burly ape was probably not courageous, but simply immune to punishment.

Suddenly the downstairs door of the house across the way opened. Instantly Doc pressed back against the side of the black doorway. He watched around the corner of the building, the breath stopped in his throat, hoping.

A man came out, a big man with powerfully broad shoulders and dangling arms. It was Punchy Gus Martin. Looking cautiously up and down the dark street, as if forewarned that he might be followed, the burly thug turned up his coat collar, tugged down his hat and hurried up the street.

Doc slipped from the doorway. He, too, glanced around to make sure this wasn't just a trap. Then he followed at a safe distance.

Punchy Gus walked three blocks to the bus line. After waiting a couple of minutes, he boarded the first bus that came along, marked "Red Point."

Doc didn't follow Punchy Gus Martin into the bus. Instead he hailed a cruising cab.

"Keep behind that bus," he instructed the driver. "Stop when it stops."

The cabbie didn't ask questions. He touched the peak of his cap, slapped down the flag on the meter and flew in pursuit of the big yellow-and-orange bus.

The bus made several stops, but Punchy Gus Martin did not get off. Through the rear window of the bus, Doc could see Martin's big head bobbing back and forth like a huge, black float.

Doc started in surprise as the bus headed across the bridge which led to Red Point. Red Point was an island just across the river from Akelton. It was part of the city, but Akelton had previously been ashamed of that fact.

On the east shore, Red Point faced the ocean. For years it had been a desolate, uninviting marshland. Recently, however, the State had decided to convert it into a public beach. There would be a ten-million-dollar boardwalk erected, facing the ocean. Even though ground had been broken on the site, it was still a deserted place after dark.

Doc couldn't for the life of him imagine why Gus Martin could be going there. He was still trying to find the answer as they roared over the bridge. A bus whizzed past them. The windows were too high and the bus was going too fast to be able to see how many people were in it. That was all the traffic they met all the way over.

The last stop the bus made was about an eighth of a mile from the bridge. It wasn't really a terminal, just a shack to protect passengers from the elements while waiting for the bus.

Doc told the taxi driver to pull up a distance from the shack. He paid him off and sent the vehicle rolling on its way back to the city.

Doc walked the rest of the way to where the bus had discharged its few passengers, squatters and workmen who lived in a squalid little settlement to the south, alongside the river.

Gus Martin didn't go that way. He kept following the twisting dirt road due east, toward the ocean side, where they had already started to drain water off the marshlands. Off in the darkness, Doc could make out the tall dredges and cranes, standing out against the night like grim, silent giants.

IT WAS a good half-mile walk across to the other side of the island. Doc could feel the difference in the air blowing in from the ocean. It was tangy, crisp, salty.

Gus Martin continued sloughing through the heavy, wet sand. Doc's curiosity was mounting with leaps and bounds. Where was Gus Martin heading? Who or what could possibly be out in this abandoned wilderness? There was not a house, not a light, only makeshift, deserted shacks jutting up here and there out of the marshy sand.

All at once a thin pencil of light cut through the blackness. Doc could see Punchy Gus Martin let out reefs in his stride. Doc quickened his pace, too. The light came from the window of one of the shacks.

Punchy Gus Martin headed straight for the door. He banged heavily with his big fist. The door opened quickly and the burly criminal vanished inside.

Doc advanced stealthily. His feet made eerie, gushy sounds in the cuppy suction of the wet sand. In various spots the light from the window slanted off shallow puddles of water, making them patches of yellow in the dimness.

Doc finally reached the window. The shade was drawn, but he could see under it, between the bottom of it and the sill.

The room was lighted by an oil lamp that stood on a rough wood table. There were a cot and a couple of chairs. Provisions lined the cupboard shelves.

A three-lung oil stove stood in the corner.

Across the table from Punchy Gus Martin sat a man only about half his size, yet he looked even uglier than the far from attractive giant. It seemed to Doc that he had seen him some place before, but he could not remember when.

Short-and-Ugly held a fat wad of bills in his hand. Obviously it was the pay-off. He counted out a neat pile and pushed it toward Punchy Gus. The big thug frowned down at the money and then at the little man before him.

"What's the idea?" he demanded. "I was to get five hundred bucks for keepin' my trap shut."

"The boss is in a tight spot right now," said Short-and-Ugly. "You'll get it later, but right now you'll have to take two hundred."

"Oh, yeah?" Rage was visibly boiling into Punchy Gus' frowning countenance. "I'm fed up with this cheap stuff. I just had my neck in the noose, see? I don't go through that kind for nobody and then get done outa my dough. You're tellin' me who the boss is and then takin' me to him. Don't forget they'd still like to find out who ordered that flatfoot plugged."

There was a disturbing *hiss* beside Doc's foot. At first it sounded like a snake, but Doc knew that snakes weren't to be found in these parts. He bent over to find out what it was. On the edge of a shallow pool of water were several thin layers of dry ice!

He had no chance to find out any more about the ice. Inside the shack there was a sudden and sharp explosion that shattered the stillness of the night. The impact jarred Doc off his feet.

CHAPTER VIII

CONDOR

BRACING HIMSELF, Miles Murdock looked through the window of the shack. The lamp had been upset and had caught fire to the dry wood floor. What he saw in its bright glow appalled him. The two men, who only a brief second ago had been wrangling about money, were now decapitated corpses, blown to pieces by a terrific explosion that must have occurred directly between them.

Doc knew it would take several moments before anyone could get here, so he dived to the door and burst inside the burning shack. An odd stench greeted his nostrils. He recognized it, but he had no time to identify it in the confusion of this awful moment.

The interior of the shack was almost completely demolished. The chairs and table were smashed, the provisions scattered everywhere. A huge section of the floor was fiercely burning.

Doc began beating out the flames. When he finally extinguished the fire, he shot the beam of his pencil flash at the smaller of the two men. Short-and-Ugly's face was beyond recognition, his clothes hanging to his mangled form by threads. Punchy Gus Martin looked even more horrible.

Then it struck Doc how uncannily similar was this explosion to the murder of old Mrs. Small. The condition of the bodies was identical, and the mysterious source of the explosion. Both had also seemed isolated to small areas.

Careful not to get blood on his own clothing, Doc fished through Short-and-Ugly's shredded garments. If anything had been inside the torn pockets of the coat, it had been entirely destroyed. But in the right trouser pocket was a handful of change, a combination jack-knife and bottle opener, a rabbit's foot, a miniature horseshoe and a small, cheaply-made lead medallion.

Doc recognized the medallion by its crude inscription. Peter de Gaul sold them to his people as "protective medals." He peddled them with the claim that whoever wore them would meet with no harm. It was just another medium of extorting pennies from the destitute, upon whom de Gaul preyed, for this one certainly hadn't done Short-and-Ugly a lot of good, nor had his other good luck charms.

Doc wasn't particularly concerned about the medallion, except that it answered one question. He remembered now where he had seen Short-and-Ugly. The thug had been a derelict who used to flop in the cellar of Peter de Gaul's mission. That meant de Gaul would certainly know who he was, maybe even something about his affiliations. Doc turned off his flash, jumped erect and sprang to the door. Through the darkness outside, he could see dim figures approaching. Men and women from Squattersville, over on the river bank, had been drawn by the din of the explosion, which had rolled like thunder out across the wasteland. That meant he must get away from this place fast.

THROUGH THE door he went, racing in the direction of the bridge, his feet fairly flying over the sand. He covered the distance in a matter of a few minutes. The bridge was just ahead of him when suddenly the wailing of police sirens halted him in his tracks!

"Police from Akelton," he muttered.

In those few moments someone must have summoned them, which meant Doc's way across the bridge, the only exit from this island, was blocked! He couldn't possibly leave without being found out and implicated. Red Point had suddenly turned into a trap!

Back off the road he ducked, out of the rays of the carlights sweeping over the bridge and roaring past toward the scene of destruction. Doc waited a moment to gather his senses. He couldn't stay here long. Sooner or later that taxi driver would reveal that he had brought a mysterious passenger over from Akelton. And they'd beat the marshes until they found him.

There was the river, of course, and Doc was a powerful swimmer. But expert as he was, he wouldn't even consider bucking that tide for that great distance.

Then an inspiration came to him.

Quickly he removed his disguise, the wax from his gums, the pallor from his face. He washed out the grease in his hair in a puddle of water.

He stayed hidden in the shadow of a cluster of reeds for about fifteen minutes, then ventured forth.

He hurried down the roadway and back to the shack where the explosion had occurred. Spotlights and headlights from the prowl cars illuminated the scene like a bizarre carnival. An ambulance and a big green emergency truck had also arrived. Police, reporters and island inhabitants were clustered about.

Someone saw Doc Murdock coming along the roadway and called him a stranger, whereupon two harness bulls pressed through the onlookers and nailed him.

"Who're you?" one demanded.

"Where did you come from?" the other added.

"I'm Doctor Miles Murdock," he answered quietly. "Just received an emergency call to hurry out here."

One of the cops shot the beam of his light into the plastic surgeon's face for a closer look. Recognition showed in his eyes.

"What screwball called you out here, Doc? You'd have to be more than a plastic surgeon to patch up the two birds inside. You'd have to be a magician."

They took Doc into the house. The lamp had been set on the shattered table and relighted. There were two interns, a couple of reporters and a handful of cops in the shack, making it too crowded for comfort. The peculiar odor that had eluded Doc was gone now.

ONE OF the men on the job was Lieutenant Riordon, a good friend of Dan Griffin's. He knew Doc.

Miles told the lieutenant about the phantom call which he insisted brought him out here. Thanks to his irreproachable reputation, no one even questioned the veracity of his statement.

"Know who either of them might be?" Doc asked innocently.

"No," Riordon replied with characteristic briskness. "Have to be a jigsaw puzzle expert to answer that one. Maybe the fingerprint gang'll be able to find something when they get here."

"Any idea how it happened?"

Riordon shrugged his wide shoulders.

"There's dynamite in one of the shacks at the far end of the island. It's used to sink the foundations for the boardwalk. Maybe these two were cookin' up a job and sort of mosied up there and 'borrowed' a little."

Doc offered what little assistance he could. Actually he was trying to determine for himself just how the blast had occurred and where it terminated. Had the explosive been planted in the floorboards? Was the lieutenant's theory accurate? Maybe Short-and-Ugly had stolen a few sticks of dynamite from the other end of the island. Perhaps it was in the drawer of the table, or hidden in the floor.

Doc hadn't seen exactly what had happened after Punchy Gus Martin's threat. Martin may have grabbed at the little man, knocked the lamp over and ignited the dynamite. But why had it been so similar to the way Mrs. Small died? Wouldn't dynamite do more damage? Also, what about that dry ice?

The door of the shack opened. A strapping man, rather handsome in a ratty sort of way and wearing foppish, expensive clothes, filled the doorway.

Doc recognized Luke Condor. He had even visited Condor's popular night club, the Red Falcon, but he knew that club was only a front. Luke Condor was the Number One Public Enemy of Akelton. He had his manicured digits dipped into every filth racket in the city. Not everybody knew that, of course, and the police could never prove it. Luke Condor's name seldom appeared in any of these shady transactions, yet there was no question that he was always involved.

"What the devil's goin' on here?" Condor barked.

Riordon shot him a nasty look.

"I can ask you pretty much the same question. What're you doin' here?"

Condor pushed into the shack. Two unpleasant-looking torpedoes followed faithfully at his heels.

"Who're them guys?" the night club owner demanded, indicating with his polished finger the two dead men.

Lieutenant Riordon's eyes were hot coals and they burned into Condor's broad back. Riordon didn't like Condor, it was plain. The gangster, ignoring him, didn't ease the situation.

"I asked you what you're doin' here," the lieutenant angrily repeated.

CONDOR WHIRLED to face him. His eyes, like a cobra's, challenged Riordan. His voice came out as heatedly as the lieutenant's and he took pains to make each word distinct.

"Don't yell at me. I ain't one of your thick-skulled flatfeet. I happen to own this shack and the property it's settin' on." He lifted his big hand and tapped Riordon's chest with the ends of his manicured fingers. "Now you start answerin' my question."

The lieutenant winced under the look, then rage suffused his lowering countenance. Doc thought it a good time to interrupt.

"Hello, Condor," he said mildly.

Condor turned with a glower. Then, as he recognized the plastic surgeon, the glower changed to a grin.

"How're ya, Doc? You here, too? What the blazes goes on?"

Doc told him in as few words as possible. Storm clouds gathered in Condor's face.

"Somebody's tryin' to frame me!"

"Who?" asked Riordon, still smarting under the sting of the gangster's rebuke.

"How should I know?"

"You don't happen to know either of these men, do you, Condor?" Doc inquired.

Condor bent forward and looked carefully at both bodies.

"Yeah," he said, straightening. "According to his clothes and size, he looks like my watchman."

"What was his name?" Riordon asked.

"Am I supposed to know the name of every bum I hand a job to?" Condor whipped back sharply. "I was out here one day and he came moochin' around for a handout. I happened to need somebody to look after the place, so I slipped him the job."

"You better come back to Headquarters with us and explain that a little better," Riordon stated.

"Sez who?"

Doc didn't wait to hear any more. He was anxious to get back to Akelton and have a talk with Peter de Gaul. Maybe the settlement worker could tell him something about Short-and-Ugly that would clear up this whole mess. Perhaps he might dump the whole rotten business right on Luke Condor's doorstep.

Doc slipped out the door. Before starting down the road to catch the bus back to the city, he took another look under the window. But what he hoped to find there was gone. The dry ice had evaporated.

CHAPTER IX

THE LOWEST RACKET

IT WAS eleven-thirty when Doc Murdock crawled through a basement window and into the mission house. The place was closed for the night. The denizens had left long ago.

Perhaps de Gaul would have willingly given Doc Murdock the information he was after with a more formal entrance, but Doc didn't deem it wise to let anyone know that Miles Murdock was interested in the case, especially Peter de Gaul. The missioner had no secrets from the world. If Doctor Murdock visited him, asking questions about a medallion found on a dead man in an explosion, everyone in the district would hear about it by morning.

Since Doc didn't wish to take the time to go back to the studio and put on fresh make-up, he wore for the first time the mask of the Purple Scar! He went noiselessly through the dark hall. De Gaul, he saw, hadn't yet retired. The missioner was still in his cubbyhole office.

At the Scar's hoarse whisper, de Gaul whirled in his swivel chair, froze. His mouth wide open. His eyes swelled in his head like a goldfish's. He was too frightened to speak. All he did was sit there and stare up at that ghastly scarred face. It looked for a moment as if he were going to faint. His colorless face went deathly white. His knees starting banging together with fear.

"I'm the Purple Scar," said the hideous apparition. "I'm not here to harm you. I simply want the answers to a few questions."

"If—if you're a thief and—and it's money you want—it's in my—my safe," de Gaul choked out. "Only please don't kill me! Please!"

The Scar tossed the lead medallion onto the desk.

"That's one of your protective coins, isn't it?" De Gaul nodded. The weird voice continued: "A man was killed tonight. He had this coin in his trouser pocket. I want to know who that man was, because I happen to know he was staying here at this mission about a month or so ago. He was a short man, not bigger than five-two, thin, very ugly, sandy hair, mouse-shaped face."

De Gaul gulped nervously. "Short, thin, ugly?"

"Right," said the deadly voice. "Who was he?"

De Gaul continued to stare at him. He swallowed again nervously. "Sounds like a description of Gyp Nolan—"

"Nolan was taller than five-two and much heavier than this man."

"Then—then maybe it was Dutch Andrews."

"Andrews had dark hair. I knew him, too."

De Gaul hesitated. "Then perhaps it was Jerry Farrar."

"Farrar? Did he live here about a month ago?"

"Yes, just about. I remember because he was here when we painted the ceilings. He helped. He was a good worker."

"Why did he leave?" the Scar asked.

"He said he had a job."

"With whom?"

"He didn't say. He never did talk very much."

"Did he ever mention Luke Condor's name?"

"Who?"

"Luke Condor, the gangster."

"Oh, no," de Gaul said with indignation. "Of course not."

"Did he ever mention a man named Punchy Gus Martin?"

"The man who was tried for killing John Murdock?"

"Yes."

De Gaul shook his head.

"Never," he said venomously. "I am sure he could not have known thatthat murderer!"

"What makes you say Martin was a murderer?"

DE GAUL'S eyes flamed with unconcealed fury.

"What makes me say so? Because I know he was. He killed my friend, John Murdock, one of my people. I sat in the courtroom. I saw. I heard. That man was guilty!"

Doc smiled behind the mask.

"Then you'd want to see John Murdock's murder avenged?"

"By all means!"

"You knew the Smalls pretty well."

If such a thing were possible, de Gaul's eyes opened wider.

"Why, yes," he faltered. "I knew them very well. They were my people also. They came regularly to hear my sermons. They were good people, very good people. But what have they—"

"Did they have any money?" the Scar put in. "Any valuables?"

"No. They were as poor as the mice in my cellar. They didn't even have money enough to buy coal for their little stove. On cold nights they often came here and stayed with me."

"Who paid for their funerals?" asked the Scar.

De Gaul paused for a long moment, his gaze riveted on the Scar's face.

"Arnold Wisply," he replied at last.

The name struck the Scar like a thunderbolt. He should have thought of Wisply before. He recalled now that he had heard of the tenement owner burying a good many of the elderly destitutes who lived in his dilapidated buildings, yet it had never occurred to him before as being significant. He should have realized the fat pinch-penny wasn't the type to give away charity, unless he had a good ulterior motive.

A talk with Arnold Wisply might prove interesting, the Purple Scar decided. Better still would be a look through his books and papers.

There was a closet in one corner of the small office. The door was warped and almost ready to drop off, but it would hold a man of de

Gaul's feeble strength until the Scar could get out of the building and away.

Doc apologized briefly for the necessity, locked de Gaul inside the closet and left the building with a fresh scent to track down.

From a drug store telephone booth, he called Dale Jordan at her apartment.

"You have a car, haven't you?" he asked.

"Yes," the girl answered. "It isn't much, but it'll take you where you want to go and bring you back—I hope. That part unfortunately doesn't depend on the car."

"Get it and meet me at the corner of Chestnut and Autumn as soon as you can. But first stop at the studio and get my make-up kit."

Less than twenty minutes later, Dale Jordan picked up Doc Murdock in her coupé. They drove to a secluded spot, where he quickly put on a fresh make-up. Then they proceeded to Wisply's residence.

Wisply lived in the suburbs, which was the principal reason why Doc had called Dale to drive him. Transit facilities were bad out there and he wanted to make sure he had a quick getaway if he needed it.

A BLOCK from their destination, the Scar got out of the car. He told Dale to drive around and return to this spot at five-minute intervals until he showed up.

"I'll be only about five or ten minutes at the most," he promised.

The Scar found the home of Arnold Wisply to be a huge house set on a lawned terrace, surrounded with dense shrubbery and trees. It was a glaring contrast to the squalor of the tenements that paid for it. Always a humanitarian, Doc could scarcely control his anger and disgust.

Keeping well in the deep shadows of the hedges that cluttered the grounds, he stole to the rear of the house. The place was in total darkness. He climbed up onto the porch and tried the back door. It was locked.

From his inside coat pocket he drew a bunch of keys, a priceless collection that would have done justice to a first-grade burglar. As a matter of fact, they once had. They once belonged to Tommy Pedlar, the Sticky-fingered Kid.

The Scar easily got the door open and slipped inside. It was black and vast as the interior of a whale's belly until he turned on his flashlight and proceeded warily through the rooms to the library. He didn't know whether Wisply was home or not, but he didn't think it necessary to put on the mask. His disguise, he knew, would be sufficient.

He went directly to the big desk standing in one corner of the library. Though he carefully went through the papers that littered the top of the desk, he could find nothing of importance. He started with the top drawer and searched the desk itself.

In the next to the bottom drawer there were several black ledgers. Each bore the name of a different street in the slum section. The Scar selected the book titled "Fleming Street," the street the Smalls had lived on.

A glance at the first couple of pages told the Scar that the ledger was divided and arranged according to houses that Wisply owned on these streets. He thumbed back to 28, the number of the tenement where the Smalls had lived. On the third floor of tenement 28 was the name "Small, Anne and Joseph." Beside their names were the words "Paid in Full. Account Closed. May 15, 1939." And there were several odd numbers.

The significance of this entry brought the Scar's altered brows together in a puzzled frown. The Smalls hadn't died until March, 1941, yet they lived rent free in Arnold Wisply's tenement since May, 1939. Why? In what way had Arnold Wisply been obligated to these people? Why had he allowed them a free apartment for almost two years?

Curious, the Scar went through the entire book. There were other names with the same cancellations, names that the Scar knew. They were all elderly people. What kind of devilish scheme was Wisply involved in? Was he really a great benefactor who didn't want his good deeds known?

No matter how he tried, the Scar couldn't picture Wisply as a philanthropist.

PLACING THE book back carefully in the drawer, he continued his search more eagerly than before. He was certain that those entries were cross-indexed some place else. When that cross-index was found, it would probably answer the question he was searching for.

There was nothing else in the desk, but in a small cabinet behind it he found a small card index.

He had memorized the numbers alongside Mr. and Mrs. Small's names. He got out the card that corresponded. It read:

109

A—$750—May 15, 1939

B—$500—May 21, 1939

Final total—$370

It wasn't hard for the Scar to figure out what those startling figures spelled. On May 15 and May 21 respectively, Arnold Wisply had taken over Mr. and Mrs. Small's insurance polices and cashed them in for a total of $1250. It was plain that this was Wisply's way of making a few extra dollars at the expense of these aged destitutes. According to the cards, he practiced it on all his elderly tenants, people with only a few more years to live.

Obviously he had them cash in their policies for what they could get, then turn the money over to him with the understanding that they would receive free burial and free rent in his house for as long as they lived. In the case of the Smalls, he had made the insignificant sum of three hundred and seventy dollars. Had Mrs. Small lived a few more years, Wisply would have lost money.

When dealing with individual cases, the profit would always be small, but Wisply housed many hundreds of aged tenants. The total must run into staggering figures. And a man who would stoop to taking such unfair advantage of these unfortunates might stoop to anything, even murder.

Disgustedly, still bewildered by it all, the Scar replaced the cards into the cabinet and shut the door. He heard a step behind him, snapped off his flash and started to turn. Something hard and heavy whirred through the air and collided with his skull.

He grabbed at the darkness. Another stinging blow hit him at the base of the skull. This one brought absolute darkness.

The Scar crashed to the floor.

CHAPTER X

FISH FOOD

RIDING AROUND in her coupé, Dale Jordan carried out the Scar's instructions to the letter. At five-minute intervals she returned to the spot where he had left her, but he was nowhere in sight.

After the third trip, her fears began to mount. He had told her he wouldn't be any longer than five or ten minutes. She forced herself to make two more trips, but still he was not there. Something was wrong!

She parked the car in the shade of a great oak tree about a half a block from Wisply's house and continued toward the place on foot. She started up the pathway that led to the house. Suddenly she heard the gravel *crunch* just ahead of her, then the sound of voices.

She sprang back into a cluster of shrubbery. Too late she learned they were brambles. The thorns clawed her face, caught at the sheer threads

in her silk hose. She tore herself away from them and turned on her spikeheeled shoes to run.

She saw a big, moving dark shape, a shape that seemed in no hurry at all, for it calmly moved toward her. The disturbance she had caused trying to escape from those thorny bushes must have attracted their attention.

For a fraction of a second she was paralyzed with fear. Then she mustered her courage, leaped to the side and tried to streak past the figure blocking her path. Just as she thought she was going to make it, a hand darted from the blackness and clutched her throat!

She went down onto the ground with fingers tightening in unhurried pressure on her slim white throat. For all their lack of frenzy, the fingers closed off her breath, gave her no chance to cry out for help. Her senses faded into a whirlpool of blackness.

The Scar heard the
splash as Dale was
thrown into the water.

TO DOC MURDOCK'S befogged brain, it, seemed that he was
in a small cramped boat that was lurching crazily over a dark, rough
sea. Then that illusion faded and he became aware of two concrete
facts. His head ached as though the brain inside it had been pounded
with a hammer. Secondly, he was not in a boat. He was bound hand
and foot and stretched out on the floor of a moving car.

He had a painful few minutes trying to collect his senses and remember what had happened, but after putting those cards back into
the cabinet in Wisply's library, he had no recollection. It didn't take a
super-brain for him to figure out that he had been sapped expertly!
Who had done it, though? Hirelings of Wisply? Or had Condor smelled
a rat in the shack at Red Point and sent a few of his gorillas to follow
him?

He tested the ropes tentatively. They were strong and well tied. His right arm was asleep under him. He attempted to turn over to work the circulation back into it and felt a limp bundle beside him.

Someone else was lying on the floor of the car with him. But the waves of pain shooting through his body from the base of his skull jumbled his thoughts out of all continuity. That last wallop had certainly been well planted.

He hadn't the least idea where the car was heading. Street lamps, flashing by at regular intervals, told him that they were still in the city. That first thought of being in a boat came back to him. He knew now why he imagined that. It was the smell of salt water. They must be nearing the river.

THERE WAS another aroma he was aware of, too, something familiar and sweet. Perfume! In the short space between two street lamps, his heart stood still. He knew that perfume, but he tried to tell himself he was wrong. It couldn't be!

Making a supreme effort, he turned his head and was able to see the indistinct white blur formed by the other prisoner's face.

It was Dale!

In his groggy mind he could not begin to answer the question of how she had got there.

Out of the corner of his eyes, he looked up and saw two men sitting on the back seat. He could make out their faces in the red glow of their cigarettes each time they inhaled, but he had never seen either of them before. There were two other men on the front seat. Miles could not see their faces.

Jolting on the floor of the limousine, he wondered just what was behind all this. Where were they taking Dale and him? What were they going to do to them? Was Wisply planning to dispose of them because Miles had uncovered his little get-rich-quick scheme, which might trace back to the murder of Mrs. Small, or was this some of Condor's doings?

Doc reached over to see if Dale was conscious. She was motionless and he could not hear her breathing. A sudden shiver passed over him. Maybe she was dead. Perhaps they had killed her.

He wanted to call to her, but he fought off the impulse. He didn't want these four men to know he was conscious. Feigning unconsciousness might be the one chance for escape.

While the car sped on and on, he worked at the stout ropes binding his arms and legs, trying to work them free.

With amazing suddenness the car careened to the right, rolled about thirty or forty feet and came to a skidding, jolting halt. It was dark and silent in this spot. Somewhere out on the water, a buoy was moaning its weird refrain. The waves rolled up and lashed against the piling of a pier.

The car doors opened, and the two thugs in the tonneau piled out, stepping on Murdock's body as they did so. Murdock heard a faint gasp beside him, and he knew Dale was now conscious. The four men conferred briefly together at the front of the car, and then three of them made off in the darkness. There was only one man left to guard the two prisoners.

"Dale!" whispered Murdock sharply. "Can you hear me, Dale?"

"Yes, Doc. What are you doing?"

"I'm about to get—free," he panted. "There! Now let me untie you. When I give the word, jump out of here and run like the devil. I'm going to tackle the man left to guard us."

"Where are we?"

"Somewhere on the waterfront is all I know," replied Murdock.

"Hey, what's goin' on here?" snarled the crook in the front seat, twisting around and peering down in the gloom.

AT THAT instant Doc Murdock hit him. It sounded like the thock of a club against a sack of sand. The crook grunted once and spilled down on the front seat like that same sand running out of the sack. Instantly Doc was up and frisking his unconcious body for guns.

He found two, and he thrust one into Dale's hand. "Pile out and run back from the rear of the car before the others return," he ordered. "I know this place. It's Foley's Wharf —a dilapidated, deserted pier and warehouse close to the slums."

Dale nodded, spilled out of the tonneau, and started running. Murdock followed. They started along the brick wall of the warehouse when somebody let out a strangled shout behind them. It was the crook Murdock had slugged. A shot sounded from down along the old pier. And then the chauffeur barged into Doc's form.

To Murdock's surprise, the fellow didn't tackle him. He simply sagged drunkenly against the retreating surgeon. He had been accidentally shot by one of his companions. At once Murdock grabbed him around the waist and held him as a sort of shield while he began firing away at the crooks returning along the length of the wharf. All the while Murdock was backing toward the street, urging Dale on.

Slugs whistled dangerously close as the night echoed to gunfire. So anxious to get Dale out of this trap and out of range of flying bullets,

Murdock retreated rapidly along the brick wall of the structure close to the old wharf. There was a lighted window just beyond a gloomy doorway, but he didn't see it. And then, just as he reached a point even with the door, the barrier suddenly opened, letting out an oblong of light that framed the figure of a man with an automatic in his hand.

Dale Jordan jerked her head around, saw this new menace, and opened her mouth to scream a warning. But she was too late. Quick as a panther the man leaped forward and caught the girl's gun wrist even as he brought his own gun barrel down across the back of Murdock's neck in a chopping blow.

Everything exploded in a flash of orange light for Murdock. But he didn't completely lose consciousness as he crumpled down, paralyzed, over the body of the wounded chauffeur. The faint hope of escape he had cherished was cruelly crushed as hands promptly seized him and began dragging him back along the pier.

He heard Dale scream faintly, and then scuffling sounds indicated that the girl was being dragged along after him. Their captors were mad, angrily cursing Murdock and each other. This, however, didn't prevent them from re-tying their prisoners.

Murdock groaned bitterly to himself. He knew perfectly well what was to become of the girl and himself. They were destined to become fish food.

The thought of dying wasn't easy to take, but that, he supposed philosophically, was part of this dangerous game he had chosen to play. Though he could steel himself to meet his own death calmly enough, he could not resign himself to the fact that Dale was to die with him. She had no part in this game. He cursed himself mentally for letting her get mixed up in it in the first place.

OUT ALONG the narrow, rickety pier which jutted far out over the inky water the men carried the girl and the doctor. The footsteps of the four men beat with a hollow eeriness over the loose planking, like muffled drums. Every muscle in the Scar's big body tensed as they arrived at the end of the pier and the two thugs holding him halted. Once, twice, they swung him and then let him go.

Far out over into the ebony-colored water he flew. He sucked a deep breath of air into his lungs just before he struck with a *splash* that almost burst his eardrums.

A coal-black waste engulfed him. He quickly collected his wits and struck out underwater with his tied feet.

During those last few steps along the pier, he had seen out of the corner of his eyes the hulk of a small craft moored to a floating buoy not more than a dozen yards off the end of the pier. That was where he headed now. If he could make it before the pressure of water fought its way into his lungs, there was a chance for Dale and himself.

He wriggled through the water inches below the surface like some strange fish, slashing his feet as though they were a tail. Battling with grim fury, he tried to close that distance before the precious air in his lungs gave out. Once the air went, the Purple Scar's short career of fighting crime would be abruptly punctuated by death. Even worse, lovely Dale would never smile and laugh again.

His shoulder-blades brushed against something hard and unyielding. The boat!

He glided underneath and came up on the other side, where the thugs on the pier could not see him. He choked out water and drew in welcome air.

There was a sudden, loud *splash*. His heart sprang to his throat. It was Dale! They had thrown her into the river. She would surely drown if he did not get to her.

To the stern of the boat he writhed, dived and reached the knifelike blades of the propeller. Desperately he sawed the bonds on his wrists against the propeller's edge. Just before his lungs gave out, he felt them part.

He didn't bother to unlash his legs, but cut through the choppy black water to the spot where Dale had gone down. The thugs spied him as he rose to the surface for a fresh supply of air. Their guns began flaming and barking in the tarry silence, but the lead that spat made harmless little dull plops in the water.

Miles had dived again. Straight down to the bottom of the black river he went. He groped frantically with both hands through the ink, trying to find her. His lungs felt as if they would surely burst. His head pounded with the pressure of the water.

And then his fingers touched her!

HE DID not stop to untie her. Together they floated to the surface. And then, still underwater, he swam her to safety behind the boat.

He saw there was no sense in trying to speak to her. She was unconscious, tossing helplessly in his arm on the water. He listened and chanced a glimpse at the pier. The thugs were not there. He wondered why.

The answer screamed out of the night at him. A siren! The police had been attracted by the gunfire.

Somehow the Scar managed to reach up and grip the boat's low railing. With his ebbing strength he pulled himself and the girl over the bulwark onto the deck.

A glance at the dull, livid color of her face gave him a terrible fright. He feared he had reached her too late, that she was already dead.

Hastily he untied her hands and feet, turned her over on her face and fought desperately to bring her back to life with artificial respiration.

A VOICE from a long, long distance hammered at Dale's consciousness.

"Dale! Dale! Snap out of it, darling!"

Her eyes flickered and opened. The first thing that came into sharp relief was Doc Murdock's wet, drawn face.

She reached up her arms to him weakly. He took hold of her and held her tightly, tenderly. She wasn't quite sure whether she was alive or dead, nor did she care much, just so long as he held her like this, always.

He got her to shore and they had to walk a half a dozen blocks before they found a taxi. Even then the driver wasn't enthusiastic about their getting into his cab and dripping all over it. But the magic of a five-dollar bill soon changed his mind.

CHAPTER XI

DEATH WALK

U NSEEN THEY returned to Doc's house through the concealed alley at the rear. They changed into dry clothes and had hot drinks. Dale was so badly shaken up by her underwater ordeal that she willingly agreed to stay here and let Doc go on alone.

The river hadn't left much of the Purple Scar's disguise intact. Being human, for all his great strength and shrewdness, he had to learn by his mistakes. This experience had taught him the value of a disguise that could be removed only by himself.

"I'll have to use the purple mask as a basic disguise," he told Dale. "When its psychological effect is needed, it must be instantly available. Slipping it on and off is clumsy and undramatic. I'll have to work out some other method."

"Have you an idea?" she asked.

"Yes," he replied, turning to his make-up materials. "I'll show you soon."

Working swiftly with clay, he fashioned a face that would not linger in any spectator's memory. After hardening the clay with his special drier, he made a plaster of paris cast, prepared a solution of melted gum elastic and poured it into the mold.

While he was waiting for it to set, he took his purple mask out of the secret pocket in his coat. The men who had tried to drown him had not discovered it, though they had relieved him of his gun. He had to get another from the wall safe.

He put on the ghastly mask, removed the second one from its mold and slipped it over the corpse face.

"Why, it's perfect!" Dale exclaimed. "You look like a—a salesman. I can't see even a trace of the purple mask through it."

"You can't?" he asked solemnly. "I'll have to remedy that."

He suddenly snatched off the upper mask, revealing the face beneath in all its scarred horror. Dale had been expecting it, yet she gasped and recoiled.

When Doc left the studio, he felt he had accomplished something. He now had two suspects, Wisply and Condor, and one motive on which to work. But he still had not visited the man who probably held the key to this entire riddle—the lawyer, Chris Korpuli.

Korpuli was the connecting link between short and ugly Jerry Farrar and the man who paid to have John Murdock killed, for it was apparent now that Punchy Gus Martin had been merely a pawn in this game of death.

As Doc had reasoned back there in the courtroom, Martin did the actual killing, but the job came to him through Jerry Farrar, who in turn got it from someone else. Martin obviously never even knew why or for whom he was murdering, but Korpuli must know. It was up to the Purple Scar to make him tell whether he was working for Condor or Wisply.

Doc knew that sooner or later his chase would lead to Korpuli. He also knew, however, that the attorney was smart. He hadn't wanted to tackle the crafty mouthpiece until he was a little better fortified with the facts. Well, that time was here right now. Korpuli was his next move.

Hailing a cruising cab from the corner, the Scar shot across to the Twenty-fifth Century Hotel, where Chris Korpuli lived. A cliff-like brick building, it towered twenty-five floors into the sky, high above the rest of Akelton.

Miles walked into the glittering lobby of the Twenty-fifth Century. He didn't know Korpuli's room number, yet he went past the desk. The clerk might start asking questions, perhaps get suspicious and notify the lawyer that someone was down here. Desk clerks are like that. So he button-holed one of the bellhops and slipped him a dollar for the information he wanted.

A couple of minutes later, the Scar was standing on the crimson plush on the twentieth floor. He located Room 2002. He made sure the coast was clear, then got out his priceless bunch of keys and inserted one into the lock. The door opened easily enough, but a chain-lock was strung across, holding it. There was not a chance in the world of getting past that barrier.

HE LOOKED about and spied a window at the end of the corridor. He hurried to it and peered out. He counted the windows away from this one. Those that would lead into Chris Korpuli's apartment were the third, fourth and fifth.

A ledge about a foot wide ran around the dark facade of the building. From the pavements, twenty stories below, came a distant rumble of traffic. The Scar knew success was the result of audacity and caution, the ability to take chances when they were necessary, but minimizing the odds by shrewd foresight. Though he was no human fly, there was only one way to enter Korpuli's rooms. He had to crawl out along that narrow ledge at that dizzy height.

Making sure the wind was not strong and that his fingers would find purchase between the bricks, he slipped off the top mask, exposing the horrible one beneath. He climbed through the window and stood up on the ledge. There was just enough room for his feet. He closed his eyes momentarily to steady himself. Then, face pressed close against the cold, rough wall, the fingers of his left hand feeling carefully for spaces between the bricks, he began moving along toward Korpuli's apartment.

He had weighed the risk against the gain, and found the chance of success worth the grave danger. In his first attempt to move along a ledge twenty stories above the ground, dizziness naturally assailed him, but he forced it off. If he lost his hold, he would tumble through space until he smashed against the sidewalk, and crime would again be free to defy decent citizens.

He clung tenaciously to the bricks, edging along without looking down. Reaching the first window safely, he stopped to let out his breath and exercise his cramped fingers. Again he drew a deep breath, flexed his fingers and continued doggedly.

His fingers touched the casement of the second window. He pulled himself to the safety of the sill. Two down and one to go!

Once more he filled his tight lungs and inched out along the foot-wide ledge. The distance between the second and third windows seemed the greatest, perhaps because his goal was close and he was beginning to tire. His fingers were scraped and numb, his legs growing stiff.

At last he reached it. His fingers wrapped on the frame and he pulled himself up to a crouching position on the sill. He peered inside.

Like the other two windows, this one was dark. Cautiously he tried the lock. It was open. People hardly expect visitors to pop in through windows twenty stories high.

Raising the window slowly and with a minimum of noise, he slipped into the room. It was dark and silent. He closed the window behind him, waited a moment, listened. No sound came.

Carefully he moved forward. His eyes had become more or less accustomed to the darkness and he could see well enough not to fall over the chairs and tables.

This, he gathered, must be the library or the living room. He proceeded to the big archway which separated this from the next room. He went through that to the next, then visited one after another until he finally came to the bedroom. He stood for a moment in the doorway, listening to heavy breathing. He smiled to himself, and felt for the wall switch and clicked it on.

BEFORE HIM in the big bed was sprawled Chris Korpuli. But the lawyer did not remain in that posture long. He bolted upright in bed and rubbed his eyes dazedly. As the hideous face of the man standing before him came into sharp focus, he drew back appalled.

"Who are you?" he demanded.

There wasn't much authority in his quavering voice. He wasn't at all the arrogant little fighter the police were used to seeing. He was terrified by the horribly scarred, dead face that stared down at him.

"I'm the Purple Scar," answered a hollow voice from the tomb. "Throw on a robe and get out of bed!"

The eagle-beaked lawyer did not argue. He snatched up a vividly colored wrapper, slipped into it and swung his legs off the bed. There were red-and-black patent leather slippers for his feet. He stood up trembling.

"Which way to the library?" the Scar wanted to know.

"Through there." Korpuli nodded his coconut head toward the archway.

"That's where you're going. You are to do some talking. While you're at it, you may as well put it in writing."

The criminal lawyer looked at him appraisingly.

"What is the meaning of this outrage?" he rapped out. He sounded a little more like his caustic self.

"You'll find out soon enough. Get into the library!"

Korpuli didn't move quickly enough, so the Scar reached out, grabbed him by the back of the neck and shoved him through the archway. Korpuli snapped on the library lights.

"Now sit down behind that desk," the Scar commanded.

The lawyer obediently did as he was told—too obediently, the Scar thought. And he also thought he detected just the faint semblance of a smile quirk one corner of Korpuli's tight mouth as he went around the desk. The Scar's uncanny sense of danger swept over him. Without appearing in the least suspicious, he glanced into the window behind Korpuli. Against the blackness outside, all objects in the room were reflected as if in a mirror.

The Scar glimpsed a glint of steel behind the portieres that masked off the archway. The nozzle of a revolver! No wonder Chris Korpuli could afford a smile. The Purple Scar knew if he tried to reach his gun, he'd be shot down before he could get it out of his holster. This was one of those moments when a quick brain spelled the scant margin between life and death.

His fountain pen was clipped to the pocket of his coat. He slipped it off.

"Get a piece of paper," he said to Korpuli.

He could see the man in back of the portieres stalk forward like an Indian after a scalp. The Scar pretended he didn't even know he was there.

Korpuli, laughing to himself, got a sheet of paper and laid it on the desk. The Scar unscrewed the top of his pen.

"You're writing a little note," he said, "telling just who hired you to defend Gus Martin, or—"

"Or what?" grated a menacing voice close to his left ear.

The Scar twisted to meet a pair of vicious snake-eyes set in a cold, impassive face. Twin cabbages seemed pinned to the man's narrow temples. The gun he held was on a direct line with the Purple Scar's third rib.

The eagle-eyed lawyer let out a grating, scornful laugh.

"Didn't you stop to think that maybe I had a valet, or a butler, or even a bodyguard?" he sneered. "You see, I've had visitors here before, so I installed push buttons at several places around the room. There happens to be one right alongside the light switch when you come into this room.

That's why I obediently pushed the button. Usually it takes only five seconds for Custer to get here after I ring. Tonight it took ten."

"I was sleeping pretty sound, sir," Custer said with a half-grin.

"Now, what was it you were telling me to write for you, Mister Purple Face?" Korpuli drawled with biting disdain.

The Scar did not reply in words. Like the swift claw of a cat, his left hand jumped up. Out of the fountain pen he was holding shot a stream of black fluid, blinding the man with the gun. With the same continuous motion, the Scar whipped out his right fist. It landed with devastating force on the point of Custer's abbreviated chin. Custer dropped the gun and staggered.

It was his last stand for the Scar lifted him up off the floor, held him a moment above his head, then tossed the "butler" half-across the room onto the leather divan. The divan gave way under his bulk.

Custer went crashing onto the floor and did not move.

CHAPTER XII

THE TABLES KEEP TURNING

EVERYTHING HAD happened in the wink of an eye, but not too swiftly for Chris Korpuli to reach the phone and try to flash the switchboard. The Scar dived over the desk, grabbed the phone from Korpuli's hands and yanked the wires out of the wall.

"Don't you touch me!" Korpuli cried out, retreating around the desk. "You'll never make me talk. I won't tell you anything!"

With that the lawyer made a mad dash for the door. The Purple Scar's hand shot out, clutched the flowing skirt of Korpuli's robe and dragged him to the window.

"Change your mind about talking?"

"No!" Korpuli spat out venomously. "Never. I'll never talk!"

A ghost of a smile crossed the Purple Scar's face at Korpuli's defiance, but the lawyer could not see that smile. The Scar had swept him off his feet. Without bothering to open the window, he shoved Korpuli through. There was a *crash* of glass and the lawyer was dangling twenty stories above the ground, held only by the Scar's strong right hand, which clutched the throat of Korpuli's robe.

"Change your mind yet?" the Purple Scar asked calmly.

"Yes, yes!" the frantic lawyer screamed out, with one glance down at the antlike traffic crawling so far below. "Yes, I'll talk—I'll talk! Pull me in!"

He clung to the Scar's wrist with grim terror. The Purple Scar could well appreciate his feelings. That walk along the ledge had given birth to this idea.

"Who hired you to defend Martin?"

"Condor—Luke Condor hired me," Chris Korpuli choked out. "Pull me in!"

Luke Condor! Ever since the gangster first made his appearance over at Red Point, Doc Murdock had been trying to figure out why Condor should have wanted John killed. Their worlds were poles apart. John's territory covered the slums exclusively and he didn't often get into Condor's exclusive section of town.

Unless Luke Condor was mixed up in the crooked insurance policy racket that Arnold Wisply was running! Condor certainly wasn't above such a dirty business. He'd rub out a six month-old baby, if he could be sold on the idea that it had gold in its teeth.

"Did Condor order John Murdock's murder?" the Scar asked.

"I don't know!" Korpuli shrilled, his bony fingers digging into the Scar's wrist like iron claws. "Condor just told me to get Martin out of the jam he was in." The lawyer was on the verge of collapse. "Bring me in! Please bring me in. I'm—I'm falling—"

The Scar believed the lawyer had told all he knew, or at least all that danger would make him reveal. He pulled Korpuli back over the sill and dumped him onto the floor, alongside the window. Korpuli lay there, a limp bundle of flesh and bone, looking for all the world as if he had been pulled through a wringer.

There was a sudden banging of fists against the door. Miles' heart beat fast. Korpuli revived, began to yell. Before the Scar could get to him to stifle his words, they were out:

"Help! Break down the door. He's in here—the Purple Scar!"

AT ONCE, in response to Korpuli's quick outcry, hard heavy shoulders smashed fiercely against the door. The Scar, revolver drawn, swept the room for an escape. There was none. He was trapped, twenty stories up!

There was a loud splintering of wood as one of the thugs struck the door with a terrific impact. The hinges wrenched loose and the door crashed down, disgorging three hoods into the room, revolvers in hand.

The Scar had not been caught napping. In that moment he had swept the lawyer in front of him as a shield and jabbed the deadly, black muzzle of his revolver into the cringing mouthpiece's right ear.

The three thugs stopped short when they spied the precarious spot the attorney was in.

"One wrong move, my friends," the Scar said with quiet menace, "and you'll see Mister Korpuli's brilliant brain splashed all over these clean walls. If you want him to go on using that brain to help you out of jams, throw down your guns."

The three yeggs knew it would be the finish for them if anything did happen to Chris Korpuli. If it hadn't been for him, Condor and the entire gang would have been imprisoned long ago. They looked from one to the other, shrugged and let their guns slip to the floor.

Miles worked his way toward the door, keeping the shivering, sweating lawyer between himself and the three gangsters. The Scar's gaze suddenly centered on one of the men before him, a broad-shouldered thug, six feet tall, with black eyes and blondish hair. Studying the contours of the triangular-shaped head, the square chin and large, angular jaw, a thought sprang into his brain.

Dealing with Luke Condor wasn't going to be simple. The racketeer was under the watchful eye of his heavily armed torpedoes twenty-four hours a day. Miles' one chance would be to get Condor away from the bodyguards. If he could accomplish this, he was certain he could make the racketeer talk. A threat to spoil Condor's handsome features would shake him more than a ten-year sentence to prison. A session on Doc's operation table would terrorize the conceited crime boss. He was sure of it.

With a few ingenious alterations, Doc thought he would be able to pass for Triangular Head. They were the same build, height and weight. The thug's mouth was wider and thinner, his brow heavier, his nose broader, his hair of a different hue. Those, however, were trifles which Doc's skill could easily overcome.

On the other hand, if he took Triangular Head, it would mean sacrificing Chris Korpuli. He couldn't hope to get out of the building with both of them. But for the immediate present, Triangular Head was the more important of the two. Besides, Korpuli was keen enough not to escape at a time like this and condemn himself. The Scar was sure he would be able to reach the wily mouthpiece whenever he wanted him.

"YOU!" HE barked at the thug with the triangular head. "Come over here!"

The man hesitated.

"Come over!" Korpuli seconded, perspiring. "If he shoots me, you're through anyhow."

Triangular Head obeyed. In a flash the Scar pushed Korpuli halfway across the room. His left arm snaked up and coiled around the neck of Triangular Head. The nose of the gun jammed into the second ear it had explored that night. A master psychologist, Doc knew the sensation of cold death pressed into the most sensitive spot on the head would break down even the most defiant criminal. He was right. Triangular Head stood passively, his eyes not daring to glance aside.

The other two gangsters made a move to retrieve their guns.

"I wouldn't," the Scar cautioned, "unless you'd like your friend to leave your gang permanently."

"For Pete's sakes," Triangular Head blubbered, "don't do nothin', fellers!"

Now that he wasn't the one in danger, Korpuli tried to goad the two thugs on. They refused to make a move, though. They thought even more of their friend than they did of their lawyer.

"Now all of you get into the bedroom," the Scar instructed. "I'll give you five seconds."

The two mobsters and the attorney hastened into the bedroom. The Scar followed, his gun still jabbed into Triangular Head's right ear.

"Down under the bed."

The three of them obediently dropped onto the floor and crawled under the bed.

"Now don't try to get out from under there for at least five minutes," said the Scar. "I'm going to be right in the next room, talking to this crook. And the first sound I hear in here is going to be too bad for him."

The Scar slammed the door shut and locked it from the outside. He had taken his arm from around the neck of Triangular Head and now held the gun at the small of the thug's back.

"March out the door to the elevator," he said abruptly. "Keep talking to me all the way down. Make believe I'm one of your pals. I'm going to have this revolver in my coat pocket, covering you every second. One wrong move—"

"I won't cross you, mister!" the crook blurted out.

"Then start marching!"

As the thug shuffled toward the elevator, the Scar suddenly whipped the ordinary mask out of his secret pocket and slipped it on over the fearful one. When they stopped at the shaft and he rang the bell, the crook glanced at him, started in surprise. He smiled, for Triangular Head was looking up the corridor puzzledly.

"I'm still here," the Scar assured him. "I'm afraid it's going to be very difficult for you criminals from now on. You'll never know who I am, or who isn't me. One of your own friends may suddenly reveal a scarred, purple face—"

"Gawd!" the thug moaned, his face white and terrified.

"How did you three know I was up here?" asked the Scar.

"The boss owns this hotel," offered Triangular Head hurriedly. "He was expectin' maybe you'd call on Mr. Korpuli, so he planted us down stairs in the lobby. He told the desk clerk to keep his peepers open. If anybody wanted to see Korpuli, we were to be sent up."

"That still doesn't answer how you knew I was here."

"You slipped one of the bellhops a buck. The kids pool their tips. The minute the clerk found out where the buck came from, he tried to get Korpuli on the house phone. There wasn't any answer, so he hot-footed us up there to see what was going on."

The elevator door slid open.

"Everything all right in Mister Korpuli's room?" the operator asked. "The desk clerk is having high blood pressure, wonderin' whether to send up the house dick or the cops."

Miles prodded his pocketed gun in Triangular Head's back.

"Oh, no," the thug said hastily with a deathly grin. "Everything's swell in there. The boys are just havin' a drink and this guy is my pal."

The driver glanced sharply at the Scar, slid the door closed and the lift descended.

CHAPTER XIII

DEATH OF A SUSPECT

OUTSIDE THE hotel, they took a cab. As Triangular Head stepped inside, the Scar hit him expertly on the back of the head. Ten minutes later Triangular Head awoke to find himself propped up in a chair under a bright domelight. He didn't know it, but he was in Doc Murdock's Swank Street laboratory. His hands and legs were tied.

Dale Jordan and Doctor Murdock wore gauze masks over their faces so that their prisoner could not identify them.

Doc took the girl over into one corner of the room, out of earshot. He told her his risky plan. She was terrified at the idea, afraid he would be discovered.

"There's nothing to worry about," he said reassuringly. "While I'm gone, though, you'll have to stay here and keep him company. See that he doesn't get any notions about trying to get away. Two of him showing up at the same time would be very embarrassing for one of him."

They went back to Triangular Head, whose name, Doc learned, was "Sleepy Harry" Russell. Doc got out his makeup materials. He sat down before the criminal he was to impersonate. Talking to him skillfully, he studied the man's face from every conceivable angle, including the way he laughed, smiled, frowned, grimaced. He watched for shadows, highlights.

His examination over, he sat at an angle where Triangular Head could not see him and began to build a face in clay and gum elastic. While he worked, he kept talking to Sleepy Harry Russell to acquaint himself with the tone and quality of the thug's voice. It was of a lower register than Miles' voice, and he was a lazy talker. He slurred words, dropped final "gs" and "hs," and mispronounced every second word.

Doc mimicked him, answering him in the same voice. Dale listened and nodded. It was perfection.

Doc Murdock had still another purpose in asking these questions. He wanted to learn where Sleepy Harry stood in the mob. What were his duties? Who were his closest pals? What did the different men in the gang look like and what were their names? He also asked what the crook had been doing these past few days, so he couldn't be tripped on that point. His questions were so adroit that his captive gave out information almost without being aware of it.

Sleepy Harry told him he had been spending a lot of time lately, driving Condor around. They had visited Red Point quite a few times.

"What's Condor been doing over there?" Doc Murdock asked. "It's not much of a place to operate from."

"I don't know," Sleepy Harry admitted. "Lookin' at some land, I guess. He's had a lot of them guys who look through a telescope on a stand. You know, the guys with tape measures."

"Surveyors?" prompted Doc.

"Yeah, that's it. They go around measuring the place."

"Is this land he's looking over the same spot where the two men were blown up tonight?"

"Naw," Sleepy Harry said. "It's up at the end of the island, where the bridge is goin'. The boss owned that place where the shack was for years. Used to use it as a hideout."

Doc went on with his reconstruction of the thug's face. When he was finished, he sent Dale out of the room while he changed into Sleepy Harry's clothes.

Dale returned after Sleepy Harry was covered and tied in his chair again. She was flabbergasted. She looked first at Doc, then at Sleepy Harry, and then back at Doc. Until the plastic surgeon spoke to her in his natural voice, she couldn't tell them apart.

Doc slid a gun into his hip pocket, left another with the girl.

"Don't take any chances with Mister Russell," he warned her. "If he moves, shoot to kill."

He left by the back door and through the twisting back alley. The Scar was off on one of the most dangerous ventures that Doc Murdock would ever assign to him.

The Black Falcon night club was one of Luke Condor's most valuable properties. With ample elbow-room, a good-sized dance floor and the best talent he could hire, it gave him a large slice of his vast income. Valuable as it was in that respect, however, the Scar had learned from the captive that it served the still more important function of front for the gang.

UNDER THE guise of Sleepy Harry Russell, the Scar approached the place. There was a resplendently uniformed doorman under the gaudy canopy.

"Hello, Pete," he said.

"Pete" was one of those little details he had obtained from his prisoner. Pete turned and recognition showed in his eyes. It gave way to surprise.

"Hello, Sleepy!" he cried enthusiastically. "I thought you had some trouble. The boss is all hot and excited about ya. He just came in."

"Yeah, I had plenty of trouble," the Scar slurred boastfully, as Sleepy Harry might have done, "but I got out of it oke. I just used the old bean." He started to go into the club, turned and asked: "You say the boss was out some place?"

"Downtown. He went out soon as he heard you was nabbed."

The Scar nodded and went into the club. The hat-check girl flipped him a big "hello" from across the half-door of her cubicle. He took off his hat and grinned back at her, then continued walking.

The fun was at its height. Bejeweled ladies in expensive evening gowns danced, chatted and sipped drinks with male fashion-plates. A marimba band was beating out a conga.

Two of the mob glimpsed "Sleepy Harry" the minute he showed his face inside the door. They came over fast, bursting with curiosity.

"What happened to you?" one demanded. "How did you get away from that guy?"

"What'd he do to you?" the other asked.

"What'd he do to *me*?" The Scar forced a sickly grin and his eyes narrowed wisely. "What'd *I* do to him, you mean. Soon as he took that gat outa my ear, I batted the ugly puss off him. Where's the boss?"

"In the office. Boy, will he be surprised to see you! He was getting ready to collect for flowers for ya."

"Yeah, come on," said the other. "We wanna get a slant at his face when he gloms you."

They took hold of the Scar's big arms as though he had suddenly become someone they were proud to associate with. They hustled him past the crowded tables, skirted the dance floor and led him through a narrow archway to the right of the band dais. Then down a narrow, blue-lighted corridor they went, halted before a green door.

One of the thugs rapped at the door three times. The door opened.

FROM BEHIND the huge flat-top desk at which he sat, Luke Condor radiated power. It had to be admitted, too, that when Condor wore evening clothes, he was a candidate for Hollywood. The club owner was tall and handsome and his black hair was long and sleek. For all his good looks, though, it was obvious that he was muscular and kept in trim.

Condor's eyes swelled in his head when he saw "Sleepy Harry Russell" standing before him on the threshold.

"What the devil!" he ejaculated. "I thought you were—"

The Scar grinned. "Naw, I got away."

"How?"

"Long story, Boss. Learned plenty of important stuff, too. I better tell you alone."

Condor was curious to hear what had happened after the Scar had abducted Sleepy Harry Russell and what he had learned. Chris Korpuli had got in touch with Condor immediately after the Scar left and told him all about the strange visit.

The club owner nodded to those in the office to leave. They filed out with dark looks. They didn't like being shut out this way.

When Condor and the man he thought was Sleepy Harry Russell were alone, the gang leader demanded:

"Well, let's have it! What's this big secret? How did you get away from this Purple Scar? Who is he?"

The Scar stood facing him, but his eyes were not on the night club owner. Instead they were focused on the door behind Condor. Obviously that door led out the back way. The Scar had spied it the moment he entered. He hadn't counted on this swift course of action, but since the breaks had come his way and he was in more danger every moment he stayed here, he decided to take this chance.

He leaped to the door through which he had just entered. His left hand flew to the bolt. His right dropped simultaneously to his gun.

Behind him was an ear-splintering explosion. The force of it hurled the Scar back against the side wall. For a moment he knelt, stunned, then dazedly turned.

Luke Condor, reduced to a smoldering, charred, mangled corpse, was sprawled across the shattered desk. There was as little left of him as there had been of Mrs. Small or the two killers at the shack on Red Point.

CHAPTER XIV

UNDER ARREST

THE DOOR behind the Purple Scar was suddenly thrown open. He turned his head. Half a dozen of Condor's prize thugs pressed whitefaced in the doorway. He continued to kneel there an instant longer, not knowing quite what had happened, still groggy from the impact of the sudden explosion.

Abruptly, though, he understood. He had been alone in this room when this horror had happened. He was the only person who apparently could have done it. Before he could rise to his feet, or utter a word in his defense, one of the thugs cried out:

"He killed the boss!"

Instantly they were upon him. The six of them flattened him to the ground, punching, hammering, beating him across the head with their gun butts and fists until the world went black and he felt no more pain.

Stars and rockets flashed big and bright inside his head. There was a blur of color—red, gold, pink, silver and blue, but mostly blue, swimming before his blurred gaze as consciousness came roaring back into his brain. He stirred, opened his eyes wider and looked around. Cops were everywhere, blue-coated cops with glittering gold buttons, silver shields, pink faces.

He blinked furiously. He could remember the exposion, Condor, his face and the entire front of his body blown away. The six menacing thugs in the doorway and the beating they dealt out. How his head pounded and his body ached from that beating!

A voice seeped through to his throbbing brain. He turned his head half-around and looked up. Out of the crazy-quilt of color and forms dancing before his eyes appeared a face. It was a square face with snapping, black eyes.

Detective Captain Dan Griffin! For that was the Scar truly thankful.

"He's come to, Captain," someone said close to the Scar's ear.

Griffin came forward. His square jaw was set hard. He glared down at the Scar, his eyes like black dots on a square white die.

"Why did you kill Luke Condor?" he demanded harshly.

Miles Murdock, the Purple Scar, gazed up at his friend. The beating he had taken must have made his face even more unrecognizable, he thought. The Scar pretended that he wanted to answer Griffin's question, but that he could not speak above a strangled whisper. The pretense worked. Griffin bent forward and put his ear close to the Scar's mouth.

"Get rid of this mob, Griff," the Scar breathed. "I didn't kill Condor any more than you did. I'm Doc Murdock."

Griffin stifled his exclamation before it reached his lips. He drew erect with an incongruous expression on his blocky face, he stared down at the man on the floor with mingled astonishment and admiration. He knew it was Doc Murdock, beyond the shadow of a doubt. Griffin had recognized his voice and, though the features were entirely different, anything Doc did with faces no longer surprised the detective-captain.

GRIFFIN QUICKLY cleared the room. When they were alone, Miles sprang to his feet and knelt beside the torn, mangled corpse of Luke Condor. He inspected it thoroughly, in his mind unraveling the answers to this baffling riddle.

Farrar, Martin, Condor and old Mrs. Small had each been killed in concentrated explosions that did little damage except to the parties immediately involved.

Doc thought back to that scene at Red Point. At the time it had looked like coincidence that Punchy Gus Martin should have been there at that precise moment, but it wasn't fortuitous. The arch-criminal behind these killings had known the time Martin was to be there, knew the bus schedule, knew just how long it would take the giant killer to walk from the last stop to the fateful shack. Also, the fiend must have arranged it so he could catch that bus, which had passed Doc on the bridge, back to Akelton.

Yes, it was all clearing now. Mrs. Small's death had been the seed from which all these other deaths sprang. John evidently had uncovered the motive behind her murder, so the killer had hired Jerry Farrar to rub him out. But Farrar had been too cowardly to do the killing himself, so he had called in Gus Martin to do the dirty work.

Martin pulled a *faux paux* by pawning the ring. The murderer got nervous, contacted Condor, who in turn called in Chris Korpuli. Or maybe the lawyer was playing possum and was the brains behind the scheme.

Korpuli, in any event, sprang Martin. Martin, having been promised five hundred dollars for keeping his mouth shut, was angry when he was cheated out of his money. The murderer welched and for fear that Martin and Farrar might get out of hand, he got rid of them.

But why and how was Luke Condor killed? How was it connected with Mrs. Small's murder?

To the last questions, Doc believed he had the answers, at least to his own satisfaction. Again he smelled that peculiar odor which he sensed in the shack following the murder of Farrar and Martin. This time, however, he knew what it was.

Captain Griffin's hard, heavy voice interrupted his thoughts.

"Now what is this all about?" Griffin demanded heatedly. "Are you the Purple Scar?"

Doc nodded without turning. Griffin twisted his face into an exasperated grimace and growled plaintively:

"For the lova Mike, what're you up to, anyway, Doc? First you scare the pants off Peter de Gaul by lockin' him in a closet. Now I find you up to your ears in a murder."

DOC'S EYES swept to Griffin's square face inquiringly.

"How did you know I locked de Gaul in a closet?"

"He happened to be at the station house, registering a complaint, when this call came in. Now what's the answer?"

"Griff," Doc said, looking at the captain steadily, "I finally got the answer to these riddles. The same person who killed Luke Condor also killed Mrs. Small."

"Because they were both killed by an explosion, I suppose," Griffin retorted, unimpressed.

"No, that's not the only reason. I'll tell you something else. Those two killers who were blown apart over at Red Point tonight were Jerry Farrar and Punchy Gus Martin."

Griffin's face fell in surprise.

"How the devil did you know that? Why, the Fingerprint Bureau handed me my report only fifteen minutes ago! It's still on my desk. It hasn't even been released yet."

"I'll answer that some other time, but Farrar and Martin were hired to kill my brother by the same party who killed Condor and Mrs. Small. Don't ask any more questions. Give me just one hour and I'll hand you your murderer. All I ask is that you have Chris Korpuli and Arnold Wisply at Peter de Gaul's mission at four o'clock."

"Have Korpuli and Wisply there?" Griffin scowled. "Why don't you ask me to hand in my shield and be done with it?"

"You've got to do it, Griff!"

"But why de Gaul's place? Why not Headquarters, if you're so sure of catching the murderer?"

"Mainly because I don't want anyone to know that Doctor Miles Murdock has any connection with this case. After all, he's a surgeon, not a detective. Let the Purple Scar finish what he set out to do."

Griffin rubbed his square jaw reflectively. He knew Doc wasn't in the habit of making rash promises. Even though Miles had been the only person in this room when the explosion occurred, Griffin was certain that he wasn't responsible for it. But now that he had been arrested, he'd have a mighty slim chance of proving his innocence.

It wasn't according to the rules in the manual, nor did it follow any of the principles Griffin had been taught. He hesitated, then shrugged resignedly.

"I'm nuts, I suppose," he grunted. "Doc, I'm likely to be dropped back to taking orders from some squirt of a sergeant out in the sticks some place, if you don't come through."

"But I will come through!" the Scar promised grimly. "I also assure you that I'll make you one of the biggest men on the force."

"I don't care about that," Griffin said worriedly, "but I'm going to play ball with you. I'll give you a fair chance to get away. If you're caught after that, I can't do anything to help you. Open the back door. It leads into an alley. I'll wait until you get to the end of it. Then I'm going to start firing. In five seconds you'll have every cop in the neighborhood after you."

MILES GRINNED appreciatively and took Griffin's big hand. No word passed between them, yet Miles knew he was wishing him luck.

Doc unbolted the rear door and flung it open. He dived out into the black alley, skidded around a row of ash barrels and began to run.

True to his word, Griffin began firing the minute Doc hit the mouth of the narrow passageway. In less time than the five seconds Griffin quoted, police were in mad pursuit.

Griffin smiled to himself. He knew the alley was dark and tricky. There wasn't a chance that anyone would catch the Purple Scar.

CHAPTER XV

"SING, BROTHER, SING!"

N **ARROW AND** dim, the beam of a flashlight shone on a small, square, black safe before the shadowed figures of Tommy Pedlar and the Purple Scar. Tommy's educated fingers spun the steel dial as artfully as the fingers of Doctor Miles Murdock wielded a scalpel. He turned to one number, felt the drop of the tumbler in his sensitive fingers, paused to sensitize the tips even more on sandpaper, then turned the knob again.

"Like openin' Janie's pig bank," he whispered. "This one musta been slapped together before Abe said his piece at Gettysburg."

Another turn and another tumbler dropped. Finally Tommy turned and looked up at the Scar. He winked with an air of triumph.

"Watch out for the moths," he said.

He gave the handle a sudden slap downward and pulled out the black door of the safe. Then he moved aside so the Scar could get to it.

The Scar brought out deeds, wills, various types of documents, leases, letters, bills of sale, citizenship papers, insurance policies—

"I'll bet he's even got the kitchen sink in there," Tommy whispered.

The Scar smiled, began thumbing through the many papers he had taken from the safe, reading each name carefully. Finally, in a little compartment devoted to it alone, he came upon the paper he sought.

It was a deed with impressive gilt edges. Age had turned the face of the paper brown, but the lettering was distinct. In part it read:

This is to verify that the Red Point Super-Development Company has this day sold to Josef Pocoapoco a five-mile parcel of land facing the ocean front at Red Point.

It went on to tell just where the land was located, the exact size of the lots and all the other legal data.

"But who's Josef Pocoapoco?" Tommy wanted to know.

The Scar, preoccupied, didn't reply. He closed the safe, turned off his flash and told Tommy to follow him.

They went across a huge black hall, through a couple of other rooms and into a smaller room. Here the Scar clicked on his flashlight again.

It was a kitchen. In one corner of the room, the beam of light picked out a tall electric refrigerator. The arrow was set at much colder than freezing.

The Scar opened the door, pulled out the cube tray. Instead of ice cubes, the tray contained several small, coinlike gray objects.

"Now why would a guy wanna keep things like that in an ice-box?" asked Tommy.

"For a very good reason, which you'll soon find out," the Scar answered.

Emptying the tray into his handkerchief and closing the refrigerator door, he silently led Tommy out of the kitchen.

DAN GRIFFIN kept his word. At four o'clock sharp he had Chris Korpuli, Arnold Wisply and Peter de Gaul at the slum mission. De Gaul had been allowed the courtesy of dressing.

Dan Griffin's life this past hour had been no rose-strewn path. He had been called down for letting a murder suspect slip through his fingers. When it came to rounding up the lawyer and the tenement house owner, it was like caging a hyena and a water buffalo. They weren't at all backward about telling the captain that they'd promptly see to it that he lost his captaincy, maybe even his job.

Griffin knew they weren't joking. They both had influence enough to do it easily.

Griffin had stationed his men in front of the hall to make sure that a man with a "scarred, purple face"—as de Gaul had described it—got in all right. The order was unnecessary. The Purple Scar was already inside. So was Tommy Pedlar.

The Scar used the sound psychological trick of making his opponents wait, hoping to get them on edge, restless. Men in that frame of mind cannot think clearly enough to pattern falsifications.

At four-fifteen, more for Griffin's sake than for the others, the Scar decided to go in. Through the rear office door he entered abruptly, alone.

"I'm sorry to have kept you gentlemen waiting," he said in a voice that seemed to have come from the grave.

The four men in the hall whirled to face him. Griffin hadn't even hinted the true reason he had summoned them here. The Scar swept each face before him. Korpuli, white, pop-eyed, was shaking as if with St. Vitus. De Gaul was as pale-faced as the lawyer, his restless eyes never leaving the Scar's grotesque features for an instant. Dan Griffin stared in awe, too, for he had not seen this horrible face since that night in the morgue.

Of those before the Purple Scar, only Arnold Wisply seemed contemptuous of his appearance.

"What's the meaning of this nonsense?" he asked scornfully.

"I am John Murdock!"

"John Murdock is dead!" Wisply retorted.

The ghastly face nodded. "I am dead—murdered by someone in this room—by the same person who killed Jerry Farar, Gus Martin, Luke Condor and Mrs. Small!"

At the mention of the last name, the tenement owner's attitude changed instantly. The scorn vanished from his fat, pasty face, was replaced by white, quivering fear.

"You bought her insurance policy and her husband's for small sums, in return for free rent in the fire-traps you own," stated the Scar. "She showed no signs of approaching death, though, and you were close to losing money on the deal. That gave you every reason for wanting to kill Mrs. Small."

The pudgy landlord stiffened in his chair and his pasty features went even whiter than before.

"I didn't kill her!" he suddenly yelled. "All I got out of her death was a couple of hundred dollars. If I wanted to kill anyone for profit, I hold policies five and six times the amount of hers—"

"I know that," interrupted the Scar. "I want to know whether you investigated Mrs. Small and her husband as carefully as you investigate all your elderly tenants when checking to learn how much insurance they hold."

WISPLY BOBBED his head nervously, ran his thick tongue over his blubbery lips and put a lumpy finger between his wilted collar and his lardy neck in order to relieve the pressure.

"They were Italians," he said finally. "They changed their name to Small right after they landed in this country. They wanted to sound more American."

"What was their original name?"

"Pocoapoco."

The Scar wheeled to face Chris Korpuli.

"Your part of the story is that Luke Condor told you to spring Gus Martin, but that you never knew who was behind it."

Korpuli was perspiring freely.

"For all I know, it was himself he was protecting," he argued.

Slowly the Scar turned to Peter de Gaul, the missioner.

"Which brings us to you, doesn't it?"

De Gaul swallowed, mustered a spiritless grin.

"Me? What have I to do with it?"

No one could see behind the mask of the Purple Scar, but his right eye-brow had become the black spade of danger.

He raised his voice and called out sharply:

"Tommy!"

The Sticky-fingered Kid came out of the office and advanced with mincing steps. Everyone watched him.

"Tommy, let me have those deeds we took from Mister de Gaul's safe," the Scar ordered.

THE STICKY-FINGERED KID passed the papers across. De Gaul's eyes were like saucers.

"This is a frame-up!" he protested savagely.

"What are those deeds for?" Griffin put in.

The Scar told him briefly. Korpuli knew the property.

"Why the city's been looking everywhere for those deeds!" he exclaimed. "That's the exact spot where the beach and the boardwalk are going. Those deeds are worth every penny of two hundred and fifty thousand dollars!"

"Which happens to be the reason why de Gaul murdered Mrs. Small and Luke Condor!"

"He's trying to frame me," de Gaul yelled fiercely.

Griffin, quiet up to this point, interrupted in the missioner's defense.

"He couldn't have killed Condor. He was at Headquarters when it happened."

"That's exactly what he wanted you to think," said the Scar. "The perfect alibi. He didn't have to be present when his victims were blown to pieces. The protective medallions which de Gaul makes and sells to his people gave me the answer. When he wanted a person conveniently out of the way—such as Condor, Martin, Farrar, or Mrs. Small—

he bored tiny holes in these coins. Into these cavities he froze nitro-nitoxide."

"Nitro-nitoxide?" Griffin repeated uncomprehendingly.

"A new and powerful explosive announced only a short while ago by Professor Hendrixson of the University of Maine. Among other ingredients, this explosive contains nitrogen, wood pulp and solidified nitrous oxide. Nitrogen and nitrous oxide have always exploded on reaching a certain temperature, but this discovery lowered that point. When frozen, nitro-nitoxide is inert. When heated to a temperature of ninety degrees Fahrenheit—lower than the external heat of the body—it detonates."

THE SCAR saw Griffin's bewilderment increasing.

"Placed in a warm pocket, or next to a person's body," he explained more graphically, "it would take only about fifteen or twenty minutes for the temperature to reach the exploding point. Only a few grains are necessary to blow a human being apart."

"Now all you've got to do is prove that fairy tale," de Gaul snarled.

The Purple Scar shook his head.

"No. I think you're going to take care of that little detail yourself." He paused to look up at the big, rustyfaced clock ticking away on the wall. "We found your medallions carefully hidden in your refrigerator, so we thoughtfully placed one inside your clothes while you were sound asleep."

De Gaul's thin face blanched with fear.

"I don't believe you! You're just trying to scare me into confessing something I didn't do."

The Scar shrugged indifferently.

"That's up to you, but if you don't start talking fast, you won't be able to talk. You've got just three minutes left."

De Gaul's hand flew beneath his coat, came out with an ornate pearl-handled revolver.

"Where is it?" he shouted, his free hand turning each pocket inside out.

Doc Murdock grinned triumphantly behind the purple, elastic mask.

"That's all the proof we need, Mister de Gaul!"

CHAPTER XVI

JUDGMENT DAY

S LOWLY THE Scar's powerful hand tightened around de Gaul's scrawny gun-wrist. He could feel the muscles tense convulsively.

"It won't do any good to pull the trigger," the Scar said placidly. "Your gun's empty. Another little detail we attended to."

De Gaul drew back in horror. The Scar quickly slapped the gun from the man's hand, sent it spinning across the floor. He grabbed the missioner by the throat.

"Now start talking!"

"But the medallion!" de Gaul choked out, twisting and squirming frantically to look at the clock. Never for an instant did he pause in his mad search through his clothing for that loaded medallion. His eyes were wild with terror. "Where is it? Where is it?"

"You can't do this," Griffin shouted harshly.

"Stay out of it, Cap!" Tommy Pedlar warned.

He had retrieved the gun which the Scar batted out of de Gaul's hand. He trained it on the detective-captain.

"That thing's not loaded," Griffin snorted, advancing.

"I wouldn't be too sure of that, Cap," Tommy said.

"We didn't even know he had a revolver," the Scar added. "Now be nice, Captain, and stand back."

"But that medallion!" Griffin cried. "It'll go off. I can't let you kill him, even if he is a murderer."

"That little matter is up to de Gaul!" the Scar shot back.

The missioner was tearing at his garments, trying to get them off his shivering body while his eyes were riveted on the clock. Only two minutes left! He fell to his knees, pleading, sobbing, still clawing.

"Where is it?" he panted. "Where is it?"

The Scar reached down, yanked the whimpering man to his feet and pinioned his hands at his sides so he could no longer tear at his clothes.

"Start talking!"

"All right, all right—I'll talk!" de Gaul blurted out. "I did kill them. Josef Small and his wife bought those deeds from a couple of swindlers when they first came from Italy. They paid every penny they had in the world for the property—over three thousand dollars. Then they learned it was nothing but marshlands, in some places six feet underwater. It broke the old man's heart, but he refused to give up the deeds.

"No one else knew he had them. I was the only one he ever told. He and his wife trusted me. When he was dying, he called for me. He gave me these deeds to hold for his wife. In his delirium he believed they'd some day turn into something worthwhile."

De Gaul glanced frantically at the clock, struggling to get his hands free to search again for that deadly coin. Only a minute and a half to go!

HE DOUBLED the speed of his words. "Neither Small nor his wife could read or write, so they didn't have any way of knowing about the beach project, that the city was trying to locate the deeds, or what they were worth. Soon as I saw them, I realized it was the chance I've waited for all my life—a chance to get out of these slums and be rich! I offered to buy the deeds from Mrs. Small.

"She wouldn't sell. She said she didn't want to go against her husband's dying wish. Well, I—I gave her one of the loaded medallions. I told her to wear it close to her heart and no harm could come to her. The last time I saw her alive, she had tucked the medallion inside her blouse and was going home."

"What about John Murdock?"

De Gaul's face was so wet with perspiration, it looked as if someone had thrown a glass of water at him.

One more minute!

In shaken tones he explained that he had hired Farrar to kill John Murdock. Farrar had split the fee with Punchy Gus Martin. The rest of the story followed as the Scar had figured it.

De Gaul had grown frightened when he learned the ring had been pawned. He went to Condor. He had done favors for the gang leader in the past. The mission cellar made an excellent spot to hide out fugitive members of the mob. He offered Condor a percentage of the deeds in return for help.

Farrar was sent to Red Point to be out of the way until things blew over, but he was getting restless and starting to ask too many questions.

"Farrar already had one of my medals, but it wasn't hard to convince him to take another," de Gaul rattled off as the minutes on the big clock ticked away his life. "His pockets were always filled with horseshoes and rabbits' feet and all kinds of good luck charms. I told him he needed protection in such a desolate spot and that two medallions would keep him twice as safe, especially if he wore them next to his heart."

"But if it takes only twenty minutes for a medallion to go off," Griffin cut in, "how could de Gaul possibly get it to Red Point? It takes at least half an hour to get there from here."

"He carried it in dry ice," the Scar said. "I found the stuff melting under the window of the shack, but I didn't understand its significance till later."

"The medallion—the medallion—where is it?" de Gaul blubbered. "Only half a minute left!"

"Just one thing I don't clearly understand," said the Scar calmly. "How did you get the gang to Wisply's so quickly?"

"Lieutenant Riordon didn't hold Condor. Condor argued his way out and came in right after you left here. He found me in the closet. I told him he could get you at Wisply's. He sent his boys. He had come to settle with me for killing Farrar in his shack, but he was more concerned with establishing an alibi in case you got away, so he went back to the club.

"It wasn't until things started to pop again, after you went to Korpuli's and grabbed Sleepy Harry, that he came back here. He claimed I tried to frame him, that the whole business was causing him too much trouble. He said he was going to take the deeds and keep everything for himself. I wasn't giving them up. While he was hitting me, I slipped a loaded medallion into his pocket. The minute he left, I went to the station house."

THE WALL clock showed there were only ten seconds remaining. De Gaul was on the verge of fainting. His face was as immobile as any dead man's and his words scarcely distinguishable as he gasped out:

"Where's the medallion?"

The Purple Scar looked down at him with contempt.

"I'm only sorry I can't tell you there really is a medallion in your clothes."

De Gaul froze with a new kind of terror.

"You mean—"

"I mean I drowned the lot of them in a pail of water in the cellar and you just wrote your own death warrant!"

With one quick shove, he sent de Gaul reeling backward into Griffin's grasp. The captain quickly summoned his men from outside and turned de Gaul over to them.

"You can take Korpuli with you," Griffin told his charges. "Accessory after the fact. And let's see you worm yourself out of this one, *Mister* Korpuli!"

"Unfortunately your insurance policy racket is just within the law, Wisply, and there isn't a lot we can do about it right now," said the Scar. "But for once in your life you can serve humanity by appearing as State's witness against these two rats."

Wisply sniffed curtly as he went out, but there wasn't any doubt in anyone's mind that he'd be there at the trial.

After the hall was clear and Griffin, Tommy Pedlar and the Scar were alone, Miles Murdock peeled off the scarred mask.

"How the devil did you know it was de Gaul?" Griffin asked.

Doc smiled. "First there was the episode I spoke about at Wisply's. With the possible exception of Wisply, no other person except de Gaul knew I was there. Second, the alibi that de Gaul thought was airtight—being at Headquarters when Condor was killed—boomeranged. If he had really wanted to report the Scar's visit, he wouldn't have waited several hours.

"Third, and the thing that clinched it, was the odor that came from each of the victim's bodies. You remember Crazy George, who used to work here around the mission?"

"Yeah," Griffin said. "Used to be some kind of chemist."

"*Some* kind is right! He was a former professor at Johns Hopkins University. The strain of work snapped his brain, but he still retained enough of his brilliance to follow directions. De Gaul must have got the formula for nitro-nitoxide and George mixed it. I remember that some time ago de Gaul brought George to the clinic with burned hands, the result of a minor explosion.

"The odor which came from those burned hands was the same as the one that came from the bodies I saw, which laid the guilt right in de Gaul's lap. He knew Mrs. Small. He knew John. He knew Jerry Farrar. As soon as I saw the name 'Pocoapoco' on the deed, I had the motivation. The Smalls were Italian.

"Since Small isn't an Italian name and there is no equivalent to Small in the Italian language, I knew the next nearest thing was 'little.' Pocoapoco in Italian means 'little by little.' The main reason I had Wisply here was to verify it."

GRIFFIN TOOK off his battered fedora and scratched his graying hair.

With a slight grin, he extended his big square-shaped paw to the plastic surgeon.

"You sure had me awfully worried for a few minutes back there, but I have to hand it to you. You came through."

"You might hand a little of it to Tommy, while you're at it."

"Heck," the Sticky-fingered Kid said with a grin, "I never knew being a cop was so much fun. We gotta do more of this stuff." He paused and looked up at the plastic surgeon wistfully. "We are gonna do more, ain't we, Doc?"

"We haven't stopped crime altogether," replied the Purple Scar gravely. "While criminals exist to prey on innocent people, the Scar must be a scourge of the underworld."

"I'm right with you, Doc !" cried Tommy in glee.

Detective-Captain Griffin said nothing, but his admiring grin showed his heart was with the gallant pair.

II

THE NIGHT
OF MURDER

CHAPTER I

VOICE FROM
THE GRAVE

THE MOMENT Doctor Miles Murdock saw the light burning in the office of his Swank Street laboratory he had a hunch that trouble was waiting. When he walked in and saw a girl sitting there, he was positive of it.

Doc Murdock wasn't in the habit of receiving after-hour patients. He was a plastic surgeon and, except in rare emergencies, his patients came to him during the day.

The girl arose the instant he entered. Doc knew that her hair was blond, even though it was completely hidden beneath a colorful bandanna. She wore dark glasses and kept her chin tucked deep in the turned-up collar of her suit jacket. It was an efficient disguise, but Doc Murdock knew complexion types and facial contours too well to be fooled.

Before he or the girl could speak, a man appeared in the shadowy doorway. A wispy little man with birdlike eyes and sparse hair, he seemed greatly disturbed about something.

"I tried to keep her out, Doc," complained Tommy Pedlar. "I told her you didn't see nobody after office hours, but she busted right in, anyway."

At one time Tommy Pedlar had been known as the notorious "Sticky-fingered Kid," a slick second-story man. But gratitude for Doc's saving his daughter's life had made him reform and become the plastic surgeon's butler-valet-handyman.

"It's all right, Tommy," Doc Murdock said evenly. "I'll speak with the young lady."

Tommy shrugged his narrow shoulders and went out, grumbling to himself. Doc smiled politely and indicated a handcarved chair beside the desk.

"Sit down, please," he said.

She sat on the edge of the seat. Her lower lip trembled. Her fingers kept clasping and unclasping the bulging black handbag she held in her lap.

"You look as if you could stand a drink," Doc stated.

He crossed to the liquor cabinet that stood at the far side of the room. Her eyes followed him.

HE WAS a striking figure, tall, slender, with an amazing breadth of shoulders. Doctor Miles Murdock was one of the most brilliant plastic surgeons of his time. The miracles he performed both here in his Swank Street laboratories and in his free clinic in the heart of the slums were known the world over. But those broad shoulders were more than merely decorative. They served a purpose in other work he did.

He returned to the girl, placed a tall glass in her hands. Sitting down in the swivel chair behind the desk, he smiled disarmingly.

"And now?"

She took a quick sip, as if to gain courage, then put the glass aside. Her mouth was the color of blood against the deathly pallor of her face.

"Doctor," she blurted suddenly, "I'll pay you twenty-five thousand dollars to change my face so that no one will be able to recognize me—and then forget that you ever saw me!"

Murdock put his fingertips precisely together and looked at the girl thoughtfully, measuringly.

"Even if I wanted to do such a thing, I'm afraid I couldn't," he said finally.

The girl's white hand slipped inside her handbag, came out with a pearl-handled .22 revolver. Her vividly red lips drew into a cold line.

"You will operate!" she declared almost hysterically.

Doctor Murdock arose to his full six feet. He reached out his big hand to her, palm upward.

"Let me have that gun, please," he ordered. "You're in trouble. Shooting me certainly can't help you."

She sprang to her feet, took a step backward, menacing him with the gun.

"Don't you dare touch me, or—"

A thin, wiry hand snaked out from behind her and snatched the gun from her grasp. She let out a muffled scream, whirled to face Tommy Pedlar.

"I figured you'd try to pull a fast one," Tommy snarled, "so I slipped back when you weren't lookin'."

She broke away from him, made a wild, desperate dash for the door. But Tommy was right after her. He grabbed her arm, spun her back into the chair.

"She won't try that again," Doc promised. "Thanks, Tommy. You can go now." When the man left, Doc faced her squarely, his eyes probing relentlessly into hers through the dark glasses. "Don't you think it might help if you talked your problem over with me—Miss Draper?"

The girl's jaw dropped with utter amazement.

"You—you knew all the time?" she gasped.

"Of course. It's my business to study and remember the contours of people's faces."

With a strangled groan, all her false courage left her. Her whole body seemed to wilt and she buried her face in her trembling hands. Then she slowly removed her disguise.

LONG, SPUN-GOLD curls tumbled to her slim shoulders, framed a lovely face which more than ten million movie fans knew as well as their own.

Carol Draper, besides being Big Four Productions' ranking feminine star, was also one of the quartette who controlled the motion picture company. Big Four had accepted the mayor's invitation to switch from expensive Hollywood to the thriving city of Akelton.

It seemed to be a wise move. In record time, at a record low cost, they were completing their initial major picture in their new home. A few days more and it would be ready for nationwide distribution. And early rushes had already stamped it a sure-fire hit.

"How can you leave the company when they can't possibly finish the picture without you?" asked Doc. "They'll lose a fortune."

"They'll lose a great deal more than that if I stay," she sobbed. "So will my husband and my two children. You must do what I ask. You're the only person in the world who can help me!"

"Then don't you think you ought to tell me what's back of all this? I want to help you, but I know what it will mean to Big Four. You can't expect me to be part of a plot that will cost your three partners close to a half-million dollars, unless I know there's a sound reason for it."

Her eyes, brown pools in which terror swam, studied his face. Strong, ruggedly handsome, it told Carol Draper that she need have no fear that this man would repeat her secret.

"When I was fifteen," she said tonelessly, "dancing in the chorus of a cheap second-rate night club, I met a man named Jess Renshaw. That was long before I ever dreamed I'd become a motion picture star, long before the name Carol Draper was even thought of.

"Jess wasn't much to look at, but from all appearances he was a man of the world. And to an impressionable girl of fifteen that meant a great deal. He wore expensive clothes, spent money freely. Every girl in the club made a play for him. I considered myself pretty lucky when he asked me to leave the club and marry him. I never dreamt what I was stepping into.

"Jess was a petty thief, confidence man, gunman. The moment I found out, I left him. He chased me half across the country, then suddenly stopped bothering me. I checked back on him, found that a man answering his description had dropped beneath a moving freight car, while attempting to escape from a bank robbery.

"I went to Hollywood, changed the color of my hair, my personality, even my name. I became Carol Draper. It was a hard struggle to the top, but finally I was graduated to stardom. I married and now have two of the grandest children alive. They're back in Hollywood with their dad. It looked just like a happy ending. Then today, late this afternoon, Jess Henshaw came back from the grave!"

"You saw him?" the plastic surgeon asked.

She shook her golden-blond head. "He sent me this letter."

DOC TOOK it, examined it. Typewritten on a cheap grade of stationery, it was postmarked at Station S, City, at 10 P.M. the previous night and addressed to "Miss Carol Draper, Big Four Productions Studio. Personal. Important."

2007 South 95th Street,
Akelton City.

Dear Mrs. Jess Henshaw:

Or have you conveniently forgotten that name with your new-found importance?

It would be rather embarrassing to have Mr. Jess Henshaw turn up, now that you are an important star, happily married.

Imagine how the tabloids or rival picture firms would relish sinking their teeth into that juicy dirt! Think, too, what it would mean to the fine gentleman who thinks he's your legal husband. And to those two kids you've got. Kind of throws a monkey-wrench into the works, if he was to find out that his wife and their mother is still married to a jail bird.

But of course you don't want that to leak out. That's why you're coming to the above address at eight-thirty tonight.

From your husband, who still adores his wife—and is determined to have her again.

Jess Henshaw.

Doc read the letter through twice. His face did not change. Only his eyes narrowed a little.

"Did your husband ever have any training in writing?" he asked. "Work for a newspaper, perhaps?"

"Not that I know of," Carol Draper replied. "When I received the letter, I was going to him. I thought perhaps it was the only way. But I couldn't. I just couldn't! Then I decided to come to you, ask you to change my face so I could disappear. Jess Henshaw wouldn't say anything then. He doesn't want money. I know he doesn't. He just wants me, his wife!"

"But suppose he didn't send you this letter. After all, anyone could type a letter. Even the signature was typed, so you don't really know whether it was your husband."

"Jess Henshaw sent it, all right," the movie star said dejectedly. "I'm positive. He wouldn't write a letter in his own hand—or even sign his name to it. He'd be afraid it would boomerang. He was clever."

She reached tremblingly for the glass of brandy, took another quick sip. Then she brought up her fevered eyes to meet his.

"You must perform this operation! If you don't—"

Her voice trailed off into silence. But that silence told Doc more clearly than words that, while she was afraid of death, she was infinitely more terrified to go on living as Carol Draper and swamp her husband and two children in humiliation.

In her confusion and desperation, Carol Draper believed that running away again would solve her problem. Perhaps at any other time she might have thought differently, or Doc might have successfully reasoned her out of it. But at the moment Carol Draper was in no condition for clear thinking. She was like a person in a black tunnel whose walls were crushing in on her, running frantically to escape.

There was no way of her knowing, of course, that inadvertently she had come to the one man who could help her out of her predicament. Not only was he able to change her face, but he might get at the root of her trouble, free her from the hideous threat of exposure.

For this highly respected young plastic surgeon, with a following that included pillars of society, stars of the theatrical and sports world, was none other than the Purple Scar, the scourge of the underworld!

CHAPTER II

INTERCEPTED

THE PURPLE SCAR was a mysterious will-o'-the-wisp character, born of murder and violence. Doc Murdock's brother, a member of the police force, had been brutally murdered and thrown in the river. When his body was fished out, only Doc's great skill had been able to prove that the water-purpled, acid-destroyed face had once belonged to John Murdock.

The killers were caught and brought to trial, but a crooked lawyer got them free. Enraged by this miscarriage of justice, Doc Murdock resolved to avenge his dead brother. And the face of the pitiful corpse had given him the idea of the Purple Scar.

Following every line of the acid-eaten features, he had constructed a gum elastic mask that hid his identity perfectly. But the purple disguise had more than that simple function. It also was an exact duplication of his brother's destroyed face, and since purple becomes black at night, it made his face invisible in the darkness.

Miles Murdock, striking swiftly and unexpectedly as the Purple Scar, ferreted out the murderers of his brother and brought them to justice. And when the case was closed, he locked the mask in his wall safe, awaiting the time when it would again be necessary for the Scar to smash crime and protect helpless people.

Placing the typewritten letter in his inside coat pocket, Doctor Murdock asked the girl:

"How did you happen to come to me?"

"A peculiar thing," answered Carol Draper. "Coincidence, you might call it. One of your cards was on the table in my dressing room. It gave me the idea immediately."

She took the card from her purse, handed it across the desk.

"Where did this come from?" he demanded. "How did it get on your dressing table?"

The movie star shrugged. "One of my friends probably dropped it there. Several have visited you and spoke very highly of you."

"Do you know if the card was there before?"

"I can't say. I don't remember."

Doc studied the card critically, an odd look in his eyes. Then, without further comment, he pushed a tiny, flat button beneath his desk. Almost at once Tommy Pedlar appeared in the doorway.

"Prepare for surgery," Doctor Murdock ordered bluntly.

Tommy was the perfect stooge. He saw nothing, heard nothing, said nothing that he wasn't supposed to see, hear or say.

Doc Murdock had told him to prepare for surgery, so Tommy promptly flooded the laboratory with bright light, washed down one of the white tables, laid out everything that the plastic surgeon would need.

Carol Draper was stretched out on the table by the time Doc finished scrubbing his hands and struggled into sterilized rubber gloves.

"Administer ether," he said. "I'll give instructions."

Tommy placed the cone over the movie star's white, frightened face. Her eyes looked beseechingly up at Doc.

"Breathe deeply," he commanded.

She began to inhale, stiffened as she instinctively fought the sweet sleep-producing aromatic. Complete relaxation swiftly came. Every troubled thought in her mind faded into blackness.

A VOICE from a long, long distance seeped into Carol Draper's befogged senses. She opened her eyes slowly. A smiling square-jawed face came into focus. In the background was another face, thin and pale.

It took several seconds before she assembled her thoughts. Then, startled by the smarting and tautness of her face, she remembered. She lifted her hand, felt bandages covering everything but her eyes, nostrils and mouth.

"You've got to be kept quiet for several days," Doc said. "Also you must stay some place where I can look after you until it's safe to remove the bandages. I can't very well keep you here. My staff would ask questions."

"But I've no place else to go!" she protested.

He gave her an address and said:

"Go there. As long as you don't leave it, you'll be safe."

She looked bewildered.

"My chief nurse lives there," he explained. "Her name is Dale Jordan. I'll phone her and tell her you're coming. Tommy will take you. I'll be over to look at you first thing in the morning. You have a habit of running away, you know. I must have your word you won't try to again."

Her eyes, peering through the white bandage that covered her face, searched his good-looking features.

"I promise I won't run away," she answered softly.

He phoned for a cab. When it drew up in front of the door, he bundled her into it. Tommy climbed in alongside.

Doc gave the address of Dale Jordon's apartment, watched the taxi pull away from the curb. Then he turned, went back up the stoop into the house and dialed Dale Jordan.

Dale had been working with him for several years. Her efficiency and resourcefulness had always made her stand out from the rest of the staff, but recently she had become more than merely another assistant to him. She was one of the three people in the world who knew the true identity of the Purple Scar. The other two were Tommy Pedlar and Detective-Captain Dan Griffin, chief of Akelton City's Homicide Bureau.

Thinking of Dale Jordan now—her reddish-brown tresses, her long-lashed brown eyes, her beautiful face—gave him a thrill of anticipation. The sound of her voice, soft, musical, made his heart pound.

"Dale. This is Miles. Tommy is bringing a patient to you. A very important patient—Carol Draper."

"The motion picture actress?"

"Yes. She's in a jam."

He told Dale in as few words as possible why Carol Draper had come to him, then hung up. He put out the light in the office and went upstairs to his studio-living quarters.

It was a huge place. Masks, busts and full-length clay figures were everywhere. In this studio Doc Murdock spent his rare moments in sculpture. Besides the relaxation it afforded him, it was invaluable for experiment before actually operating on a patient.

Adjoining this studio was a fully equipped gymnasium, where a daily workout kept his reflexes quick, his muscles firm and supple. At college he had earned letters in four major sports, and he would no more think of allowing this training to go to waste than he would neglect his surgical practice. A sound body to Doc Murdock was as important as a sound mind.

HE WAS tired. It had been a trying day, climaxed by a dinner speech at one of many civic clubs to which he belonged. Tomorrow promised to be even more hectic, with half a dozen tedious operations.

Doc was almost undressed and ready for bed when the phone suddenly rang. He lifted the transceiver to his ear.

"Hello. Speaking. Yes. Where? Right away. Thanks."

He banged the instrument back into the cradle and scowled down at it. His hands knotted into tight balls. His right eyebrow and the lines shadowing it twitched to form an oddly-shaped black spade.

It was not actually a scar, but a peculiar paralysis of certain muscles over the right eye, sustained in a college football game. He could have had it corrected, but it in no way impaired his vision, nor did it alter his appearance. But when rage gripped him, that black spade appeared—and it was an omen of danger for someone.

Hastily he began to dress again. He put on a white shirt, dark tie, black suit and black shoes. Donning his black felt hat, he went to a panel in the wall, pressed a carefully concealed button. The panel slid away to reveal a wall safe. He spun the dial, opened the thick metal door. From the far corner of the safe he took the mask of the Purple Scar!

He tucked it into a secret pocket, stowed a revolver into the hip-holster strapped beneath his coat. He rushed down the stairs and ran through the heavy black fog that intensified the night.

As he turned the corner of Hoyt Street where it bent into Arrow, only half a dozen blocks from his office, he spied a knot of people through the fog. Three green-and-white prowl cars stood at the curb, a short distance from a shiny, jet-black ambulance.

Doc started to elbow through the crowd, and a policeman with a blue-black jaw thrust out a white-gloved hand.

"Where d'ya think you're goin'?" he demanded.

"I'm Doctor Murdock."

The cop squinted beady eyes, looked at the plastic surgeon through the black haze. "Yeah, of course," he growled. "Come on through, Doc."

Tommy Pedlar lay on his back on the sidewalk. His head was resting in a policeman's lap. Another had the beam of a flashlight on him. An intern in a long black raincoat, which almost hid completely his short white coat and white pants, knelt beside Tommy.

"Tommy!" Doc cried out.

But the trusting, worshipful eyes remained closed.

MISSING STAR

A DEEP VOICE that was trying hard to be soft and sympathetic yanked Doc Murdock's harassed eyes up from Tommy Pedlar. It was Detective-Captain Dan Griffin.

The Homicide man was square-shouldered, square-bodied and square-faced. Griffin's character fitted right into that square motif. He was an all-around square policeman.

Miles nodded, thanked Griffin for phoning him. Then he asked, indicating Tommy:

"Serious?"

"Shot twice," the detective answered.

"Take a look for yourself, Doctor," the intern spoke up.

Doc got down on one knee. The intern showed him where the bullets had lodged. They were nasty wounds, one in the thigh, the other in the groin. Tommy was still unconscious. Doc examined them carefully, the spade growing more prominent than before over his right eye.

"Better get him to Emergency fast," he said tersely.

They got Tommy into the ambulance. Doc and Captain Griffin wedged in alongside the stretcher.

"Anyone see how it happened?" Doc asked the Homicide chief as the ambulance clanged on its way.

"Some woman stuck her head out the window when she heard the shots. Said she saw a cab tear away from the scene, but she couldn't read the plates." He studied Doc Murdock's stern face in the blurred reflection of the street lamps which flashed past through the fog. "Tommy Pedlar out on a job for you?"

Doc nodded.

"Then maybe you have an idea who did it," Griffin said.

Doc shook his head. "I'm afraid we'll have to wait for Tommy to answer that one."

Griffin tried to find out exactly what the job was, but Doc just dug his hands into his coat pockets and refused to answer.

Actually it was more than a refusal. Bitterness pervaded Doc's mind. Helping Carol Draper had been merely a kindly act, but now it had turned into something personal. Tommy Pedlar meant a lot to Doc Murdock. So did Tommy's seven-year-old daughter Janie.

It was because Doc Murdock had saved Janie's life that Tommy turned over a new leaf. Doc took the Sticky-fingered Kid and his daughter out of the slums, made Tommy over into a first-class helper. The little girl he sent away to a good boarding school in the country.

Doc felt they were both his own personal responsibilities. If anything should happen to Tommy, Janie would be heart-broken and Doc would have lost one of his best friends.

What had happened to Carol Draper?

Had she just used Doc, induced him to change her face so that no one would know her, then doublecrossed him and run away? Was it possible that she had shot Tommy? Doc found that difficult to believe.

THE AMBULANCE made a sharp turn and came to a screeching halt in front of the platform which led into the emergency receiving ward at the city hospital.

Tommy was quickly shifted onto a waiting stretcher. Two white-clad orderlies whisked him immediately to Surgery.

Doc took a moment to call Dale Jordan from the hospital. When she answered, he told her not to expect Tommy Pedlar or Carol Draper and explained what had happened.

"But you can do something," he added. "Find out where Carol Draper was staying in town. Go there. See if she has a typewriter. If she has, type out this letter."

He dictated a stream of words.

A few moments later he was dressed in white, his eyes sharp, black pinpoints above his white surgical mask. He stood in the white-walled operating room and looked down at his friend, lying senselessly before him on the table.

Doc had served his internship in this hospital. As a member of the staff, he was allowed to stay there to perform the operation.

A rubber suction-cup was fitted over Tommy's nose and mouth. He had no way of knowing how near death he was, that his life lay in his friend's hands.

Doc waited a precious thirty seconds, praying that he would not fail. Then he gave the nurse beside him the signal for the scalpel.

Dan Griffin was pacing the anteroom of the emergency ward when Doc Murdock emerged.

"How is he?" the captain asked worriedly.

"Bullets came out clean. Now if he doesn't have an internal hemorrhage, he'll be okay by morning."

"And when'll he be able to talk?"

"Not before morning." Doc looked at Griffin squarely. "Dan I'd like you to keep your eye peeled for a girl."

He turned toward the locker room to get his hat and coat.

"What's she look like?" Griffin asked, following him.

"Gray business suit, red-and-blue bandanna, carrying a black bag. Her entire face is covered with a bandage."

Doc opened the door and went into a small room, lined with tall green lockers.

"Her face is covered with a bandage?" Griffin echoed. "And who's under the bandage?"

Doc paused in the act of opening a locker door. His voice was so low that Griffin had to strain to hear.

"Carol Draper."

The Homicide chief let out a disgruntled sigh.

"That movie company's starting to get into my hair," he growled.

"What do you mean?" Doc demanded, startled. "What happened?"

"This afternoon we had some real trouble. Dave Winters is the big-shot director at Big Four. Owns a hunk of the company, too, I hear. He's the guy who's directing their first important picture, the one starring Carol Draper. Well, this afternoon somebody tried to get into his safe. Anyhow, that's what his butler called in and reported."

HE PAUSED to shake his head gloomily before continuing.

"It seems it was the butler's full day off. But he happened to drop back at the place about 4:30 in the afternoon and found the safe open. I sent one of the boys right over to have a look. He says the safe was rifled, all right. But while he was there, Winters walks in. Winters flies off the nut, says the butler is whacky. Claims he simply forgot to lock the safe.

"He takes a look inside just the same, says nothing was gone. But the cop reports that Winters had a worried look on his face. You can't third-degree a guy into admitting something of his has been stolen, though, if he wants to keep on saying it hasn't been. So we scratched it off the blotter.

"But it doesn't let us forget it. Tonight about 7:30, out at Lou Kerkin's Lullaby Club, Winters gets a bun on. He has a row with another of the picture company's owners. There are four of 'em altogether, you know. That's where the name 'Big Four' comes from. There's Winters, Carol

Draper, a fellow named Victor Banco and another gent called Jules Gunther."

"I've heard of Jules Gunther," Doc Murdock put in. "I understand he's the brains of the company. Through his insistence and foresight, I believe, they moved to Akelton."

"Whatever he is, Gunther's the baby Dave Winters picked on tonight. Winters, they say, was at the club when Gunther came in, and I hear he was spoiling for trouble. In practically no time at all he starts insulting Gunther. Somebody said he even took a swipe at the guy. We got the call. A prowl picked it up.

"By the time they got there, Gabby Newel—that's Big Four's loud-lipped press agent—had Winters and Gunther quieted. He said that it was strictly a personal matter and neither party wished to press charges. Gunther agreed and wouldn't discuss it. Dave Winters wasn't in any condition to talk about anything. He'd passed out."

"From what I've heard, this Winters isn't a very pleasant chap to get along with," Doc said.

"And from what I hear, that's a very polite way to put it. Anyway, the boys hung around the club until they saw Winters tucked into a cab and sent home. I was sort of hoping we'd heard the last of it. But now Tommy has been shot and you tell me Carol Draper had something to do with it."

"I didn't say she had anything to do with it," Doc objected hastily. "The fact is, I'm going to ask you to forget everything I told you, at least for the time being."

Griffin's left eyebrow raised quizzically.

"What's you trying to do—pull another Dave Winters?"

THEY WERE out of the locker room now, walking down the long, silent, white-walled corridor to the front door. Doc was grinning to himself. It was odd that Dan Griffin should have put his question that way, because at that moment Doc happened to be thinking that maybe the fight with Jules Gunther at the Lullaby Club had something to do with Carol Draper's mysterious disappearance.

Doc was wondering how he could find out. It was plain that Jules Gunther wouldn't talk, by what Captain Griffin had just said. Gabby Newel, the press agent, wouldn't talk, either. He was paid to see that only pleasant things about Big Four Productions got around.

But there was still Dave Winters.

Maybe Doc could find out if anything had really been stolen from his safe and what it was. Did it in any way have some bearing on this evening's argument? Maybe it would all lead to Carol Draper's whereabouts and the ugly mess in which she was implicated.

Standing on the sidewalk in front of the hospital, Doc pulled two tiny gauze-wrapped objects from his inside pocket.

"The slugs I took from Tommy," he said, placing them in the Homicide captain's outstretched palm. "See what you can find on them. I'll call you later."

Before Griffin could ask even one of the many questions he had on the tip of his tongue, Doc sprang into a cruising taxicab and was away.

CHAPTER IV

MURDER STEW

IT WAS 11:30 the same night. Doctor Miles Murdock stood in the dark doorway around the corner from the apartment hotel in which Dave Winters lived. The movie director had rented the penthouse apartment for his stay in Akelton.

There was an elevator inside the building, but it was not self-service and Doc didn't want anyone to know he was calling on the director. How could he get to an apartment twelve stories up without being seen?

The fire escape crawled up the front of the building. If he used it, anyone passing would spot him. But the building next door had an escape which came down in a dark alley, and it was slightly taller than the apartment hotel.

Doc slipped into the alley. From inside his coat pocket he drew out the purple mask, fitted it over his face. Then, leaping up, he gripped the lower rung of the extension ladder and pulled it down. He climbed with a speed and agility a circus trapeze artist would have envied.

On the roof he looked across at the penthouse. The windows were black. The space between the buildings was at least eight feet wide and a high spiked railing enclosed the roof of the apartment hotel.

The Purple Scar eyed the awful chasm thoughtfully, then stepped back a few paces to get a running start. He raced to the edge of the roof and leaped.

Through black space he flew, landed on the roof opposite with a jarring *thud*. His hands furiously sought and grasped the iron pickets of the fence.

He let out his breath at last, climbed over the fence and advanced warily to the big double doors which led into the penthouse. He tried the knob. It was locked.

He took a bunch of keys from his pocket, a priceless collection that had once belonged to Tommy Pedlar, the Sticky-fingered Kid. The fourth key he tried did the trick. He nudged the door open and slipped inside.

He waited a moment until his eyes became accustomed to the darkness, then moved silently through the rooms.

He came to what he judged must be the master bedroom, paused a moment on the threshold and tiptoed to the bed.

There was a figure sprawled upon it, fully clothed. Naturally it would be Dave Winters.

The Scar leaned forward to shake him awake, but a strange tightening gripped his chest. There was no sound of breathing from the man on the bed!

Taking a pencil flash from his vest, the Scar shot the beam at the man. Involuntarily he stiffened at the ghastly sight.

It was Winters, all right. The Scar recognized him at once from pictures in the newspapers. But he had been stabbed through the heart. Blood from the wound had left a vivid splash of color against the white sheets.

Doc leaned forward, pressed sensitive fingers against the chill skin. From his brief observation he gathered that death had been instantaneous and must have occurred no less than four hours ago—before Carol Draper had come to his office!

She could easily have killed Dave Winters first, typed the letter to herself and made Doctor Murdock an unwitting accessory after the fact—

A floorboard creaked behind him. As he whirled, a heavy object crashed down upon his wrist and sent the flashlight spinning to the floor. Before he could recover from the suddenness of the attack, the heavy bludgeon rose again. In the darkness he could not escape it. It came smashing down upon his head with a sickening impact. He made a wild grab at his adversary's coat, felt something rip away in his hands. Then blackness closed in and he slid to the floor.

THE ROOM was still dark when he opened his eyes. Slowly he raised himself to a sitting position. His head felt as if someone were deliberately pounding his brain with a huge hammer. He sat there for several moments. Then, as if the door to his mind had suddenly been flung open, his thoughts came roaring back in a torrent.

His mysterious assailant had obviously not been an expert scrapper, for he had not chosen a really vulnerable spot. Nor had there been a great deal of force behind the blow. It had had barely enough to drop him for a few minutes and leave him with a dull, heavy ache in his head. Moreover, the prowler must have been in a great hurry to get away. He hadn't even stopped long enough to search the Scar or make sure that the chase would not be taken up too soon.

The Scar got to his feet, staggered to the side of the bed. He made another quick examination of the corpse. Maybe the first time he had been wrong. Perhaps Winters hadn't been dead only four hours. Maybe this prowler who felled him had killed Winters just a short time before.

But Doc Murdock found his first guess had been correct. Why, then, had this person come back to the penthouse? What was he after—the contents of the safe?

The Scar picked up his flashlight from the floor. It still worked. He slipped through the rooms to the library-den, swept the walls with the beam until it came to a sudden stop on the open wall safe. Papers were strewn about the floor in front of it.

He approached the safe, looked inside. It was empty. Whatever the prowler was after, he had taken, unless someone else had got to it first.

The Scar plodded back into the bedroom, his head pounding. In the very spot where he had fallen he stepped on something small, round and hard. He pointed his light down at the carpet. It shone on a button.

He remembered grabbing hold of his assailant's coat. He must have torn off the button. He picked it up. Small and gray, it could have come off either a man's coat or a woman's suit jacket.

He recalled that Carol Draper had been wearing a gray business suit when he last saw her.

The scream of a distant siren came to his ears. He didn't pay any attention to it at first. Probably it was an ambulance or fire engine answering a hurry call. But louder and louder it swelled and suddenly was joined by several more, all heading in his direction.

He frowned, leaped to the doors that led out onto the roof. He stared through the picket railing, his eyes searching the streets below.

Several police cars were pulling up in front of the building. One poked its green-and-white nose into the alley. That effectively cut off all avenue of escape.

The person who had sapped him must have put in that call for the police, thinking it an excellent way to trap the Purple Scar. Doc had to admit it was far from stupid. Caught near the corpse, he would be unmasked—if not worse.

HE RUSHED back into the library, snatched up the phone, dialed the operator and got Police Headquarters. Captain Griffin's voice answered.

"I'm in a spot, Griff," the Scar said hurriedly. "Dave Winters has been murdered. I know you know. But listen. I'm cornered in his apartment. You've got to get over here fast. Say that you called me, wanted me to look at the body. I'll try to keep out of sight until you get here. But hurry! Bluecoats are starting to swarm around like hornets."

He slammed down the receiver, leaped for the door. He heard voices outside in the corridor and saw the knob turn. A step took him back out onto the roof. Police were patrolling every inch around the apartment house. His one chance was to get down the fire escape without being seen. At such a height, no one might notice him.

Over the iron-pronged fence he clambered, slipped to the edge of the parapet and reached the escape. Hugging the side of the white wall, he climbed down to the eighth floor. The window facing him was dark. He whispered a silent prayer that no one would be inside.

Without a sound he opened the window, scrambled through into the room. He waited, not daring to breathe. There was no sound. The apartment was empty.

He stayed dose to the window, staring out. Some moments later a squad car screamed to a halt in front of the building. He saw a squat man in a black suit and pulled-down hat step out onto the sidewalk and hurry into the building. It was Griffin.

The Scar gave his friend time enough to ride up to the top floor. Then he slipped to the door, turned the snap lock and opened it. The hallway was dimly lighted.

As he hurried to the back staircase, Doc Murdock peeled off the purple mask and hid it away carefully in the secret pocket of his coat. He went swiftly up the marble stairs to the penthouse.

A bluecoat, stationed outside the door of the murder apartment, frowned inquiringly as Miles Murdock approached.

"Hello, Doc," he greeted. "Where the devil did you come from? I hope you didn't hike up twelve flights of stairs."

Doc grinned blandly. "The elevator boy let me off at ten by mistake. Nervous after what happened, I guess."

"Captain Griffin's waiting for you inside," the policeman said, opening the door. "Said to send you right in."

Doc nodded and entered. Griffin was standing in the middle of the carpet. He met the plastic surgeon with a censuring stare. Doc grinned calmly.

"I got here soon as I could," he said.

His eyes roved the corpse in the next room. As if it were the first time he had laid eyes on it, he started and exclaimed:

"How did it happen?"

Griffin's square brows gathered together darkly.

"Maybe you can tell us?" he said with biting irony.

"Maybe. I'll have a look-see."

He held Griffin's gaze for a moment with his eyes that contained an almost exaggerated amount of candor.

DOC AND Griffin had been friends for many years. The square detective had been Miles' dead brother's friend before that. He had always had great respect for the young doctor's prowess in surgery, but it was not until he saw the efficiency with which the Purple Scar brought to justice his brother's murderers did Griffin believe that the Scar could really assist the force.

Still Griffin was one hundred per cent policeman. And while he knew that Miles was merely continuing his brother's fight against crime, he had to be less than open in his co-operation and enthusiasm.

Doc brushed past into the bedroom. This time he made a more complete survey of the body. He found something that his previous hurried examinadon had failed to disclose. Under the eyes, at the angles of the mouth, and over the jugular vein were tiny, almost invisible hypostatic spots, such as were usually found in severe cases of opium or morphine poisoning. This prompted an even more intense study of the body.

Pulling Griffin aside, Doc said:

"Griff, you've got to call the medical examiner. Have him get this body to the morgue immediately. The post-mortem must be held tonight."

"Tonight? A fat chance!"

"It's got to be done. It's very important."

"Why?"

"Winters has some kind of poison in his system. Whether it was the cause of death or not, I don't know, but we've got to find out. And how long that dope will remain in the body is problematical."

"Alcohol is what you'll find in his system, most likely."

Doc shook his head, unconvinced.

"You're a good cop, Griff, but you'd better not try doctoring yourself. You're a rotten physician."

CHAPTER V

GABBY

SEVERAL BLUECOATS were drifting around the place, making notes. Doc watched them apparently with an impersonal interest. After calling the medical examiner's office, Griffin watched, too. Then, when he saw them leave the library and go out the roof, he grabbed Doc Murdock's arm and steered him into the library. Bursting with curiosity, he demanded:

"Now what's this all about? How and why did you get into this place?"

Doc told him what had taken place, how he discovered the body and the blow on the head. When he had concluded, he asked:

"Now you answer one for me. What about those bullets I gave you?"

"Nothing. They came from an unregistered gun."

"Which means we're out of luck, as far as tracing them is concerned."

As he spoke, Doc moved to the desk. A small writing pad next to the telephone caught his eye. The number scribbled upon the pad was black and deep, as if it had been written with an angry hand.

Doc leaned forward, read the number. South 8974, 7:30 pm. He made a mental note of it. Maybe it would lead to something later on.

It was then that he spied the portable typewriter standing uncovered in the corner. He took a piece of plain paper, inserted it, tapped out a brief note.

Griffin wanted to know what he was up to. Doc had refrained from telling him about the letter which Carol Draper had received. He grinned.

"Typewriters are very fascinating, just like people. Each one has its own individual characteristics and faults."

He tore out the paper, stuffed it into his pocket. That was something else he'd check later.

The detective-captain's inquiring frown followed Doc as he browsed around the book-lined walls. The titles on the shelves surprised the plastic surgeon a great deal. "How to Win Friends and Influence People," "Self-expression Self-taught," "Master Thyself," "Power of Will."

"Looks as if our friend, Dave Winters, wasn't the terror in his own mind that he wanted people to believe he was," mused Doc, "with his barking, bellowing and slave-driving. I'd say he had more than a slight inferiority complex, which he hid under a rough exterior." He scratched the tip of his nose reflectively. "I wonder whose standard he was trying to reach."

Captain Griffin was about to ask what he meant, but the cop on duty in the hall opened the door and poked his head inside.

"Gent here to see Mister Winters, Captain," he announced.

"Okay, let him in," Griffin instructed.

The man whom the police officer had announced took a step across the threshold, stopped with a frown.

"Say, what's going on around this place?" he complained. "Cops everywhere. Everybody so secretive."

"Who are you?" Griffin demanded sharply.

"You can say that again for me, mister," the newcomer flipped back.

Griffin's answer was to flash his gold-and-blue shield.

"Oh, that's different." The big fellow came inside with a mirthless grin as the policeman closed the door behind hem. "I'm Gabby Newel, press relations counsel for Big Four Productions."

NEWEL WAS tall, solidly built, with meaty shoulders that bulged under the expensive tuxedo he wore. His wide-jowled face was pleasant and his hair a fiery red. He was apparently in his late twenties or early thirties. The big black cigar stuck in his mouth was the badge of his profession.

"What's cookin' around here, anyway?" he protested.

"Dave Winters has been murdered," Griffin answered impassively.

The redhead's face reflected pure incredulity.

"Murdered?" he gasped. "But he couldn't be! Why, I was at the Lullaby Club with him only this evening, a few hours ago. That's why I came here now, to check and see if he was all right. When he left the club he was drunker than a lord. And Big Four has almost a half million dollars sewed up in the picture he was making. Gosh, what a slap in the eye this is going to be!"

"Gunther and Winters had quite an argument tonight, didn't they?" Doc Murdock asked.

The press agent's eyes came around to meet the plastic surgeon. There was recognition in them.

"Aren't you Dr. Murdock ?" When Doc nodded Gabby shoved out his big hand. Doc, as he shook it, couldn't help but notice the huge, oddly shaped ring which adorned Gabby's middle finger. It was shaped like two wrestlers locked in a death-hold. Gabby saw him eyeing it and grinned proudly.

"College memento. Intercollegiate wrestling champion. Had it made over into a ring." He suddenly remembered and his face saddened. "But what about Winters? I don't get it. Who killed him?"

"We were hoping you'd be able to give us some idea," Griffin said drily.

"Well," Gabby replied bluntly, "offhand I can think of a couple of dozen people who won't shed any tears."

"What was the argument about that Winters had with Jules Gunther tonight?" Doc persisted.

Gabby smiled. There was something genuinely handsome about his face when he smiled, yet it was far too rugged a handsomeness to meet cinematic standards.

"If you're thnking it had anything to do with Winters' getting killed," Gabby said, "I can save you a lot of foul-ball chasing. I admit there wasn't any great affection between Winters and Gunther, but Winters happened to be the best director in the flicker business. He made hits out of duds. And Jules Gunther never allows his personal feelings to stand in the way of that old pocketbook of his."

"What were they arguing about?" Griffin repeated stubbornly.

Gabby shrugged his wide shoulders.

"Production costs. That was always their sore spot. Winters had a habit of running into high figures when he was shooting a picture. Gunther acted as sort of a stabilizer. I always said it was a whacky setup at Big Four. They tried to pattern it after United Artists. The company was made up of a director, a star, a writer and Gunther, the only sound business head of the whole gang."

"Who was the writer?" Doc asked casually.

"Victor Banco. He used to do a Broadway column some years ago. Married to a swell dish, Stella Stanly, former Zeigfeld beauty."

DOC DROPPED the subject quickly and began on another tack.

"How will Banco and his two partners manage after this death?"

"Okay. Banco, Carol Draper and Gunther'll each grab themselves off a bigger slice of the company. That was the agreement when the company was formed. If anything happens to one, the others split his share. But on the other hand, Winter's death is going to be costly to the company. Regardless of whether he was liked or disliked, his label on a picture spelled box office. Directors like that don't grow in bunches like grapes."

"How about the personal issue, as far as these remaining three partners were concerned? Banco, for instance. How did he and Winters hit it off?"

Gabby's shoulders moved uneasily under his tuxedo jacket.

"That's a ticklish proposition, in view of what's happened. First of all, Winters was something of a Don Juan. You know what I just said about Stella Stanly, Banco's wife, or rather I should make it Banco's wife in name only. They're not putting up at the same tepee at the moment."

He shifted his enormous black cigar to the other side of his mouth.

"I know that's going to point the accusing digit at Banco, so I'm putting in my say right now. I've known Vic a long time, ever since the days when he used to pound out the dirt in that column he ran in the old *Graphic*. He rates tops in my book. I don't think he'd hurt anybody. Besides, there's no real proof that Winters was responsible for the Bancos' split."

"Now what about Carol Draper?" Doc inquired.

Gabby's eyes narrowed wisely and he smiled just enough to show a hint of white teeth.

"Ya got me there, pal, right in the old soft spot. Far as I'm concerned, Carol Draper is the golden-haired gal. You couldn't beat a wrong word out of me about her. Carol gave me my first big chance in Hollywood. I've handled her ever since she made a grab for that first rung."

His smile expanded.

"Of course I'm not saying I didn't give her a couple of good healthy boosts. But the point is she's not like the rest of these half-baked hams you meet. She didn't forget little Gabby after she made the top."

Griffin cut in at that point. He told Gabby Newel that he wanted him to look at the body for obvious reasons. Gabby's face drained a little. He sighed deeply and shrugged.

"Okay, if you can stand the sight of a man who can't stand the sight of blood."

All the effervescence that was part of the voluble redhead's make-up left him as he turned toward the bedroom. The corners of his mouth twitched and for a moment, as he stood there on the threshold, he looked as though he were going to cave in. But he got a fresh grip on himself and went inside reluctantly with Griffin.

Doc Murdock took advantage of the opportunity to pull the two typewritten sheets of paper from his pocket and compare them. The note he had just pounded out on Winters' portable and the letter Carol Draper had received from Jess Henshaw were identical in contents. But there the likeness ended. They had not been written on the same machine.

Griffin and Gabby Newel returned to the library. The detective-captain was asking confidentially:

"Just what was your slant toward Winters, Newel?"

Gabby seemed shaken by the ordeal of viewing the corpse of the movie director. But he quickly recovered his composure and answered:

"We got along. Nobody was his bosom pal, of course. He didn't bother me much, though, and I kept away from him."

"How did you happen to choose the Lullaby Club?" Doc questioned, walking toward them.

GABBY GRINNED. "You seem kind of interested in this case, Doc."

"The success of Big Four Productions means a lot to our city," Miles answered soberly. "And this publicity is unpleasant to anyone who loves the place that gives him a home and a living. Perhaps you don't know what it means to take pide in your city and its people. If not, I pity you."

"You mean you're afraid Big Four'll hoist anchor and rush back to good old Hollywood?" Gabby chuckled. "You don't have to get gray about that, Doc. Big Four'll be around these parts when your children's children have whiskers down to here."

"How did you happen to choose the Lullaby Club tonight?" Doc repeated. "Did Gunther know that Winters was going to be there tonight, waiting for him?"

"He didn't say so to me," answered Gabby. "All I know is this. About 4 o'clock this afternoon, Carol Draper's maid brought her a letter while she was on the set. I was hanging around, watching them shoot close-ups. I don't know what was in the letter, or even whether that had anything to do with it, but all of a sudden Carol said she had a splitting headache.

"She looked it, too. And she certainly wasn't in any condition to have close-ups taken, so Winters called it quits for the afternoon. Everybody working on the picture, including himself, went home. The next time I saw Winters was at the club."

"And did you see Carol Draper again?"

"Nope, but I called her apartment several times to find out how she was feeling. The clerk told me she had gone out and hadn't got back yet. Another funny thing—he said she fired her maid, all of which has me sort of worried, especially on top of Winters' getting killed. It's not like Carol to act so mysteriously."

"According to reports," Griffin interjected for the record, "Winters left the club at 7:45. He must have gone straight home and been killed around 8:30. Where were you at that time, Newel?"

"Right after Winters left the club, Jules Gunther and I returned to the studio. We had some releases to get out. In fact that's why Gunther originally asked me to go with him to the club. He wanted to talk them over. But after what happened there, we didn't care much about staying."

"Of course you can prove you were with Gunther at that time?" Griffin persisted.

Gabby grinned. "Call him now, if you want. Beechview one-two-four-five. Or if he's not at home, try the studio. They're shooting a quickie out there tonight. South eight-nine-seven-four is the number. That's his own private wire."

South 8974 was the number on the telephone pad, Doc remembered. So that number led to Jules Gunther's private phone. That meant Dave Winters had probably come home about four-thirty, found the bluecoat in his apartment and the safe tampered with. As soon as the patrolman left, he must have called his partner and told him to meet him at 7:30 in the Lullaby Club.

Did Winters think Gunther had something to do with that safe being opened? What could have been in there that Gunther might have been interested in? Why, also, didn't Gunther tell Gabby Newel that he was going to meet Winters? Or was it the press agent who was withholding information? If so, Doc decided, it might be wise if he did not reveal his knowledge of the call until he found out for sure.

ONE OF the cops came into the library from the bedroom.

"Captain, look what I found under the mattress that Winters was layin' on!" he exclaimed.

He held up his hand. Wrapped in a handkerchief, in order not to destroy prints that might be on it, was an odd-shaped mother-of-pearl-handled paper cutter. There was congealed blood on the long blade.

As the police officer came closer, red-haired Gabby Newel's eyes almost bulged out of his head as they settled on the blade. The hint of a surprised gasp escaped his lips. Griffin caught the gasp. His face came around, his black eyes intent.

"Well, do you know whose it is?" he demanded.

Gabby appeared to be fighting for self-control.

"No— I don't know—" he stammered.

"Holding back evidence or informaton in a murder case is no joke, Newel," the detective-captain rapped out. "If I were you, I'd start talking. Whose cutter is this?"

Gabby's eyes traveled hopelessly from Griffin's square face to the blade, then back to Griffin's face.

"It—it belongs to—to Victor Banco!" he gasped.

CHAPTER VI

LEAD!

QUESTIONING SOON revealed that Victor Banco lived in this same building. His apartment was on the fifth floor. Promptly Griffin, Doctor Murdock and Gabby Newel went down there.

In response to Griffin's ring, a tall man with a sallow face and sleepy green eyes opened the door. He had gray-streaked black hair which he wore long at the back and full above the eyes. Blue pajama legs flapped beneath a vividly-colored dressing gown. His none-too-powerful chin fell with surprise as he saw the three men standing there, but he had the presence of mind to invite them into his study.

Griffin let Gabby Newel handle the introductions and tell Banco briefly what had happened upstairs. The manner in which the writer received the news of this tragedy was strange.

At least Doc Murdock thought so. He could not put his finger on whether the former newspaper columnist who had become a motion picture executive was happy, surprised or worried. Banco had a face that never betrayed emotion. But one thing Doc Murdock knew—Banco was not sorry about Winters' death.

"Where've you been all night?" Griffin asked.

"Here in my apartment," Banco replied. "Since 7:30. I came here directly from dinner."

"Any way of proving that?"

"Only by the people downstairs who might have seen me come in—the desk clerk, the doorman, and the elevator boy who brought me up here."

"But there's no way of proving that you didn't leave this room after you got here, sneaked up the back stairs to the penthouse and stabbed Dave Winters to death!"

"Are you insinuating—"

"I'm not insinuating anything," Griffin shot back.

Dramatically he held up the paper-cutter. Banco's eyes fastened on it. His mouth fell open.

"You seem to recognize it," Griffin said quietly.

Banco gulped, stared at the dried blood on the blade. Definitely his face was not inscrutable now. He was greatly disturbed and he made no pretense at hiding it.

"Of course I recognize it," he faltered. "That paper cutter used to be mine."

"What d'ya mean—used to be?"

The gray-haired writer wetted his lips.

"I gave it to Carol Draper."

"Carol!" Gabby Newel shouted.

The flame from his fiery hair seemed to communicate itself to his brain. With one bound he was across the room. He clutched Victor Banco by the throat, bent him backward across the desk. Doc Murdock and Captain Griffin had all they could do to prevent Gabby from strangling the man. They pulled him back several feet. His eyes blazed, his mouth was an ugly slash.

"He's lying!" the press agent spat out venomously. "He's trying to frame Carol Draper. He wants to ruin the company!"

"But why should he want to do that?" Doc Murdock questioned. "He has a great deal of money tied up in Big Four."

"He's got a lot more invested in property out in Hollywood. If Big Four does happen to click in this town and other companies decided to follow he'll lose a fortune. He fought tooth and nail to keep Big Four from moving here, but his three partners out-voted him. He and Winters were at each other's throat all the time. Winters kept changing his scripts and you know what that means to a writer."

"You didn't talk like this upstairs," Griffin reminded curtly.

"Because I tried to give him a break. I knew how it'd look for him. I even stuck up for him about his wife. But I see now that he wouldn't stop at anything to keep his money—killing Winters and trying to frame Carol Draper!"

HE MADE a wild, desperate lunge to get at Banco's throat again, but the writer backed away in fright. And Gabby could not shake the steel grip of the two men holding him. They quieted him down finally and got him out of the apartment. Then Griffin went on with his routine questions.

Nothing much of importance was revealed. As Gabby Newel had said upstairs, Banco and his beautiful wife were estranged. But Banco insisted doggedly that Dave Winters was in no way responsible for the separation.

Banco, however, admitted he had never had any use for Winters. He also admitted owning considerable property in Hollywood, as Gabby had stated. He said he had been opposed to Big Four's coming to Akelton City, but as far as killing Winters or framing Carol Draper were concerned, he claimed it was utterly preposterous.

Doc Murdock, using the excuse that he wanted to type a full report of the case for Griffin, asked Banco if he might use the portable typewriter. Banco told him to go right ahead.

It was another dead end. The type did not match the one in the warning note…

It was long past midnight when Doctor Murdock said goodnight to Detective Captain Griffin on the sidewalk in front of the apartment house. Griffin told Doc to be sure to be at H.Q. in the morning. The Homicide chief was herding together all suspects in the case for questioning.

But Doc was not content to wait until morning for further developments. First of all, there was the mystery of Carol Draper's whereabouts to be cleared up.

Was Victor Banco trying to frame Carol Draper, as Gabby insisted? Or was he telling the truth when he said he had given the paper cutter to the movie actress. If so, it made things look black for the girl.

Doc hailed a taxicab on the corner, gave an address and settled back in the rear seat, his mind a swirl of thoughts. Who was actually behind this mystery? Had Carol Draper been kidnaped, or was she playing possum? Was it really Jess Henshaw, her first husband, who had sent that letter to her, or was he dead?

What had been stolen from Dave Winters' safe—love letters written by Victor Banco's wife, that might involve her in this murder? Or was Doc's first guess correct, that it was Gunther with whom he had tangled in the darkness of Dave Winters' apartment? He did not know, but he meant to find out.

The taxicab in which Doc Murdock was riding came to a squealing halt in front of the City Hospital. After he paid off the driver, he went directly to the little room in which Tommy Pedlar lay.

Doc had told a white lie to his friend, Dan Griffin. He had known that Tommy would quickly snap out of the ether, but he did not want anyone hurling questions at the Sticky-fingered Kid until he found out for himself what had happened.

THOUGH TOMMY had regained his senses some time before, his head was still throbbing when Doc came in. He mustered a feeble grin and mumbled:

"Guess I kinda bungled this one, eh, Doc?"

"Of course you didn't," Doc stated flatly. "Just take it easy and you'll be okay in a few days. Tell me how it happened."

Tommy nodded painfully. "That cab driver was a phony. The real driver must've been ambushed. Me and the Draper dame rode only a few blocks when the driver says somethin's wrong with the engine. He gets out to look at it. First thing I know, the back door opens and there's a gat aimed at my belly. Like a dope I make a dive for the rod, but he shoots twice. Somethin' hot burns my leg and my side and then everything goes black."

"Just one more question, Tommy, then I'll be all finished. Did you get a look at the man who shot you?"

Tommy nodded slowly, his eyes beginning to close. Doc could see that unconsciousness was starting to catch up with the wounded Sticky-fingered Kid. But he had learned who had shot his friend.

He snatched the smelling salts off the dresser, yanked out the cork, shoved the bottle under Tommy's nose. Tommy struggled to escape the pungent odor. His eyes flickered and he made a spiritless grin. Doc repeated the question. Tommy swallowed and mumbled almost inaudibly:

"Guy they call—'Penguin Pete' Barrow—"

His head fell limp. His eyes closed and his brain was once more enveloped in merciful surcease from unbearable pain.

Doc looked down at the little man sadly.

With an almost fatherly hand, he tucked the blanket in, flicked off the bed light and stepped out of the room.

"He'll be all right by morning if we let him rest," he instructed the white-uniformed nurse on duty outside the door. "And don't let anyone disturb him, not even the police."

He turned and went down the white-walled corridor to the telephone booth, which stood just inside the main entrance. He dropped a nickel into the coin slot, got Captain Griffin on the wire and asked a hurried question.

"Sure, I know Penguin Pete Barrow," the captain replied. "Tough egg. Lives uptown in the smoke section. Plays around some in the numbers racket. Packs a gat for anybody who'll slip him the price. Never with the same mob for more than two jobs in a row. What do you want with a rat like him?"

"I want to know where he lives," declared Doc.

"Why?"

"Something personal."

"Anything to do with Tommy Pedlar getting shot, or this movie murder mixup?"

"Can you or can't you give me Barrow's address?" Doc demanded.

"Hang on," Griffin said wearily. In a couple of minutes the deep-throated voice came again. "Here it is, Doc. Seven-seventy-two Fennox Avenue. Bad neighborhood. If you want me to, I'll send a couple of boys up to bring him in."

"Thanks, but I'd rather it stays off the blotter. Incidentally, any word from the medical examiner yet?"

"Everything except a report. He raised the devil about performing a midnight autopsy."

"How about the paper cutter? Any prints?"

"Clean as a cloud."

"Okay. Give me a ring soon as you hear about the autopsy."

He hung up and left the booth. He was looking for trouble and he meant to find it.

CHAPTER VII

MEET THE PENGUIN

DALE JORDAN was waiting for Doctor Murdock when he returned to his Swank Street laboratory. A green summer dress set off to advantage her slim, highly attractive figure. Far back on her reddish-brown curls perched a ridiculously small beret with a long green feather.

She darted up the stairs to the studio after him.

"How's Tommy?" she asked anxiously.

"He'll be all right in the morning. What did you find out about Carol Draper?"

"She lived at the Hotel Pierre, only you neglected to tell me one little detail. How was I supposed to get into her suite?"

"But you got in didn't you?"

"Of course. Luckily she discharged her maid this afternoon."

That verified what Gabby Newel told Doc. The actress must have let the servant go right after receiving the note, when she decided to run away.

"The manager of the hotel asked if I was the new maid when I wanted to know the number of her room. Naturally I said yes, so he had one of the boys let me into her apartment to wait."

Doc smiled appreciatively. He had been sure Dale would be able to figure out a way of getting into the apartment. That was why he had her helping him with this dangerous work. Dale could always be depended upon, no matter what the emergency was.

"Did Carol Draper have a typewriter?" he asked.

She nodded, handed him a neatly typed sheet of paper. When Doc compared it with the original which Carol Draper had received from Jess Henshaw, his brows came together.

He had sent Dale to the movie star apartment to type the note, merely to satisfy himself that he had left no stones unturned. He had not actually believed that the note she received had been typed on *her own machine!*

That could mean that anyone with access to the machine could have typed the letter. A clever burglar like Jess Henshaw could certainly have broken into the rooms and written the message.

"Don't forget she could have done it herself," Dale pointed out after Doc explained his find to her. "Suppose it turns out that she did do it."

"I'll lose my faith in human nature."

"But that gray button, the paper cutter Banco gave her, those two notes typed on her machine, the neatness with which she was abducted and her wanting her face changed after Dave Winters had been murdered—every single clue points squarely at her."

"Almost too squarely," Doc objected. He looked at the two letters again and added: "Besides, she never worked on a paper, at least as far as I could discover."

Dale was about to ask what he meant, but the telephone bell jingled. Doc lifted the receiver to his ear.

"This is Griffin, Doc. Cause of death—knife wound penetrating the right ventricle of the heart. No trace of opium, morphine or any other dope."

IF DOC MURDOCK was disappointed or surprised at Griffin's report, his face did not show it. His jaw merely seemed to set a little and his eyes narrowed.

"How about the alcoholic content in the body?" he asked.

"Surprisingly little."

"Thanks, Griff," Doc said. "You'll be hearing from me soon."

Dale had worked with Miles Murdock too long to ask questions when that preoccupied look appeared in his eyes. She silently watched him walk to the tall cabinet that stood at one corner of the studio. From the bottom drawer he took out make-up materials.

Working swiftly with clay, he fashioned a wide-nosed, high-cheeked face. After hardening the clay with his special quick drier, he made a plaster of paris cast, prepared a solution of melted gum elastic and poured it into the mold.

While he was waiting for it to set, he pulled out the purple mask from the secret pocket in his coat. He put on the ghastly mask, removed the second one from its mold and slipped it over the corpse face. A greasy, waterproof substance temporarily flattened down the wave in his black hair and turned it blond.

Experience had taught him the value of a disguise that could be removed only by himself and would not be affected by hard usage. The purple mask he used as a basic disguise for, when its psychological effect was needed, it had to be instantly available. Slipping it on and off would have been clumsy and undramatic, so he employed it as a foundation for all other disguises that became necessary.

He stood up, examined his revolver and slipped it back into his hip holster.

"May I help?" Dale ventured at last.

"Not right now," he said. "Stay where I can reach you. I'll probably need your help later."

She clasped his big hand warmly, told him she would wait here, and added her usual parting prayer:

"Please be careful!"

He left by the back door. It led into a winding black alley that ended a half a block away. This secret exit had been built by the original owners of the old-fashioned mansion which Doctor Murdock had converted into his laboratory and home. He found it an excellent way of getting in and out of the building without being seen.

Where 129th Street crossed Fennox Avenue, Doc discharged his taxicab. The night fog seemed to have grown worse, cloaking all objects in a thick, obscuring veil.

Crossing the street, he studied the numbers on the tall brownstone houses. The fog masked their aged, dirty faces. Here and there a yellow patch that was a window sent a tunnel of light through the haze.

Almost at the end of the block stood a crumbling rooming house. He checked the number, went up the stoop briskly. A dim light shone through the ragged lace-curtained glass door. He found a row of bells to one side, but no names over them.

It looked as if he would have to pick a bell at random to get in. But the knob turned and the door creaked open. A heavy blond woman purred:

"Looking for me, mister?"

"No," he said. "I'm looking for Pete Barrow. Penguin Pete, they call him."

The purr went out of the blond's voice.

"Nobody here by that name!" she snapped.

The Scar had anticipated that response. As she started to close the door, his right hand came out of his pocket, holding a five-dollar bill.

"It's yours for the right answer," he told her.

Her eyes gleamed and said quickly:

"He lives on the top floor, second door to the right."

She snatched the bill and hurried into her room, slamming the door behind her.

The Scar slipped into the dim-lighted hallway, noiselessly went up the stairs two at a time. The upper landings had no lights. The higher he climbed, the darker it became. The top floor, seven storeys up, was as black as ink.

Down the narrow corridor to the second door he went, making sure his revolver was loose in his holster, ready for instant use. He rapped lightly on the door. There was no answer. He tried the knob. It was locked. He hammered again, louder. Still there was no reply.

From his pocket he took his bunch of keys. A brief investigation of the lock with the aid of his pencil flash told him which key to use. He was about to insert the key when suddenly the door swung open.

A short, brutish-looking man with anthropoid features stood there. His bull neck sloped into beefy shoulders. His unbuttoned coat revealed a broad spread of white shirt front which undoubtedly had earned him the "Penguin" sobriquet.

"What's the idea tryin' to bust into my room?" he demanded ferociously.

"Why don't you answer the door when you hear somebody knocking?" the Scar shot back.

"Who are you, anyway?" the man in the doorway snorted.

"John Pryor's my name. You Pete Barrow?"

"Why?"

"I want to talk to you."

"Tomorrow. I'm too tired tonight. Scram!"

He tried to slam the door, but the Scar's powerful shoulder stopped it.

"I hear you're a taxi driver, among other things," the Scar said. "I want to know what you did with a certain passenger you picked up tonight—a young lady with bandages on her face."

The killer's ape-like face grew several shades darker and alarm showed in his eyes.

"I don't know what you're talkin' about!" he snarled. "And I said scram!"

A gun suddenly appeared in the Scar's hand. He rammed it against Penguin Pete's stomach. The killer's startled eyes dropped, caught the glint of the steel. He managed a sickly smile.

"You can't plug a guy for nothin'—" he began.

As he spoke, his hand crept to his belt. His eyes came up and met the gaze of the man before him. Abruptly his hand leaped, brought up a glittering six-inch length of knife blade, slashed viciously at the Scar's gun-hand.

The Scar tried to pull back, but the hallway was too narrow. The blade slashed across his knuckles, made him lower the gun. Before he could bring it up again, Penguin Pete Barrow had lunged past him and shot up the stairs.

SWIFTLY THE Scar wheeled, went after the man three steps at a time. He had expected Pete Barrow to be reluctant to talk, but he hadn't figured the hood would actually put up a fight like this. But if he wanted a battle, that was what he would get.

The Scar heard a door burst open above him, caught a glimpse of the fugitive racing out to the roof. He would have shot the man, but that would have been unwise. He continued the chase.

Reaching the roof door, he crouched low and sprang through it. He scanned the dark, mist-swept rooftops for any moving silhouette. There was none. He moved forward cautiously, gun in hand, eyes wary.

From one roof to another he went. On the sixth he heard a footstep crunch the gravel behind him. How could Penguin Pete have circled around and got back there so quickly?

The Scar pivoted, saw fire streak out of the blackness again and again. He thought he heard someone groan. Flat on the tar roof he flung himself. He could not hope to see through the darkness and fog. Besides, he had no desire to kill anyone.

He fired high, back in the direction from which the shots had come. He heard footsteps pound back across the roofs. A door slammed.

Bandaging his hand with his handkerchief, the Scar worked his way back to the roof he had come from, keeping low and in the shadows of the chimneys. He stopped short as his toe struck something soft and yielding that felt like a bundle of wet wash. He bent forward, cursed softly the instant he snapped on his flash.

Stretched out on the roof at his feet lay the body of Penguin Pete Barrow. He was dead.

For a moment the Scar thought he had killed the man. But then he realized that he had pointed his gun in the air and hadn't fired in this direction at all. Someone else had been up there on the roof with them—someone who had deliberately committed murder to keep Penguin Pete Barrow from talking....

The Scar saw no one, heard no one as he left the rooming house. Evidently the neighbors were accustomed to hearing gun shots in the middle of night and wisely tended to their own business.

Reaching the street, he was busily asking himself baffling questions. Who had followed them onto the roof and killed Penguin Pete Barrow? How did the killer get up there? Could it be possible that he had been hiding in Pete's room while the Scar had been talking with the doomed man?

It seemed logical. Perhaps the killer had learned that Penguin Pete had not succeeded in killing Tommy Pedlar and that the victim could identify him. If so, in all likelihood the gunman had come to remove Penguin Pete from the scene. The intrusion of the Scar had fitted nicely into this scheme.

Penguin Pete had probably thought he was doing the right thing by drawing his questioner up onto the roof, where the killer could take a bead at him, or else clear the way for the killer to slip out of the room and escape. Instead the murderer had doublecrossed Penguin Pete and taken the opportunity to get rid of him.

DOC MURDOCK was pondering all this as he walked several blocks to an all-night drug store. He went inside, entered a phone booth, and dialed Police Headquarters. He reported the killing of Penguin Pete Barrow. Then he waited a moment and called Beechview 1245. A sleepy voice answered.

"Is Mister Gunther at home?" asked Doc. "Still at the studio, eh? Thank you."

He hung up, his brow furrowed. Never had he encountered as heartless a group of business associates as Big Four Productions. Though one of their number had been murdered and another reported missing, they went right on shooting pictures all night long.

He hailed a cruising cab in front of the drug store.

"Big Four studios," he told the driver.

Settling back in the rear seat, he drew a blank card from his pocket, scribbled a few words on it and signed it. He studied it for a moment and nodded with satisfaction. The Sticky-fingered Kid had been a good teacher in the Purple Scar's battle against crime. When necessary, the Scar was an excellent forger.

CHAPTER VIII

SAFE

U NDER A dim light the man at the main gate of the Big Four studios scrutinized the card that the blond, broad-featured man before him had proffered. It said:

PLEASE ADMIT BEARER TO STUDIOS.
VICTOR BANCO

He was passed without question through the gate. As he entered, though, he saw the guard reach inside the booth, take down a sheet of paper which was tacked to a flat slab of wood and write something down.

"What's that?" asked the Scar.

"A record we keep. Tells what time people come in and go out."

"Employers, too?"

"Everybody."

A smile widened still further the broad face of the strange visitor.

"Would that sheet tell whether Gabby Newel, the press agent, left here with Jules Gunther about 7 o'clock?"

The guard nodded. "But we ain't supposed to give out any information."

The Scar pulled a dollar bill from his pocket. The guard looked around cautiously, pocketed the bribe and looked down at the sheet.

"Left here together at exactly 7:10," he whispered.

"What time did they come back?"

"Two minutes to 8."

"Either of them leave again?"

The man's bony finger raced down the sheet.

"Mister Gunther left the studio about 11 o'clock," he said. "Came back again before 12."

"How about Gabby Newel?" asked the Scar.

"Didn't leave the studio until about midnight."

"You're sure of that?"

"That's what it says, and nobody's touched this sheet since I came on duty."

"What time was that?"

"Seven."

"Okay. Thanks a lot." The Scar was about to turn away when he suddenly thought of something else. "What kind of suit did Mister Newel have on?"

The guard checked back in his mind. "Tuxedo," he said finally.

"All night long?"

"Far as I know."

"How about Jules Gunther?"

"Gray I think. Yeah, sort of a dark gray."

"Thanks."

The guard, fingering the dollar in his pocket, watched the blond stranger melt into the foggy darkness, wondering why the stranger had smiled at the mention of a gray suit.

The Scar found the interior of the studio interesting. Far over in a corner of the lot, one sound stage was booming with activity, like a little world set apart. There were lights, people, noise, camera and sound crews. This was where the night scenes were being shot for the quickie.

He sauntered over, careful to keep in the shadows where no one could see him. He scanned the faces watching the scene that was being taken. One face seemed to stand out from the crowd. It was Jules Gunther. He couldn't miss that famous parrot-beaked, bald-topped man with tufts of steel-gray at the temples. That face had adorned almost every story the Big Four Productions press department had released.

But the face wasn't what interested him at the moment. It was the black suit Jules Gunther had on. That meant the movie executive had changed clothes since returning to the studio tonight.

PROMPTLY THE Scar turned, walked back through the grounds. The rest of the lot was like some graveyard of forgotten ages. Here was a time-worn stage coach used in Westerns. There was a "flat" that photographed as the front of a boom town saloon. Farther on he came to a huge Spanish galleon used in sea epics. Actually it was only the prow, jutting high overhead into the black, murky sky. The rest of the ship was a tangle of spars and crossbeams, with cables holding it together.

There was no end of odd and interesting sights, some beautiful, some grotesque. Floodlights, cables and sound contraptions were everywhere, but all were lying idle.

He continued on to the administration building, where the offices were located, found the directory. Jules Gunther had his office on the ground floor, Room 12. The Scar went there, found the door locked. He had no trouble gaining admittance with one of his many keys.

It was dark inside, but he drew his flashlight and played the beam around. The huge office was decorated with exquisite taste, the floor carpeted in deep maroon plush. At one side stood a massive desk of African mahogany with hand-carved chairs to match.

His flashlight picked out a closet door. He tried the knob. It was locked, too. The second key he tried opened it. The light from his flash pushed aside the darkness, settled on a gray business suit. The coat of the suit was minus one button. The cloth where the button had been was partly torn away!

Beyond all doubt, Jules Gunther was the man who had struck him in the darkness of Dave Winters' penthouse. But that did not necessarily mean that Gunther was the man who had killed the movie director.

In the first place Gunther, according to the time sheet, had not left the studio from 8 o'clock until 11. And Winters had been murdered somewhere around 8:30, not before. Why then had Gunther gone to the director's penthouse? What had he been looking for?

The more the Purple Scar wrestled with the thought, the more certain he became that something had been stolen from Winters' safe when the butler found it had been tampered with and called the police. That something was evidently important to Gunther. Nor did he think Gunther had succeeded in getting hold of that something the first time, else why should he have gone back there? It was up to the Scar to find out what Gunther wanted from that safe, or what he had been trying to keep someone else from getting.

Closing the closet door quietly, the Scar moved to the big desk. Quickly he examined papers littering the top of the desk, found nothing of value, went through the drawers. He found nothing of interest there, either. The Scar frowned. There must be something here! Perhaps in his anxiety he had overlooked it. He started again with the top drawer. The first thing his eyes lighted on was a mirror.

He had heard that Jules Gunther was pompous, arrogant, filled with contempt for all those who did not meet his specifications. But he never heard that the man was so vain that he kept a mirror in his desk drawer. But was it really vanity?

THE SCAR snatched up the mirror, opened the wide, flat center drawer of the desk. With the aid of his flashlight he worked the mirror around inside the drawer. He stopped suddenly, a faint smile on his face.

There, pasted to the top of the desk drawer, was a row of figures—obviously the combination of a safe?

He played the beam around the office again. There was no safe, or anything that resembled a safe. But as he scanned the walls, he noticed that the picture of one of Gunther's stable of racing thoroughbreds was tilted.

The Scar stepped to it, pushed the picture to one side, exposing the wall safe. He followed the combination and in a moment had the steel door open. He dug his hand inside, brought forth a stack of papers and a black ledger. He glanced through them rapidly.

They showed clearly that Jules Gunther, as the brains of the firm, had complete charge of production and distribution of all films. Included were details of all transactions, corporation reports and other data pertaining to these important duties. From what the Scar could gather in this brief survey, all seemed to be in perfect order.

But then, farther back in the safe, he found another bundle of papers, fastened to a smaller ledger with several elastic bands. These dealt with precisely the same subjects, yet the entries in this ledger were plainly in code.

The Scar was familiar with the more simpler forms of cipher communication, of course. This was one of the most simple, especially since the reports were at hand to check against the figures. The answer leaped right off the pages at him. Jules Gunther had been guilty of embezzlement that had cost his partners fabulous sums!

Taking advantage of the fact that his three partners were not business-minded, he had carefully kept two complete sets of books. One set his partners and their auditors might inspect. The other set, though, was for his own personal use.

Yet in this second set of books an odd thing was apparent. Systematic payments had been made to someone whose name did not appear even in code. Why?

At this particular moment the Purple Scar could not take the time to try to figure out the answer. But a return glance to the second batch of reports told him plainly that if one of these had been intercepted, and put into the hands of one of his partners, Jules Gunther would have been ruined.

Suddenly the Scar heard the sound of a door opening outside in the corridor. Footsteps approached through the long hallway. His heart skipped fast. He threw the ledgers and reports back into the safe, shut the heavy door, spun the tumblers and let the picture drop back into place.

His eyes swept the room for an escape. The footsteps were coming toward the only door. The single window was barred securely on the outside.

HE DIVED for the clothes closet, pulled the door shut just as the other one opened. A switch clicked and light flooded the office from twin cut-glass chandeliers.

"I thought I locked this door when I went out," said the heavy voice of Jules Gunther. "I must be growing careless."

The Scar, inside the dark, stuffy closet, crouched and tried to see through the keyhole. But Gunther and the person with him took seats at an angle which made it impossible for him to see.

"Well, Lou, what seems to be on your mind?" asked Gunther affably. "Certainly must be important to bring you here at this hour."

"Yeah, I didn't want to talk to you about it over the phone," said the man named Lou. "And I had to wait till things slowed down at my place before I could break away." He lowered his voice and asked in a cautious tone: "You're sure nobody can hear us in here?"

"Positive."

"I'm here about a friend of yours," Lou went on. He had a voice that was both silk and sharp, deadly steel. "I got orders to wrap about twenty feet of river over this friend's head. But I thought maybe you might like to change that order."

Shocked surprise sprang into the motion picture executive's voice. "What do you mean?" he demanded.

"I mean I'm holdin' somebody that the city's got the fine comb out for."

Gunther made a gasping sound.

"You mean you're holding Carol Draper?"

"I never mention names, Mister Gunther," Lou said smoothly.

Gunther sprang to his feet, coming into the Scar's line of vision. His parrot-beaked face was flushed crimson.

"You're a kidnaper! You abducted Carol Draper and have the audacity to come here and try to bargain with me!"

"Now calm down," purred Lou. "I happen to know where it is."

"Where what is?"

"A body you wouldn't want dug up." The way Lou said it, it was plain that "body" was merely a figure of speech. "You see, my boys've got very good ears. And those ears happened to pick up what you and Winters were arguin' about tonight in my club."

Those last two words—"my club"—struck the Purple Scar like a thunderbolt. Now he knew to whom Jules Gunther was speaking. It was "Lullaby Lou" Kerkin, owner of the Lullaby Club, where Winters and Gunther had had their memorable argument.

Lullaby Lou Kerkin, a throwback to pre-Repeal days, had his fingers in every racket in the city. By some miracle he had always managed to avoid the fate of other racketeers who had either been shot by their own kind, or imprisoned by the Government for income tax evasion.

So Lullaby Lou was the one who was holding Carol Draper! Naturally it was for him that Penguin Pete Barow had kidnaped the movie star. Maybe he was also the killer who erased Penguin Pete and came so close to ending the career of the Purple Scar, back there on the rooftops.

CHAPTER IX

A CAPTOR ESCAPES

JULES GUNTHER had seated himself behind his desk again. The Scar could no longer see him, but it wasn't hard to guess that the movie executive's face was covered with perspiration. Lou Kerkin, in that silk-steel voice which was now more steel than silk, since he had gained a jump on his opponent, continued:

"That's why I didn't have any worries about coming to you and laying my cards on the table. You won't tell anybody I'm holding her. If you do, I'll blab that you've been rookin' your partners."

"Shh, don't talk so loud!" Gunther cautioned fearfully.

Kerkin laughed. "I hear Draper's right near the finish of a picture that Big Four's got a barrel of dough sunk in—close to half a million. Well, I'm willin' to give her back to you nice and cheap."

"Cheap?" blurted Gunther.

"Sure, to complete the picture. The company can afford to fork over a hundred grand to protect half a million."

"But what about your orders to throw her in the river?"

"I'm in business for dough, not for my health. She goes to the highest bidder!"

"But I don't know whether I want her back," Gunther confessed after a moment's deliberation. He apparently felt he could afford to admit this since he was dealing with a crook as ruthless as himself. "Now that she and Winters are out of the way, there are only two of us left to split the company."

The Scar's neck acquired a sudden kink from the cramped position he was in, trying to keep his ear to the keyhole. He straightened. As he came up, his shoulder inadvertently brushed against one of the coat hangers. It evaded his fingers as he tried to catch it from falling, and struck the floor with a loud clatter.

He heard the intake of breath from the two men in the office, then utter silence. Every muscle in his body tensed, his heart pounding against his hollow ribs. He pressed back against the wall of the closet, waited. He could visualize what was happening outside. The two men must be padding cautiously over the heavily carpeted floor toward the closet.

He heard the knob turn slowly. Then abruptly a voice barked menacingly: "Come out with your hands in the air, or I'll fire!"

The Purple Scar knew that was sheer bluff. They didn't want to attract an audience any more than he did. But they might have fired if he invited it by drawing his own gun, so he left it in his holster. Instead he picked up the fallen coat-hanger, waited in the dark silence of the closet, the breath bunched in his throat.

Suddenly the door swung open. An unsteady white hand, grasping a black automatic, moved inside the closet like the head of a cobra, ready at any instant to spit death.

Down on the gun-hand the Purple Scar brought the hangar. The gun thudded to the floor. With the same swift motion the Scar lashed out with his right fist, and felt the solid impact as it landed flush against Jules Gunther's jaw. Gunther teetered, then crashed to the floor.

THE DOOR leading into the long corridor slammed shut as the Scar sprang over the fallen body of the movie executive and into the office. His eyes swept the big room, but Lou Kerkin was not there. He had chosen that moment to flee from the man he had trapped.

Out through the door and into the corridor burst the Purple Scar in pursuit of Lullaby Lou Kerkin. The corridor was deserted. He hesitated. He could have returned to Gunther, but right now he felt it was more important that he help Carol Draper. And Lou Kerkin was the only person who could tell him where she was.

Outside he caught a glimpse of a figure hurrying down the black path that led to the main gate.

Kerkin, in his flight, turned his head and looked back. He saw the man chasing him, broke into a run. But the Scar was much swifter. He closed the gap rapidly.

They had just reached the old Spanish galleon and were about to pass under its upturned prow when the Scar, only a short step behind the fleeing night club owner, looked up. He saw something move above them, hurl over the side of the ship and come down directly in the path of Lou Kerkin.

He cried a warning, but Kerkin did not heed it. The Scar lunged forward. He struck the night club owner with a flying tackle that sent both of them sprawling out of the way of a giant flood-light that smashed murderously against the ground.

But Lou Kerkin did not seem grateful. As the two of them scrambled to their feet, he wheeled and sprinted away.

The Scar started in pursuit, but from the shadow of the galleon jumped a hulking black shape. It struck him hard. As he fell, he brought this new attacker to the ground with him.

A hand reached toward his throat. He grabbed the wrist in an iron hold, tried to penetrate the darkness and see whom he was fighting. It was impossible.

His adversary's left hand snaked through an opening and gripped the Scar's throat. The grip was anything but puny. He found himself choking and felt a sharp pain in his gullet. His eyes felt as though they were going to burst.

He doubled his right fist, hooked his elbow and swung. The first blow landed on top of the man's head. The second time he crashed his cut knuckles against the other's jaw.

The assailant's head snapped back and he let go his hold. He sprang to his feet, staggered a moment from the sting of that last blow on the jaw. Then, convinced that his opponent was a little too tough, he disappeared at high speed into the shadows.

John Pryor arose, too. He moved his head slowly from side to side. His windpipe felt as if it were made of squeezed sponge-rubber. He knew it was useless to chase after his attacker, for he could never hope to find him in the queer tangle of riggings, spars and ropes through which he had gone. He then looked down the path that led toward the gate. Kerkin was not in sight, either.

The Scar frowned at his right hand, opening and shutting his fingers. The two smashes he had planted on the mysterious man's head and jaw had reopened the slash on his knuckles. He started to wipe away the blood, found that his knuckles were greasy and that several hairs from the man's head had clung to the grease. In the yellowish light from his flash, they looked coarse and white.

PLACING THE hairs carefully in a folded piece of paper, he stuffed them into his pocket.

On the way to the gate he passed by the wardrobe department. He glanced in through the barred window, shot the beam of his torch inside. No one was there.

When he reached the main gate, he asked the guard several questions, then hailed a cab and drove to the Lullaby Club.

The night club was one of the most popular spots in town, about fifteen minutes' ride from the studio. The prices were high, but the food and the show that Lullaby Lou served were worth the stiff tariff.

When the Purple Scar, still in the blond, broad-featured character of John Pryor, came into the club, the last show had just bowed off. The band, an aggregation of seven dusky swingsters, was beating it out for a handful of couples on the postage-stamp dance floor.

The Scar went to the bar, swung a long leg over one of the blue-leather-topped stools and ordered a straight rye.

"Boss in?" he asked the bartender when he was served his drink.

"Ain't seen him around."

The Scar lifted his glass, looked through it at the light, set it down again.

"I hear that movie director who got bumped off tonight was in here," he said, "arguing with his partner just a couple of hours before he got it."

"Yeah," answered the bartender, setting a couple of freshly wiped glasses on the shelf behind him. "Had it out hot and heavy for a few minutes."

"Arguing about business, I suppose."

The bartender shrugged. "I wasn't listenin', mister."

"I hear Winters was plenty plastered."

The bartender took a damp rag and polished the mahogany in front of his blond customer.

"That's where you're wrong," he stated bluntly. "He was sober as you and me when he came in. I was talkin' to him while he was waitin' for Gunther."

"Certainly must have had plenty after that," the Scar surmised.

"About two or three shots."

The Scar looked at the bartender with an odd frown, drained his drink and placed the glass atop the counter. His brain was busy with a fresh thought. How could Winters, a habitual drinker, get drunk on two or three drinks?

Before he could get the thought straightened out, Lullaby Lou Kerkin came in with two ugly-looking bodyguards at his heels. He went through the club like a cyclone. Without even nodding to customers, he disappeared into the office. The pair of thugs stayed on guard outside.

In the fleeting glance the Scar had caught of the night club owner's face, it was plain that what had happened in the movie studio had upset Kerkin. In all probability it had made him stop off to make sure that Carol Draper was still safe.

THE SCAR took a dollar from a healthy roll of bills and laid it on the counter. Slipping off the high stool, he sauntered to the door of the office.

The guards blocked his way.

"I'd like to see Mister Kerkin," he announced.

"He ain't seein' nobody tonight," one of the guards snapped. "He's busy."

"It's important."

"He ain't seein' nobody," the thug repeated ominously.

The Scar looked from one bodyguard to the other. He could not miss the tenseness of their muscles. To try to slug or argue his way through would be useless. He shrugged and walked away.

When he got outside, he looked up and down in the fog to be certain no one was watching. Then he slipped cautiously to the rear of the building. He came to a lighted window about nine feet above the ground and knew it was the office.

He found an empty ash-barrel, overturned it noiselessly and placed it beneath the window. By standing on tiptoes he could see inside.

Lullaby Lou Kerkin, seated behind his desk, had the phone to his ear and was dialing a number. Evidently there was no answer, for he slammed it back into the cradle and snorted.

The Scar was laying plans to maneuver his way into the office when his thoughts were painfully interrupted. Something hard and unyielding whacked him brutally across the shins.

His hand dropped like a plummet to his gun, but the ash-barrel went flying out from under him. Unable to reach the sill to hang on, he went crashing heavily to the ground.

He managed to get his revolver out of his holster. Immediately, though, a heavy shoe clamped down on his gunwrist, pinning it securely to the damp ground. He made a desperate effort to twist his hand free, but the muzzle of a revolver jabbed into the back of his neck. Then a pair of stout hands wrenched away his own gun.

"Get up!" a cold voice rasped close to his ear. "And keep your meat-hooks high, where they won't get you into trouble."

The Scar squinted up through the darkness. Above him stood the two guards who had been watching Kerkin's office door.

"Yeah, it's us," snarled one of them. "We figgered you'd try to pull somethin' smart, so we kept an eye on you. Get up!"

CHAPTER X

DANGEROUS BARGAIN

WHILE THE Scar was rising to his feet, the window above him opened. Lullaby Lou Kerkin's dark, ugly head poked out into the black fog.

"What's goin' on down there?" he demanded angrily.

"Some guy grabbin' himself an earful and an eyeful of what you were doin'," one of the thugs explained.

"Bring him in the office through the back way."

The gun prodded deeper into the Scar's neck.

"Move, and move fast!"

The Scar went willingly. He had meant to get into the office somehow, and even being accompanied by armed killers while he was weaponless was a victory of a sort. He could figure out a way of handling them, he was sure.

Lullaby Lou Kerkin was compactly built, with a round, hard head, short black hair and a face that was almost unbelievably homely. An enormous diamond stud, too large even for bad taste, centered his white tuxedo shirt, while its twin sparkled in a gaudy platinum setting on his sausage-like little finger.

He stood with his feet apart in the middle of the office and stabbed a savage glance at his prisoner.

"What's the big idea?" he snarled.

The Scar shrugged. "I wanted to see you, but it seems these two friends of yours had other ideas."

"Who are you?"

"John Pryor."

"What d'ya want from me?"

A thin smile etched the Scar's broad face. He jerked his head at the two men flanking him.

"I think you'd rather hear about it privately."

"C'mon, c'mon, quit stallin'!" Kerkin growled impatiently. "I'm busy. The club's closin' up in a couple of minutes."

"Okay, if you want it that way. It's about your visit to the Big Four studio tonight. I'm the guy you had that hundred-yard dash and tackle with."

Kerkin's homely face grew still blacker. He scowled at the man before him. "Beat it!" he barked at his two guards. "But keep your rods handy, just in case."

The two hoods nodded. With dirty looks at the Scar, they went out to guard the entrance again. Kerkin faced the broad-featured, blond man.

"Okay, start spillin'!" he rapped out.

"There's no sense wasting words," said the Scar with a grin. "You know and I know what you went to see Jules Gunther about. You're holding a certain young lady prisoner."

Kerkin's eyes narrowed to murderous pinpoints.

"If you think that information's gonna get you anything but a dose of lead, you're nuts."

"Oh, I don't know," the Scar replied. "You see, I happen to know that you've been doublecrossed."

"What d'ya mean—doublecrossed?" Kerkin spat out. "Who'd doublecross me?"

"Since you don't like to mention names, we'll call the party in question Mister X," evaded the Scar. Though he felt certain by now that he knew who "Mister X" was, there was still the possibility that he had made a mistake. If he mentioned the wrong name, Kerkin would know instantly that he was bluffing and his little game would be terminated before it had even begun. He continued: "Mister X told you to snatch Carol Draper, didn't he? Well, that was a gag. He wanted you to grab somebody else, someone he knew would be at Doctor Murdock's office."

"What're you tryin' to pawn off on me?" growled Kerkin.

"Did you look under the bandages the girl had on her face?"

"Sure. What about it?"

"Was it Carol Draper you saw?"

"Yeah, of course it was. She had a plastic surgery job done on her map."

THE SCAR feigned an easy smile. He shook his blond head in a pitying negative.

"That's where you're dead wrong, you poor sucker. It wasn't Carol Draper at all."

"Then who was it?" whispered the club owner menacingly.

"A patient of Doctor Murdock's, some woman who's in a nasty jam. She had her face changed. That's why Mister X had your stooge Penguin Pete Barrow pick up this woman at Doctor Murdock's office. Murdock knows that you're holding her, too, because I told him. He wanted to send the police here, but I convinced him to let me see you first. But if anything goes wrong and I don't come back—"

"What's the connection?" Kerkin interrupted.

"Mister X doublecrossed you into thinking that you were grabbing Carol Draper, to throw you off the scent. Then, after he's collected for this other girl you're holding, he'll say you made a mistake and he doesn't have to pay off. He's using you for a sucker."

Kerkin sprang clear across the office, grabbed the Scar by the front of the coat.

"Don't say that again to me, lug! Nobody takes Lou Kerkin for a sucker. Nobody!"

The blond, broad-shouldered nemesis of crime could easily have broken Kerkin's grip, but he felt it was more to his advantage to pacify the club owner than to fight with him.

"Okay, if you want to think he didn't doublecross you," he said casually. "I was just trying to help you and at the same time get back at Mister X for a couple of scurvy tricks he pulled on me."

Kerkin's hot eyes bored into the other's face like twin coals. The corners of his mouth were white with fury.

"Suppose you are tellin' the truth," he grated. "Suppose he is pullin' a cross, what happened to the real Carol Draper? Where is she now? How do I know you ain't lyin'?"

The Scar fought back a grin. While talking to Kerkin he had worked out a desperate plan. There was a chance that it might be accomplished, but if it couldn't be, it would be the end of the Purple Scar—and Doctor Murdock as well.

"Well, if I produce Carol Draper right here in this office," he bargained, "will you agree to release the girl you're holding and not try to grab Draper? You can't lose anything. You've still got enough on Jules Gunther to keep the squeeze on him. Besides, he already told you he doesn't want any part of Carol Draper, so this is your chance to triple Mister X's doublecross."

It was a difficult problem for Lullaby Lou Kerkin to decide. He placed his hands behind his back and paced the floor. He stopped pacing at last and faced the Scar.

"Okay, I'll play ball with you," he stated. "You show me Carol Draper, prove to me it was a cross, and I'll deliver the other dame."

"And they'll both go free?"

"Not if you try to pull a fast one."

The Scar's eyes were black agates as they met the night club owner's eyes.

"How about yourself?" he asked. "How do I know you'll keep your word?"

"That's up to you. You made the terms. But remember—if you tip the cops, or make one wrong move, I'll plug all three of you on the spot."

The Scar looked at him for a long moment. Kerkin was not lying or bluffing. In order to learn whether he had been tricked, he would keep his word.

"I'll be back in about an hour," the Scar said quietly.

He pivoted on his heel, walked to the door and went out.

"SURE IT'S crazy," Doctor Murdock admitted to Dale Jordan about ten minutes later in the privacy of his studio. "But it's a chance to save Carol Draper's life."

"You know Lou Kerkin's holding her," objected Dale. "Why can't you turn the whole thing over to the police? Let them get her."

"In the first place," Doc explained, "it would guarantee her death. Kerkin would put her out of the way so fast, we'd never know what happened to her. Second, we couldn't prove that he does have her. And the police could wear out every strip of rubber hose they have, but they wouldn't make Kerkin talk. They've tried that too many times and failed."

"But how do we know he'll keep his word to you?" Dale asked.

"Well, we can count on his wanting to see proof. And I saved his life on the movie lot. While he's not the type who'll come right out and say thanks, I have an idea he appreciates it. Even so, it'll be dangerous enough. You don't have to do what I asked, darling. If you think it's best not to, we'll figure out something else."

She studied Doc's transformed face. He still wore the broad nose and blond hair of "John Pryor," but that unstudied, thoughtful look was pure Doctor Miles Murdock. She shook her head in mock disgust.

"You don't have to use a blackjack," she said. "I'll do it."

He grinned at her gratefully.

"I figured you would," he admitted. "That's why I went to the trouble of digging out a stack of Carol Draper's stills."

He showed her the photographs of the movie star, taken from every conceivable angle. He took out his make-up kit and other necessary materials. Studying the actress' face intently, watching particularly for shadows and highlights, he began to pat a lump of clay into the rough shape of a head.

"Are you sure it'll work?" Dale asked nervously. "I don't look anything like her—anywhere."

He followed the features of the actress with minute detail. Under his nimble fingers a face began to form.

"Lou Kerkin won't be interested in the 'anywhere,'" he answered abstractedly. "He just wants to know whether he's being played for a fool. I don't think he'll even notice that she's almost an inch taller than you. All he'll be interested in is whether your face is hers and if you sound like her."

"Well, I should be able to mimic her," she said. "I've heard her often enough on the screen and radio." She lowered her voice a full octave and asked throatily: "Do I sound like the famous Miss Draper now?"

He looked up and grinned appreciatively.

"Not bad. Even if it were a lot worse, though, you'd sound more like her than she will through those bandages covering her face."

WHEN THE head was fully formed, he made a plaster of paris cast, melted a solution of gum elastic and poured it into the mold. This method of duplicating faces he had found much more effective than working with cosmetics and artificial devices. For one thing, it invariably produced a startling likeness, and it also was impervious to water and rough wear. Moreover, it was as close to being indetectable as any disguise could possibly be.

He dried the mask, removed it from the mold and slipped it over Dale's face. Then, using a harmless dye that did not remove the wave from her hair, he changed her tresses from fiery red to spun gold. His clever fingers, adaptable to almost every art that required fine handwork, quickly dressed her hair in the well known Carol Draper fashion.

Finished, he stepped back and allowed her to look in the full-length mirror. An involuntary gasp escaped her lips.

"It's unbelievable!" she exclaimed. "Why, I actually feel like Carol Draper, it's so real!"

"Let's hope Lullaby Lou Kerkin is as impressed," he said fervently.

"He will be. I know he will. I was afraid it wouldn't work before, but now I can't see how it could fail."

Doc Murdock looked at her and smiled, because he could imagine at least a dozen ways in which they might be detected and unmasked.

CHAPTER XI

A RINGER

KERKIN'S LULLABY CLUB was closed to customers when a blond man and a blond woman emerged from their car in the horseshoe drive that led to the front entrance. The woman wore a heavy veil over her face.

One of Lullaby Lou's hoods met them at the front door, brought them through the dark, deserted night club to the office. He rapped politely on the door. "Come in!" Kerkin snapped impatiently.

The Scar smiled blandly at the homely night club owner, who sat behind his big desk, furiously puffing on a black cigar. But inside the

Scar was not smiling. He knew the seriousness of this tense moment. He was fully aware of what would happen if this desperate impersonation failed.

"Well," he managed to say, almost confidently, "I had a tough time persuading her to come here, but here she is. Carol Draper, in person."

Kerkin drew deeply on his cigar, then emitted a column of smoke that hung over his head like a storm cloud. With narrow, suspicious eyes he appraised the girl before him as she lifted her veil.

She, too, was fighting a terrible uneasiness inside her.

Kerkin's ugly, stone face did not change as he chopped out the word: "Talk!"

The girl smiled wanly.

"What would you like me to say?"

"Tell me about you last picture."

"Sunup?"

"Yeah."

Dale Jordan thanked her lucky stars that she had seen it. She gave a brief, hurried synopsis of the story in her best mimicry of Carol Draper. Before she was finished, Kerkin cut her off.

"What's your husband's monicker?"

"His name? William C. Cornelia. He's a broker. His office is on Sunset Boulevard in Hollywood."

Kerkin's face was still a frozen mask.

The Scar wondered where the club owner was getting all these questions, until he glanced over the top of the desk and saw a sheet of paper lying there.

"Walk up and down the office," Kerkin said to Carol Draper's double.

The Scar felt his heart sink. This was one possibility he had dreaded. Dale looked at him sideward, with a tiny inquisitive frown that only he could detect. He said a silent prayer and nodded.

She turned, walked sedately to the door, turned, walked back to the desk. Kerkin's brows came together. He sucked in a long breath, then announced: "Okay, it's her." He raised his voice and called through the door: "Charlie!"

The door swung open. A thug, gat in hand, poked inside.

"Take 'em back to the car," instructed Kerkin. "Tell 'Trigger' to give 'em the girl."

The Scar paused with his hand on the knob of the door, looked back and asked:

"What are you going to do about Mister X?"

"Don't you worry about that," Kerkin growled, fighting to keep down the seething hate inside him. "I'll take care of his wagon."

PERHAPS DOC MURDOCK'S hunch had been right. Maybe it was the night club owner's quaint way of showing his appreciation for having his life saved. Whatever his motive for keeping his word, when the made-up plastic surgeon and his made-up assistant seated themselves in the car, the real Carol Draper was immediately delivered to them.

The movie star was shaken up badly and frightened half out of her wits, but she had not been harmed.

"You need be upset no longer, Miss Draper," the Scar said as they drove away. "You're on your way back to Doctor Murdock's laboratory. You're safe now. We're his friends."

He did not accompany them all the way back to the office. Instead he had Dale drop him off at the apartment hotel in which Dave Winters had been murdered. Before he stepped from the car, he asked Carol Draper a few questions. Then he told Dale to continue on and take good care of the blond star.

The Scar knew that now he must move with the speed of lightning. Lullaby Lou Kerkin had promised to take care of Mister X, which meant that the Scar had to beat him to the punch.

The Scar went into the glittering lobby of the lavish apartment hotel. At this hour it was quite deserted. The desk clerk looked up and tried sleepily to put a polite inquiring expression on his face.

"Name's Pryor," said the Scar. "I'm working on the Winters case with Detective-Captain Griffin. Are you acquainted with Mister Jules Gunther and Gabby Newel, the press agent?"

"Yes, sir," the clerk replied. "I am."

"And you've been at this desk since early this evening?"

"Since six o'clock."

"Did Jules Gunther visit anyone in this hotel tonight?"

The clerk thought back.

"Yes," he said at last. "He came to see Mr. Banco at about eleven o'clock."

"Know how long he stayed?"

"I can't say. I must have missed him when he left."

"How about Gabby Newel? What time did he come into the hotel?"

"Shortly after Mister Winters'—death, I'd say a few minutes before twelve. At any rate, around midnight."

"Neither of these two came in at any time before that?"

"Not while I was at the desk, sir. And they couldn't very well get upstairs without my seeing them."

"Thanks. Now will you please give Mister Banco's room a buzz? I'd like to speak to him."

A MOMENT later the Scar had Victor Banco, the screen writer and motion picture executive, on the wire.

"I'd like to ask you several questions, if you don't mind, Mister Banco," he began.

"Not at all," answered the voice. "I'm only too glad to help if I can."

"You can. Did Jules Gunther visit your apartment tonight?"

"Yes."

"At what time?"

"Eleven o'clock."

"You're sure it was that time when he called?"

"Positive. I'd been waiting for the symphonic hour on the radio. It had just started when he rang the doorbell. That was almost exactly eleven."

"How long did he stay?"

"Not more than five minutes. He merely came to assure me that he couldn't let Winters make any further changes in my script for 'Moon Over Me.' Winters and I had a great deal of trouble over that issue."

"Why didn't Gunther give you this assurance over the telephone?"

"I really don't know. I thought perhaps he was passing by and decided to drop in and give it to me personally."

The Scar thanked him and hung up. He returned to the desk clerk.

"How many white-haired guests do you have registered?" he asked.

The clerk gazed at him in amazement.

"White-haired guests?" he repeated. He had to mull that one over in his mind. Finally he replied: "Three. Two men and an elderly woman."

"Anyone of them check in recently?"

"Yes. Mister Greener checked in this afternoon. Room eleven-thirty. Wanted to be high up, the day clerk told me."

"Does Mister Greener happen to be in now?"

The clerk twisted to look at the keyrack to make sure.

"No. He went out about nine o'clock. Hasn't returned yet."

The Scar smiled wryly. "And he won't ever come back."

He thanked the clerk for his co-operation, turned and walked into the public phone booth. He dialed a number. When he stepped out of the booth, he left the apartment hotel. He caught a taxi and snapped at the driver.

"The Unicorn Apartments and don't spare the horsepower!"

GABBY NEWEL was greatly taken aback to see a man with a hideously scarred purple face standing before him in the corridor. Gabby might have slammed the door of his apartment shut on that face, only the purple-masked stranger held a revolver leveled at his stomach.

"What in the devil do you call this?" Gabby gulped. "Who are you?"

"The Purple Scar," answered the ghastly character. "In my own humble way, I try to see that justice comes out on top occasionally. May I come in?"

Gabby looked down at the gun.

"I—I don't seem to have much choice."

The Purple Scar entered. It was a pretentious layout, flashy, furnished with the very latest in everything, just the sort of apartment he had expected the brash young press relations counsel to have.

"Strange as it may seem," said the Scar quietly, "I came here only to ask your help on a very important matter."

"My help?" Again Gabby's eyes were on the gun. "With that persuader in your hand, you don't need anybody's help."

The Scar lowered his gun and quickly holstered it.

"Sorry," he apologized. "I didn't mean to keep it pointed at you. But it did seem like a pretty good sales talk to get me in here."

Gabby was visibly relieved to see the gun disappear. He mopped his brow with the silk handkerchief that he took from the top pocket of his pajama jacket.

"Now I can talk a little easier. What makes you say you want my help? Surely the Purple Scar doesn't need a press agent!"

"No, the underworld does all my advertising for me. It's about Dave Winters' murder."

Gabby Newel's face suddenly turned serious. The Scar's eyes, alert black dots through the shriveled slots in the purple mask, were fixed on Gabby's as he went on:

"I think I can put my finger on the guilty party. Before I do that, however, I want to enlist your help, since you're well acquainted with everyone involved."

"I'll be glad to help," Gabby volunteered eagerly. "But who did it?"

"We'll come to that in a moment. First I'd like to outline my theory, step by step, so you'll know where we stand. For the time being we'll call the guilty party Mister X."

"I'm listening," Gabby assured him tensely.

"Then we'll begin with the statement that Jules Gunther was embezzling his three partners."

Gabby's face blanched.

"Embezzlement? How do you know that?"

"There are reports to prove it, reports that Gunther never entered into his books. Somehow Dave Winters might have got hold of one of them, threatened to expose Gunther and ruin him. That's only a theory, of course, but it seems to fit right in with the other answers. Dave Winters, in spite of his great success as a motion picture director and executive, probably never could really meet Jules Gunther on an equal level.

"It's my belief that Winters actually suffered from a strong inferiority complex, an impression that is proved by the type of books he read. Gunther's egotism, for which he was well known, must have gnawed at Winter's mind like a cancer. Getting hold of the telltale report was Winters' one chance to disgrace Gunther and at the same time appease his own complex."

"Then Gunther must have killel Winters to keep him from showing the report," Gabby suggested.

THE SCAR shook his horrible head.

"I don't think so. I believe someone else found out about Gunther's little game a long time ago and has been successfully blackmailing Gunther ever since. Gunther's private books show a systematic leakage, as if he might be paying huge sums of money to keep somebody quiet. That goes back to my theory that Gunther wasn't the person who killed Dave Winters. If he wanted to kill anyone, he probably would have killed the person who was bleeding him all this time."

"It sounds reasonable enough," Gabby agreed.

"Winters, however, apparently couldn't be silenced with money. He wanted the satisfaction of seeing Gunther dragged in the dirt, so he probably threatened to expose Gunther, but wanted to make him sweat first. This Mister X who's been blackmailing Gunther evidently learned that Winters had this incriminating report. He realized that if Winters did make it public, his sweet little graft would be gone.

"So he must have gone to Winters' penthouse yesterday afternoon, cracked the safe and stole the report. The cop who answered the call swore that Winters looked as if something very important had been taken from the safe. Winters then called Gunther at the studio, as a notation on his telephone pad showed.

"He perhaps figured that Gunther had something to do with the disappearance of the report and made an appointment with his partner to meet at the Lullaby Club at seven-thirty. Common sense tells us that he must have told Gunther that he was going to talk, even that he thought the report was stolen. That meant Mister X had to act fast to get Dave Winters out of the way.

"He went to Winters' penthouse at eight-thirty and stabbed him to death. Gunther, not knowing that Winters was dead but thinking him unconsciously drunk, went to the penthouse to make sure that the report was stolen. If it hadn't been stolen, he meant to take it. That was when I happened along. The result was that he slugged me and ran away."

"Then, since it wasn't Gunther who killed Winters, who did?" Gabby asked bewilderedly.

"Before I tell you that, I want you to meet me at Winters' penthouse in one hour. I'll have everyone else connected with the case there, too. Can I depend on you?"

"You sure can," the red-headed press agent stated bluntly.

He put out his right hand to his masked visitor, as if to seal the bargain. The Scar also lifted his hand, but his iron fingers closed over the press agent's wrist like a vise.

CHAPTER XII

THE CASE IS BROKEN

GABBY NEWEL struggled desperately to break free, but the Purple Scar knew the workings of human anatomy like a book. There were certain nerve centers in the wrist that, when twisted the proper way, could render a man powerless. Gabby, even though he had held the intercollegiate wrestling championship for three successive years, dropped to his knees, helpless.

"Now, Mr. Gabby Newel," the Scar intoned, "I don't have to wait until later to tell you who killed Dave Winters. *You* did! You're the man who's been blackmailing Jules Gunther all these years."

"You're crazy!" gasped the press agent wildly.

"I don't agree with you. You found out Gunther was embezzling his partners and made him agree to pay you to keep quiet. And then, when you learned that Winters was going to spoil your racket, you killed him. You knew Banco had given the paper cutter to Carol Draper, so you stole it and stabbed him to death with it. Your intention was to pin the murder on her. You see, she told me that part of the story on her way back from Lou Kerkin's night club."

Gabby's face went whiter than ever.

"Back from Kerkin's?" he echoed in horror. "What do you mean?"

"That's a little surprise, isn't it? Well, you made a mistake when you wrote that letter from 'Jess Henshaw' and left Doctor Murdock's card on her dressing table, figuring she would immediately get the idea of having her face changed. Doctor Murdock didn't operate on her. He used collodion to draw apparent scars in her face, under my suggestion. I found a girl who could easily be made up to resemble Miss Draper and brought her to Lou Kerkin. He thought you had doublecrossed him and released the real movie actress, believing her to be someone else.

"Carol Draper told me that you tried to marry her some time ago, but she refused. You pretended to be a good sport about it. Actually you were smoldering over the refusal, because you really loved her. And when she married the broker, Cornelia, you were determined to get even. You waited until this chance, when you could kill two birds with one stone by pinning Winters' murder on her. And all this time she trusted you, gave you the run of her place and considered you her best friend. You can't deny evidence like that."

"And I would have done it, too!" yelled Gabby hysterically. "She deliberately led me on, and then jilted me!"

There was a loud commotion on the fire escape outside the window. The door of the bedroom burst open at the same time. Blue-coated figures piled into the room. From out of the blue pattern stepped a square-shaped man in civilian clothes. Detective-Captain Dan Griffin addressed his words directly at the Purple Scar.

"Your message was delayed in reaching me. I almost didn't make it on time."

Gabby looked up with new hope at the squat detective.

"This man's a manac!" he cried out.

"Did you hear the whole story?" the Scar asked Griffin, ignoring the press agent's out-bursts.

"I couldn't miss it," answered Griffin with a grin.

The Scar let Gabby arise and handed him over to two husky cops.

"You can't make what I said stick!" Gabby was yelling. "He got it out of me under pressure. He made me say those things. They were lies, every one of them. I didn't kill Winters. I never took a cent of blackmail in my life!"

THE SCAR smiled behind his hideous purple mask. He reached forward and slipped the ring with the twin wrestlers off the middle finger of the press agent's right hand. When he pressed one of the figures on the ring, a tiny prong sprang forth, emitting a sticky, colorless fluid.

"I wonder how you'll explain this one," he said.

"What the devil's that?" Griffin cut in.

"This is how Dave Winters was drugged at the Lullaby Club," the Scar explained. "Winters wasn't drunk, as the medical examiner's report showed. The bartender at the Lullaby Club verified that report when he told me that Winters, a habitual drinker, had passed out on only two or three drinks. Newel gave him a shot of this needle at the same time that he gave him a pat on the back, which is a characteristic of press agents all over the world.

"You see, it isn't poison. It's a drug made from Chinese Thunder God weed. The Department of Agriculture has been making extensive experiments with this weed recently. It's a Chinese plant which kills insects and other parasites. When mixed with certain other chemicals, it produces a drug which, when administered into an open wound, will cause a drunken sleep.

"This drug, however, is subject to quick evaporation. That was why it was so important that the medical examiner perform an immediate autopsy. Even then it proved to be too late. The drug had entirely evaporated. However, Newel drugged Winters because he had a perfect course of action planned, a means by which he could follow Winters to his penthouse and kill him.

"During the afternoon, this very ingenious young man engaged a room at Winters' apartment hotel under the name of Greener. Mister Greener was an elderly-looking man with white hair. This room, being on the eleventh floor, made it quite convenient to walk up one short flight of stairs to the penthouse."

"He trying to frame me!" Gabby shouted frantically.

"You knew," said the Scar, "that if you came into the apartment hotel as Gabby Newel, you'd be recognized immediately. Also you had that time sheet at the studio gate to think of. You wanted that as a concrete alibi. So, having access to the studio wardrobe and being more or less familiar with the art of make-up after all your years around actors and actresses, you transformed yourself into the white-haired Mister Greener."

He then told about the battle in the studio under the prow of the old Spanish galleon. He explained how the white hairs from the man's head had adhered to the grease he found on his knuckles. That grease turned out to be ordinary theatrical greasepaint which Gabby had used to make up his face as the elderly man.

"And if you'll have laboratory technicians check his face," the Scar concluded, "I'm pretty sure they'll find particles of greasepaint still in the pores."

Apparently he remembered something else at that point. He stepped to Gabby, made a thorough search through the press agent's pocket, found nothing. Then he strode to the solid oak desk which stood against the wall. He brushed through the papers atop it, rummaged through the drawers until at last he came to a sealed envelope addressed to Police Headquarters.

"I thought perhaps I'd find this somewhere around here," he said, "typed and ready for the grand climax to what would have been the perfect crime—if it had worked."

HE PASSED the letter across to Captain Griffin. Griffin tore it open with anxious fingers, read:

> To whom it may concern:
>
> This is the end of Carol Draper. Today Dave Winters was murdered. You need search no farther for his murderer. There were certain things he found out which would have brought many heartaches and great disgrace to several innocent people. That is all you need know.
>
> By the time you receive this letter, Carol Draper will have ended her life by her own hand.
>
> Carol Draper.

"The signature, of course, doesn't mean a thing," said the Scar, reading over Griffin's shoulder. "It could easily have been traced, because Carol Draper's autograph wasn't hard to secure."

"But how could you have known it was already typed?" Griffin wanted to know. "He could've written it any time."

"No," the Scar replied. "He had to type it on Carol Draper's machine if he wanted it to look authentic. He probably typed it at the same time he did the first letter he sent to Carol Draper from 'Jess Henshaw.' But in his haste he made a little slip which suggested that whoever wrote both letters must have been a trained writer, a newspaperman, most likely."

Griffin looked at the note again, then back at the Purple Scar, puzzled.

"How do you figure that out?"

"There is no first person pronoun in either note, yet in both letters the writers were presumably describing themselves, the things they did. Elimination of 'I' or 'me' from personal descriptions of acts requires training. It isn't necessarily difficult to acquire, but if you haven't learned it, you're not likely to use it. That narrowed our list of suspects down to just two people who were experienced writers—Victor Banco, a former newspaper columnist, and Gabby Newel, a press agent.

"There is also the fact that Gabby had access to Carol Draper's apartment, where he could use her typewriter, steal the paper cutter with which Winters was killed and learn about her first husband, since he was her personal press agent for a number of years. Finally then is the fact that he was with Gunter and Winters at the Lullaby Club when they argued and Winters was drugged. All that leads directly to him."

"You'll never make it stick!" Gabby screamed, his big face sweaty and as crimson as his flaming hair.

"I wouldn't renew the lease on this place, if I were you," Griffin said sarcastically, "at least not until after the trial." He turned back to the Scar and asked: "There's still one thing that hasn't been cleared up—the murder of Penguin Pete Barrow."

The Scar smiled. "I think Lullaby Lou Kerkin'll be able to give you some interesting data on that subject. And you won't have to bother going out of your way to find him."

"Why?"

"Wait right here. I have an idea he'll be showing up any minute now to take a shot at your prisoner." With that the Scar pivoted toward the door.

"But where are you going?" Griffin questioned.

"I? I've got a date with a couple of beautiful blonds."

Detective-Captain Dan Griffin could not see him grin, for the Purple Scar had already vanished. Griffin knew, however, that Doc Murdock, acting as The Scourge of Crime, had not walked out until the case was tightly closed. He also knew that, when a call for help again arose from tormented people in the grip of relentless criminals, the Purple Scar would come forth to do battle.

III

MURDER IN GOLD

CHAPTER I

HOT SHOT

EVER SINCE Jimmy Morgan had reported on the job tonight he had felt that something was wrong.

Not only was there a tenseness about everything at the Playhouse Night-club. But Jimmy, struggling into his powder-blue waiter's coat, had strange foreboding that something was going to happen here tonight—something terrible!

When "Buck" Langhorne, owner of the night spot, failed to give his full attention to Peggy Pan's specialty—that was the clincher. Because Buck Langhorne had a lot more than a passing interest in Peggy Pan, he never missed her turn.

Peggy did a male impersonation at the club. She was good, too. In the two weeks she had been working there, she had caught on nicely with the crowd. That, coupled with the fact that Peggy had a face and figure designed to interest any man, had made Buck dive off the deep end for her.

Every moment Jimmy Morgan was not busy, waiting on tables, he kept his eyes glued on Buck Langhorne. The night-club owner was as jittery as a flea on a hot plate. His none too handsome physiognomy was sweaty, worried. He couldn't stay put for more than two or three minutes at a time.

At least half a dozen times during the evening, Jimmy saw him duck into his office as if he were expecting someone.

The last time he went into the office, it must have been two-thirty. The club had reached its highest pitch of excitement. The band, an aggregation of six white-coated swingsters, were playing at fever pitch. A bright colored spotlight swept back and forth across the crowded dance floor.

Jimmy Morgan watched the office door for a long time, growing more and more curious. He waited until the coast was clear, then ducked into the kitchen.

A beet-faced man in a chef's hat looked up from behind an array of pots and pans.

"Gonna grab a smoke out in the alley," Jimmy said to him.

He went out of the kitchen with its smell of frying meats and its thick, acrid smoke, into the back alley.

IT WAS black dark out there, but Jimmy found his way to the back door of the office. He regretted there were no windows.

He peered into the darkness cautiously, as far as he could see, to make sure no one was watching. Then he put his ear to the door.

Voices filtered to him from inside. Three voices, arguing violently. It was a hard job for Jimmy even to make out Buck Langhorne's voice, but he did.

"You guys have got your gall bustin' into my safe, helpin' yourselves!" Buck was raging.

"Yeah," sneered another voice. "Helping ourselves to what's *mine!*"

"Why you worn-heeled bum!" thundered Langhorne. "If I called the cops they'd slam you behind bars so quick it'd make you dizzy." Then apparently he spoke to the third man in the office. "And that goes for you, too!"

"Only I don't think you will call the cops," rapped the distorted voice of that third man.

"Well, if you think I'm gonna let you two rats ankle out of here with somethin' worth fifty Gs—without doin' somethin' to stop you, you got a lot less brains than I gave you credit for havin'!" came from Buck Langhorne, savagely.

Jimmy could hear one of the desk drawers open. The eavesdropping waiter had more than half an idea what Buck Langhorne was going after. His gun!

There was a sudden scuffle of feet inside. An agonized outcry that could not be heard in the club proper above the din of the band. Then there was the sickening thud of a falling body!

Jimmy could feel his scalp tighten. And his tanned face, which somehow made him seem out of place as a night-club waiter, constricted with alarm.

Instinctively he was reaching for the knob—when the door opened. He could see that, though the light in the office had been turned out. Then he had a brief glimpse, in the darkness, of two hulking figures that loomed before him in the doorway.

He tried to stop them. He flung up his hands to block their way. But a hard, blunt object came down out of the blackness and struck him across the temple. He sagged back against the wall, half stunned for a moment.

When he straightened and tried to give pursuit, there was no trace of the two culprits. He followed the alley to its end, but they were gone!

He came back to the office. The door was still open. He slipped inside, called Buck Langhorne's name, softly. There was no answer.

Fear hammered at his brain as he groped his way to the light switch on the far wall. He clicked it on—and stopped cold in his tracks. His tanned face was a mask of horror. The short hairs on the back of his neck bristled, and he felt suddenly weak all over.

For there, sprawled out at his feet on the floor, lay Buck Langhorne, flat on his back. Blood was seeping onto the floor from what must be a wound on his back.

JIMMY MORGAN dropped to his knees beside the body. He turned it over. In Langhorne's back was an ugly purplish-red knife wound, through which life had flowed. Jimmy was far from an authority on

Sprawled at Jimmy's feet lay Buck Landhorne, flat on his back.

the subject. But he could tell in a glance that Buck Langhorne was beyond all earthly aid. Buck Langhorne was dead!

Arising slowly to his feet, his mind clouded with the shock of this tragedy, Jimmy's eyes were held by the open wall safe.

He frowned darkly, as if the discovery affected him personally. He hurried to the safe, stuck his hand deep into the round, black cavity—

That was what he was doing when he heard a startled gasp behind him. He whirled. A man Jimmy knew well stood in the doorway that lead into the club.

Jimmy had not heard him enter. He was Dan Davis, Buck Langhorne's partner in the Playhouse. He was rather a tall man with light brown hair and a face which, though cut along nice lines, did not reveal an over-abundance of character. And he wore his clothes with a carelessness in accord with his rangy figure.

He just stood there, staring at Jimmy with pale eyes, the door to the club closed behind him.

Jimmy Morgan, looking into those eyes, felt a new wave of fear sweep over him. His insides writhed. He wet his thin lips and blurted out an explanation.

"I was in the alley, catching a drag when two men burst out of the office, almost knocked me down. I tried to stop them, but they hit me over the head. By the time I could go after them, they were gone. So I came into the office to see if everything was all right—and found Mr. Langhorne like this!"

Dan Davis did not say anything. He moved forward into the room and stooped over. He picked up the revolver which Buck Langhorne must have just managed to get out of the drawer the instant before death struck him down.

Davis pointed the gun at a spot that approximated the second button on Jimmy Morgan's jacket.

"I'd sit down if I were you," Davis said, in a low, but emphatic voice. "And I'd be quiet—until the police get here."

Jimmy's bronzed face blanked with astonishment.

"The police?" he gulped. "You don't think that I—"

"It's not my place to think anything," interrupted the partner of the dead man with a terrible coldness. "That's for the police to decide."

He reached the telephone that stood atop the desk, and dialed the operator.

"But that's ridiculous!" Jimmy insisted shrilly.

Davis ignored the remark. He got the operator, then the police, and told them to hurry right over.

"There's been a murder committed here," he said, and gave only the briefest details.

Then when he hung up, he indicated a chair with his gun.

"Sit down, Morgan, and wait!" he ordered.

Jimmy opened his mouth to protest, but clamped it shut again without saying anything, as he looked down the long, menacing barrel of the revolver. With a shrug he turned toward the chair.

And then a strange thing happened! The light in the office went out, plunging the room into sudden darkness.

Jimmy's mind flashed. Here was his chance to get away. And he must get away! If he didn't the police would be sure to hold him and maybe find out certain things about him that he did not want known—not in the face of this killing!

Without a second thought, Jimmy wheeled on his heel and dived for the door that led into the alley. He sprang out into the night and started to run. Behind him he could hear Dan Davis's angry voice, calling to him to stop.

Then there was a bright yellow flash in the darkness behind him. The crack of a gun! Something hot and stingy ploughed into Jimmy Morgan's left shoulder. The impact of the bullet drove him stumbling forward. He straightened then, clapped his hand over the bleeding mark that the bullet had made, and pushed on.

A short distance from the mouth of the alley, he was lucky enough to hail a cruising taxicab. Hiding his wound, he gave the driver an address and piled inside.

As the cab was gunned on its way, Jimmy Morgan settled into the back seat, took out a handkerchief and plugged his wounded shoulder.

CHAPTER II

EMERGENCY CALL

DOCTOR MILES MURDOCK opened his eyes at the touch of something cold and rigid against his right cheek. He came out of pleasant dreams. A man is likely to have pleasant dreams with his engagement to the "one girl" just recently announced.

Doc squinted in the light of the globelike bowl suspended on long chains from the ceiling's center. He raised himself on one elbow, twisted in bed.

A figure was standing before him. The figure of a man wearing dark glasses, a pulled-down felt hat, and with the collar of his dark coat turned up high. An efficient disguise. But—most important of all—the intruder had a gun leveled at Doc.

It was not the first gun that that ever had been pointed at Doc Murdock. But certainly it was the first time it had ever happened in the privacy of his bedroom.

Still Doc was not excited or afraid. As one of the truly great plastic surgeons of his time, his training had taught him more than his professional art. He had learned to master his emotions, to control his fears, even in the face of death.

His keen black eyes took in the figure before him in a glance and noticed a false in the dress. At the same time a peculiar scent tangled with his senses. A puzzled frown gathered together his brows. He started to speak, but his nocturnal visitor was before him.

"You're coming with me!" said Dark Glasses, in a deep voice, never for a moment taking the gun off the surgeon. "Get out of bed and get dressed!"

Doc nodded his head, thatched with black curly hair that was touseled now. Reaching for his robe, he draped it across his football shoulders, pushed back the covers, and swung his feet off the bed to the floor.

His muscles were tense, taut—he was about to make a quick grab for the gun-wrist before him—when the light suddenly caught the gutter of a diamond in the center of Dark Glasses's extended, gloved, left palm. It sent myriad pinpoints of light into Doc's eyes.

He blinked furiously, looked again. He saw the ring into which the diamond was set. He could hardly believe his eyes. It was the engagement ring he had given to Dale Jordan only two days ago!

He went white, hammering back the fear that for once threatened to break out of control.

"Where did you get that ring?" he demanded.

White lines of fury etched the corners of his mouth, and above his right eye his brow and the tiny lines and muscles surrounding it twisted to form a deadly black spade. That mark which now showed was a characteristic of Doc Murdock, as everyone who knew him was well aware, it was the scar left from a cleat wound he had received in college.

Doc might have had it cleared up. But it did not impair his vision or his looks. And it appeared only when terrible rage gripped him. But then it was prophetic of danger for someone!

"I got this ring from your fiancée," the mysterious stranger said evenly.

"I brought it with me only to convince you that you must do as I say. You needn't worry though. She's perfectly safe—so far. But I can't guarantee how long she'll stay that way if I don't return, or if you refuse to go with me."

DOC'S EYES were still angry. That spade was still prominent. But he saw there was nothing else he could do except go with the stranger. Dale was more precious to him than anything on earth. If anything should happen to her—

He stood up, the spade washed away.

"I'll be dressed in a minute," he said, then took his clothes and stepped behind a tall screen.

"Don't try anything funny back there," Dark Glasses warned.

Doc did not reply as he peeled off his pajamas quickly. Standing there in his bare feet, he was exactly six feet tall. A handsome man of splendid physique, with that black curly hair of his, and a strong face, out of which stabbed coal-black eyes. Expressive eyes that could be cold and deadly as the point of a saber, or as friendly as an outstretched hand, whichever the occasion demanded.

His muscles moved in perfect coordination, like well-oiled springs, and although he had never mixed with one hundred and eighty-five pounds of wildcat—which was his own weight—it was worth a good bet that he could give said wildcat a good run for the laurels.

He began to dress. In short order he stepped from behind the screen, ready to go.

"You'll need your surgical kit," said the man with the gun.

Doc twisted, frowned inquiringly.

"For Miss Jordan?" he demanded.

"No. You'll find out all about it when you get there."

Then Dark Glasses told him exactly what he would require.

Doc procured the necessary instruments and materials, stuffed them into his bag. Then he led the way out of the place and to his car which he kept in a small private garage in the rear. He climbed behind the wheel and with the nose of Dark Glasses' gun resting against his ribs, he got the car under way.

In front of a dismal, dirt-streaked building in the heart of the slum section of the city, which Doc knew perhaps better than he did any other part of town, he was told to halt the car.

It was in this very locality that Doc Murdock had served his internship with the City Hospital. It was to this spot, also, that he had returned to build his own free clinic, a place where slum people could come and receive his expert services without cost. The selfsame services for which the wealthy on the other side of town paid so much.

Emerging from the automobile, Doc paused a moment to look up at the tenements that stared across at each other in the bleak silence, it was like standing in a deep deserted canyon, with only an occasional square of yellow light shining out from the steep walls. Then his companion with the dark glasses prodded him on.

Up a couple of brown-stone steps of one of the tenements, Doc, surgical kit in hand, preceded Dark Glasses. Then into a dark hallway. They climbed three flights of mournfully creaking stairs, finally pausing before a warped, unpainted, wooden door. Faint light showed beneath the door. It went out the instant Dark Glasses rapped.

"Who is it?" a voice from inside whispered cautiously.

"Me. I've got the doctor."

A key turned in the lock. The door squeaked open. Doc and Dark Glasses stepped inside. The door closed behind them and light came on again to reveal a youth with a tanned face and a shock of tousled brown hair that hung before his frightened cat's eyes.

It was Jimmy Morgan, the young waiter from the Playhouse Nightclub. Doc frowned at him. He had never seen this young fellow before, but he had his own way of knowing his name was Jimmy Morgan. And he could see that the kid was weak from pain and in bad shape.

No one said anything. But Jimmy turned and led the way into the next room. Doc saw Dale Jordan.

She was sitting in a chair, hands tied behind her. Her disheveled reddish-brown hair fell over her face, half-hiding her starkly staring emerald-green eyes.

Her slender silk-encased legs were tied, also, and a gag was wrapped around her mouth so that she could not cry out.

The gun which was jammed in his ribs kept Doc from going to her. Infuriated, he wheeled to face his captors. But before he could speak, Jimmy Morgan said:

"I've got a slug in my left shoulder, Doc. I want you to take it out."

He ripped open his shirt and showed Doc the blood-stained packing he had over the wound. Swiftly Doc removed the packing, and his fingers probed the shoulder in a hasty examination.

"How long's the bullet been in there?" he demanded.

"Few hours."

Doc frowned. "You'll have to go to a hospital."

"I can't go to a hospital," Jimmy said flatly.

"But you need surgical attention. And I can't remove a bullet without reporting it."

The gun bit into the plastic surgeon's side.

"I'm afraid you're wrong, Doc!" Dark Glasses informed him tersely. "This is one operation you'll perform—and not report it. Or somebody will be probing for bullets in your girl friend."

Doc's eyes were on Dale. She shook her head.

"Don't do it because of me," her eyes were saying. "I'm not afraid."

Doc smiled at her, faintly.

"We've got the big table," Dark Glasses said sharply, "a gas range for hot water to sterilize your instruments, and we've even put a five-hundred-watt bulb in the fixture. Everything you need."

"My clinic's only a couple of blocks away," Doc suggested.

Dark Glasses' head moved in a slow refusal.

"Thanks," he said flatly, "but you'll do the job right here."

Doc flexed his fingers, aching for a chance to wrap them around his captor's throat. Then he shrugged.

"Okay," he gave in. "But if you want a good job done, you'd better release Miss Jordan. I'll need her to assist me."

Dark Glasses looked across at Jimmy Morgan. The wounded waiter nodded slightly.

The moment Dale's bonds were removed she flew to Doc's arms. He kissed her and told her not to be afraid.

"Sorry," Dark Glasses cut in. "But there's work to do."

The four of them went into the kitchen of the small railroad flat. Doc laid out his instruments. Dale took them and placed them in boiling water.

JIMMY MORGAN ripped off what was left of his shirt and climbed up onto the table. He hesitated a moment, then said:

"This isn't all you're going to do, you know, Doc. While I'm under the ether, you're going to change my face. That's the real reason we picked you. I don't want it changed much—just enough so it won't look like me."

"So the police won't recognize you?" Doc supplemented acidly.

That seemed to surprise Jimmy. "How did you know?"

"Your description's been broadcast over every station in the city," Doc said coldly. "Killed Buck Langhorne at the Playhouse Nightclub, didn't you?"

"No!" Dark Glasses was quick to contradict for Jimmy. "He didn't kill Buck Langhorne!"

Doc turned with the ghost of a smile on his mouth. "What makes you think so? Did you?"

"Neither of us killed him!" Jimmy said.

"Then why are you trying to duck the police?"

"Because they *think* I killed him—and there's no way I can prove I didn't," Jimmy replied. Then in a sharper tone. "You just take the bullet out of my shoulder and fix up my face! That's all you've got to worry about."

"So you can play Hawkshaw, I suppose?" Doc said with mild derision. "Find the killer, clear yourself, and then come back to me to have your face restored to normal?"

Jimmy's eyes slitted. "Yes, that's exactly what I want to do!" he snapped peevishly.

"But don't you think that's sort of silly?"

"You've said enough!" Dark Glasses barked. "Never mind what we think or what we're going to do. You just get started with that operation. And remember! One funny move or one slip and you and your girl friend don't live for that coming wedding I read about in the newspapers."

"So that's how you found out about Miss Jordan and me," said Doc.

"Get started with the operation!" Dark Glasses snapped sharply.

Doc smiled ironically, but said nothing more.

Jimmy was prepared on the table. Doc scrubbed his hands and struggled into sterilized rubber gloves. He signaled to Dale to administer the ether through the cone. Dale placed it over Jimmy's face.

Jimmy's eyes, terribly frightened, looked up at Doc in silence over the top of the ether cone. Then they closed and he began to inhale.

Doc waited until Jimmy's senses had faded, then his fingers signaled to Dale for the scalpel. Dale had it ready and waiting. She had worked side by side with him for so long she could almost anticipate his every move, every want.

She slipped the scalpel into his hand. Doc's fingers wigwagged to her again. He knew that Dale would read what they said.

He leaned across the prostrate figure on the white kitchen table. Out of the corner of his eye, he could see that Dark Glasses' entire attention was riveted upon him. That gave Dale, according to his signaled instructions, a chance to duck to cover.

Doc straightened, and with the sharp point of the scalpel at a spot directly over Jimmy Morgan's heart, he said to Dark Glasses:

"Drop that gun—or Jimmy Morgan has a hole in his heart as big as Buck Langhorne had!"

The face of Dark Glasses went pale. The gun-hand stiffened.

"You better drop it!" Doc repeated sternly. "I'm not fooling!"

COMPLICATIONS SET IN

MURDOCK SAW Dark Glasses ponder a precious thirty seconds, watching the point of the scalpel indenting Jimmy Morgan's flesh. Then, slowly, the gun lowered and dropped onto the floor with a thud.

At Doc's order, Dale sprang forward, snatched up the gun and leveled it at Dark Glasses.

Doc removed the scalpel from Jimmy's flesh. Looking directly at Dark Glasses, he said:

"Now let's see what you look like without those glasses and that hat—young lady!"

"Young lady?" Dale echoed with shocked surprise. "You mean he's a—"

The dark glasses and the turned-down felt hat came off. Golden curls tumbled down to the girl's shoulders and there stood Peggy Pan, the male impersonator from the Playhouse! Both of them had seen her on occasional visits to the club.

She dropped her head, shame-facedly.

"You knew all the while?" she asked Doc chokily.

He nodded. "Men don't as a rule wear the kind of perfume you were wearing, nor do they button their coats on the left side. Had an idea you were a girl the minute I saw you. After I got here and saw Jimmy and remembered that the story of Langhorne's killing, I read in the papers, had mentioned how the lights had gone out when he made his get-away, I figured you must be somebody who worked there and had helped him escape. Since I knew a male impersonator was working at the club, it didn't take much detecting to figure out the answer."

"Yes," Peggy Pan admitted finally. "I put out the lights. I was looking for Jimmy in the alley, when I saw that the office door was open. I reached it just as Dan Davis—Langhorne's partner—was phoning the police. I could see in a minute that Jimmy's chances of proving his innocence would be mighty slim. I knew where the main switch was in the club, so I ran to it and threw out the lights so he could get away."

"If Jimmy's chances were slim then, what do you think they are now?" Doc asked her.

The blond club entertainer covered her face with her gloved hands and commenced to sob. All her pent-up emotions were finally giving way.

"You think a lot of him, don't you?" Doc asked quietly.

She nodded, without speaking.

"I thought so—taking the chances you did," Doc said. "That's why I had an idea you'd drop the gun—if it meant saving his life."

She looked up at Doc. Her eyes were blue pools in which terror swam.

"You're not going to help us?" she cried.

"I'll remove the bullet," he said simply.

"And his face—"

"We'll talk about that when Jimmy comes to again," Doc told her quietly.

He turned back to the unconscious man and his nimble, skillful fingers moved with quick precision. He made a slight incision in the wound, took a pair of forceps and probed inside the gash for the lead slug. After a few seconds he found it, gave it a slight twist and brought the bullet out neatly. Then he cauterized and packed the wound.

HE STEPPED back and felt Jimmy's pulse. Normal. He put the wrist down on the table and peeled off his rubber surgical gloves.

"Is—is he going to be all right?" Peggy Pan got out through trembling, colorless lips.

"Good as new," Doc consoled.

In about fifteen minutes Jimmy Morgan was sufficiently recovered from his ether bout to listen to the sound argument that Doc Murdock offered to him and the girl.

"In the first place," Doc pointed out to them, "hiding out and ducking the police won't get you to first base. They'll trace you, even if you have a new face. And then it'll be a lot worse. You'll not only jeopardize yourself but Peggy as well."

"I don't care!" Peggy was quick to put in.

"Just the same, Jimmy," Doc said, "you'll be a lot wiser if you give yourself up. The police will hold you—that's only natural. But you'll save yourself and Peggy an awful lot of bumps. Especially if, as you say, you didn't kill Langhorne."

"I didn't!" Jimmy insisted.

Doc looked at the waiter's intent face, long and steadily. There was something in the kid's eyes that made Doc believe he was telling the truth.

"Okay," Doc said finally. "I'll make a bargain. If you'll give yourself up, I'll do what I can to help you."

"But how can you help?" Jimmy wanted to know, hopelessly. "You're a doctor—a plastic surgeon. What we need is a detective."

Doc looked across at Dale Jordan. Both hid their smiles.

For Jimmy, though he had no way of knowing it, was actually talking to one of the greatest sleuths alive—the Purple Scar! A mysterious will-o'-the-wisp character that had been born of murder and violence.

John Murdock, Dr. Miles Murdock's brother, a member of the city's police force, had been shot down by cowardly gangsters. His face had been mutilated with a powerful acid to obliterate all possible identification. Then his body had been thrown into the river. On the flood tide two days later the purple-discolored body had come to the surface.

Dr. Miles Murdock, called to the morgue by his friend, Detective-Captain Griffin, to rebuild the mutilated features in an effort to establish identity, had stood there with the police officer and viewed the purplish, acid-ravaged face of—his own brother!

For the doctor's skill had made it possible for him to prove that this pitiful body once had been the virile one of John Murdock.

The killers had been caught and brought to trial, but because of the skill of another man—the vicious skill of a lawyer trained in defending crooks—they had got off scott free. Not for good and all, though, nor for long.

For it was at the moment that Doc Murdock had faced the bitter realization of a miscarriage of justice that the Purple Scar had been born. It had come to Doc to use that name in memory of his brother's water-purpled face as he had last seen it. And in his soul was a fervent vow to avenge his brother's death.

IN PREPARATION for that he had built for himself a gum elastic mask that should be the trade-mark of the Purple Scar, the newly evolved Nemesis that was in his mind. He had followed the lines in the police photograph of his brother's ghastly, mutilated face in making the mask and, since purple becomes black at night, Doc's own face, when wearing the mask in the darkness, was invisible.

Striking swiftly and unexpectedly as the Purple Mask, he had avenged his brother. He had ferreted out proof against the killers until they could no longer escape. He had brought them to justice—and they had paid.

But even that, he had discovered when it was all over, was not enough. The only way he could thoroughly avenge his brother was to throw himself into a campaign to prove that crime does not pay, and to that purpose he had dedicated his life. Now he had become insatiable as an avenger of injustice, as one who brought criminals to time when all police methods failed.

The name, the Purple Scar, had become a grim one to criminals and the criminal underworld. And always, when such protection was necessary, he wore the mask. He also wore it when he wished to work openly as the Purple Scar.

When Doc Murdock turned to crime fighting, he was no less talented and efficient than he was in his chosen field of plastic surgery. And he had kept himself in top trim for that purpose. A daily workout in the big gym atop his Swank Street mansion kept his body as fit and supple as it had been when he had taken down four letters at college.

His laboratories were second only to those of the F.B.I. He had also made a thorough and complete study of every phase of criminology and the fighting of crime. And his knowledge of plastic surgery and the human anatomy made him a past-master in the art of disguise.

As Doc now focused his gaze once more on Jimmy Morgan, he made up his mind that here was work for the Purple Scar. But he could not let young Morgan know that the Purple Scar would take an interest in his difficulties. For only three persons knew his identity. They were Dale Jordan, Tommy Pedlar, once the notorious "Sticky-fingered Kid," a slick second-story man who had become Doc's chief factotum after Doc had saved the life of his little daughter, and Detective-Captain Dan Griffin of Homicide, a lifetime friend of Doc and his brother John. Only three persons knew his true identity.

"You're quite right, Jimmy," Doc said. "You do need a detective. Perhaps we can arrange for one to help you."

Jimmy's eyes filled with a sort of faint new hope.

Doc continued talking persuasively, to put his own viewpoint across. He was a good salesman. Eventually he won. It was finally decided that Jimmy Morgan would surrender himself to the police and Peggy Pan would return to her job at the club, tomorrow night, and pretend that she had no interest in the young waiter's plight.

"There are just a couple of points I'd like cleared up first," Doc said. "Did you see either of these two men who came out of the office, Jimmy? Could you recognize them?"

"No. It was too dark."

"Did you hear them say anything?"

Jimmy paused, looked at Doc for a moment, and then for some reason he lied.

"No," he denied flatly. "I didn't hear them say anything."

IT WAS not much later that Detective-Captain Dan Griffin, Doc Murdock's friend of long standing, looked up from his flat-top desk, with an incredulous expression on his face as Doc and Jimmy Morgan walked into his office at Police Headquarters.

Doc knew if he brought Jimmy Morgan straight to the head of the Homicide Bureau in Akelton that young waiter would be more courteously treated than if Jimmy surrendered to the routine man in charge. Of course, they would sweat and grill the kid to try to find out if he was telling the truth. But Jimmy would be sure to get a square deal. Because Dan Griffin was known, even by those on the other side of the fence, as a square detective.

He was even built of squares. His body was shaped like a squat cement block, and he had a pleasantly hard, square-jawed face, and eyes that were black agates. His hair, squared at the temples, was graying black.

Dan Griffin recognized Jimmy Morgan at a glance. He could not figure out, though, how the devil Doc Murdock had managed to snare him, with the entire police department combing the city for the waiter.

Doc did not keep Griffin in the dark for long. He told the detective-captain about removing the bullet from Jimmy's shoulder—except that he twisted the details a trifle. He said that Jimmy had come to his office seeking medical attention. And he did not mention Peggy Pan at all.

For though Griffin was his pal and a square-shooter, the Homicide man was still one hundred percent cop! One peep about the male impersonator from the Playhouse, and Peggy would be dragged in for questioning and probably slapped into a cell for assisting a murder suspect to escape.

"Between you and me, Dan," Doc told Griffin after Jimmy had been taken to be booked, mugged, fingerprinted and locked up, "I don't think he killed Langhorne."

Griffin eyed Doc inquiringly. "So? Who did?"

"I don't know," Doc tossed off lightly. "It's your job to figure that out."

Griffin's eyes were still studying Doc. He could almost read what was going on in the plastic surgeon's brain.

"You know you'll have to be at the D.A.'s inquest in the morning," he said. "Taking that bullet out of Morgan's shoulder sort of earns you a ringside seat."

Doc showed sudden interest. "Who's going to be there?"

Griffin smiled. "I thought that'd get a rise out of you," he bantered. "My job to figure out, eh?"

"Who's going to be at the inquest?" Doc repeated.

"Dan Davis. Karl Kirkland, Langhorne's mouthpiece. A dame named Peggy Pan who works in the show. A lot of waiters—"

"What's the girl being brought in for?" Doc broke in.

Griffin shrugged. "Langhorne's doll."

Doc frowned. Langhorne's doll? Now there was a nice complication rearing its ugly head. Hadn't Peggy just admitted that she "thought a lot" of Jimmy Morgan? Could it be possible that this was one of those inevitable triangles? Had Jimmy Morgan killed Langhorne after all?

Somehow Doc still did not think so. First of all, there was the open safe. That would have nothing to do with a "love murder." Then, too, the murder weapon had not been found. And Dan Davis had come on Jimmy too soon after the killing of Langhorne for him to have disposed of the weapon.

No, Doc decided, there was more to this than a jealousy motive. Perhaps tomorrow's inquest would drag out a couple of leads.

CHAPTER IV

BLOOD AND GOLD

I T WAS late in the morning when Doc Murdock arrived at District Attorney Barret's ofice in the Criminal Courts Building. A last-minute emergency call had detained him.

Dan Davis was on the grill as Doc came in. Everyone else was present and accounted for.

Doc went over and sat alongside Captain Griffin at the far side of the room. Fragmentarily he obtained a picture of what had transpired.

The medical examiner's report had been submitted and read. Buck Langhorne had died of a knife wound, it was said. The blade, penetrating the right ventricle of the heart, had caused instant death. Griffin also said that the report contained something about "gold particles being found in the wound," but Doc didn't have a chance to go into details. The district attorney was talking to Davis and Doc did not want to miss any of it.

Barret, a slim man with a stub nose upon which his pince-nez balanced precariously, said to Davis:

"You discovered Jimmy Morgan at the open safe and seem to be of the opinion that he killed Langhorne. Can you give a reason why he should have done this?"

Davis's pale eyes swept to Jimmy Morgan's drawn face, then traveled to Peggy Pan, who was sitting a few chairs away. Peggy, as Doc had suggested for her to do, was trying to appear as unconcerned as possible.

"Jealousy!" Davis snapped out in answer. "Morgan insisted on hanging around Peggy Pan. And Langhorne didn't like it. Everybody at the club knew she was Langhorne's girl. Several times I heard Buck Langhorne bawl Morgan out, tell him to stay away from Peggy. The last time he threatened to fire Morgan if he didn't obey."

"Is that true?" the district attorney rapped at the accused waiter, his eyes distorted black dots behind his glasses.

Jimmy looked about like a frightened, trapped animal. In spite of his coat of tan, his face was pale beneath it. He saw Doc Murdock looking at him. Doc wagged his head in an encouraging "Go ahead."

Jimmy swallowed and told the truth.

"Yes," he said. "Langhorne did threaten to fire me."

The D.A. did not dwell on the subject. He returned to Davis.

"To your knowledge was there anything of great importance in the safe?" he asked.

"I couldn't say for sure," Davis replied. "Buck and I had our own private offices and individual safes. But I do know that, as a rule, he carried about a thousand dollars in cash in his safe."

"Was the money there when you looked into the safe?" Barret snapped at Morgan.

"I didn't have time to see what was in the safe," Jimmy replied unflinchingly.

"Was it there when your men searched the office, Captain Griffin?"

The Homicide chief shook his square-shaped head in a negative.

Barret took off his nose-glasses, wiped the lens with his handkerchief. Then, setting the glasses back on his stub nose, he directed his next question at Karl Kirkland, Langhorne's attorney.

KIRKLAND, TALL, rather slim with a smallish, triangular-shaped head and neatly-combed, straight, black hair, was the essence of sartorial splendor. He wore clothes like a movie star and incessantly smoked a cigarette through a pearl inlaid holder.

"You handled Buck Langhorne's affairs for several years," the district attorney said to him. "Who would profit mostly by his death?"

Kirkland took his time answering. He studied the lighted end of his cigarette a moment, then allowed his eyes to lift and travel slowly across the room to Dan Davis. Davis stared back at him, heatedly. Doc Murdock could read implacable enmity in that torrid look.

In a draggy-sounding voice, that weighed each word carefully, Kirkland said:

"About the only person who would directly benefit by Buck's death is his partner—Davis! Davis now becomes sole owner of the Playhouse—and the Playhouse is no small paying proposition."

Davis's pale eyes were murderous. His hands knotted and unknotted.

Kirkland paused to draw smoke through his cigarette holder. Then, as it drifted up in a bluish veil before his steady eyes, he went on talking.

"And," he said slowly, punching each word for its full dramatic worth, "I feel it only my duty to tell you that Davis wanted the Playhouse—very much. I, personally, know that he tried to buy out Buck Langhorne. But Buck refused to sell."

"Is that true?" Barrett rapped at Davis.

"Yes," Davis admitted, fighting to keep his voice low and level. "But it wasn't half as bad as he's trying to make it sound."

"But you did try to buy out Langhorne?" the district attorney persisted.

"Yes—when I found out what sort of a person he was."

Davis knew that it was no secret that he and Langhorne had been as far apart as the poles. Langhorne, a product of the slums, had a long and unenviable police record. Davis was college bred, with a family tree with roots that went all the way back to the hull of the Mayflower.

Unfortunately for himself, however, Davis had bright lights in his blood. A couple of years before he had been one of the Gay Way's most popular playboys. Then he had met Buck Langhorne. Buck had showed him the way to have his fun and make money at the same time.

Davis had invested what was left of his fast-dwindling inheritance with Langhorne—and the Playhouse Nightclub was the result. That this weird combination of opposites had made a howling success of the night spot caused more than one head-wagger to stop and gape with surprise.

"When I learned that he was mixed up with a lot of petty crooks and gangsters," Davis went on, "I naturally offered to buy him out."

"And when he wouldn't sell, you threatened him!" Kirkland bluntly accused. "You told him that one way or another you'd get the club!"

"Is that true?" the district attorney asked Davis sharply.

"Yes," Davis said coolly. "But I didn't kill him. What I said to him meant only that something would happen to make him sell me his share."

"What, for instance?"

"I don't know what." Davis' face flushed as he tried to untangle himself. "All I do know is that I didn't kill him."

AND SO it went on for the rest of the morning. Questions, answers, accusations, denials. Everybody in the office was quizzed. Peggy Pan, the waiters, Jimmy Morgan. Even Doc Murdock went through the query mill.

It was almost noontime before Jimmy was led back to his cell and the others excused.

Doc left the office with Captain Griffin and together they walked down the lengthy corridor.

"I think for once you're wrong, Doc," the captain of detectives remarked. "Morgan's as guilty as a kid with jam on his hands. He killed Langhorne because of that Pan dame. And you can't sell me otherwise."

Doc smiled faintly. "A gent named Davis seems to be pretty well fortified with a reason for wanting Langhorne out of the way, too."

"Davis?" Griffin's square face came around with an incredulous expression. "Aw, Doc, you're slippin'. Davis ain't no killer. Why, just look at the family he comes from! Bluebloods! Real class stuff."

Doc shrugged as they approached the door that led down the high stone steps to the sidewalk, where the noonday mob from the surrounding office buildings was milling about.

"Maybe we're both kicking at the wrong rock," he suggested. "Don't forget that missing thousand. Maybe it'll turn out to be just a plain case of robbery, and manslaughter. Another thing—there's that missing murder weapon."

"Aw, Morgan was probably working with somebody," scoffed Griffin. "The Pan dame maybe? Slipped her the dough and the knife through the alley door."

"And then came back to the open safe, I suppose, and had himself caught red-handed?"

Griffin didn't get a chance to answer. For behind them at that moment, a short way back up the corridor, came the sound of angry voices. Doc and the captain paused with the front door half-open, turned to look back.

The altercation was between Dan Davis and Karl Kirkland. They had just come out of the district attorney's office and were arguing heatedly. It was impossible to tell what they were saying, but obviously Davis was sore because Kirkland had pointed the accusing digit at him.

And then—without warning—Davis lunged at the lawyer. His right fist snaked out and struck Kirkland below the left eye. The attorney staggered back into the wall.

A crowd started to collect in the hallway. Doc Murdock and Captain Griffin were already racing back to the spot. They shoved through the morbidly curious crowd. Davis was set to sail back at Kirkland again, when the plastic surgeon grabbed him.

At the same time, Griffin blocked Kirkland.

"A fine demonstration for two men like you to put on," Griffin sharply reprimanded.

It rolled off Davis like water off a duck's back. He struggled with all his might to get at the lawyer. But Doc's powerful hands held him.

"Take it easy," Doc cautioned. "This won't get either of you anything but a lot of sour publicity."

"I don't care what it gets me!" Davis barked. "He's trying to frame me! He'd like to see me swing for Langhorne's murder! He never has liked me—not since I first met him—because I told Langhorne I didn't trust him. And I still don't!"

HE MADE another vain attempt to break away.

A couple of detailed officers came up then. They dispersed the crowd.

Kirkland was bathing his injured eye with a damp handkerchief that had been dipped in one of the wall fountains. He was mad as a bull with a red flag waved at it. His own face was aflame.

"Don't think you're going to get away with this!" he snarled at Davis. "I'll fix your wagon pretty."

Griffin took him by the arm then, steered him down the corridor, and outside the door into the street.

Doc Murdock held onto Davis until he was sure the lawyer was gone. Then he let him go. Davis had quieted down considerably.

"Too bad you had to do that," Doc told him.

Davis straightened his rumpled clothes.

"Yeah," he said, a little shamefaced. "I guess I did make sort of an exhibition of myself, didn't I? But after he deliberately tried to pin the murder on me…. And that smirk he had on his face when I met him out here in the hall!"

"You did your best to accuse young Morgan," Doc reminded.

"But Morgan's guilty!" protested Davis. "I was only doing my duty."

"I recall Kirkland's speech sounding something like that," Doc said, with an odd quirk at the corners of his lips.

Davis plainly did not care for the comparison. Without further comment, he and Doc walked to the door and down the tall stone steps where Griffin was standing alone on the sidewalk.

"Kirkland gone?" asked Doc.

"Yeah. I just put him in a cab."

The Homicide chief nodded upstreet, and fished a package of cigarettes from his coat pocket. He proffered the pack to Davis, for he knew Doc did not smoke. Davis said he didn't, either. Griffin mouthed a butt and looked hard at Davis.

"You got yourself a nice spread of trouble," he said, "when you hung that crepe on Kirkland's optic. I don't know what he's going to do—he wouldn't tell me. But I got an idea he's gonna dig plenty deep to get back at you. Maybe you'll find yourself with a nice juicy assault and battery rap pinned around your neck."

"If that's all it amounts to, I won't care," Davis said, staring moodily in the direction Griffin said Kirkland's cab had gone. "That sock was well worth it."

He hailed a cab for himself, piled inside and left Doc and Griffin standing on the sidewalk.

"Well, there's one guy with enough mad in him to commit mayhem," was Griffin's observation.

"Your blue-blood friend," Doc ribbed good-naturedly.

Griffin scowled and grunted. Doc did not rub it in.

"You said something about gold dust particles being found in the knife wound in Langhorne's back," he remarked, to change the subject.

Griffin nodded. "Yeah. Screwy, ain't it?"

Doc's black eyes narrowed reflectively. "Maybe not so screwy. Chances are those gold dust particles were on the blade of the knife that killed Langhorne."

"Which means the person who killed Langhorne must have been around gold?" Griffin said, with a rising inflection.

"Maybe a jeweler," Doc offered.

"How about a prospector?" Griffin suggested. He paused, studied the expression on Doc's good-looking face. "Any ideas?" he wheedled.

Doc smiled. And Griffin knew that smile. The smile of the Sphinx, he called it.

CHAPTER V

CLUES

AFTER A crowded day, operating, consulting, keeping appointments with his patients, visiting the clinic, Doc Murdock and Dale Jordan retired to the privacy of his top floor studio. It was somewhere between eleven and midnight then.

That studio was an odd looking sanctorum, furnished to a man's taste. Death masks and other weird objects adorned the walls. Bits of sculpture littered the place.

What few idle moments Doc could manage he spent at sculpturing. Not, however, as an idle hobby. The work kept his fingers quick and supple for the delicate operations he performed. Also he found this art an invaluable aid in working out clever disguises.

Dale watched Doc go directly to the wall. He pressed a carefully concealed button and the panel slid away to reveal a small safe. Opening the deep depository, he took out two small objects, then closed the safe again.

With the objects in his hands, he sat down before a mirror. Dale half smiled as she watched him spread out carefully and fit over his face—the mask of the Purple Scar!

The reflection of the horrible face in the mirror wiped Dale's smile away, made her shudder. She should have been used to it by this time, she told herself. But it was so fearful-looking that she doubted whether she'd ever become accustomed to it.

A ghastly network of scars it was, that hugged to his face skin-tight. A hideous purple—as Doc's brother's face had been when he had been dragged from the water. Eyes empty, shriveled sockets. Mouth a twisted slash.

The second object Doc had withdrawn from the safe was another of those skin-tight masks of his own contrivance, but this one allowed for facial expressions.

This he fitted over the purple mask. The lifelike disguise changed him into a broad-nosed, square-jawed, high-cheek-boned individual.

From sad experience Doc had learned that ordinary disguises were unsafe for the dangerous work he had undertaken. Tireless experimenting had brought these outer rubber masks to perfection. They were masks that could be made to resemble any person Doc Murdock found necessary to impersonate.

Already Doc had changed his clothing to conform with the character he intended to portray. Now one final transformation completed his work.

A greasy substance which temporarily removed the wave from his black hair and changed it to light blond gave Doc that finish for a disguise that only the keenest eyes could possibly detect. If any could.

Dale did not lift her gaze from him until the transformation was complete.

"Isn't there something I can do to help?" she asked then.

Doc stood up and looked down into her lovely, though slightly worried face.

"I'm afraid not, darling," he said. "I'm not quite sure what I'm up against this time."

It was not that Doc did not have a wholesome respect and admiration for the ability of the Police Department, but he realized they were not infallible, and it was in such cases the Purple Scar took a hand.

Perhaps now, in their zeal to pin the murder of Buck Langhorne on young Morgan, the waiter, they had overlooked something that might be twisted into an important clue. Such things had been known to happen in the Purple Scar's experience. That was why Doc's first visit was going to be to the Playhouse to see just how things shaped up there.

Dale laid a trembling white hand on his arm.

"Be careful, darling," she whispered, and it was a prayer.

His mask contracted to form a smile. Then he leaned forward and kissed her. The next moment he was gone. Downstairs, he left the house via the back door route....

THE ALLEY at the back of the Playhouse was midnight dark. Hemmed in on three sides by tall brick buildings, it twisted like a black shoe-lace for almost half a block.

Through the darkness came the Purple Scar. Cautiously he approached the rear door of the nightclub, the door leading into the office where Buck Langhorne had been killed the night before.

In the club, business was going on as usual. Dan Davis obviously was not grieving over his partner's death.

The Scar took a bunch of keys from his coat pocket. He smiled a little, thinking of that bunch of keys. Once they had belonged to Tommy Pedlar, the "Sticky-fingered Kid" whom Doc Murdock had long since taken under his wing. A swift memory of the time that had happened came to Doc now. Tommy had been convalescing from a session with a yegg's bullets when he had turned those keys over to his friend, Doc Murdock. The fresh page he had already turned over....

The third key the Purple Scar tried proved to be the right one. It turned easily in the lock. He nudged the door open and toed into the dark, tomblike office.

From the club beyond the door opposite came the clamor of the band, laughter, tinkling glasses, voices.

The Purple Scar closed the outer door, snapped on his flashlight, and shot its beam about the office. Everything was precisely as it had been last night, as it had been described to him. Even the safe door had been left open.

He moved quickly to the safe, fished inside. It had been cleaned out. He played his torch on the safe door. He could see the powder marks where it had been dusted for finger prints. But, according to Captain Griffin, the only prints found any place on the safe had been Jimmy Morgan's.

Hanging on the wall alongside the safe was a huge oil painting of a racehorse. A sleek-looking animal with pricking ears. The name on the gold frame said, "Finale."

The Scar turned and went softly to the desk. A lot of papers were scattered atop it, but nothing that seemed important.

Then his gaze caught a wire spindle to which a stack of tabs were attached. The Purple Scar tore off the top few and glanced at them, to make sure he had all the tabs from last night. He read the scrawled signatures, above Buck Langhorne's okay.

He recognized several of the names. Prominent night-club rounders. But one name in particular seemed to leap right off the paper at him. Ben Trexel!

That snapped the Scar's thoughts back to the man now in the morgue. The gold dust in Buck Langhorne's wound. The fact that the killer *might* have been a jeweler. And Ben Trexel was one of the city's most important jewelers!

Still, Trexel bore a fine reputation and though he had been a customer of the night-club, it did not seem reasonable that he could have had any connection with a thug such as Buck Langhorne had been. On the other hand, the fact that Trexel had been here last night was worth filing away for future reference.

NEXT, THE Purple Scar tackled the desk drawers. He went through each one, carefully. About the only thing he could find of any importance was a stack of bank statements fastened together with rubber bands. He withdrew last month's statement and scrutinized it.

One entry popped his eyes. A fifty thousand-dollar check had been deposited by Langhorne on the fifteenth of last month!

Fifty thousand dollars all in one lump is a lot of money, the Purple Scar thought, even for a man like Buck Langhorne. It must have been a whale of a deal that had pulled in that kind of lucre. That was one item the Scar meant to check on at the first opportunity.

He was placing the statements back into the drawer when he heard a key rattle in the door that led into the club. He turned for the alley-door, but saw that he could not make it! But he also spied a closet door that he pulled open and ducked inside as the club door opened.

He heard the lights click on, and the door close. He ventured opening the closet door a crack, and saw three men standing in the office.

One of them was Dan Davis, his face pale, eyes protruding as if with fear. The other two—big, surly, beefy-looking guys—the Purple Scar had never seen before.

They began pushing Davis around, banging questions at him.

"Come on!" one of them barked. "This is the last place left. Now where is it?"

"I don't know," Davis got out.

The bigger of the two bruisers gave Davis a shove that knocked him back against the desk.

"Don't keep handin' us that line," he growled. "Langhorne was your partner. He'd tell you what he done with it!"

"But he didn't!" Davis was perspiring freely. "I swear he didn't!"

The smaller of the thugs was already yanking out desk drawers, overturning furniture, looking behind pictures, pushing back the rug to make sure there were no loose boards in the floor where something might have been hidden.

And then he turned toward the closet!

The Purple Scar pressed back against the wall. But the closet was so shallow that even a blind man could not miss him. His breath held in his throat. His heart pounded.

The knob began to turn.

There was no alternative for the Purple Scar but to swing into action. He struck the door with the sole of his foot, the full weight of his body behind it. The door swung outward and smashed the thug opening it, full in the face!

The Purple Scar surged out of the closet, swinging. The suddenness of his attack worked to his advantage. He caught the bigger of the two strong-arm men flush on the jaw, with the first blow he fired.

It sent the big fellow reeling back against the wall with a jarring impact. The Scar turned in time to see the second lug, the one who had been handed a faceful of door, snatch up a chair.

BUT BEFORE the chair could be brought down upon the Purple Scar's blondish head, the Scar lashed out with his right foot, lashing the chair-swinger's chin. As neat a demonstration of *la savatte* as anyone ever saw.

The chair crashed to the floor and the man who had tried to wield it rocked groggily. The Purple Scar set himself and was ready for an attack from either of the two hoods. But no attack came. Stunned and confused, they had all they desired of this blond tornado who fought with hands and feet.

They darted past him and almost tore the door from its hinges as they hurled themselves out of the office.

The Purple Scar did not chase after them. A row in the club would leave him open to as many questions as they. And he had no desire to have his identity made known.

Instead, the Scar turned to Dan Davis, who was standing beside the desk, his eyes almost popping out of his chalky face.

"Who—who the devil are you?" Davis managed, with an incredulous look.

The Purple Scar's broad face lighted with a grin and from his pocket he took a dummy badge. He showed it to Davis, but too quickly for the night club owner to make out accurately what was on it.

"From the district attorney's office," the Scar said. "A couple of things cropped up during the day. I came here to find out if you could throw any light on them. My name's John Pryor."

Davis was still fog-bound.

"How did you get in that closet?" he demanded.

"I was doing a little sleuthing around in here," the Purple Scar said truthfully, "when I heard you and your friends coming in. I thought my absence would save a lot of explaining, so I made myself scarce." He eyed Davis sternly. "Incidentally, who were your friends?"

Davis shook away the cobwebs from his brain.

"I never saw them before," he said. "They forced their way into my apartment tonight, insisted that I knew where some gold was hidden. They declared, finally, that it must be somewhere in the club here."

The Scar's eyes widened with sudden surprise.

"Gold?" he ejaculated. "What gold?"

Davis shrugged. "I don't know. They said Buck Langhorne had it, and that it belonged to their boss."

"Who is their boss?"

"They didn't say. But they tore my place, at home, apart. Then they brought me here to the club, went through my office with a fine comb. They came in here to look as a final gesture. I haven't the slightest idea what it's all about. I never heard of any gold before."

The Purple Scar's thoughts were on that gold that had been found in the wound in Langhorne's back. Was there any connection between that gold and the gold the two thugs were looking for?

Also, was Davis telling the truth about not knowing about the gold, where it was hidden? Suppose he did know.

Suppose it turned out to be a sizable amount. Would he have surrendered it to them, regardless of how much they pushed him around? It was not likely.

At Davis' invitation, "John Pryor" sat down in one of the big easy chairs in the office. Davis sat down behind the desk. Pryor stated his business briefly.

"Do you know whether Buck Langhorne had any business dealings with Ben Trexel?" he asked.

Davis frowned. "Trexel? The jeweler? I'm sure he didn't. Trexel comes into the club frequently. But as far as he and Langhorne doing any business together—that's absurd."

The Scar smiled noncommittally. Then he asked:

"Do you know anything about a deposit made by Langhorne on the fifteenth of last month—a check for fifty thousand dollars?"

A look of profound surprise wreathed Davis' face.

"Fifty thousand dollars? Are you joking? I don't believe Langhorne ever had that much money all at one time in his life."

Before the Scar could make further comment the door that led into the club swung open. The man who entered wore dark glasses, but it needed no second glance to tell that behind the glasses was Karl Kirkland. And there was no question why he wore those dark glasses. That sock Davis had planted on the attorney's eye in the corridor at Criminal Courts' Building had raised an unlovely purplish-hued mouse under it.

In view of that run-in, the presence of the lawyer here in the Playhouse caused a wrinkle of surprise in the Scar's brow. This was no social call!

CHAPTER VI

SURPRISE PARTNER

KIRKLAND'S SHADED eyes traveled from Davis to the Purple Scar, then back to Davis. He scowled.

"I've been waiting outside in the club all night for you, Davis," he said coolly. "I thought I'd find you alone—after seeing your two friends just leave. I'll be back. I want to talk to you." He reached for the knob of the door.

"Just a minute, Kirkland!" the Purple Scar's voice interrupted. "I want to talk to you."

Kirkland twisted, with a frown. "I don't believe I've had the pleasure—"

The Scar arose and came forward. He flashed the phony badge again, quickly, and gave out the "John Pryor from the D.A.'s office" line. He didn't waste time after that. He asked Kirkland about Trexel and the fifty-thousand-dollar bank deposit.

The lawyer gave about the same reply as Davis.

John Pryor then rubbed his stout jaw with the back of his big hand and eyed Kirkland, critically.

"I don't suppose you'd care to tell me why you came here to see Mister Davis, after what happened this noontime?" he asked.

Kirkland looked across into Davis' narrowed eyes. The lawyer's mouth formed a straight wintry line.

"On the contrary," he said, "I think it would be a good idea if I did tell you. It might help in case anything happens to me—as happened to Buck Langhorne."

Davis' hands were tight balls at his sides.

"You never miss a chance to put the finger on me, do you?" he snapped.

Kirkland, ignoring the remark, dipped his left hand into his pocket, took out a legal-looking paper. He waved it in front of Davis' face.

"A warrant for what happened this noontime?" the Purple Scar guessed.

Kirkland shook his head slowly, a grin of satisfaction smearing his thin face.

"A marriage certificate!" he announced elatedly.

"A marriage certificate?" the masked man echoed.

Kirkland nodded, with an air of triumph.

"Buck Langhorne's marriage certificate."

"That's a lie!" Davis exploded. "Langhorne wasn't married."

Kirkland smirked. "I thought you'd be surprised. Langhorne was married. Married when he was a kid. Tried to get a divorce. But because of her religion, his wife would never give him one. He never wanted it publicized, because it might hurt his Don Juan rating. And so—Mr. Davis, after all your careful planning, the Playhouse still isn't all yours! Legally Langhorne's widow has a claim to half of it. And believe me, I'm going to see she fights that claim to the highest court!"

The Purple Scar craned to try to read the license. But a fleeting glance was all he could manage, for at that moment Dan Davis' fury, for the second time that day, broke out of control.

With a snarl, he sprang across the room at the lawyer. He got his hands on Kirkland's throat and exerted pressure. Only the Purple Scar's immediate intervention saved Kirkland from worse than a black eye.

The Scar broke Davis' grip and pushed him back into a chair.

KIRKLAND'S EYES were murderous pin-points behind his dark glasses, as he fingered his throat which felt like squeezed sponge rubber.

"I suppose I can spot you that," he said with an angry snarl, "and what happened at noontime—for the pleasure I'll get out of this."

He waved the certificate once more before Davis' face, then stowed it back into his coat pocket. From the same pocket he withdrew his pearl-inlaid cigarette holder, inserted a cigarette. With it between his lips he gave Davis a last disdainful glare, turned on his heel and went through the door, banging it behind him.

The Purple Scar waited in the office with Dan Davis until he was sure that the debonair, but angry, attorney was safely out of the club. Then he left by way of the alley door.

When he reached the street, he was debating with himself. Should he call Ben Trexel and find out whether he had a finger in this mess? If Langhorne had had gold in his possession, he would have needed someone with a permit through which to fence it. Trexel being a jeweler would have been in a fine spot to dispose of it.

While Trexel had an untarnished reputation, at least so far as Doc Murdock, the Purple Scar, knew, he was still in business to make money. And Doc had met more than a few reputable business men who did a little "off the bottom" dealing.

The Purple Scar finally decided to call Trexel's home. By carefully wording his conversation, he could easily tell whether Trexel had had any dealings with the murdered nightclub owner.

He found an all-night drug-store, sought Trexel's number in a directory, and ducked into the booth. In a couple of minutes a soft feminine voice was answering him over the wire.

"Is Mr. Ben Trexel at home?"

"No, he isn't," the soft voice said. "This is Mrs. Trexel."

"Have you any idea where I might find your husband?"

"I'm sorry, I haven't. Mr. Trexel left early this morning. I haven't the faintest idea where he went, or when he'll be back."

The Purple Scar couldn't help but ask:

"Aren't you worried about him?"

"Worried?" A musical little laugh came over the wire. "Not in the least. Mr. Trexel often leaves town on such trips. Stays away for as long as a week, without telling me where he's gone or when he'll be back. But he always comes home again."

Nothing gained there, the Purple Scar thought, as he hung up the receiver. Ben Trexel's being out of town could have nothing to do with the case.

He turned from the booth, went out into the street, and on home, to get the rest that was essential to a man of his profession....

BRIGHT AND early the next morning Doc Murdock, again assuming his John Pryor character, was at the National Park Bank, shortly after it opened. He went directly to the cashier, convinced him that he was from the district attorney's office and had the bookkeeping department check on that fifty thousand dollar deposit.

Even to a bank of this size a fifty-thousand-dollar check was not of common occurrence. In a few minutes John Pryor had the desired information. The check had been drawn on the Banner Trust Company, made out by Joe Rossini.

Dr. Murdock needed no introduction to Joe Rossini. Neither did anyone else who ever read the sports pages. Rossini had illusions that he was one of the city's outstanding sportsmen.

Actually he was no more than a roughneck gambler—one who was none too ethical, at that.

He had a stable of crooked fighters well versed in the art of plain and fancy diving. And a string of racehorses that ran hot and cold to his order. It was said that some years ago he had tried to slip a ball player ten grand to chuck an important series. The player got nailed and the judge ruled him off the diamond. But Rossini had managed to ease his fat neck out of the mess, and had lived to don a new white collar. Definitely not nice people was Joe Rossini.

And it was he who had given Buck Langhorne those fifty Gs! Why? Joe Rossini was not one to squander greenbacks. It must have been for a mighty important transaction.

The Purple Scar put on his thinking cap. What did Buck Langhorne and Joe Rossini have in common—aside from being of the same breed?

Suddenly across the silver-screen in his mind flashed the picture of the racehorse, Finale, which had been hanging on the wall in Langhorne's office at the Playhouse. The horse, as Doc recalled, was a top fighter. But what connection Buck Langhorne might have had with the horse, Doc was not well enough acquainted with the "sport of kings" to say.

But he had a pretty good idea where he could find out.

He ducked into the first phone booth he came to, and got the office of the racing secretary on the wire.

"Could you give me some information about a horse called Finale?" he inquired. "I'd like to know for whom the horse runs."

There was a pause while the information was checked. Then he was told:

"Finale has been running for the Red Tree Stables."

"Who owns the stables?" he asked.

"Niccolo Lo Sasso."

"Does he still own the horse?"

"No. The horse was sold last month to Mr. Joe Rossini."

The Purple Scar said "Thank you" and dropped the receiver onto the hook. Over and over on his tongue he rolled the name "Niccolo Lo Sasso." Where had he heard that name before? Then it came to him. He had never heard it, but he had seen it—on the marriage certificate that Karl Kirkland showed him last night in the club! Niccolo Lo Sasso was none other than Buck Langhorne!

ON HIS way back to his Swank Street laboratories, he dropped into the local offices of the *Morning Form,* a racing sheet. He asked to be shown the files for a month or two back, and scrutinized the charts.

Finale's last winning race had been almost two months ago. The filly had made three straight wins to draw down a ten-thousand-dollar purse. She had been running for the Red Tree Stables.

Going through the papers carefully, he found a small item that told of the sale of the horse on the fifteenth of last month to Joe Rossini.

Back to the charts. Two weeks ago Finale had finished last in a seven-horse race. She had been rested for a week or so, then entered again. And again she had trailed the field and pulled up lame!

The Scar left the offices of the racing daily with a new thought playing around in his brain. Buck Langhorne had sold Joe Rossini a crack racehorse for fifty thousand dollars. But as soon as Rossini got the horse it failed to win. Finally the horse had pulled up lame.

That meant Rossini was stuck for fifty grand. And anyone who knew Joe Rossini was aware that he was not the type to be taken over by anybody!

Figuring it out on that basis, Joe Rossini could know a lot about Buck Langhorne's murder.

Doc Murdock had only one regret. He had to wait all day long before, in his role of John Pryor, he could get to Rossini and play a little "information please" with the gambler. Because Rossini was as hard to get to during the day as that funny-mustached guy who lives on that mountain in Berchtesgaden in the Bavarian Alps.

Rossini made book. From twelve noon until after six P.M. he sat closeted in a big room, surrounded by a couple of dozen quick-triggered gents, answering phones and taking bets.

So the Purple Scar returned to his own office to shed his role of John Pryor, for the time being, to resume his normal character of Doc Murdock and attend to the important work that had piled up in his absence.

CHAPTER VII

GOLD IF YOU FIND IT

SOMEWHERE AROUND five o'clock that afternoon Doc Murdock had just finished the final and most delicate of a series of four grafting operations. They were to restore the entire left side of a man's face, a face that had been ravaged by fire.

He was standing over the sink, in one corner of his fully equipped, white-walled laboratory, scrubbing his hands with antiseptic soap when Dale Jordan came in. Besides being the girl he was going to marry, Dale was Doc Murdock's chief of staff, a nurse and first assistant of remarkable efficiency.

"Captain Griffin is in the reception room, waiting to see you," she announced. "He just came in and he looks plenty excited."

"Send him in, darling, and keep everyone else out," Doc directed.

Dale nodded her copper-topped head and went out. Almost at once the square-faced head of Homicide loomed in the doorway. Dale had been correct. He was excited all right. His eyes showed that.

"Doc," he said, with no preliminary, "I need your help."

Doc nodded, noting the big burlap bag that Captain Griffin held.

"What've you got there?" he asked.

"I'll show you," Griffin quickly replied. "New case just cropped up. Have to drop everything else for a while and work on this. It's red hot."

He walked to one of the white-topped operating tables, under a bright overhead light. He placed the bag atop the table.

As Doc advanced, drying his hands in a towel, Griffin opened the bag. Out tumbled the severed head of a man, and two human arms!

"A couple of kids, picking berries, stumbled across this out around Red Point," said Griffin. "These things were stuffed in this bag and hidden in the bushes."

The plastic surgeon's face was expressionless as he looked down at the grotesque objects on the table. The blood on the head had long since dried, but it was a gruesome thing. For it had been battered and gouged and mutilated beyond all possible recognition. The hands and the arms had been hacked at, also. The fingers obviously had been scraped so that they could not be identified with fingerprints.

"Lord only knows what became of the torso or the legs of this poor devil," Griffin said sadly.

"Any idea who it is?" asked Doc.

Griffin shook his head. "That's why I brought the things to you. The medical examiner took one look and threw up his hands. You're our only chance to make identification."

Doc took another look at the remains and rubbed his stout jaw.

"I don't know, Griff," he said thoughtfully. "After all, I'm a plastic surgeon—not a jig-saw puzzle artist."

"It'll mean a lot to me if you can do it, Doc," urged the captain.

Doc studied the head a moment, then shrugged.

"Okay, Griff," he gave in. "We'll take a crack at it. But I won't make any promises."

THAT WAS plenty good enough for the detective.

What happened in the silence of that white-walled laboratory during the next fifteen or twenty minutes made restorative art history. With nothing more than the battered shell of an almost shapeless skull to go by, Doc Murdock rebuilt that hollow-eyed, caved-in face.

Apparently it was the head of an undersized man of some fifty-odd years, with a markedly receding chin and forehead, hollow eyes and slightly buck teeth.

"And according to the state of the limbs and head," was Doc's final analysis, "I'd say he was killed night before last. Same night Buck Langhorne was killed. Do you know him now?"

He gestured to his completed work, and Captain Griffin studied the rebuilt face carefully. Then he shook his head in a slow negative.

"Never saw him before. Looks like we're just as bad off as before."

"Well, we might be able to find a clue as to where he was or what he was doing when he was murdered," Doc suggested hopefully.

He picked up one of the dead limbs, studied the hands. Then he took a bistoury, the small surgical knife he used for making minor incisions, and scraped the dirt from under each of the dead nails.

Placing this dirt on small flat specimen glasses, Doc carried it to a microscope that stood on one of the racks. Deftly he adjusted the apparatus and took a good peek. The particles of dirt and other substances became giant boulders under the magic lens.

"What do you see?" Griffin asked anxiously.

"Look for yourself."

Griffin peeped into the microscope as Doc readjusted it.

"See that yellow substance?" Doc pointed out.

"Yeah. What is it?"

"The same thing found in the wound that killed Buck Langhorne—particles of gold dust!"

Griffin's eyes came up away from the microscope, his square face a mask of profound astonishment.

"Holy smaltz!" he gasped. "What do you make of that? You don't suppose this is gonna dovetail back to the Langhorne case?"

Doc's brows wrinkled in deep ridges as his nimble brain grappled with a dawning idea. Without comment he turned and walked to one of the tall white cabinets that lined the far wall of the laboratory.

He opened the door and took out a photographer's large camera. This he used for taking "before and after" pictures of his patients, for his files.

He loaded the camera with plates and, as Griffin looked on with wonderment, Doc shot the remodeled head from every conceivable angle. Then he left Griffin for a spell and went upstairs with the plates, into a small dark-room.

When he emerged sometime later, he had half a dozen photographs of the rebuilt skull. And anyone who had known the man in life would surely have been able to recognize him from these pictures.

"NOW WHAT?" asked Griffin.

"I've got a couple of visits to make. I have an idea that I'm going to need your help later in the night. Where will you be?"

"Home in bed," Griffin said promptly. "I haven't had a decent sleep since Langhorne was bumped."

"Okay," Doc Murdock announced briefly. "If I need you, I'll call."

Even before Captain Griffin left, Doc Murdock knew on whom his first call would be made that night. He said nothing of it, however, but as soon as the Homicide officer had gone he sat down to figure out what his further moves would be—after he had made his call on Peggy Pan.

There were many important matters to be attended to first, however, so it was after eleven o'clock that night when Doc Murdock, the Purple Scar, but again in his role of John Pryor, approached the Castle-Front Apartments where Peggy Pan lived. It was a nice apartment house on the west side of town; not too ritzy, not too cheap. The sort of a place a girl like Peggy might be expected to live.

There was a clerk behind the switchboard in the lobby. "John Pryor" did not care to have the clerk see him. He went around to the back, made use of the rear door, and mounted the stairs.

He had called Peggy at the club and, introducing himself as John Pryor, a friend of Doc Murdock, had asked her if he could speak to her some place besides the club. She had suggested her apartment and said she would slip out between shows and meet him there.

He found Peggy's apartment on the third floor, and admitted himself with one of his many keys. He clicked on the lights. There were two small rooms that reflected the girl's character—a sort of solid femininity, hers was, he thought.

He had scarcely seated himself in one of the three big chairs in the living room when someone halted before the door and inserted a key in the lock. He clicked off the lights and darted into the coat closet to his right.

The door opened. He saw a girl's figure outlined in the square of yellow light from the hall. She fished for the wall switch, turned on the lights and closed the door. She gave a low, startled cry as John Pryor stepped out of the closet.

"It's all right," he assured her. "I'm the man who called you at the club."

"Oh!" She relaxed a little. "You're the detective Dr. Murdock promised would help us?"

Her pretty face, beneath her piled-up blond curls was drawn with worry. She wore no hat, and a sports coat covered her evening frock.

"How did you get in here?" she asked.

"That's not important," he told her. "What I'm here for is to ask a couple of questions. Do you know whether Buck Langhorne was hiding any gold any place?"

SHE HESITATED, took a cigarette from her purse, lighted it and inhaled deeply. Her visitor's eyes were fastened on her face. There was no change of expression. But he was not forgetting that she was a proficient actress.

"I never heard about any gold," she said finally through the smoke that drifted out of her curved red lips.

He reached into his pocket. He took out the photos of the mysterious dead man and showed them to her.

"Ever see this man?" he asked.

He was sure he saw her facial muscles tighten a little. But there was no change in her tone.

"No," she said evenly. "I've never seen him. Is he—"

She stopped abruptly, and started as a knock came on the door. The two stared at each other in silence. The girl's eyes showed sudden fear.

"John Pryor" stepped toward the next room.

"See who it is," he said softly, as he ducked into the darkness behind the thin wall that separated the two rooms.

Peggy crushed out her cigarette in an ashtray and opened the door. Two men pushed into the room. The Purple Scar needed but a glance to recognize them. They were the same two tough nuts he had chased out of Dan Davis' office. He might have done the same thing now, but he was curious to learn what they were doing here. What did they want of this girl?

He didn't have long to wait to find out.

"Well, sister, we told you we'd keep an eye on you," said the larger of the two thugs. "What are you up to—sneakin' out of the club between shows? Tryin' to give us the slip? Maybe take a run-out powder with the gold, huh?"

The girl took a step backward. "I told you I don't know anything about any gold!" she cried indignantly.

"Don't give us that! Langhorne had a case on you, trusted you. And the boss has an idea Buck gave you the gold to hang onto—and that you're hidin' it."

"But I'm not!" the girl insisted. "I told you last night I never even saw the gold. If there is any—why don't you ask Dan Davis about it? He was Buck Langhorne's partner, wasn't he?"

"We did ask him," the smaller hood declared surlily. "He gave us the same line you're handin' us. One of you is lyin', and I'll lay a hundred to one on it."

"What about his safe?" Peggy Pan asked quickly.

"What safe?"

"His safe at the club—in his office. A wall safe, behind one of the panels."

The big thug scowled. "You wouldn't be tryin' to kid us, lady?" he asked dubiously.

"Of course not!"

"Okay, you better not be, or we'll be back to have another talk with you—a nice long talk!"

They left as abruptly as they had appeared.

The man who called himself John Pryor came out of the next room. His face was twisted into a scowl.

"So you didn't know anything about any gold?" he barked at Peggy Pan.

Her eyes were filled with appeal as she faced him.

"I only knew about it through—" she began, but the Scar chopped her off short.

"Why didn't you tell the police about it and try to save Jimmy?" he demanded.

"Because I don't know whether there actually is any gold!" Peggy cried pleadingly. "And I didn't think the police would believe me."

"How much did those men tell you the gold is worth?"

Peggy hesitated an appreciable few moments before she said simply: "Fifty thousand dollars!"

CHAPTER VIII

MIDNIGHT VISITS

FIFTY THOUSAND dollars! That was the exact amount Rossini had paid for the lame racehorse. Could it be possible that Rossini had killed Langhorne and stolen the gold?

Then who were those two gorillas who had just left Peggy Pan's apartment? The answer to that seemed reasonably easy. From all indications they were Rossini's men.

"Fifty thousand dollars would take two people a long way," the Scar, whom Peggy knew as John Pryor, said to the girl with a hint of accusation in his voice.

"Are you sure you didn't tell the cops about the gold because you have it? And are living with the hope that Jimmy can slip his neck out of the noose?"

"That's not true!" she cried heatedly.

He studied her a moment. "Do you know who their boss is?" he finally asked her.

"The two men who just left?" She looked at him with a question. "No—I don't know."

"And you're sure you never saw the man in the photographs I showed you?"

"I never saw him," she firmly declared.

He kept on staring at her, icily.

"You and Jimmy are in a pretty uncomfortable spot," he reminded her with inexorable accusation, "and I'm trying to help you. So don't you think it might be a good idea if you tried pitching 'em where I can hit 'em? Is there anything you haven't told me—and want to tell me?"

She met his gaze with an odd look. She *did* want to tell him something. He could see it in her eyes. But for some reason she could not. Something would not let her tell him.

Maybe it was because she didn't know for sure whether she could trust him. Maybe it was just fear. Whatever the reason, though, he knew that no degree of pressure or persuasion would get it out of her now. He gave it up, for this night.

"If you need me," he said finally, "you can contact me through Dr. Murdock."

Then without questioning her further, he went to the door, opened it and went out. He could not swear to it, but he was fairly sure that he heard footsteps preceding him down the back stairs. As if someone had been listening at the door, had heard him coming, and had beat it.

He reached the sidewalk, looked around. No one was in sight.

A drumroll of thoughts beat at his brain. At least he knew now that beyond the shadow of a doubt the gold that seemed to command the attention of several people had something to do with Langhorne's murder. And he still had a canny intuition that, as little as anyone would believe it, Ben Trexel fitted into this jigsaw somewhere.

Maybe by now the jeweler had returned home. Or maybe his wife had heard from him. Always the Purple Scar followed his urging instincts. He did now.

Ducking into the first phone booth he could find he dialed Trexel's number. The same soft feminine voice he had heard before said "hello."

"Hello, Mrs. Trexel," he quickly replied. "Has Mr. Trexel returned home yet?"

Evidently she didn't recognize his voice for she said:

"No, he hasn't. Is this Mister Rossini?"

THE NAME smashed into the Scar's brain, shattering what else was in his mind as if it had been a bombshell. Of all the names he might have expected to hear that was the one which was furthest from his mind.

Quickly he assembled his scattered thoughts. Only a dullard would have neglected to take advantage of a lead like that.

"Yes—yes, this is Rossini," he said.

"Well, Mr. Trexel called early tonight from Bobbsville, Mr. Rossini," the voice on the wire said. "He left a message for you."

The Purple Scar listened intently to every word.

"He wants you to meet him at his lodge," Mrs. Trexel said. "He's waiting there for you. He said he left a message at your home, but also left it here, in case you called. You know where the lodge is, of course?"

The Purple Scar took a gamble. "In Bobbsville—"

"Yes. On Route Sixty-two."

She gave brief instructions just how to get there. Thanking her, the Scar hung up.

The Purple Scar left the phone booth with a brand new lead to chase down. So Trexel and Joe Rossini had something in common! That was interesting. Now it was up to the Purple Scar to find out what that "something" was.

He hopped a taxicab and shot across town to a small public garage that was open all night. Past experience had taught him the value of having a car he could make use of. This one, a roadster, was kept in the name of John Pryor.

Not three minutes after he paid off the driver of the cab that brought him to the garage he was in the roadster roaring toward Bobbsville.

Perhaps if he had not been so intent on where he was going, and on speculation as to what he would find when he got there, he might have spotted the darkened car that crept out of the shadows after he pulled out of the garage. It followed at a safe distance behind him.

It was past midnight when the Purple Scar braked his roadster to a halt in front of Ben Trexel's lodge on the edge of a lake some twenty-five miles from the city. A dark, desolate place.

As the Scar saw the upraised knife coming down at him he fell back—too late.

He snapped off the lights of the car, climbed out and, with the aid of his pocket flash, found his way along the dirt path to the door of the lodge. It was a two-story, cottage-like affair in absolute darkness.

He banged on the door with the heavy knocker that sounded like thunder in the stillness of the country. When there was no answer after repeated knockings he tried one of his keys in the door and went inside.

It was dark and dank, with the atmosphere of a place that not often was opened up. He swept his light around the big room, and it showed up a scene of disorder. The chairs, the table, made of rough unfinished wood, were overturned. Dishes and glassware on the floor, smashed. There was no question but that a terrific struggle had taken place here.

He walked to the center of the room and studied the mess on the floor. One small object caught his eye—a cigarette butt. He bent and picked it up. Though half-burned, it bore no mark to show that anyone had smoked it.

Placing it in his pocket he went to the stairs. He first shot his torch light up, then mounted the steps gingerly.

There were two rooms upstairs. Twin beds were in one of them. And one of the beds had apparently been slept in quite recently. Also, there was an empty Gladstone bag under the bed. The initials "BT" were stamped on it. But there was no sign of the missing jeweler. Strange!

THE PURPLE SCAR went downstairs and looked around the living room again. He spied a small door. It was locked. But he soon had it open. It led down into the cellar. He followed the beam of his flashlight down the rickety wooden stairs.

At the farthest end of the cellar, covered over with tarpaulin was a huge, weird-looking object. He hurried to it, uncovered it. It was a small smelter! A furnacelike contraption in which metals might be separated from the ores. Gold could be melted down in an apparatus like this.

It didn't take much imagination to figure out why Ben Trexel had this smelter hidden in the cellar of his lodge, twenty-five miles from the city. Trexel was mixed up in some kind of crooked business! Probably he—

But the Purple Scar never quite got the rest of his observations figured out in his mind. For at that moment he heard a crack behind him on the stairs.

Before he could turn, a man sprang at him off the staircase, knocking the flashlight out of his hand. So swift was the attack that he had no single chance to glimpse his attacker.

But in the dimness, he did see the faint outline of an upraised knife coming down at him. He tried to pull back—too late. The cold steel of the blade ripped into his left arm. He could feel the hot blood gushing out of the stinging wound.

Nevertheless he grabbed for the wrist that held the knife, clung tenaciously. The knife wielder tugged to break away. His hat flew off and sailed into the open smelter where it flared up an instant, then smoldered to nothing.

When this attempt to knife his antagonist failed, he lowered his hatless head and, goatlike, butted the Purple Scar fiercely in the pit of the stomach. The Scar had tried to block the attack with his injured arm—but to no avail.

The impact of the blow broke the Scar's hold, made him momentarily dizzy. He stumbled back against the wall to brace himself, his knees almost touching the floor.

When he straightened and his head cleared he was alone in the darkness. His attacker had gone.

From his back pocket, the Purple Scar took a clean handkerchief. He wrapped it just above the bleeding wound in his arm, applying it as a makeshift tourniquet. He realized that it incapacitated him, but he had an idea he would not need his arm for strenuous defense again this night. For he was equally assured that the man who had knifed him had fled.

Convinced, further, that he had seen all he could in this place and that Trexel definitely was not here, he staggered up the stairs and headed for his car.

He had a little difficulty driving back to the city, one-handed, but even so he was not quite through for the night.

The Purple Scar did not go directly home as perhaps he rightly should have done For his wounded arm was bothering him, even making him slightly weak. Firmly he determined that he would not go home until he had made another visit—a most important visit. A visit he would have made earlier had he been able to. A visit to Joe Rossini!

The Scar parked his car a block and a half from where the gambler lived in the suburbs. He walked the rest of the way.

ROSSINI'S HOME was truly something out of an architect's dream folio, although not much of it could be seen at night. A Lannon stone dwelling, it set back about several hundred feet off the roadway, on a high terrace. Trees and carefully trimmed hedges cluttered the grounds.

Vaulting over the roadside hedge, the Purple Scar approached the side of the house, cautiously. He took a moment to slip off the mask of John Pryor, baring the ghastly mutilated face of the Purple Scar!

The Pryor mask he stuffed into a secret compartment in his clothing. Then he clambered up onto the porch, found the double French doors open, and slipped noiselessly into the library.

He knew that Rossini had half-a-dozen men sleeping in and about the house and he didn't want to bring them down on his head. To avoid that he must be cautious in discovering which of the many rooms in the big house was Rossini's bedroom, get into it without disturbing anyone, and have a nice quiet little confab with the gambling thug.

Salted away in a shoulder holster beneath his coat was a .38 revolver. It was not for display, nor for intimidation purposes. It was for use, if necessary. Like the Northwest Mounted Police, the Purple Scar never liked to use a gun as a threat. But this was one occasion when using a gun for such an end was essential. Joe Rossini would understand no other language.

The Purple Scar crossed the deep-carpeted library floor and made for the massive hand-carved staircase that led upstairs from the hallway. He was passing the desk—when suddenly the lights came on, shocking him to his heels! He had underestimated the vigil of Rossini's faithful watch-dogs!

"Don't move!" a surly voice from the doorway barked.

But he was already moving. With one sweep of his right hand he grabbed up a heavy cut-glass inkwell from the desk. With the same motion he sent it sailing at the man in the arched doorway.

A shot cracked out and death in the form of a lead slug whined past the Scar's left ear.

He heard a dull, sickening *whock!* His aim with the inkwell had been much more accurate than the aim of the man who had sent the bullet. The inkwell had caught the gunman a glancing blow on the temple and dropped him in his tracks like a poled ox.

In one bound the Purple Scar was leaping over the prostrate figure stretched out in the doorway. But scarcely had he reached the hall when he heard Rossini's trigger men heavy-footing it down the stairs. One quick glance showed the gambler himself bringing up the rear.

CHAPTER IX

THE LONG COUNT

PHYSICALLY, JOE ROSSINI was not big. His bald pate, tufted here and there with fireman red hair, his protruding forehead, pancake nose and broad, jutting jaw seemed neither to harmonize with nor fit his ferocious reputation. He looked more like a burlesque comic.

Now he was wearing a tailor-made, bright-flowered bathrobe over equally gay pajamas. There were scuffs on his big feet.

The Purple Scar took all this in in a glance, then his eyes swept the hallway and spied a hatrack, filled with coats and hats. He ducked down behind it.

The mob thundered downstairs like a herd of buffalo. They saw their fallen henchman and surged into the library with drawn guns. The Scar knew at that moment that if he didn't get the upper hand on them, they would shoot first when they caught sight of him and ask questions over his corpse.

Rossini was left in the hallway, alone, for a moment. The Purple Scar was quick to grab this opportunity. With one long step he was behind the gambler and jammed the snoot of his revolver deep into the small of Rossini's back.

Rossini let out one yelp. His mob poured back into the hallway.

The Purple Scar was beginning to feel a little weak and nauseated from loss of blood. But he battled that with grim determination. He let the mobsters get a good look at his gun and they stopped as short as if they had run into a stone wall.

Rossini was sweating profusely. "Do somethin'!" he was pleading vainly with his men. "Do somethin'!"

"If they do," the Purple Scar warned in his left ear, "you'll have a hole in your right side big enough to put your fist through. Tell them to get rid of their guns. Throw them into that umbrella stand." He sank the gun deeper into the gambler's back.

Rossini had a squeezy feeling that this man who was jabbing the gun in his anatomy was not kidding. And he was in no spot to argue the matter further.

"Okay guys," he growled sullenly. "Get rid of your rods. We'll straighten things with this smart guy—whoever he is!"

"For your information, Joe—I'm the Purple Scar!"

The Scar could tell by the expressions that washed the hard faces before him just what the name of the Purple Scar meant to them. None too willingly they dropped their guns into the deep, tubular umbrella stand—but they dropped them.

"Now!" The Scar indicated a small coat closet in the hall. "The lot of you, in there!"

When they didn't move fast enough, he prodded Rossini with his gun.

"Go on!" Rossini ordered surlily. "Do what he says. But he won't get away with this—Purple Scar or no Purple Scar!"

Rossini was trying to put up a bold front before his men. It would never do to lose their respect. He was trying to show them that he was

The Purple Scar
sprinted for the river.

not intimidated by the Purple Scar. But—perspiration was rolling down his bull neck in rivulets.

ONE BY one the men, growling angrily, filed into the closet. The Purple Scar worked Rossini around toward it, slammed the door shut with his foot. He turned the key in the lock and pocketed it.

"And don't try to get out until your boss tells you to," he instructed through the panels. He nudged Rossini with the gun. "Now you get into the library."

Reluctantly, Rossini obeyed. They stepped over the unconscious gangster still sprawled in the doorway and went into the library. The Scar ordered Rossini to sit down in one of the big chairs.

"You ain't gonna get away with this!" Rossini repeated, in a growl so deep in his throat he sounded like an animal at bay.

"Sit down!" commanded the Scar.

Rossini sat. The Purple Scar was thankful for the chance to sit down, too, for he was growing weaker every moment. The tourniquet had helped, but the cut was deep and still bleeding, draining his strength.

"Now, start talking," he said peremptorily. "I'm interested in freeing a kid who's being held for murder of Buck Langhorne."

"So what's that gotta do with me?" Rossini rasped.

"Maybe you killed Langhorne yourself," said the Scar laconically. "I'd like to know."

"You're nuts!" snapped Rossini. "But I wouldn't be sorry if I had."

"Because he sold you a lame horse?"

Rossini's red brows clashed together. "I'm not talkin'." He clicked his teeth together with finality.

"Oh yes, you are," the Purple Scar said, lifting the gun a little. "Unless you want to spend the night picking lead out of your insides. You gave Langhorne a fifty-thousand-dollar check for a lame horse, and—"

Rossini's gaze riveted on the black eye of the gun. He swallowed.

"Okay," he mumbled. "So he stuck me with a lame horse."

"And you were sore."

"Yeah. I was sore."

"Now tell me about the gold?"

"Gold?" Rossini merely shrugged.

"The gold your two gorillas were shaking down Davis and Peggy Pan for. Fifty thousand dollars' worth. The same amount as that check. You stole that gold!"

The Purple Scar did not believe that. But he thought he might be able to trick Rossini into talking.

Rossini bit—hook, line and sinker.

"You're nuts!" he ground out again. "I'm lookin' for that gold myself. It belongs to me!"

"You mean Langhorne got it from you?" the Scar pressed.

"Naw," snapped Rossini. "I mean he promised it to me. I told him if he didn't want trouble, he'd cough me back my fifty G's—and take back his spavined-legged nag. He said he didn't have that much dough, but he offered to give me the gold. He said it was worth more than fifty grand if I wanted to hold onto it a while."

"There's a Federal law against hoarding gold, you know," observed the Purple Scar.

"There's laws against lots of things," Rossini scoffed. "But you can get around 'em. Same as you can get rid of hot gold if you try hard enough."

"How were you going to get rid of it?"

"Look, Mac—I ain't no canary."

"You'll be a dead pigeon if you don't answer my questions."

THE NOSE of the gun was on a level with Rossini's heart. The sweat was still pouring off the red-headed gambler and into his eyes. He wiped it away with the sleeve of his bright robe.

"You were going to get rid of the gold through Ben Trexel, weren't you?" the Purple Scar went on inexorably—only probing, but a doctor was accustomed to hunting for the sore spot that would make a man wince.

Rossini's red beetle-brows came together with a frown at the mention of Trexel's name.

"How did you find out I had anything to do with Trexel?" he demanded.

"Never mind that. Answer my question!"

Rossini eyed the gun. Licked his dry lips. He decided to answer.

"Trexel," he said, "was buyin' stolen gold; gold stolen from different mines. According to law, only the registered owner of a mine can sell new gold and the mint can trace in a minute what mine, or what locality the gold came from. There's been lots of this gold stolen all over the country and it was hard to sell. Trexel bought it cheap, and resold it to other crooked jewelers to be made into jewelry."

"After he melted it down in the smelter he had in his lodge in Bobbsville," the Purple Scar supplemented.

That almost popped Rossini's eyes.

"How the devil did you find out about that smelter?"

Again the Scar didn't answer. Instead he asked:

"What was your connection with Trexel?"

"He was a friend of mine."

"Why did he want to see you tonight at his lodge?"

"Who said he wanted to see me?"

"You were there, weren't you?"

Rossini frowned darkly, gave no answer.

"Weren't you?" the Scar hammered.

"So what if I was?" came the surly, reluctant admission.

"Where is Trexel now?"

"How should I know?" Rossini's thick shoulders lifted. "He told me to meet him at the lodge, but when I got there he wasn't any place around."

"That's your story?" The Scar leaned forward, his livid face brightening, the burning eyes compelling.

"Yeah, that's my story! I couldn't even get inside the place."

"So you waited until I got in, followed me, and knifed me."

"You're nuts!" That seemed to be Rossini's favorite accusation. "I never saw you before in my life."

The Scar stared back at him, unwaveringly. Maybe the man was telling the truth. Maybe he wasn't.

"You still haven't told me what Trexel wanted of you."

The gun was still there, backing up each question. Rossini ran the sleeve of his gown across his sweaty face again.

"He wanted to see me about the gold," he said slowly. "He said he knew where it was now that Buck got his."

"Wasn't Trexel being just a little too concerned about your interests?" insinuated the Scar.

"Why shouldn't he look out for me? I've done plenty of favors for him."

"Was it he who originally put the bug in your ear that Langhorne had the gold?"

ROSSINI'S EXPRESSION answered that one in the affirmative.

"Now how did Langhorne get hold of the gold?" the Scar hurried with his next question.

"How should I know?"

"You know all right. You wouldn't take a chance and accept fifty-thousand-dollars' worth of gold unless you knew where it came from."

Rossini reflected a moment, again licked his parched lips. And again decided that in this case frankness was the better part of valor.

"Okay," he said. "Trexel gave me the story. The gold came from a small mine up in the motherlode country. Two kids owned it—a girl and her husband. The mine was left to them. There was a lot of trouble about who the real owner of the mine was, so until it could be settled, no gold from the mine could be sold. A corkscrew named Flarity—"

The Scar held up a hand to stop him. He showed Rossini the photos of the dead man.

"Is this Flarity?"

Rossini craned. "Yeah. That's the corkscrew. Where is he?"

"Never mind that. What about Flarity?"

"He's a crooked geologist. He got wind of this small mine and that it had a lot of good stuff in it. He got Langhorne to back a trip out there. Then he got a job working in this mine, analyzing gold or something—and swiped over fifty grand worth of nuggets and dust. He brought it to Langhorne for the split. He said that it had been found out that he was stealing the gold and he couldn't go back there.

"Everything would've worked out swell—only Langhorne got wind that Flarity had held out on him. Flarity had gone and peddled about two grand worth of the gold on the Q-T. So Langhorne grabbed the gold and wouldn't give Flarity enough to buy peanuts. Flarity was in a stew. He couldn't go to the cops because he was up to his ears in the mess.

"And that's all I know about it. What happened to Flarity? I can't find out nohow. Maybe he's got the gold. Maybe Davis got it. Or maybe the dame got it. All I know is that I ain't got it—and I want it because it belongs to me!"

"The gold belongs to the two kids who own the mine," the Purple Scar contradicted tonelessly. "But we won't argue that point now. Right now you're going to stand up!"

As he spoke the Purple Scar arose. That sickish, sinking sensation came back to him again. His knees started to buckle and he thought surely he would go down.

With the gun in one hand, the other useless, he was in a bad way to support himself. But he finally managed to brace himself by placing his legs firmly against the side of the chair. He could not for a moment allow Rossini even to suspect his weakened condition. For Rossini would be quick as a cobra to take advantage of the situation.

"Come on, move!" barked the Scar. "Out of that chair!"

Rossini took his own sweet time getting up. His face was so red it was almost a match for his hair. He was not accustomed to taking orders and he didn't like, one bit, the grilling he had just undergone.

The Purple Scar thought of something. It didn't seem pertinent at the moment. But the Scar never overlooked his hunches and he had his reasons for asking what he did now.

"What brand of cigarette do you smoke?"

"Me smoke cigarettes?" Rossini snorted indignantly. "Who said I smoke them things? I smoke cigars. A man's smoke."

"Okay," the Scar said, and abruptly instructed: "Now turn around and face the wall."

ROSSINI OPENED his mouth to protest, but clamped it shut again at sight of the revolver. He turned his face to the wall.

"Now start counting good and loud," said the Scar.

"Now wait a minute!" Rossini dragged out more time that meant so much to the Purple Scar, in protest.

"I said count!" barked the Scar. "And keep on counting so I can hear you. Or I'll come back and finish what I should do right now!"

Rossini with his face to the wall, made a lot of ugly, angry grimaces and mumbled undertoned curses. But nevertheless he began to count:

"One—two—three—"

The Purple Scar backed slowly, unsteadily, toward the open French doors.

"Four—five—six—"

And the Purple Scar was gone, out through the doors to be swallowed up in the darkness.

CHAPTER X

RAT-MADE TRAP

WHEN DOC MURDOCK arrived home, the first thing he did was pour himself a liberal drink of whisky. He got it down in a gulp. It braced him considerably.

Then, in his laboratory, he examined the deep gash in his arm under the powerful microscope. He was looking for one thing with great care—and was rewarded.

There in the open wound, mixed with the congealed blood, were several glittering telltale specks, invisible to the naked eye but pronounced under the strong lens. Particles of gold dust! Doc was sure he must have been slashed with the same knife that had killed Buck Langhorne. A knife with gold dust on it.

Doc also made another discovery. Adhering to his clothing, held by his dry blood were several black hairs! They must have come from the murderer's head when he butted Doc in the dark cellar of Trexel's lodge.

When he studied them under the microscope he found something else. These hairs were dead, rootless! And where there should have been roots were spots of dried glue. Wig glue!

Whoever it was he had struggled with in Trexel's lodge must have worn a wig of some sort. A wig! In Doc's eyes dawned a horrible realization.

Peggy Pan was a male impersonator, wasn't she? And she wore a black wig as part of her makeup. Could it be possible that after all, she was the guilty person?

As Doc removed the makeshift tourniquet from his arm and cauterized and dressed the wound, he checked back to that session with the knifer in the darkness. He had been butted while he had been holding his assailant's wrist. He had tried to block the head-smash with his injured left arm.

If he had been holding the knifer's right wrist, it would have been impossible for him to hit with his head, because of the position of his right arm. Crossed in front of him, it would have automatically blocked the butt. Therefore Doc must have been holding the knifer's left wrist. Which meant that the person he was after now was left-handed!

That gave him three things to look for. A left-handed person, someone who wore a wig, and a long-bladed knife that in some way or other had been in direct contact with gold dust. Now in the possession of his own unknown assailant at Trexel's.

The ringing of the phone bell disturbed his musings.

When he answered he heard a woman's voice that was little more than a whisper.

"Dr. Murdock?"

He replied in the affirmative.

There was breathless agitation in the voice of the caller. Her words rushed at him, spilling over each other in her haste.

"This is Peggy Pan. That man, that detective—"

"John Pryor, you mean?" asked Doc.

"Yes. He told me to contact him through you if I needed his help. Can you get a message to him, please?"

"Yes. But what—"

"I just received a phone call from Ben Trexel, the jeweler."

"Are you sure it was Ben Trexel?" Doc tried to keep the sudden excitement out of his voice.

"He said he was," Peggy said breathlessly. "He wants me to come to him. It's about the missing gold. He says he can tell me what's happened to it. I'm afraid to go alone. Will you ask Mr. Pryor if he'll please go with me?"

"I'll have him meet you at Main and Walnut Streets in about fifteen minutes," Doc said promptly. "Bring your car."

THERE WAS a wealth of relief in her "Thank you." She thanked him, too, for his own interest, and for keeping his word to Jimmy and her about helping them....

Peggy Pan was waiting in her shiny, black coupé at Main and Walnut when "John Pryor" arrived. He got into the car and asked:

"Where to?"

"Seven hundred and eight Pearl Street."

"Nice section of town," he commented ironically. "Certainly not the sort of a neighborhood in which you'd expect to find a man like Ben Trexel."

"That's what I thought," Peggy agreed as she maneuvered the car away from the curb.

She drove in silence. The Scar, known to her as John Pryor said nothing, either. But he watched her intently. Her pretty face was tight and set; the tiny muscles in her jaw rigid. Her eyes were focused straight ahead through the windshield. Her fingers with their red lacquer tips trembled slightly as they gripped the steering wheel.

Pearl Street separated the gas works from the river. It was a dirty, crooked little street that ran for about half a dozen blocks ending up in a coal yard.

Seven hundred and eight proved to be a five-story, dirt-streaked building, one in a row of four that housed unpleasantness of more than one variety. To the rear of the houses ran the river; cold, black, clammy.

The windows of these houses were in total darkness. There was no sound, except for the occasional blast of a boat whistle. The place seemed asleep, entirely deserted. Frankly, the Purple Scar did not blame Peggy Pan for not wanting to visit this place alone.

As she pulled the car to a halt alongside the curb, and looked up at the gloomy buildings, she touched his arms, trembling.

"I'm scared stiff," she whispered in a quavering voice.

He covered her hand with his own big comforting one, reassuringly.

"You stay in the car until I have a look around," he told her.

"I'd be terror-stricken sitting here alone," the girl quickly objected.

The Purple Scar's broad, blondish John Pryor face lighted with a warm, understanding smile.

"Okay," he gave in. "Keep driving around and come back here in a couple of minutes. Then if everything looks all right, you can go in with me. What was the floor?"

"Fourth floor. Rear door."

She threw into gear and the car rolled away. He turned and went into the hallway. It was as black as a tub of tar. Fumbling in the darkness a moment, he found the bannister and started to climb the carpetless wooden stairs, slowly. The place was all but falling apart with decay, and as musty as a fisherman's cellar.

He was puffing a little when he reached the fourth floor landing, for the stairs were steep. He paused a moment, dipped his hand inside his coat and withdrew his revolver. Then he continued along the dark, narrow corridor.

WHEN HE reached the rear door he paused, listened. There was no sound inside. He tapped lightly on the door with the tips of his fingers, a slight sound that was distinct in the stillness. He rapped again, a trifle harder; still no reply.

He turned the knob then, and the door opened under his touch. Something queer was tightening in his chest as he slipped inside.

The room was even darker than the hall. He felt along the wall for the light switch, found it and clicked it on. Light poured from the single bulb that was suspended from the ceiling's center on a long black cord.

He stopped dead still, staring, his heart battering his ribs. Peggy Pan's phone caller had told her the truth. Ben Trexel was here—and so was death!

Trexel's body lay on the bare wood floor, directly under the unshaded light. The floor was stained with the blood that had seeped from his throat, which had been cut clean from ear to ear!

The shock of seeing the jeweler like this passed quickly. The Purple Scar went forward and knelt beside the body. Trexel had not been dead long, for the body was still warm.

Apparently he must have been held prisoner in this place before he had been killed. For his wrists were raw—red with rope burns and skin was off his face with the tape that must have been stuck across his mouth for a gag.

As the Purple Scar knelt there, the door suddenly burst open behind him! He twisted around quickly.

Three uniformed policemen filled the doorway. He recognized the seriousness of his plight instantly, just as it was flashed to him that this had been a carefully laid trap. The killer had attempted to lure Peggy Pan here, then pin the murder on her by calling the cops who would be certain they had caught her in the act.

Or—could she herself have arranged all this because the man she knew as John Pryor was getting too close to the solution to Langhorne's murder and the mystery of the gold, and she wanted him out of the way?

At any rate, he had walked right into the setup.

Two of the cops came into the room with revolvers drawn. The third bluecoat remained in the open doorway.

The Purple Scar's mind was a swirl of thoughts. If he were arrested, sooner or later they would penetrate his disguise and it would come out that he was not only the Purple Scar—but also Dr. Miles Murdock!

Not only that, but there was every reason to believe that this murder would be pinned on him. The absence of the murder weapon would not strengthen his case a hoot. Such a thing had not helped Jimmy Morgan.

His eyes studied the three hard faces looking down at him. These men, he decided, could not be reasoned with. Trying to talk to them would be like batting his head against concrete.

He started to get up slowly, almost brushing the suspended light bulb with his head.

One of the cops made an unwise move then.

As he grabbed for the Purple Scar's arm, the Scar drew back, clipped him on the jaw with a short right hook that didn't travel more than six inches, and with the same continuous motion struck the swinging light bulb with his fist, as if it were a punching bag.

The bulb exploded with a pop!

The Purple Scar dropped to the floor beside the corpse. The cops would not risk shooting in the dark for fear of hitting one another. But they started to call out, telling each other where they were.

In that way, the Scar knew that one of the uniformed men was still in the doorway. As he crept closer, he could see the silhouetted outline filling the black frame.

Then one of the bluecoats fumbled his flashlight from his pocket. But he was too late. Before he could snap on the beam, the Scar lunged at the man in the doorway. He hit his midriff with a powerful shoulder.

He heard the bluecoat grunt and saw the black figure stagger backward and slump to the floor with the wind knocked out of him. The Purple Scar leaped past into the hallway.

Down the stairs, two at a time, he raced. He had reached the third floor landing when he heard voices on the stairs below. More police!

He turned to go back. But the police above him had already started down. He spun on his heel and raced the length of the dark third floor corridor.

The rear door was locked. But he struck it twice with his shoulder and almost tore it from its rusted hinges.

Fortunately the room into which he plunged was vacant. He raced to the window. The drain-pipe that ran from the roof to the ground was rusted and rotted, but he could only trust it would hold his weight.

Out across the window-ledge he scrambled, reached the drain-pipe and started down. He heard the police burst into the room he had just left just as his feet touched the ground.

He heard them yelling as he sprinted toward the high fence that separated the yards from the river. If he could make the river, he would be safe!

Pistols barked and sharp brilliant flashes showed at the window through which he had climbed. Bullets whined close to his ear, pelted into the wooden fence as he scaled it.

A couple of policemen were coming down the drain-pipe by which he had made his escape. They reached the fence as he reached the edge of the water. The Purple Scar dived, with a splash, under the waves.

The police, guns coughing, smoking, stood on the shore playing their flashlights over the black water. But the man they were after did not reappear.

They waited for several minutes, then cautiously climbed back over the fence.

"Guess we must've got him," one of them called up to the others at the window.

"Yeah," agreed another. "No human being could keep under water that long and live."

BUT THESE men in blue did not realize that the man they had been chasing was the Purple Scar. Many before them had wondered, many more would wonder whether the Purple Scar was human, or whether he was endowed with a cat's number of lives and could not be killed.

In reality what the Purple Scar had done was simple. Instead of swimming away from shore, he swam back to it. Huddling close to it, he kept his head below water, except for brief intervals when it became necessary to replenish his supply of air.

When he was sure the police were gone, he swam a safe distance away and climbed out of the water.

There was no sense in looking for Peggy Pan now. Even if this cute trap, from which he had miraculously escaped, had not been of her making, then surely the fleet of police cars piled up in front of the gray-faced buildings would have scared her away.

CHAPTER XI

—A BONER, A HANK OF HAIR—

BY THE time Doc Murdock reached home, he had a lot of things figured out. Not only about Buck Langhorne's murder, but about the missing gold.

It was not guesswork on his part, either. At least, most of it was not. He had arrived at these solutions in his own methodical way. There were a few loose ends still to be gathered together and a couple more things to be proven. But for the most part, Doc Murdock was nearing the climax of one of the most baffling mysteries he had yet tackled.

After removing the two masks from his face, he changed into dry clothes and sat down to make his plans. Then he called Captain Griffin.

It was well past four o'clock in the morning. But he wanted to finish this case before something else happened. And things were bound to happen, unless this business was cleared up tonight! The murderer was getting bolder all the time.

"Griff," Doc said to his friend, "I want you to round up several people for me. I don't care how you accomplish it, but I want them in Langhorne's office at the Playhouse in about half an hour. Now don't argue until I explain—"

And he went on to tell Griffin his plan in detail.

Griffin listened without interruption until Doc concluded. Then he yawned into the phone and said:

"Okay. I'll have 'em there. Who are they?"

"Peggy Pan. Dan Davis. Karl Kirkland. Joe Rossini. And bring Jimmy Morgan along, too."

"You're certainly giving me a sweet job," grumbled Griffin. "You know that, don't you?"

"Yes," Doc admitted. "But I think the results will be worth it."

"I hope so," Griffin remarked as Doc hung up....

Captain Dan Griffin was a man of his word. Within half an hour after he grunted "Good-by" to Doc over the wire, the Homicide detective captain had the desired five people herded together in Buck Langhorne's office at the night-club.

Only Joe Rossini had put up a squawk. He had ranted and raved about it being the second disagreeable thing that had happened to him that night. And he had made a lot of threats about "getting Griffin's badge." But that was old stuff to the Homicide officer and didn't stop him from dragging the big shot gambler to the club.

Outside, in the club, now emptied of help and customers, the detective-captain had stationed several uniformed policemen with instructions that no one be allowed to leave, until he gave the word.

The back alley was left unguarded. That was the way, Dan Griffin knew, the Purple Scar would make his entrance.

Even now through the long shadows of the alley the grim figure was moving silently, pantherlike, toward the office door with the purple, elastic mask fitted over his face.

He banged his fist against the panel of the door. There was a shuffle of feet inside. The catch was thrown and light shone on him as the door was opened.

Six strained, startled faces stared into that horrible face. Peggy Pan let out a sharp scream, and Jimmy Morgan slipped an arm around her to quiet her.

Then everybody began chattering at once. Rossini, for one, demanded to know what the Purple Scar had to do with this party. Also he began shooting off his mouth about "his rights."

GRIFFIN FINALLY got him and the others quieted. Then he turned the floor over to the Purple Scar.

The Purple Scar lost no time getting down to brass tacks. He informed the five suspects why they were here. One of them was the murderer, he said, of Buck Langhorne, and had stolen the fifty thousand dollars in gold that was missing.

There was plenty of indignation expressed. Each of the five vigorously denied being guilty.

"In that case," said the Scar, "I'm sure each of you will be willing to cooperate with us to prove your innocence. We have several clues to investigate. First, we'd like to compare signatures. So I'm going to ask you to sign your name to a piece of paper."

Again Rossini was the only one to put up an argument. But when it was pointed out that if he didn't write, he would automatically be considered the murderer, and at least detained, under arrest, he quickly consented.

Griffin passed out slips of paper and saw that each of the five had pencil or pen with which to write. Actually it was not a specimen of handwriting that the Purple Scar wanted. This was simply an attempt to discover which of the five was left-handed.

But the killer amongst them was shrewd. Not one of them wrote with the left hand.

Then from his coat pocket the Purple Scar withdrew, a man's crumpled felt hat. He pressed it out neatly.

"This hat," he announced, "was found in the cellar of Ben Trexel's lodge. It was dropped by the killer after I had a run-in with him. There's a blood stain on the brim of the hat. Blood from my arm."

That was not true, either. The hat was a discarded one of Doc Murdock's. In fact the attacker had lost his hat, it had been burned up. Therefore, the Purple Scar knew that the murderer would have no qualms about trying the hat on.

"I'd like each of you to try on this hat for head size," he said. He handed the hat to Rossini. "You try it on first!"

Rossini made a sour face. He kept right in character by putting up a squawk.

"I told you I wasn't inside the lodge! How could I have dropped any hat?"

"And if you did drop this one, I suppose you'd admit it?" the Scar snapped at him curtly. "Try it on!"

"Aw!"

Rossini snatched the hat out of the Purple Scar's extended hand and, without looking inside it, slapped it on his head.

It was at least a couple of sizes too small, sat on top of his big bald head like Hooligan's tin can. Disgustedly, he threw the battered hat back at the Scar.

"Satisfied?" he snapped.

The Purple Scar made no answer. He turned to Karl Kirkland who sat alongside the desk, his cigarette holder stuck in his mouth at an ironic angle.

"Mr. Kirkland, do you mind trying it on next?"

The debonair lawyer placed his cigarette holder on the desk, took the hat and put it on. It was quite a bit too large for him, settled down on his small-sized head almost to his ears. He smiled serenely.

"I guess it's not mine, either," he observed placidly.

But when he started to take the hat off a startling, and for him an embarrassing, thing happened. Not only did the hat come off, but tiny, almost invisible wires that were like fishhooks and had been attached inside the top of the hat-band, entangled in the lawyer's black hair. And off came his toupee! His head was left a shiny ball almost as naked as Joe Rossini's.

This was precisely as the Scar had anticipated, had planned for. The wires were so cleverly hidden in the top of the hat-band that it was necessary to put the hat on to know they were even there. The Purple Scar had purposely selected Rossini first, because Rossini's head was far too large to fit inside the hat. He would not even know they were there.

The Purple Scar also had taken that brief moment of confusion to snatch up the cigarette holder which Kirkland had laid on the desk.

He took out the cigarette and examined it.

"Your murderer, Captain," he announced to Griffin. "Karl Kirkland—Langhorne's trusted attorney."

"You're insane!" Kirkland denied, wild-eyed, still trying to unsnarl his toupee from the fish-hooks. "Why should I kill Buck Langhorne?"

"For the fifty thousand dollars' worth of gold stored in his safe," the Purple Scar whipped back.

"So!" Joe Rossini stormed, starting toward the lawyer. "He's the guy who swiped my gold!"

The Scar blocked his way.

"Wait a minute, Rossini. I told you before that the gold doesn't belong to you."

"No," Peggy broke in shrilly. "It's our gold! Jimmy's and mine."

The Purple Scar looked at the girl and smiled wisely. He had waited a long time for her to admit that. For since Joe Rossini had first told him that the gold had originally been stolen from a small mine owned by a young married couple, the Scar had suspected that Peggy and Jimmy Morgan were that couple.

Besides, Jimmy's out-of-place outdoor complexion did not altogether become a night-spot waiter.

Because the Scar had believed that had been one of the principal reasons he had requested the presence of Peggy and Jimmy here at this quiz session. He had hoped that when the lid was finally pried off they would admit the truth, and perhaps add a word or two to seal the killer's fate. Peggy did all the Purple Scar had hoped she would now.

"We knew the gold was stolen from our mine but couldn't prove it," she went on hurriedly. "The mine ownership hadn't been cleared and didn't yet belong to us. Therefore the gold couldn't be legally sold by us.

"Jimmy knew that if the gold was sold by anyone else it would be eventually traced back to our mine. We'd have a mighty slim chance proving that we didn't have some hand in the sale of the gold. So we traced the gold through Flarity to Langhorne. We thought maybe we could get the gold back ourselves. So we came here to Akelton.

"Being a performer before I married Jimmy, it was easy for me to get a job with Langhorne. I played up to him and he fell for me. I figured in that way I might be able to find out what he'd done with the gold. Finally, one day, it slipped out that he had the gold in the safe. I contacted Jimmy and had him get a job in the club as a waiter. We were waiting for our chance to get at the gold—when Langhorne was killed."

ROSSINI LEAPED to his feet angrily.

"Are you trying to tell me that he had the gold in his safe all the time?" he shouted.

"Yes," Peggy enlightened. "He told you he had to get it from some place only to stall you off, hoping that something would turn up so he wouldn't have to give it to you."

"How come Flarity didn't recognize you or your husband since he worked at your mine?" the Purple Scar wanted to know.

"He worked there only a short while, and at the time Jimmy and I were away. The mine was in charge of the foreman. It was he who suspected that Flarity was stealing the gold—but before he could prove anything Flarity got away. We might have told the police about the gold, if Jimmy hadn't been unfortunate enough to be caught at the safe and with Langhorne's body.

"We were afraid to tell them then, because that would give Jimmy an even sounder reason for killing Langhorne. He'd never have been able to prove his innocence. Another thing, we found out that Flarity had held out some of the gold on Langhorne and sold it. That meant that sooner or later the government would find out about it and trace it back to our mine. Which would leave us right in the middle of the whole mess."

"Quite interesting," Kirkland cut in irritably, finally having untangled his toupee from the wire hooks. "But what I'd like to know is—how does all this implicate me?"

The Purple Scar squared around and faced the lawyer, who with his toupee in place again, looked like his debonair self.

"Chances are that Flarity, when Langhorne refused to split the gold with him, came to you," the Scar said, "told you about the gold in the safe, and offered to split with you if you'd help him get it. Being Langhorne's lawyer made it easy for you to get the combination to his safe. You and Flarity must have been robbing the safe when Langhorne barged in and caught you in the act. The only thing you could do then—was kill him."

Dan Davis, quiet all this time, but seething with rage, suddenly erupted.

"And he's the one who's been trying to pin the murder on me!" he shrieked.

CHAPTER XII

MURDER PARTY CLIMAX

CAPTAIN GRIFFIN could see Dan Davis' muscles stiffening, his hands knotting until they were tight across the knuckles. Sidling to the club owner, the detective-captain laid a restraining hand on his shoulder. "Take it easy, Davis," he whispered. "He'll get what's coming to him without your help."

The Purple Scar was going on, as if there had been no interruption.

"You killed Flarity, Kirkland," he accused, "because you didn't want to split the gold with him, and because you were probably afraid that a man of his type would be likely to blackmail you later on. You hacked up his body with the hope that it couldn't be identified and in that way eliminate all possibility of it dove-tailing back to the gold.

"Another thing, Flarity was under suspicion for having the gold. If by any chance, Jimmy Morgan squirmed out of the noose, it would be well to have everyone believe that Flarity was still at large. People might think he had the gold—and erase all possibility of anyone suspecting you.

"It's quite obvious that you next went to Ben Trexel, tried to get him to fence the gold as he was going to do for Langhorne. Trexel either didn't want to get mixed up in a murder, or he figured he owed it to Joe Rossini to tip him off that you had the stolen gold. Maybe he even threatened to turn you in. At any rate, it was dangerous for you to let him go around with the knowledge that you had a hand in the Langhorne killing. So since you couldn't use him anyway—you killed him!"

Rossini's mouth looked mean.

"The bum!" he exploded, and tried to push forward toward Kirkland. "Lemme at him!"

But again the Purple Scar interceded. After a lot of ugly faces and "barking dog" remarks, the gambler finally took a back seat. The Scar resumed his remarks to Kirkland:

"You killed Trexel and tried to pin the murder on Peggy Pan. Because you probably figured out, as I did, that she and Jimmy were the mine owners. And you knew that sooner or later it would be discovered that they were. But I mussed up your plans when I went to the tenement on Pearl Street tonight and walked into the trap you had set for Peggy Pan."

"Theories!" Attorney Kirkland thundered. "You haven't proven a thing! You've nothing on me. Just because I happen to wear a toupee, just because I chanced to be Langhome's attorney doesn't mean I'm his murderer—or Flarity's murderer—or Trexel's murderer!"

"You won't deny that you were at Trexel's lodge tonight, shortly after he called Rossini and told him that he wanted to see him about the stolen gold!" the Scar said sternly. "That you struggled with Trexel, overpowered him and brought him back to the city!"

"I'll deny everything you've said!" Kirkland snapped back.

The irate attorney was so convincing in his argument that even Captain Griffin had to admit that the Purple Scar had to do some mighty fast thinking to out-fox him. But the Purple Scar had known from the start that he was dealing with a shrewd article. And he didn't expect for a minute that Kirkland was going to come right out and confess. Even dullwitted murderers seldom do that.

The Scar had his next move mapped out accordingly.

Shielding what he was doing from the others with his broad back, the Scar picked up an ornate brass paperweight from the desk. He walked about five or six steps across the room, waited until a moment when Kirkland was completely off guard, then whirled, threw the weight at the lawyer. "Catch it, Kirkland!" he yelled.

Kirkland looked up with a start, saw the weight coming at his head. Instinctively he threw up his hand to shield his face and at the same time caught the paper weight—in his left hand!

"Explain that, Mr. Kirkland!" the purple Scar exclaimed quickly. "Both you and the man with whom I fought in the cellar of Trexel's lodge are left-handed!"

AT ANY other time, when his wits were less frenzied, when all these accusing eyes were not staring at him, Karl Kirkland might have thought up an excuse. But as it was, and as the Purple Scar had anticipated, Kirkland's only thought was that he was trapped—discovered! That he must escape!

From his coat pocket, with his left hand, he drew a clasp knife, an ornate affair with a pearl handle. His grin was twisted as he touched a spring and a fat, dangerous-looking blade shot out.

Then he did a desperate thing. He grabbed the nearest person to him, who happened to be Peggy Pan. Using her as a shield, with the point of the knife at the base of her slim neck, he growled: "Don't any one of you make a move or I'll drive this blade through this girl's brain!"

It was as good as if the lawyer had signed his own confession!

Slowly he worked the terrified girl toward the back door. There was an evil expression on his thin face. All his suavity, his evidences of culture had left him.

Jimmy, fever-eyed, made a move toward him. Davis and Rossini would have liked to get their hands on him, too.

The Purple Scar caught Jimmy Morgan's arm and pulled him back.

"But do something!" Jimmy cried in desperation. "He'll get away—he'll kill her!"

"He won't get far," the Purple Scar said calmly. "Not with the alley filled with cops."

Kirkland's eyes slitted, distrustfully.

"I don't believe you!" he snarled.

The Purple Scar shrugged mildly. "Open the door and see for yourself."

The lawyer was near enough to the door to reach the knob. This he did with his right hand, keeping the blade of the knife close against the back of the girl's golden head. But in so doing it was necessary for him to twist his head the fraction of an inch.

That was enough of an advantage for the Purple Scar. With one quick leap he was across the room, his right fist cutting an arc through the air and smashing with devastating force against Kirkland's jaw.

Kirkland tottered back into the wall, straightened, and tried to slash at the Scar with the murderous blade. But the purple-masked detective was too quick for him. He was all over the attorney in a flash. He wrenched away the knife and sent him spinning into Captain Griffin's waiting arms.

"THERE ARE several things I still don't savvy," Griffin said as he and the Purple Scar rode back toward the plastic surgeon's Swank Street residence in a taxicab. "How did you know it was Kirkland?"

"Several reasons," said the Scar, glad that he could soon resume his rightful identity of Doc Murdock. "First of all, he was the only one of the suspects with black hair. And since he was vain to an almost exaggerated degree, there was the chance that he might wear a toupee. Next, I recalled that in the club office last night, he used his left hand several times—to show Davis and me Langhorne's marriage certificate, and to take his cigarette holder from his pocket.

"Then there was the cigarette I found at the lodge. He and Peggy Pan, of all the suspects, were the only ones who smoked cigarettes. Davis didn't smoke at all. Rossini smoked nothing but cigars. And Jimmy, whether he smoked or not, was eliminated because he was in jail when Trexel was killed. Not only that, but the cigarette I found was the same brand that Kirkland uses."

"But a few million people smoke those cigarettes," objected the Homicide captain. "Maybe Peggy Pan smokes them."

"If Peggy had smoked the one I found there would have been lipstick on it. This cigarette hadn't even been in anyone's mouth. Instead it had a peculiar indented ring around it, where it had been inserted in a holder. And I don't think it escaped you that Kirkland uses one of those. While that didn't actually convict Kirkland it did throw plenty of suspicion his way."

"Okay. Now what about Rossini? Where did he fit in?"

"Rossini and his stooges were interested in only one thing—the gold. He had nothing to do with Kirkland, and Kirkland wanted no part of him." Briefly the Scar explained about the gambler's associations with the jeweler.

"And Davis?" asked Griffin.

"Davis was apparently sincere in his belief that Jimmy Morgan murdered Langhorne. Davis and his partner hadn't been on the friendliest of terms lately, so naturally he knew nothing about the gold or the racehorse deal. He just happened to be the unfortunate pawn who got mixed up in this crazy swirl of events."

Captain Griffin shook his head.

There was still much he did not understand.

"If you knew or suspected all the time that it was Kirkland," he said, "why did you want Rossini, Davis, Peggy Pan and Morgan brought to the club?"

"Because Kirkland knew that each of them was implicated," the Purple Scar explained. "It was not so much a trap to catch them, as it was one to snare Kirkland. If the hat trick, the writing gag and the paper-weight business had been pulled on Kirkland alone, he might have objected, or been too cautious for us. But with the others present he had confidence enough to believe that he could hold his own. He couldn't very well have refused to try the same experiments in front of the others. Another thing, it's nice to have a lot of witnesses when it comes trial time."

"What about the gold in Langhorne's wound? How did it get there?" asked Griffin.

"The gold was in dust and nuggets that Langhorne kept in bags in his safe. Chances are that when the safe was opened Kirkland, to make sure that Langhorne hadn't out-foxed them and put dummy bags in there, cut one of the bags open to see. Gold dust particles are minute, clingy. Some stuck on the knife and came off a little bit at a time."

They were at the front door of Doc Murdock's home now. Doc climbed out of the car.

Griffin stuck his square face out through the open window and he offered his hand. As Doc Murdock shook it, Griffin declared: "Well, Doc, you sure did another swell job—and earned a nice, long quiet rest."

Doc smiled. Because somehow he didn't think it was going to work out that way.

IV

THE CHAIN
OF MURDERS

CHAPTER I

WHAT MAKES STEVE RUN?

STEVE MULLENS was running. Odd. No one could remember Steve Mullens running before.

Thick-bodied with short, bowed legs, Steve Mullens had always been a study in slow motion. But he was now picking his way through the crowd like a broken-field runner.

Hatless, his face contorted into an agonized expression, he tried to coax more and more speed into his short legs.

His breath was bunched in his throat as if he dared not spare the time to let it out. His watery eyes screamed fear.

Dr. Miles Murdock's clinic was on the ground floor of a white-faced building that was pinched between two, tall, grimy gray tenements. It stood out like a beacon in the surrounding gloom of these slums.

Inside the office, behind a polished, flat-top white desk sat Dale Jordan. Tall, gracefully slender, with long copper-tinted brown hair, Dale, even in her stiffly starched nurse's uniform with its uncompromising lines, was someone around whom to weave a dream.

At least, Doc centered his dreams around her. For besides being his chief of staff, Dale wore his blue-white diamond on the third finger of her left hand.

Dale heard the heavy hob-nailed shoes of the running man beat upon the stone steps that led to the door. The next instant the door swung open. Steve Mullens burst inside.

The pretty nurse, looking up from behind the desk, was about to remind him that the clinic closed at five, and that it was quarter after now. But one glimpse at the mask of terror which was the man's face, and she was on her feet, her brows drawn together in an anxious frown.

"What's the trouble, Mr. Mullens?" she asked him quickly.

Steve Mullens swallowed convulsively.

"Ida! My wife, Ida!"

Dale saw the solid block of flesh before her tremble and start to sway. She hurried forward and laid her hand on his stout arm to help support him.

"What's happened to your wife?"

STEVE MULLENS shook his head like a man in a daze. His words tumbled out of his mouth, rough-edged with emotion.

"I—I don't know. When I came home from work just a little while ago, I found Ida doubled up on the floor—holding her stomach—groaning. I tried to pick her up, but she screamed like I was killing her. I tried to find out what was the matter with her, but she was out of her head. Couldn't answer me—just groaned. First thing I thought of was Doc Murdock. So I came, fast. He's gotta help me!"

A door at the far side of the office swung open. Dr. Miles Murdock emerged, his head tilted slightly, inquiringly. It was an exceedingly well-shaped head that would have interested any sculptor. A head

As Doc ducked into the store a burly man was brandishing a cleaver in Charlie's frightened face.

crowned with wavy black hair and crowded with burning genius that looked out of his jet eyes.

Exactly six feet tall, Doc had shoulders that needed no padding under the snug white doctor's coat he wore. His profile could have earned him a screen test for the asking.

The moment Steve Mullens saw the doctor, he hurled forward. His hands clutched frantically, desperately, like a drowning man, at Doc's wide shoulders. His lips moved again, pouring out unintelligible words.

Dale made them understandable. Doc whipped several pertinent questions at Steve Mullens, who answered them to the best of his ability.

Doc faced Dale again.

"Call for an ambulance. Tell them to meet us at Steve's place—and make sure they bring a stomach pump."

Even as he spoke, Doc was out of his white jacket and getting into his suit coat. Then, snatching his black surgical kit off the desk, he shot out the door.

The moment the phone call was completed, Dale grabbed her belted tan coat off the rack and, with Steve Mullens, chased after Doc.

Doc was half-a-block ahead of them by the time they reached the corner. With a skill that would have outshone Tommy Harmon, Doc was weaving in and out through the crowd, his black bag tucked under his powerful right arm.

He was racing like some small town country doctor answering his first call, instead of being the great plastic surgeon he was. A surgeon whose patients included pillars of society, greats of the stage and screen, luminaries of the sports world.

But the unfortunates of these slums were his people. Here, in the very heart of the slums, he had served his internship with the City Hospital. Here he had gained at first hand the experience that was to make him the most brilliant young plastic surgeon of his time. Here, too, he had learned how desperately these poor folk needed medical assistance that a crowded city hospital could not begin to supply.

When success came to him and moved him over to the more prosperous part of the city he did not go with an eye to personal profit or to satisfy ambition. He went to earn money, that he might give the poor the benefit of his services, the medicaments and necessities that they could not buy.

So he charged the rich exorbitant fees, which they would never miss. And, with this money, he had built his free clinic on Swank Street in the midst of the tenement district.

DOC HAD reached the dirty, gray-streaked building in which Steve Mullens lived. It was like all the rest in the neighborhood, reeking with filth, inside and out.

Doc went up the short brown-stone stoop in two bounds. Dale and Steve Mullens were now a block behind him.

Pushing open the door, Doc charged into the dark, dank hallway. A conglomeration of smells greeted him. Cooking food. Lingering mustiness. Filth.

He grabbed hold of the rickety bannister and, still hugging his black bag, raced up the thin-carpeted stairs. One—two dirty landings he clicked off.

On the ill-lighted third floor landing, people were gathered before an open door, mumbling. Poorly clad people, men and women. Doc started through the group.

"One side!" he thundered. "Let me through!"

Someone recognized him. "It's Dr. Murdock!"

Instantly they cleared a passage for him. He went into the rooms. They stretched out in railroad fashion and were crudely furnished with mismated tables and chairs that had probably been picked up in some second-hand store.

There were more people inside, chattering inanely. He pushed through to the kitchen. There he saw Mrs. Mullens. She was doubled up on the linoleum-covered floor.

Her knees were almost touching her chin and she was moaning in agony.

Doc swept aside those clustered around her. He bent forward and made a hasty examination. The woman had been poisoned!

Doc turned at the sound of a woman's voice clearing the morbid curious from the rooms. It was Dale.

They got Mrs. Mullens to the crude brass bed in the next room, where Dale and Doc gave first aid to the woman. While they were working the wail of the ambulance siren came from the street. Then the screech of brakes as it careened to a stop in front of the door.

Doc left Dale with the now-quieted woman, and went back into the kitchen. There was a tall black pot on the stove. It was warm, although someone had turned out the gas beneath it.

Docs' gaze roved the room, fixed on a tablespoon on the floor. He picked it up. It was moist. He smelled it, returned to the stove. Lifting the lid off the black pot, he dipped out a spoonful of the stew. He made a grimace as he sniffed it.

Taking a fork from the table drawer, he stabbed the stew meat and brought it out of the pot. He examined the dripping meat with the eye of a critic. Then over his right eye there appeared the impression of a black spade. Not actually a spade, of course. Just an illusion created by certain lines and shadows. The resuit of a cleat wound at college. It appeared only when rage gripped him, and then spelt danger for someone!

Doc returned to the bedroom as the intern and the ambulance driver came in with the stomach pump.

The intern greeted Dr. Murdock, asked what was the matter.

"Sodium cyanide poisoning," Doc told him. "She must have sampled the stew she was preparing. The meat in it's overloaded with cyanide. Lucky she didn't eat any of the meat. One good bite—" he broke off.

THE INTERN'S face twisted into an incredulous mask.

"Odd!" he exclaimed. "We just came from a place over on Wallace Street—party named Forbes—Big Jake Forbes, they call him. His wife just died from eating poisoned meat. D.O.A. Might easily have been sodium cyanide."

Doc knew "Big Jake" Forbes. He was one of the slum toughs.

The plastic surgeon's face set in stony lines. His eyes narrowed, musingly. *Were* these two poisonings coincidence?

Doc left Dale Jordan and the intern to pump the poison out of Mrs. Mullens' system. It was just routine work.

He went back into the kitchen. Steve Mullens was there. His face a take-off for death, his eye dull and lifeless, he stared at the plastic surgeon as he came into the room.

"Will—will she live, Doc?" Mullens muttered, fearfully.

Doc nodded. "She'll be as well as ever in a couple of days," he assured.

Steve Mullens clasped Doc's hand in his stubby-fingered paws, in an outburst of emotion. There were unrestrained tears in his eyes.

"I won't forget this, Doc! You saved my wife's life."

"Where did your wife buy the meat that's in the stew?" Doc asked.

Mullens shrugged. Then a thin voice came from the other side of the room.

"I bought it for Mama," Steve's ten-year-old son Jimmy said. "It came from Charlie the Butcher's."

CHAPTER II

POISON STEER

C HARLIE THE Butcher's shop was on Down and Doffet Streets. Doc knew trouble was waiting there before he had gone half a block. A crowd milled on the sidewalk in front of the store, grumbling, shouting, waving their arms in the air.

Doc Murdock kept on going. He shoved and elbowed his way through the stormy aggregation, gained the door. There stood a big man in rough work-clothes with a sawed-off bat in his fist.

Doc ducked past him into the store. Another burly guy had Charlie the Butcher pinned back against the wall, behind the tall chopping block. He was brandishing a cleaver in Charlie's sweaty, frightened face. The man was Jake Forbes.

Doc didn't stop to try to do any reasoning with the man whose wife had just died from eating poisoned meat. He didn't believe Jake Forbes would be in a state of mind to do any listening. Right now Jake would understand only one language.

Around the chopping block, Doc swept and hurled himself at Jake. He caught the wrist of the hand that gripped the cleaver, spun Big Jake around.

Jake's face was vicious.

"Lemme go!" he spat out of the ugly slash that was his mouth. "He killed my wife! Sold her poisoned meat!"

"I didn't!" Charlie the Butcher screamed in contradiction. "I didn't sell nobody poisoned meat!"

His bloated face was almost entirely drained of color. There was blood on his white apron from the meat he sold, but in another moment his own blood might have been there also.

Jake made a desparate attempt to wrench his arm from the plastic surgeon's viselike grip.

"Lemme go—or I'll kill you, too! This ain't none of your business! Keep out of it!"

But Doc didn't scare.

Jake took his left hand from Charlie's flabby throat, balled it, and threw it at Doc's head. Doc bobbed to one side and played his fingers along Jake's stout right wrist.

Doc knew the exact location of even the tiniest nerves and muscles. The most sensitive of these he found in Jake's wrist. The next moment, Jake's knees banged against the floor. He let out a wail, the cleaver dropped out of his hand and bounced in the sawdust that covered the floor.

The big man on guard at the door stalked forward like a redskin, the bat in his upraised hand like a tomahawk. Doc twisted, and in one swift motion snatched up the cleaver and aimed it at the threatener's head.

"If you don't want to be guest of honor at a scalping party, you'll pick up those size tens of yours and carry them out the door," Doc barked.

The man with the bat hesitated. He looked down at Jake, still groveling on the floor, then at the poised cleaver in the plastic surgeon's hand. Evidently the prospects of a "scalp treatment" did not appeal to him. Because he turned promptly and took Doc's advice.

Doc allowed Jake to scramble to his feet. Brushing the sawdust from his clothes, Jake scowled blackly at Doc. His eyes traveled to the cleaver.

"Sorry we had to get tough with each other, Forbes," Doc said. "But I've got an idea you'll thank me when your head clears. Now I'd get home, if I were you. I'll attend to this. I'm just as anxious to clear up this poisoned meat business as you are."

FROM THE distance came the wail of a police siren.

Jake stiffened. It was plain by his expression that he knew this would not be a healthy spot in which to be caught. He turned, glowered at Charlie, then mumbling something deep in his throat, he hurried out the door.

Charlie let out a sigh of relief and his pudgy hand mopped sweat from his fat, chalky face.

"Thanks, Doc," he said. "That's one life I owe you. Even if I don't know what it's all about. He runs in here like he's crazy, grabs a cleaver, backs me against the wall—and starts sayin' I sold poisoned meat to his wife."

"You did sell poisoned meat." Doc told him the story quickly, then asked, "Where's the side of beef you cut if off?"

Charlie thought a moment, then led Doc into the ice-box. There, hanging from one of the meat-hooks, they found a half-carved side of beef. It had the government stamp on it, okayed by an authorized inspector.

Doc examined it carefully.

"This entire side of beef is loaded with sodium cyanide," he finally said.

Charlie's face was almost stupid in its blank amazement.

"Sodium cyanide?" he exploded. "What—"

"You sell any of this meat to anyone except Mrs. Forbes and the Mullens family?"

Charlie blubbered out frightened words.

"Yes. To a few people."

He racked through his mind and rattled off three names and addresses.

"You're sure that's all?"

"Positive." Charlie perspired.

The door opened and two policemen burst inside.

"What's goin' on here?" one of them demanded hoarsely. He recognized Doc Murdock and his voice changed. "Hello, Doc. What's cookin'? Just got a call to shoot over here—somethin' about somebody being murdered."

"More than one person *will* be murdered—three entire families— unless you two get back into your car and move fast!" Doc snapped.

He explained briefly. Then Charlie repeated the names and addresses of the three who had purchased the poisoned beef.

Out the door the cops tore, into the prowl car and sped away on their errand. Doc turned back to Charlie.

"Where did you get the meat?" he demanded.

"From the Landon Meat Company. Fresh in this afternoon. Driver delivered it. Put it in the refrigerator himself."

"Anyone else go in there?"

"Nobody but me."

"Okay. Hold that meat aside. The police'll be in for it later."

Without further comment, Doc left the butcher shop. In a drug-store on the corner, he used the telephone.

"Griff," he said into it when he got his number, "things are happening down here. Things you ought to be in on. Heard about Mrs. Forbes, didn't you?"

Detective-Captain Dan Griffin on the other end of the wire said that he had heard. But it had been reported as just another routine poisoning. And people were always dying of something or other in the crowded slums.

HE PERKED up with sudden alarm as Doc filled in the "blank spaces," told what he had learned about the poisoned meat. Dan Griffin knew that Doc was not a man to get unduly excited. Not only that, but Griffin had a profound respect for Doc Murdock's judgment. Mainly because the detective-captain was one of the few people alive who knew that behind his sleek outer covering of plastic surgery, Doc Murdock was actually the Purple Scar! A phantom-like figure born in blood and dedicated to the proposition that lawlessness must not pay.

Cowardly gangsters had murdered Miles Murdock's brother, a member of the city's police force. Then, mutilating his face with a powerful acid, they had dumped his body into the river. Two days later the bloated, purplish corpse had come to the surface.

Miles Murdock had stood in the morgue alongside his friend, Captain Griffin, and had viewed the acid-destroyed face of his brother, turned a ghastly purple by its days in the water. From this he had conceived the nemesis of evil known as the Purple Scar! A name to be reckoned with whenever and wherever men broke the law.

From police photographs taken of the horribly scarred face, Miles Murdock had made a grim mask of purple-dyed gum elastic. This mask he wore over his handsome features when such protection was needed, or when he wished it known that the Purple Scar was at work on a case.

Having attained as near perfection as was humanly possible in his chosen field of plastic surgery, Doc Murdock had climbed to similar heights in his career of fighting crime. A daily workout in the big gym atop his Swank Street quarters kept him fit for this arduous task, and he had not neglected the practical part of his self-chosen profession for his laboratories were second only to those of the F.B.I. in Washington. And his knowledge of plastic surgery and the human anatomy made him an expert in the art of disguise.

In every way he was fitted to cope with the intricacies of crime in all its phases, and with the assuredness of an eventual solution.

But whether this case of the poisoned beef was work for the Purple Scar, Doc Murdock did not know. He had a strange feeling, however, that there was something far more sinister behind it than the accidental killing of a few innocent slum people, and would not pass the matter up until he had satisfied himself.

"I'm on my way to the Landon plant," Doc concluded to Captain Griffin over the wire. "Thought maybe you'd like to come along.... Oke. I'll pick you up in fifteen minutes."

The Landon Meat Products Company was located on Water and Front Streets, overlooking the river. Including its vast stockyards, it took in several square blocks, with a private dock and railroad siding. The plant closed for business at six o'clock, but there was still quite a bit of activity going on around the place when Captain Griffin and Dr. Murdock drove up in the doctor's underslung black sedan.

Dan Griffin, seated beside the plastic surgeon on the front seat of the car, was captain of detectives of Akelton's police. Some called him the "square detective." And he was square, inside and out. His face was square with a straight-across, graying hairline that met flat temples which formed another square. A square nose was above a generous mouth and square chin and jaw. His eyes, snapping black agates, alone broke up the square motif. But it was picked up again by his powerful, square shoulders and body.

FROM THE man at the gate of the Landon meat company Doc and the detective-captain learned that Roger Landon, head of the firm, was still in his office. A flash of Griffin's badge and they were passed through.

The lowing of cows, the grunting of hogs and the bleating of sheep came from the pens that lined each side of the narrow, crooked streets along which they drove. There were sections and "wards," and each held it own kind of animals, with each variety making its varying kind of vocal complaints.

Finally they came to the immense red-brick building at the extreme end of the yard, close to the river. This was the slaughter-house and meat-packing establishment in which the beeves, hogs and sheep were turned into food and other commodities and shipped all over the country.

On the second floor of the building, outside Roger Landon's private office, sat his secretary, flanked by typewriter, dictograph, filing cabinets and telephones. As Griffin and Doc approached, the plastic surgeon took cool stock of the girl.

In a gray business suit, horn-rimmed glasses, and with her naturally blond hair pulled back into a tight bun and wearing a minimum of lipstick and powder, she was making a firm attempt to create the impression of a young business woman.

But she did not fool Doc Murdock. Doc's business was faces. Behind that austere primness she was assuming, he saw real beauty. Her features as well as her figure approached perfection in their symmetry.

"Business woman by day," was Doc's silent summation. "I wonder what by night?"

Doc said aloud: "We'd like to see Mr. Landon."

"Mr. Landon is—"

"Yeah, we know, Blondie," Griffin cut in as he glanced at the door behind her, tight-shut. "We know he's in conference. But he'll see us!"

The girl flushed indignantly, then quickly paled as Griffin flashed his badge again. Doc thought he detected a hint of fear creep into her eyes, behind those horn-rimmed glasses, as she clicked on the key of the inter-office communicator.

"Two gentlemen to see you, Mr. Landon. One of them is a police officer."

"Detective-Captain Griffin, tell him," supplied the square detective.

The girl echoed that into the communicator.

There was an unintelligible cackling in the box. Then the girl looked up with smiling blandness.

"Mr. Landon says to come right in."

As they turned and went through the door marked "Private," Doc could feel the girl's eyes following them, never leaving them until they were inside.

Roger Landon's private office was large and neatly furnished. There was a wide desk at the far side before three tall windows. Landon sat behind the desk majestically, a hatchet-faced man of about sixty-five with a shock of white hair and colorless cheeks. He was a distinguished looking man, but his eyes were his outstanding feature—eyes quick, sharp, and expressive.

LANDON WAS not alone. Alongside the desk, in a brown leather chair, sat a big-boned, dark-complexioned man who wore his smart clothes with an air.

"You wished to see me?" asked the meat packer. Apparently he sought to make his voice cordial, but there was a distinguishable challenge in it.

Griffin nodded, and came directly to the point.

"You sell meat to a butcher in the city named Charlie Schmidt, don't you?"

Landon straightened with a jerk.

"My shipping department takes care of such matters," he said, his tone annoyed and short. "See them!"

"What we gotta say'll interest you more than them," Griffin shot back caustically. "The meat you sold Schmidt today was poisoned!"

Landon's white brows pulled together with an incredulous frown. "Poisoned?" he snapped angrily, and the man beside him made an odd guttural sound in his throat.

"Yes," Griffin snapped. It always did him good to slap a man off his high horse. "One woman's already died from eating it. And a few more just ducked the morgue by the skin of their teeth."

Landon leaped to his feet.

"I don't believe it!" he flared, his eyes blazing. "It's a lie! Another trick! You're in with him!" He waved his white-knuckled fist toward the door. "Get out! Get out of my office before I—"

He did not finish, for the door was burst open with a bang. The blond who had been parked at the desk outside hurtled into the office. Her face was flushed, her eyes terrified.

"Mr. Landon—look out the window!" she cried frantically. "A riot in the yard! Men with sticks and clubs!"

CHAPTER III

RIOT

ROGER LANDON whirled to the big, triple windows behind him, peered out, scowling. Doc Murdock, Captain Griffin and the other man in the office who had not been introduced were instantly at his side.

A mob was surging into the yard, sweeping tumultuously toward the main building. A thick, black mass moving forward like a seething swarm of giant black ants, voices raised in shouts, and threats that, mingled with the moaning and groaning of the penned animals, made awesome sounds.

The guards and the workers in the yard tried to stop the onward rush of enraged men, but their efforts were wasted. They were overwhelmed and carried along bodily with the mob.

"The slum people!" exclaimed Doc Murdock.

"Slum people?" Landon whirled around to face the plastic surgeon, tiny beads of perspiration on his high forehead. "What do they want?"

"I just told you," Griffin growled. "Your meat killed one of their people. Made a lot more of them sick. They're not taking that lying down—they're not dumb."

"They must have traced the meat here, as we did," said Doc.

"Well, right or wrong," snapped Griffin, "this is a job for the riot squad." He spun to the phone. But before he could lift the receiver, Doc clapped a hand over the instrument.

"That's only going to spill a lot of blood," he argued earnestly. "Can't you see, Griff? These people are half-crazed. Caught up in mob hysteria. Seventy-five per cent of them don't know what they're doing. After all, it was one of their friends, one of their number who was killed. And others have seen their loved ones suffering from the poisoned meat that came from this place. Wait—"

The rioters coming on with a rush had reached the front of the building. Their crazed faces were turned up to the lighted windows. Then someone threw a well-aimed rock. It smashed through the center one of the three windows with a resounding crash.

Landon leaped back into the middle of the room. His face was white, etched with fear. Then there came the sound of running footsteps from the outer office and a man dashed through the doorway, a man of about forty, tall and with sturdy shoulders. His sparse brown hair was tousled, one sleeve of his expensive suit was ripped almost completely off, and the left side of his white face was smeared with blood.

"Uncle Roger!" he shouted. "That mob—they're going to lynch you! Something about poisoned meat! I tried to stop them at the gate—tried to reason with them—but they wouldn't listen. If one of the guards hadn't rescued me—"

Landon whirled to Griffin angrily.

"Police officer, are you?" he snarled. "Then why aren't you doing something?"

"Keep your shirt on!" Griffin fired back at him. His hand went for the phone, again. Then his glance went to the door. "Doc! Doc! Come back here! You're crazy! They'll tear you apart!"

But Doc Murdock already was out of the office, running through the reception room and out into the hallway. He went down the steps two at a time. The big, front double-doors were locked and barricaded by a handful of guards. Rocks and clubs were banging against them. The menacing roar of the mob filtered through.

THE GUARD who seemed to be in charge spun around as Doc Murdock approached on the run. His sweaty face was a mask of fear.

"I don't know how much longer these doors'll hold," he shouted.

"Open them up!" Doc said quietly.

The guard faced him belligerently, with a look of incredulity.

"Open them up?" he gulped. "And have that wild pack murder us?"

"Open them up!" Doc repeated, more sharply.

The guard hesitated a moment. He could not see Doc's face well in the semi-darkness, but he could tell by the sound of his voice that here was a man used to giving orders—and having them obeyed. Muttering, he unbolted the doors and threw them open.

There was the mob, surging, snarling, waving arms and fists and clubs savagely. Doc took a couple of steps forward and, standing on the top of the three steps, looked out into the faces of the mob. Angrily distorted faces, yet faces that he knew. And in the very front rank, leading the pack, was Steve Mullens.

Mullens took one look at Doc and halted in his tracks.

"Doc—Doc Murdock!" he shouted, as if the plastic surgeon were an apparition that had suddenly materialized.

Then other men in the blood-thirsty ranks recognized the man who treated them and their families in his slum clinic. To those too far back, drifted his name.

"Listen to me, all of you!" The surgeon's voice rang out as sharp as the crack of a pistol, in the sudden silence that held the mob tense. "You're making a mistake!"

Steve Mullens found his tongue. "I wouldn't get mixed up in this, if I were you, Doc," he growled surlily. "This ain't none of your fight." Doc stared down at him. "It is my fight. I'm your friend. You're going to do things here that you'll regret. Things you'll have to pay for, dearly."

"That's for us to worry about," a man farther back in the mob shouted.

"Yeah!" came the growled chorus, and "That's right!"

"Better get out of the way, Doc," Mullens said, "so you won't get hurt."

The mob started to mutter again, and to move forward slowly, dangerously.

Doc stood his ground in the open doorway, defiantly. His keen eyes bored into Steve Mullens, whom he singled out as a ringleader.

"Less than an hour ago, Steve," he said, "you vowed you'd never forget that I saved your wife. And now you're going to trample over me. Okay, come ahead. But I've an idea I'll remember it the next time you come running into my clinic for help."

Mullens shrank back into the crowd.

"That goes for the rest of you," Doc said coldly, as his eyes swept the angry mob. "Trouble and sickness has a way of cropping up, pretty often. What will you do if you find the doors of my clinic closed to you? And the city hospital too crowded to help you and your families?" His eyes swept the mob accusingly, then he shook his head. "Believe me, I want to help you," he said earnestly. "I'm here now trying to help you. I'm trying to find out about the poisoned meat. I want to get to the bottom of this business as much as you do. His lips tightened grimly. "And you can believe me that whoever is responsible will pay. I promise you that. But he'll pay the right way."

AND THAT did it. The angry mutterings died down, and men broke ranks, though there were a few in the crowd, men like Big Jake Forbes, who were not impressed. But for the most part the mob just wasn't a mob anymore. Fear for themselves and for those dear to them had made them individuals again, small, frightened people who scattered and hurried out of the yard, their angry passions curbed for the time being and without the mob at their backs, Jake Forbes and the remaining few belligerents were easily chased by the guards.

Doc had not known it, but Captain Griffin had been standing directly behind him all the time he was haranguing the mob. Doc was first aware of it when the captain laid his block-fingered hand on his shoulder and sighed gustily.

"What a fool trick *that* was—even if it did work," he growled. "Good thing I can afford to lose weight, 'cause I lost plenty just then. You're a lucky guy to be alive."

Doc smiled wryly.

"Suppose we get back upstairs and see what our friends have to say now?" he suggested.

Roger Landon was standing in the middle of the private office, wiping sweat from his face as Doc and Griffin came back into the office. His blond secretary, back at her desk, had flashed Doc a smile as he went past.

Still in the office with the meat packer was the big-boned man who had been with him on the arrival of the police officer and Doc Murdock, as well as the chap who had come running into the office with his clothes torn and his face bleeding.

Doc took a look at the fellow's cut face. The blood made it look a lot worse than it actually was. It was little more than a superficial scratch.

"I caught a part of what you said to that mob down there," Landon said to Doc. "Why didn't you tell me you were Dr. Murdock? I—I guess I was pretty rude."

Doc shrugged his wide shoulders.

"I guess you had reason to be," he said. "Apparently something was bothering you considerably before that mob broke loose."

Landon nodded soberly. "How right you are!"

Then the meat packer introduced the other two men in the room with him. The big foreign-looking man was Donato Cabral.

"My South American buyer," Landon informed.

Doc remembered then what the newspapers had reported about Landon taking advantage of the recent act by the government which cut in half the import duties on competitive agricultural products produced in the Argentine for shipment and sale in the United States. One editorial had lambasted it as a "foul and fatal blow" to the American farmer. And the Western ranchers who raised beef, and with whom Landon had been dealing, far from approved of his buying Argentine beef.

Doc wondered if this poisoned meat business was going to dovetail into this disapproval. For it was not long before Landon admitted that Cabral had just brought a shipment of cattle from the Argentine, and was here now to make arrangements with Landon for another shipment.

The other man in the office was Walter Faber.

"My nephew," Landon explained, "and superintendent of the company."

EVEN THOUGH Faber seemed affable enough, one look at the man gave Doc the impression that he evidently was not much of a superintendent. More than likely his job was just "one of those things" passed out to relatives.

Maybe it was just his appearance that failed to impress. His pince-nez, with the black ribbon, his foppish clothes which seemed almost too tight for comfort, the three or four fountain pens stuck in his vest pocket gave him an air that distinctly was not businesslike.

Again Landon apologized for his rudeness and gave a brief explanation.

"I've been upset lately. Everything going wrong—shortages, dissension among the workers, business falling off."

Doc, in fact, had heard rumors to that effect. For years the Landon Company had been one of the leaders in the meat-packing industry. But recently something had happened to the firm, and it had fallen far behind its competitors.

"Have you any idea what's behind this set-up?" Griffin asked. "Who might've poisoned the meat?"

In Landon's eyes was a sudden flare of anger.

"Yes," he shouted. "Sam Ziggley and his crowd, that's who!"

"Uncle Roger!" Faber began to protest, but was silenced by his uncle's glare.

"Who is this Ziggley?" Griffin inquired.

Roger Landon seemed more than willing to explain; anxious, to be more exact. Apparently, with the recent happenings, he had reached the boiling point, and his accusations came with a rush.

Sam Ziggley, he told Griffin, was a rival meat packer with a plant up the river in Chesterfield.

"Nobody in the business has ever had much use for him," Landon said bitterly. "He's no good. Uses unethical means to sell inferior products."

As he spoke, Doc was quickly remembering that not so long ago Sam Ziggley had been mixed up in the "meat pumping" racket. He had been accused of selling "watered" meat, that is meat filled with salt water, in order to give it increased weight. Water pumped deep into the tissues of the meat with a hypodermic syringe gave the cut a full juicy appearance, but of course evaporates when cooked.

These charges against Ziggley never had been proved, however. But the mere rumor had not helped Ziggley's reputation as an honest businessman.

Griffin was interested in Landon's accusation of his business rival.

"Why should Ziggley want to bother you?" he asked.

"He wants to expand," Landon said readily enough. "Until recently he's been content with a local business, but now he wants to branch out nationally. He wants to use our name on his inferior product. Figures he can buy something that has taken us years to build for a few paltry dollars. Sam Ziggley was right here in this office with an offer to buy. But, believe me, he got his answer—quick! And ever since then we've had nothing but trouble. But if he thinks he can intimidate me into selling, he's got another guess coming! I'll never sell the Landon Meat Products Company—to him or anyone else!"

WALTER FABER'S eyes flickered. He caught Doc Murdock's eyes and shook his head slowly, as if to say that he did not agree with his uncle, but was hardly in a position to argue.

On the other hand, Donato Cabral was in perfect accord with Landon's denouncement of Sam Ziggley.

"Meester Landon ees right," the big South American said in his deep voice with the heavy Spanish accent. The voice went well with his velvet-black hair and flashing teeth. "Even back home een the Argentine thees Ziggley he has baad reputation. He makes contracts weeth many ranchers down there. They ship cattle to heem. Then after the cattle arrive, he cuts the price. Thees ees in legal litigation now. The Argentine ranchers, they do not like trouble. They like to be good neighbors—like our government ask. But they want their money, and they weel fight thees Ziggley for eet. He ees one bad actor."

Cabral appeared to be "wound up" for the rest of the day. So Doc interrupted and got back to the poisoned meat. Again he asked Landon what was his theory about it.

"I can't see how it could have happened," the meat packer said.

"Nor I," Faber was quick to supplement. "Our meats are inspected and reinspected by government inspectors and our own men, before they're loaded onto the trucks for delivery."

"Would the inspector who examined the meat that was delivered to Charlie Schmidt still be on duty?" Doc inquired.

"We can easily find out," Faber said. "I'll call the loading platform."

Doc suggested going there instead.

Faber shrugged. "If you wish."

The scratch on the superintendent's face had dried now. He had cleaned off the blood and patched his torn sleeve as well as possible, and was more like his spick-and-span self when Doc and Griffin followed him from the office. Cabral and Landon did not offer to accompany them.

Passing the blond in the reception room, the plastic surgeon's keen eyes caught the open key on the inter-office communicator which stood atop her desk. She had been listening to every word spoken inside the office.

"A most dutiful secretary—or a most inquisitive one," Doc thought.

CHAPTER IV

DEATH ON ICE

IN A cubicle-like, one-windowed shack at the extreme end of the loading platform at the rear of the warehouse, Jim Stone, the government inspector assigned to the plant, looked up as Faber approached with Doc and Captain Griffin.

Stone, a medium-sized man with a bald head, was wearing a butcher's soiled coat. He readily answered the questions asked him.

"I've been on duty for the past eight hours," he said. "And I've examined every chunk of meat that left this warehouse. I'll stake my job that no poisoned meat passed me."

Doc pointed out that the small quantity of sodium cyanide required to poison an entire side of beef would be extremely difficult to detect. Jim Stone nodded his bald head.

"I know, Doc," he admitted. "But no matter how small a portion was used, it couldn't get past me. Not after the tests that are given."

"Maybe the meat was poisoned *after* it reached Schmidt's butcher shop?" Faber suggested.

"That's hardly probable," Doc pointed out. "Charlie Schmidt has been selling meat to the slum people for a long time. He's only small fry—doesn't do enough business to warrant anyone wanting to do such a thing to him. And, from what your uncle told us about the firm, it's more logical that the meat was poisoned as part of a scare campaign to keep people from buying your meats and products."

Faber laughed a little wryly. "You don't want to take what Uncle Roger said too seriously," he said, apologetically. "He's had a persecution complex ever since business began to fall off. He imagines everyone is trying to ruin him."

"Then you don't think Ziggley could be responsible for these things?" Griffin cut in.

Faber grinned broadly. "Sam Ziggley just happens to be Uncle Roger's pet peeve. Ziggley used to work here in the plant. Held a rather responsible job. But he was a little too ambitious to work for anyone. He wanted his own plant, and to be his own boss. So he quit here and started his own firm. And became our rival. Uncle Roger never forgave him. For which you can't altogether blame him. But, frankly, my uncle has no one to blame for what's happened to business—except himself."

"Meaning?" Doc asked.

"He could easily be tops again. But he refuses to listen to suggestions from anyone. He won't advertise. Still believes in the old bunk that a good thing needs no ballyhooing. 'If a product is any good it will sell on its merits.' That's Uncle Roger's slogan. And that bit of philosophy is one of the main things wrong with the business!"

"What about the shortages your uncle mentioned?" Doc questioned.

Faber frowned. "That's something else again. We are losing a tremendous amount of our goods. But where it's going, how these things manage to slip out, is something we can't seem to account for. Certainly nothing could be taken out during the day, because they couldn't get past our platform checkers. And at night every gate is heavily guarded. Yet these losses run into hundreds of dollars a week."

"How about the river? The warehouse is close alongside it."

"Yes. But to get from the warehouse to the wharf, it is necessary to lower a sort of drawbridge. At night this bridge is drawn—and enough racket would be made in lowering it to attract the attention of anyone in the yard."

"One more question, Mr. Faber," Doc put in. "What's your opinion about this poisoned meat?"

Faber shrugged. "I *can't* explain it. I can't *believe* it!"

"Well, I can assure you the meat was definitely poisoned," Doc said. "I examined it."

"Oh, I'm not questioning you, Doctor," Faber said quickly. "I meant it seems so improbable that anyone would want to do such a terrible thing."

"Well, since the meat couldn't have been poisoned when it left the loading platform and wasn't poisoned after it reached, Charlie Schmidt's, then it must have been poisoned en route," Doc declared.

"Which would leave it up to the driver who delivered the meat, since he'd be the only person who would have access to it," Faber said.

GRIFFIN, WHO had been listening attentively all this while, turned to the timekeeper.

"Is the driver who delivers to Charlie Schmidt around?" he asked.

He was not, a checkup revealed. But his name was Sandy Phail and the time sheet showed that he had signed in from his route at four-fifty-five that afternoon.

"But it's funny," the time keeper said, poking his head out through the door of the shack. "He didn't leave his keys. They ain't on the rack. All the drivers leave 'em there."

"You see him when he checked in?" Griffin wanted to know.

The timekeeper nodded. "But he must've left right after that, because I didn't see him again." He glanced sideward at Faber. "Gets kinda busy here at that time of day."

"Do you know where to get in touch with him?" asked Griffin.

"We keep a list of the drivers' names and phone numbers written right here on the wall in case we need 'em." He pointed a scrawny finger to a list of names and numbers scribbled on the plaster-board wall of the shack.

"Call him and tell him to get back here right away," Griffin instructed. "We'll wait for him."

The timekeeper looked at Faber inquiringly. Faber told him to call.

Someone was driving in under the tin roof of the loading platform. A 1930 Ford sedan badly in need of a paint job. Behind the windshield sat a thin-faced, middle aged man. He brought the car to a shivering halt, slapped open the door and jumped out. As he climbed up onto the loading platform and hurried forward, Doc got a better look at him.

He was fairly tall, with a sharp face that was seamed and leathery. Just now his black, lusterless eyes were wide with excitement.

"What's going on here, anyway?" he demanded. He spoke with a slight wheeze and hesitated after every few words to take a breath, as if he might be suffering from asthma.

"I heard there was a riot down here," he hurried on. "Something about poisoned meat, and—"

"Who're you?" Griffin whipped at him.

The man drew himself up indignantly. But before he could say anything, Faber introduced him.

"This is Mr. Coyne, Carl Coyne. Our plant manager. Mr. Coyne's been associated with Uncle Roger for the past twenty-five years or more."

Coyne's black eyes narrowed. "I'll speak for myself!" he snapped.

Doc saw in the look that passed between the two men that showed neither held any great love for the other.

Once more Griffin showed his badge then gave Coyne a thumbnail sketch of what had transpired. It was the same old story all over again.

"Impossible for the meat to have been poisoned before leaving the loading platform," Coyne stated positively.

"Where were you while all this riotin' and other stuff's been goin' on?" Griffin wanted to know.

"I was home," Coyne said shortly. "I'm on the job every morning at five, so I leave every afternoon about three-thirty. I've got to sleep sometime!"

THE TIMEKEEPER'S white-thatched dome was poked out of the shack.

"Sandy Phail ain't got home yet, accordin' to his missus," he informed.

"Keep calling till you get him," Griffin snapped back, then turned to Faber. "We'll have a look at Phail's truck while we're waiting."

"Mr. Coyne will show you," Faber replied. "That's his department."

Which seemed to remind Coyne of something. He reached into his inside pocket and brought forth a sheet of paper on which something had been typed.

"This is a release you're supposed to sign," he said to Faber, then went on to explain to Doc and Griffin: "We're transfering the new shipment of Argentine beef from the pens to the slaughter-house tomorrow," he said.

It was clear by the way he spoke, that it irked him no little to have to give things to a man like Faber to sign.

Coyne obviously considered this man incompetent, yet his particular job made him Coyne's superior.

Faber took the paper and made a pretense at studying each word, while the plant manager looked on with contemptuous eyes. Finally satisfied that all was in order, Faber reached for one of his pens. He began to unscrew the top, then hastily returned it to his pocket, chose another, and signed his name at the bottom of the page.

Doc watched that episode with interest. Then with Griffin and Faber, he followed Carl Coyne around behind the warehouse to the big garage. Stone, the inspector, remained with the timekeeper.

Against the far wall in the garage stood nine bright red, ten-ton refrigerator trucks. Sandy Phail's truck bore a huge number "6" on the side. It was an up-to-date side-door load affair with a safety lock sunk in the center of a big, shiny, chromiumed door handle.

"Our drivers are instructed to keep the doors of their trucks locked at all times," the thin-faced plant manager explained. "So that it would be next to impossible for anyone to get into the truck."

Doc couldn't help but think how much evidence was piling up against Sandy Phail. How many questions the poor guy would have to answer when he finally did manage to put in an appearance.

Griffin reached up and gave the door-handle of the truck a slap. It was locked.

"Mr. Coyne has a duplicate set of keys that will open the locks," Faber spoke up.

Doc caught the look that Coyne shot Faber. It was as deadly as a deathray. For which he couldn't altogether blame Coyne. Because Faber had certainly buried a nice, long knife between the plant manager's shoulder blades.

"Okay, Coyne," Griffin ordered. "Start opening the lock!"

Coyne dug his hand into his trouser pocket and withdrew a bunch of keys. He fumbled with them a moment, rather awkwardly, Doc thought. Then he chose one and inserted it into the truck-door lock.

A blast of cold air rushed out of the refrigerator compartment at them as Coyne opened the door. Griffin took out his pocket flashlight and poked its beam inside the truck. He stopped and froze there, with a choked cry trembling on his lips.

DOC TOOK a single step forward and looked into the truck. There in the narrow ray of light, hanging from one of the hooks that was meant for sides of beef, was the figure of a man.

His throat had been cut. The blood that had flowed from the wound was frozen on his clothing. His features were strangely set, his body rigid. He looked like a waxen figure that had been sprayed with a gallon of crimson paint.

There was a frightened gasp alongside Doc's left ear. He twisted to see Coyne's white face staring at the dead body hanging inside the truck. Directly behind Coyne was Walter Faber, mouth open wide, eyes starkly staring.

Coyne's words seemed to have jammed somewhere between voice box and lips. Either that or he was putting on a great act, for he was speechless.

It was Faber who finally managed to get out:

"It's—it's Sandy Phail!"

CHAPTER V

MORE MURDER

JAMES DONNELLY, prosperous investment broker, sat at the big redwood desk in his library and puffed luxuriously on his fat cigar. Life for James Donnelly was good.

Paunchy, fat-jowled, he was one of the most successful businessmen in Akelton. His fine house, located in the most fashionable section of the city, had been decorated and furnished with artistic care. He had a retinue of servants, a town car.

It was no great secret to those who knew James Donnelly, or who had done business with him, that much of his success and wealth had come from deals that leaned to the shade. He made no bones about the fact that he was out for James Donnelly.

Right now he was involved in a deal that spelled upwards to a million dollars or more. It had practically been dumped into his lap. It had been left for his conscience to decide whether he should brush it out of his lap, or grab it and stuff it into his already overflowing pockets.

The answer was obvious. A million bucks "ain't hay," and James Donnelly had less conscience than Pinocchio before he met Jimminy Cricket.

Donnelly flicked the long ash of his cigar into an inlaid tray and looked down at the desk, which was strewn with travel folders that told of the wonders and beauties of the land south of the border—South America.

Then the telephone at his elbow burred softly. Reaching the handpiece, he put it close to his mouth.

"Yes—Donnelly speaking.... Oh, hello. You're late. I expected your call half an hour ago.... Yes, I've got the money. Have you the deeds? Good.... No, don't come here. It's better for no one to see you until everything has been settled. Then let *him* and anyone else who wants to, squawk their heads off. Where are you now?"

He jotted down an address on the phone pad at his elbow.

"I'll be there about nine thirty," he said. "And stop worrying. I'll bring the money with me. G'bye."

He dropped the receiver back into its cradle and fingered the folders on the desk. Then he dug his left hand inside his coat and withdrew a gold-edged ostrich-skin wallet.

Flapping it open, he took out a neat stack of greenbacks from the center fold. He counted them again to make sure they were all there. One hundred thousand dollars in cold cash!

Satisfied, he stowed the wallet with the money in it back into his pocket. There was a grin on his face that did not match the deceit in his eyes. This one hundred grand was going to grow into more than a million dollars, he was thinking. And the whole transaction was going to be as simple as taking a bottle away from a six-month's-old baby. There would be a squawk, but it could be easily throttled. At least, that's what Donnelly thought.

Flicking his ash into the tray again, the investment broker mouthed his cigar and arose. His short legs carried him to the arched doorway. Triumph and self-confidence oozed from him as he fingered the black button of the wall switch and plunged the room into darkness.

So intent had he been on his illict scheming that he had not seen the figure that had stolen into the library and stood behind the heavy drapes that separated the rooms. Stealthily now the figure moved up behind Donnelly. The instant that the lights went out, it sprang like a black panther at the investment broker.

Strangely Donnelly made no outcry or struggle as the figure dragged him to the floor....

DR. MILES MURDOCK was with Detective-Captain Dan Griffin in the lab at Police Headquarters when the call came in, saying that James Donnelly had been found dead. Doc had gone out there with the square detective after they had accompanied Sandy Phail's body to the morgue to pick up what scraps of evidence they could find. At the same time, they had examined the body of Mrs. Forbes, the woman who had died from eating the poisoned meat.

Doc doubted that any more could be learned about Sandy Phail's death even after the autopsy. It was plain how he had been killed.

"But one thing puzzles me," Doc told Griffin. "Phail must have been six-three and tough as a two-bit steak. How did the killer get close enough to a man like that to slit his throat without him putting up a fight? And if Phail did put up a fight, why didn't someone in the garage hear it?"

"Maybe the killer sapped him?" Griffin said, but before the words were out of his mouth, he recalled that, except for his cut throat, Phail hadn't had a mark on him.

When the two had reached Griffin's office they had fallen to discussing the keys to the refrigerator compartment of Phail's truck. The timekeeper had said that the driver had not turned them in. Yet the keys had not been on Phail's body.

"Phail was probably killed because he knew who poisoned the meat," was Doc's theory.

"You mean he was in on the job? And was killed to keep his mouth shut?"

"Not necessarily," Doc said. "Phail probably didn't know the meat was poisoned. But he would have known as soon as someone died from eating the meat he delivered. Phail was probably slated for the slab from the very start of this business."

"Coyne!" Griffin exclaimed, narrowing his eyes wisely. "There's the man. He left the plant at three o'clock in the afternoon. He had duplicate keys to the truck. He probably laid for Phail, waited until he made a delivery some place, then sneaked into the truck and poisoned the meat. Phail spotted him, but figured that Coyne had a right to be in the truck. Coyne knew Phail would talk as soon as it leaked out that the meat was poisoned. So Coyne bumped him."

"But why would Coyne take Phail's keys? Coyne had a set of his own. And it still doesn't clear up why Phail made no fight?"

It was then that the call came announcing that James Donnelly had committed suicide.

"Suicide?" Doc echoed, piqued with sudden interest.

Doc had known James Donnelly. He had been in the investment broker's company many times, since he and Donnelly were both prominent Akeltonites.

Griffin shook his head thoughtfully.

"Why a guy like him wants to blow his brains out, is something this block of mine can't figure," he said. "The guy had everything in the world to live for."

"Exactly," Doc agreed.

Griffin's square face came around with a lifted eyebrow. "What are you hintin'?"

Doc shrugged. "Going to take a run over and look at him?"

It wasn't really a question—more a suggestion.

Griffin watched Doc a moment, calculatingly.

"Yeah," he said then. "Maybe it'd be a smart idea if we run over."

DOC MURDOCK and Captain Griffin were admitted to James Donnelly's palatial home by one of the frozen-faced butlers, properly and immaculately attired despite the hour and the tragedy.

A couple of bluecoats who had picked up the broadcast on the shortwave were already on the scene. And the district attorney was on his way.

The atmosphere of the mansion made it seem as though there must have been some mistake, that this thing could not have happened. But when Doc and Griffin were led into the library and into the presence of the corpse, that feeling disappeared.

The first thing that wafted to Doc's sensitive nostrils as he entered the death chamber was a faintly unpleasant odor. Sort of a smoking smell. He tried to identify it, but could not.

On the floor lay the body of James Donnelly, clad in a light gray business suit. There was an ugly purplish-black bullet-hole in his right temple, and he lay on his back. Blood was smeared in a messy pattern on the floor under his head.

The D.A. had given explicit instructions to touch nothing until he arrived. But Doc didn't care to wait that long. As the Purple Scar, he had found that it was often necessary to move swiftly, scissor the red tape that too often retarded the forward march of justice. So without actually disturbing anything, he began to drift about the room.

On the surface it seemed plain that the pudgy investment broker had taken his own life. In his right fist was a .45 Colt automatic with one chamber exploded. Nothing in the room seemed to have been disturbed. No chairs or other furniture had been overturned.

At Griffin's request, the butler stepped forward. That grave-faced individual looked enough like a movie butler to hold his Screen Guild membership. He said he and the rest of the staff had been downstairs in the servants' quarters when they had heard what "sounded like a shot."

Grave Face had reached the library first and found his employer just as he was now—sprawled out on the floor, dead.

"How long did it take you to reach the library after you heard the shot?" Griffin questioned.

The butler checked back. "I'd say a couple of minutes at least, sir. You see, I was having a late snack. I had to wash and get into my coat. Mr. Donnelly was rather a stickler for appearances."

"You took all that time after you heard a shot?" Griffin rapped.

The butler looked hard at the detective-captain.

"We didn't know it was a shot at the time we heard it. I told you it only sounded like a shot. For all we knew, it might have been a car backfiring. I decided to come upstairs to make certain."

"Were the lights on when you came into the library?" Doc cut in.

The butler turned his head, frowned. "No, sir."

Griffin looked at Doc. But the plastic surgeon made no further comment. As far as he was concerned that was the clincher. This was murder!

NOR WAS that an entirely new idea, for from the first moment when word of James Donnelly's "suicide" had reached him, Doc had smelled a fat-bellied rat. Donnelly had not impressed him as the sort of person who would take his own life, no matter what kind of a spot he was in.

Here in the house were several more tangible reasons to back up Doc's suspicions. A man about to commit suicide would hardly go to the bother of putting out the lights. Nor would he carry a lighted cigar in his mouth. And obviously he had been smoking one. Because almost directly under the wall light switch, Doc found a half-smoked cigar butt, which had burned a small brown hole in the carpet.

Doc picked it up and found that the tip was still slightly warm, while the other end was moist.

Doc wondered if that peculiar smoky odor had come from the cigar burning the carpet. Maybe. But somehow it didn't smell like that.

As Griffin went on with his quiz session, Doc continued to move about the room, his keen eyes alert to even the most insignificant details. Finally he came to the big redwood desk and saw the travel catalogues spread out on the desk.

Doc wrinkled his brow. More evidence that this was murder. A man about to blow his brains out would hardly be interested in where and how to spend his time in the Argentine.

His gaze traveled a little farther to the phone pad. Two notations were jotted on it.

Each one was written in a different hand.

The top item read:

Call Blackstone 8-2152, before six-thirty

The other was:

Room 602, Eureka Hotel

Doc caught Grave Face's eye and beckoned him forward.

"Which of these notations was written by Mr. Donnelly?" he asked.

"The bottom one, sir," the butler said. "The top is mine."

"When did you write it?"

"Late this afternoon. A gentleman called, left that phone number, with the request that Mr. Donnelly call him."

"Did you know this gentleman?"

"No, sir. He wouldn't give his name. Said Mr. Donnelly would know for whom to ask, then hung up."

"Was this second notation on the pad at that time?"

"No, sir. That must have been written recently—shortly before Mr. Donnelly—"

The butler did not finish, for sudden emotion had choked up in his throat.

"You have any idea why Mr. Donnelly would want to do a thing like this?" Doc asked.

"Not the slightest. At dinner, Mr. Donnelly was in particularly high spirit. Asked me how I'd like to go to South America and live."

"Mr. Donnelly intended going to South America?"

"Evidently, sir." The butler's eyes moved to the travel folders.

"Thank you," Doc said.

The butler rejoined the other servants who were being questioned. Doc scrubbed his chin reflectively. Then when Griffin had concluded his questioning, he called the detective over.

"Griff, I'd like to use the phone to trace a number."

Griffin gave permission.

Doc dialed "Information," told the girl it was a police call and gave her the number he wished traced.

There was a wait, then the girl's voice again in the phone.

"Blackstone Eight-two-one-five-two is listed under the Landon Meat Products Company."

Doc's face was set as he let the receiver drop back into place. He echoed the girl's words to Griffin. Griffin's black eyes popped.

"What the devil do you suppose that means?"

"Search me," Doc said laconically, and moved to a window as a police siren wailed outside.

CHAPTER VI

THE PURPLE SCAR

BRAKES SCREAMED and tires burned to a crunching halt in the gravel driveway. One of the bluecoats in the library pushed aside the heavy curtains of another front window and peered out.

"It's the D.A. and the medical examiner," he informed.

"Better let the D.A. find out about the phone call himself," Griffin whispered to Doc. "He'll raise the City Hall roof if he thinks we did too much snooping before he got here."

Doc nodded.

A moment later, lacking only a fanfare of bugles and drums, District Attorney Barret and his cortege of deputies made their majestic entrance into the library. The mild-looking man with the black bag, at the tail end of the procession, was the medical examiner.

Barret, a slim man of medium height, adjusted his pince-nez to his snub nose and glanced about the room. He appraised the corpse with a grunt. Then he saw Captain Griffin and Doc Murdock. He shook hands with the plastic surgeon.

Griffin told Barret how Doc happened to be with him.

"Yes," Barret said. "I heard about the poisoned meat. Sad thing. We'll go into it in the morning. Right now, we'll straighten out this mess."

The D.A.'s staff was already at work, fingerprinting everything in sight, making notes, taking photographs of the room and the body. The medical examiner was busy, too.

Doc and Griffin stood off to one side and watched. Griffin seemed well satisfied that the district attorney's office was taking this unpleasant duty off his hands. James Donnelly had been a big pigeon. A slip in a case like this could stir up a political furore.

One of the investigators came across the half-smoked cigar butt. It was cooled now, so it didn't mean much in the way of evidence. But he stowed it away for future reference just the same.

"Well, Doc, how about it?" Barret finally asked the medical examiner.

"Bullet entered the right temple. Death instantaneous."

"Self-inflicted?"

"Off-hand I'd say yes."

Barret shrugged his narrow shoulders.

"Keep on looking anyway, boys. Can't afford any mistakes in a case as important as this one."

One of the men was rummaging around the desk. He discovered the writing on the pad, called over one of the "shutter mob" and took a picture of it. Then he opened the top drawer.

Doc saw him take out a large flat black checkbook. He opened it and emitted a long, low whistle.

"Chief, take a look at this."

Barret walked to the desk. Doc craned in, too. The last stub in the book was for a check for one hundred thousand dollars, payable to "cash," and drawn *today!*

"More evidence that this is murder," Doc told himself.

A man contemplating suicide would not draw one hundred Gs out of the bank. But what had happened to this money? It was not on Donnelly's body, nor in his desk, nor his safe, nor any place else that they looked.

DOC'S MIND was made up. It was finally time to call upon the Purple Scar!

Covering his yawn with the back of his hand, Doc said to Griffin:

"Getting kind of sleepy. Had a big day—and will have an even busier one tomorrow. So long as nothing else seems to be happening here, I think I'll run. Mind?"

"Go to it, Doc," Griffin said. "I'll ride back with the gang."

"If you can spare a little time in the morning, Doctor," Barret put in, "I'd appreciate if you'd drop in at my office. Like to get that poisoned meat business cleared up."

Doc said he would be there. Then he bade good night to "the gang" and sauntered slowly out the door. But once the night air hit him and he was alone, his sleepiness suddenly left him. With one quick bound, he was into his black sedan and gunning out of the oak-tree-lined driveway, his brain busy with what his first move would be.

The first phone Doc came to, he called Dale at his Swank Street quarters. He knew that Dale would be there waiting for him, in spite of the hour.

"Dale, darling," he said when he heard her voice, "I want you to meet me at Main and Walnut Streets as soon as you can. And—"

He rattled off a string of instructions, then hung up.

Doc was sitting on the fender of his car, the ground before him littered with stamped-out cigarette butts when a yellow taxicab drew up behind him. Fifteen minutes had gone by since he had called Dale Jordan. But here she was now.

Doc hurried back, dropped a dollar into the driver's outstretched palm and opened the door. He helped Dale to the sidewalk and, as the cab wheeled away, hurried her back to his own car.

Dale looked a lot different now. She was not wearing that stiffly starched nurse's uniform. Instead a tan dress of thin woolen stuff did nice things to her figure.

Doc helped her into the front seat behind the wheel. He climbed in beside her.

"Drive," he told her.

She drove a couple of blocks while Doc explained all that had happened.

"Did you bring what I asked for?" he asked then.

Dale nodded and took a carefully wrapped package from her large leather handbag.

Doc told her to stop the car. Then he got out, climbed into the back seat, and drew the shades. By the time the car was under way again, he had the package open.

It contained three small articles. One was a bottle filled with a sticky, yellowish fluid. Doc yanked the cork from the bottle and smeared the sticky stuff into his thick hair. It was a dye of his own special make, one that changed his hair from black to a sort of straw color and removed every hint of a wave.

He spread the second of the articles out on his lap. The mask of the Purple Scar! A perfect reproduction in gum elastic of his brother's acid-scarred face, copied skillfully even to the slightest detail. A face so horrible to look at, that even the least sensitive recoiled at sight of it. It was the face of a corpse!

DOC FITTED it over his own handsome face. Looking up into the overhead mirror he could see Dale shudder at his reflection. He saw the look of repulsion that came into her eyes, and he could not blame her.

Quickly he took the third article. Another skintight rubber mask. But this one was not hideous. This was the face of a commonplace, uninspired-looking individual, the kind of face it would be hard to remember, or describe. Which was exactly as Doc intended it to be.

The business end of a revolver was shoved into Cabral's chest.

This lifelike mask he slipped on over the purple mask. From costly experience, he had learned that ordinary disguises were too risky for this dangerous work he had chosen, and after tireless experiments, he had hit upon these rubber masks. Such masks could be made to resemble any person it might be necessary for Doc to impersonate. And they were so perfect that even the keenest, most critical eye would find it difficult to discover that they were masks.

His disguise completed, Doc went through his pockets and turned over to Dale his credentials and everything that might reveal his identity. All he kept was his cigarettes, a book of paper matches, his pencil flash, a bunch of priceless keys that would open any lock this side of the one on the Pearly Gates, and what money he thought he might need.

"See how fast you can make Henshaw and Moffet Streets," he told Dale then.

The address that Doc Murdock, now the Purple Scar, gave was two blocks from the Eureka Hotel. When Dale and Doc arrived there he told her to wait, and climbed out onto the sidewalk.

"Oh—I almost forgot something," Dale called.

Doc frowned as he watched the girl dig her lacquer-tipped fingers into her bag and come out holding a blue-black automatic between her forefinger and thumb. He smiled as easily as though he wore no mask, for they were so sheer and pliable that they even allowed for expression. He took the gun and stowed it into his pocket.

"Do be careful, darling," Dale breathed.

He held his smile as he leaned inside the car and kissed her. Then he turned and walked briskly to the Eureka Hotel.

The Eureka was one of the finest hotels in the city. Whoever was occupying Room 602 must have a fair-sized bankroll, Doc mused, or he had immediate prospects of getting one.

He went into the glittering, palm-filled lobby with a sprinkling of guests and walked straight to the elevators.

"Six," he told the boy as the door was shut behind him.

A moment later, he was deposited in the sixth floor corridor. It was deserted. He waited until the elevator door closed, then walked to the door marked "602."

He rapped. There was a brief wait, then the sound of feet coming toward the door. The barrier swung open.

Doc Murdock had all he could do to fight back the exclamation of astonishment in his throat. For there standing before him in the open doorway stood the big-boned Latin whom he had met that afternoon in Roger Landon's office—Donato Cabral!

"Are you Mr. Cabral?" he asked evenly.

THE LATIN'S brows, as bushy and black as John L. Lewis' brows, came together in an inquiring frown.

"Yes," he replied hesitantly.

"You had an appointment with Mr. Donnelly, didn't you?" Doc asked.

Cabral took about thirty seconds to study the unimpressive character before him.

"Why?" he asked then.

Doc took a long chance.

"I'm John Pryor," he replied. "I'm associated with Mr. James Donnelly. That is, I sort of work for him. He told me to come here and tell you that he was detained."

Doc was playing a long shot, on the premise that Cabral was not the murderer, and also that Cabral did not know that Donnelly was dead.

"Why didn't he call me?" Cabral demanded.

Doc felt a little easier. At least, Cabral didn't know that Donnelly was dead. Or was he just acting?

"He was with some people," Doc answered. "He didn't think it was a good idea. You see—he won't be able to make it tonight, so he asked me to come and settle things for him."

Cabral was cagey. "What things?"

Doc allowed a wise grin to twitch his lips.

"Can't we talk better inside?"

He glanced up and down the hall. Cabral's eyes narrowed, a little suspiciously. His hand groped for the knob of the door. "I'll call Donnelly myself," he grunted.

He gave the door a quick shove to slam it in Doc's face. But instead it jammed against the plastic surgeon's inserted foot. The next thing Cabral knew the business end of a revolver was in his chest, and he was being backed into the room.

CHAPTER VII

MIDNIGHT ADVENTURE

DONATO CABRAL'S eyes gleamed wrathfully as Doc closed the door behind him.

"What's the idea?" the South American demanded heatedly. "Who are you, anyway?"

Doc made Cabral turn and face the wall for a moment, and when the South American looked again—he was staring into the horrible face of the Purple Scar! A ghastly network of torn, acid-destroyed tissues, features almost totally eaten away, eyes only empty, shriveled sockets, mouth a twisted slash.

Cabral turned deathly pale. For it was plain that the name and the exploits of the Purple Scar had been whispered even in far-away Argentine. Sweat was standing on his face, and he ran his tongue over his thick lips.

"What do you want with me?" he asked hoarsely.

"You had an appointment with James Donnelly tonight, didn't you?" asked the Scar in a hollow, toneless voice that seemed to come from the grave.

Cabral nodded nervously. "What was wrong about that?"

"Nothing. Only about an hour or so ago—James Donnelly was killed!"

Cabral's whole body seemed to tremble.

"Killed?" he repeated in a husky whisper.

"Murdered!" the chilling voice said.

Cabral slumped into a chair and looked up unblinkingly into the purple face that stared at him accusingly.

"I didn't kill him—I swear I didn't!" he gulped. "I haven't left this room since I came in at eight o'clock."

"But you know who did kill him."

"No. No—I don't know."

There was an unsteadiness in Cabral's words that did not seem sincere to the Purple Scar.

"Why were you meeting Donnelly here?" he asked.

Cabral's gaze traveled from the Scar's awful face to the leveled gun, then back to the two black dots that seared him from somewhere back of those empty eye-sockets.

"I—was handling some business for him in South America," Cabral muttered.

The Scar's mind flashed back to those travel folders on Donnelly's desk.

"It couldn't have been a very upright business for you to meet him in a hotel room in the middle of the night."

"It wasn't because it was dishonest," Cabral was quick to correct. "It involved a big property deal in the Argentine. Donnelly was going to start some kind of a project down there. I never did find out the details. I don't think anybody ever knew except himself."

The Scar suddenly noted something strange about Cabral's speech. This afternoon in Landon's office he had spoken with a decided Spanish accent. Now that he was excited, it was almost entirely lacking.

"All I know is that he figured to clear a fortune on the deal," Cabral went on. "But he didn't want anything known about it until after it was closed, and the property his. He was afraid someone would cut in, and that the property would be jacked up to the sky."

"Is that why Donnelly drew one hundred thousand dollars out of the bank today?" demanded the awesome voice of the Scar.

"Yes. He was to give the money to me tonight. Tomorrow I'm sailing for South America on business for Mr. Landon, the meat packer. This was just something I was doing on the side. But if Donnelly's dead—"

Something vicious showed in Cabral's eyes and his lips drew back almost in a snarl.

DOC COULD understand the man's attitude. If his story was true, his commission on a one hundred thousand dollar deal would buy a lot of hair oil. But it remained for the Purple Scar to find out whether it was the truth, or whether the South American was just a good actor.

"Get up!" the Scar ordered sharply.

Cabral arose quickly and the Scar prodded him into the bathroom.

"And don't try to come out until a good five minutes after you hear the hall door slam," the Scar added.

He closed the bathroom door and hurried out of the apartment. But he did not slam the door. He didn't even close it. Cabral wouldn't know whether he had left or not.

The instant the Purple Scar reached the hallway, he slipped the mask of John Pryor over the face of the Scar. He did not ring for the elevator. Instead he went down the back stairs.

Dale was still waiting for him when he got to Henshaw and Moffet Streets. Doc leaned into the car and rattled off detailed instructions.

"Darling," he said, "you and I go to work now. You in one place, I in another."

Dale was alive with curiosity.

"Your job," Doc said, "will be to drive to the Eureka Hotel, park the car where you can grab it in a minute. Then you're to go into the lobby of the hotel, wait for a gentleman named Donato Cabral to show his Latin physiognomy, and follow him every place he goes."

Dale grinned at him. "Every place, darling?" she murmured....

Doc's job took him to Landon Stockyards.

It was dark and deserted in this section of town at this hour. The wind, blowing from the river, made it chill and disagreeable.

As Doc approached the tall, wide-webbed wire fence that enclosed the yards, he saw that Faber had not exaggerated the situation. The gates were well fortified with guards. Only the Invisible Man could get past them with stolen goods.

Doc followed the fence until he came to a spot where he could climb over without the guards seeing him. But certainly no one could have smuggled out several hundred dollars' worth of meats this way.

Inside the yards, it seemed even darker. And the mooing, grunting and bleating of the hundreds of penned animals made it a weird place at midnight.

Doc picked his way along the narrow, twisting, pitch-black avenue that separated the pens, until he came to the red brick warehouse. He went around to the side door and found it locked.

But locked doors never stopped the Purple Scar. At least, not for long. From inside his coat, he withdrew his invaluable collection of pass-keys. Almost instinctively he selected the right one and slipped it into the lock.

A fraction of an inch at a time, he eased the door open, until he could peer into the huge place, crowded with canned and packed foodstuffs, and lit with two ghastly pale bulbs. It smelled dry in there, like a huge public market that had been shut tight for several days. There was, however, no time to conjecture about that.

MAKING SURE that his revolver was free in his hip pocket and ready for instant use if he needed it, the Scar stepped boldly into the high-ceilinged place. From all indications it was deserted. But he had to be sure.

He paused a long moment just inside the doorway, listening intently. It was an utter stillness that greeted him.

Then he moved slowly toward the rear wall that faced the river. It was totally blank and as smooth as the shell of an egg.

What he expected to find here, he didn't rightly know. But he had hoped that it would at least partly reveal some answer to the shortages that were occurring in the company.

That's why he had come here tonight. He knew that hundreds of dollars' worth of foodstuffs do not vanish into thin air, and since the gates were so heavily guarded and the drawbridge to the wharf too noisy to lower, there must be some answer. But what was it? How were these things carried out of the warehouse, unseen?

Of course, there was the chance that the guards might have been bribed. But that seemed illogical. There were so many of them that surely one of them would have dropped a word.

No, there must be some other entrance to this warehouse. It was while he was on this thought, playing the beam of his flashlight along the sheer blank wall that he had come up against that he spied a faint track mark on the floor. It was a mark that a rolled up-ended barrel had made. Doc followed the impression to the wall.

Doc's brow wrinkled with deep ridges. The mark of a barrel would not lead right, straight up to the wall. It would have to curve away from the wall, because a barrel is round and couldn't possibly get that close—unless it continued to go right on through the wall!

Even now the Scar was searching the wall carefully, with his flashlight. But he could not find a crack nor the hint of a door any place.

Killing the light, he raced his hands over the entire area carefully, trying to locate a concealed button that he was certain must be there. It was about six inches from the rubber-tiled floor that his fingers brushed something that gave way under his touch. The next thing he knew there was the sound of metal-sliding against metal and a small portion of the wall had opened up—just space enough for him to squeeze through. Then, automatically, the door slid back into place.

The Purple Scar was in a narrow pitch-black passageway, not more than five feet high. He dared not light his flash now. He waited a moment to try to accustom his eyes to the darkness. Then drawing his automatic, he took about a dozen short steps.

Then the ground seemed to come to an abrupt end. But he had merely come to a stone staircase that led straight down.

Pressing against the wall, he descended the steps. Twelve in all. Then another black passageway, damp and musty. The Scar figured that this one must lead to the river.

He took a few more steps, and stopped suddenly as a mutter of excited voices came from behind a stout, fireproof door, directly ahead. He could see a faint sliver of light shining from beneath the door.

He listened. But whoever was in there was talking a foreign gibberish he could not make out.

Dare he go closer?

Suddenly down out of the darkness came a blunt, pliable object. It struck the Purple Scar across the base of the skull and exploded a bombshell of vivid color inside his brain. His senses melted into the blackness that followed.

CHAPTER VIII

TUNNEL
OF DANGER

S **LOWLY THE** Purple Scar opened his eyes. He blinked and closed them again, quickly.

There was a blinding light in his eyes. He tried to move. But he could not. His hands and his legs were well tied.

In a torrent thoughts rushed into his brain. He remembered now. The black passageway. Voices. Then a terrible blow on the back of his head that had brought senselessness.

Someone directly ahead of him was muttering. He opened his eyes slowly, squinted, and tried to see past the light. As well as he could make out, he was in a small room, musty and smelly, as the passageway had been. It must be the room behind the door at which he had listened.

There seemed to be several people in the room with him. He could sense them, even though he could not see them, because of the two bright lights focused in his eyes.

"Who are you?" a voice boomed out of the darkness at him.

The Scar ran his tongue over his lips. His mouth tasted like the morning after, and there were shooting pains in the back of his skull.

"Who are you?" the voice repeated, in a tone so loud it almost split the plastic surgeon's throbbing head.

He tried desperately to distinguish something in the voice that would betray the speaker. But all he could make out was that it sounded Teutonic. That was an accent for which the Purple Scar did not care— not with his country at war with Germany and Japan.

Doc Murdock had been hoping every day that his own volunteered services to the Army would be accepted. He knew that surgeons like himself were badly needed, but so far the authorities had decided that he was also badly needed where he was.

A sort of fury swept him now. If these unknown men *were* Germans—

Someone stepped into the patch of light. A man in seaman's garb, and with a week-old stubble on his face. Without warning this rough-looking man drove his grimy fist into the Scar's mouth.

"Talk!" he roared.

The Scar strained at the bonds that held him. Rage gripped him.

Week's Growth grabbed him by the front of the coat and shook him roughly.

"I said talk!"

The Scar looked up with narrowed eyes. But common sense told him that nothing could be gained by keeping silent.

"Okay," he murmured. "I'll talk. I've got nothing to hide. I'm John Pryor, and—"

"What were you doing in the plant tonight?" demanded the voice of a man beyond the wall of light.

"I work there, on one of the machines. I forgot something. Came back to look for it."

There was a sibilant whisper. Then the foreign-accented voice barked savagely:

"You're lying! You do not work in the plant!"

The Scar smiled grimly but wisely behind the twin-masks. So someone had just whispered that he didn't work in the plant. Someone afraid to speak for fear Doc might recognize the voice. Someone who knew enough about the plant to know every man who worked there.

That fitted several people, and at the same time limited the list to those he had met or was likely to meet in the near future. Providing he got out of this present mess!

Someone wheezed in the darkness, cleared his throat. The Scar's brows wrinkled. But whatever thought he had was rudely shattered. For the stubble-faced man had made a dangerous discovery—dangerous for the Purple Scar!

IT WAS true that his rubber mask was so perfect that it could pass the scrutiny of even the severest eye. But it was hardly a mask that could pass the critical, exacting glare of what amounted to a spotlight. Besides the stubble-faced man was literally on top of the Scar. The man's foul breath was being breathed in his face. Therefore, Week's Growth did what no one else had ever done—he discovered that his prisoner was wearing a false face!

With one swift motion, he reached forward and ripped the upper mask off the Scar's face. Whatever else he and the others in the room may have expected to find beneath the mask, they never could have dreamed in a million years that it would be the dreadful, purplish face of a corpse that stared out at them!

The Scar heard several of them gasp with horror.

"It's—the Purple Scar!" someone cried out in alarm.

At the mention of the Purple Scar's name tenseness could be felt in the room. It was a tenseness that was born of hate and fear. For these men, whoever they might be, were lawbreakers, and every criminal big and small had heard of the Purple Scar. And they knew that he was their sworn enemy, that they had cause to hate him!

For a moment the Scar wondered if the glare of the lights would reveal that this, too, was a mask. But either the men never thought that a man would wear two masks, or they were willing to concede that this hideous face was his own and his reason for wearing the outer mask. At any rate, they did not touch it.

"Most unfortunate, Purple Scar," said the voice with the Teutonic accent. "You might've escaped with your life. But now that we know who you are, it would be too dangerous for us to let you live."

He issued a curt command. At once, Week's Growth tied a blindfold over the Scar's eyes. Hands then seized him and hauled him out of the room. As he was leaving, he caught someone's muffled voice, apparently giving instructions.

They carried the Scar down the long passageway that twisted like an underground cowpath. The smell of salt water became stronger. The *lap-lap* of waves reached his ears.

There was a brief halt while more whispered instructions were exchanged. Then the Scar felt himself transferred to other hands, carted a little farther down what appeared to be a short flight of stairs. Then he was dropped onto the floor.

The floor seemed to be moving, lurching from side to side. Only it wasn't exactly a floor. It was the hold of a ship.

It didn't take a quiz expert to figure out what was in store for him. He could visualize Davey Jones preparing a nice cozy guest room for him down there under the waves.

The Scar strained at the ropes binding his wrists and ankles, but whoever had tied them was no amateur. He waited a short while to make sure that he was alone. Then, twisting his body so he could scrape the back of his head against the rough flooring to rasp at the knots of his blindfold, he soon had it off.

He lay there awhile longer until he could make out large objects in the darkness—barrels, crates, sacks. Through the portholes above his head, he could see the reflection of the dim wharf lights.

He snaked across the floor toward one of the larger crates. It was bound with sheet metal straps.

Twisting his big body around, he got his powerful fingers under one of the metal bands and worked it back and forth, until it snapped off, leaving a sharp ragged edge. After that it was merely a matter of sawing through his wrist bonds.

He was about to start untying the rope on his ankles, when he heard the hatch at the head of the stairs squeak open. Now he was in for it!

WHILE THE Purple Scar was undergoing his trying experiences in the warehouse of the meatpacking company, Dale Jordan was having some interesting experiences of her own.

Less than five minutes after Doc Murdock had left her, Dale was seated in the palm-decorated lobby of the Eureka Hotel where a continuous stream of guests were moving to and fro. She had parked her car a quarter of a block from the entrance to the hotel, where it would be readily accessible if and when she needed it.

Her heart beat fast with the excitement this adventure offered. How should she know Donato Cabral? Doc had given her a thumbnail description of the South American, but he had airily disdained assuring her that this would serve. It was definitely up to her to make mighty sure that she was following the right man.

Dale had that arranged with the desk clerk. For a crisp piece of folding money, he was to point out the South American to her, if he came down.

For about ten minutes Dale waited in the lobby. She watched men and women get on and off the elevator. And as each man passed her she would look at the desk clerk and he would shake his head in a slow negative.

Finally she began to think that Cabral was never going to put in an appearance. Perhaps, she thought, this was Doc's quaint way of sidetracking her, while he tackled some dangerous work without her insisting on sharing it.

It was during this dark moment of doubt that a tall man wearing a wide-striped gray suit and a large gray sombrero stepped out of the elevator and walked toward the front door. Dale's eyes flashed to the desk. The man behind it quickly nodded his head.

Throwing down the newspaper she had pretended to be reading, she hurried out the door after Cabral. She saw him pile into the first taxicab in the feed line, and tried to hear the address he rattled off to the driver, but could not.

She shook her auburn head in answer to the hawking cabbies in the line and ran back to her parked sedan. She got behind the wheel just as Cabral's machine spun around the corner.

Pressing the starter with her open-toed shoe and throwing off the brake, she gunned away from the curb with a grind of gears and flew in pursuit of the cab carrying the South American. She picked up his red tail-light at the corner and followed at a safe distance.

Dale wondered where on earth the man could be going at this hour. Obviously Doc's visit to him had stirred the South American to action. Maybe Cabral was the man who had killed James Donnelly, Sandy Phail and poor Mrs. Forbes. Or maybe he was going to lead her to the guilty party.

Doc had told Dale that he believed all these deaths were linked together in some way, and that they tied in with the poisoned meat, the sabotage and shortages at the Landon plant, and the big deal that Cabral said Donnelly had been consummating in South America.

Dale was thinking of all this as she kept her car roaring after Cabral's taxicab. She started in surprise as the route led to the river where the Landon factory and stockyards were located.

That was where Doc had gone. He had said something about wanting to find the answer to "the leak in the Landon Company." Whatever that meant.

SUDDENLY DALE'S heart leaped into her throat. Could it be possible that Cabral suspected that Doc was going to the stockyards and was on his way to ambush and kill him?

For what other purpose could the South American be going there at this hour? The plant was closed.

Cabral's cab whirled around the next corner, rolled a short way, then came to a halt in front of the side gate to the stockyards. Dale braked her car to a stop a short distance behind.

She saw the South American emerge and pay the driver. The taxi wheeled away. Dale sat in her car and watched Cabral go past the guard at the gate. Apparently the guard knew that the man had business with the company. But that trick would not work for Dale.

Still Doc had told her to follow Cabral every place. And that was precisely what she intended to do.

She started the car rolling again, went past the gate and continued alongside the high fence in the direction of the river. Presently she came to a spot which, although she had no way of knowing it, was approximately the place where Doc had climbed the fence.

She got out of the car and approached the high barrier, reconnoitering. It was going to be no easy job getting over that fence. But she could not let Doc down. Maybe right this moment, his life might be in danger inside the yards. She must get in there!

She walked to the wire fence, got her fingers into the webbing and drew herself up, muttering angrily as she felt a run spring in one of her brand new stockings.

With her fingers cramped and rubbed raw from the rough wire, she finally managed to get one leg crooked over the top of the fence, her skirt giving a loud *rrrrip* in the bargain. She hung there in that rather precarious and undignified pose, until she got her breath. Then she swung her body over and looked down at the long drop to the ground. She held her breath.

"*Wooooo,*" she let out and jumped. She landed inside the yards with a dull thud.

Dale never had known a place could be as dark as this. And the weird sounds that the animals made caused chills to dance along her spine.

She could barely discern the tall buildings at the far end of the yard, in the darkness. She remembered that Doc had mentioned something about "a warehouse," and decided one of those buildings must be the place he meant.

She hurried forward, fearful that at any moment one of the bars would drop off the wooden pens and that the animals would barge out at her. Or that someone was lurking in the shadows that the pen-posts cast, ready to leap at her....

Determinedly she put such thoughts aside and quickened her footsteps. This certainly did not smell like a perfume factory, she thought.

Dale was weary when she reached the first of the red brick buildings. Her stockings were ruined, her hands cut and bleeding, her expensive suit ripped. What next would happen to her?

SHE WENT to the door of one building, not knowing whether it was the warehouse or not. As it happened, it was not. It was the building in which the meats were prepared and canned, and where Landon's office was located. In fact, it was right on this spot that Doc Murdock had stood in the afternoon and dispersed the slum mob.

At any other time it might have struck Dale as odd that this door should be open at night, when the rest of the place was closed. But she was not in a very observant mood just at present. Her sole concern was in finding Doc Murdock or Donato Cabral.

Pushing the door open gently, she slipped into the corridor. She stood there a moment. The size of the place in the darkness oppressed her. It was like standing on the rim of a slumbering volcano in the darkness, not quite sure what the next step would bring.

Then she decided to risk going forward. She took about half a dozen short steps toward the staircase—and heard muffled steps behind her!

She wanted to scream, but something made the sound jam in her throat. Her hands were clenched and she tried to move but her feet refused.

She managed to turn her head. Then she just stood there, helpless, unable to move a muscle, until she saw a big moving shape in the darkness blocking her way to the door.

That was like a spur. She sprang to one side and tried to dart past the figure. But a hand came from the blackness and caught her by the throat!

She went down on the concrete floor with the hulking figure on top of her, and with fingers pressing against her throat, tighter, tighter!

CHAPTER IX

ESCAPE!

WHEN THE Scar slipped back to the spot where the men had dropped him, he snatched up the blindfold. Draping it over his eyes, he lay motionless on the floor, his hands tucked behind his back.

The hatch door opened and closed. Heavy feet thumped down the rickety wooden steps. Then the beam of a flashlight filtered through the fabric of the blindfold.

The Scar tensed his steely muscles and waited until the man who had entered came closer and bent forward. Then the Purple Scar went into action.

His hands came from behind his back and grabbed at the man bending over him. The blindfold fell away, his right fist crashing with terrific force against the man's lantern jaw.

The man grunted and fell backward. The Scar was upon him in a wink, pounding lefts and rights into his face and body. The man stiffened out and lay as motionless as a corpse.

Doc Murdock, the Purple Scar, fished through the man's pockets and found a jack-knife with which he cut the ropes on his ankles.

Then he took the man's flashlight and walked to the crates, barrels and sacks that lined the walls of the hold from floor to ceiling. Each was stamped with the words: "Landon Meat Products," and told what each contained. Hams, bacons, sausages, lard, soups, extracts, and so on.

Here was the answer to how shortages were occurring in the Landon plant. At night, through the secret passageway, hundreds of dollars worth of provisions were being stolen and smuggled onto this ship.

But what happened to them after that? The Purple Scar was determined to find out.

Killing the light, he went quickly up the stairs. A fraction of an inch at a time, he eased the hatch open until he could peer out into the night. After the stuffiness of the hold, the crisp air refreshed him. The sea was rather calm, causing the boat to toss only slightly.

The Scar had slipped onto deck, thankful for the darkness and the elongated shadows that were cast by the masts, when he heard footsteps coming toward him. He leaped back behind one of the tall masts. A man lumbered past within arm's length of him and headed straight for the hold.

The Scar knew that the instant the man opened the hatch and saw his crony knocked out down there, that the Scar's chances for escape would be greatly lessened. He sprang from his hiding place and began to sprint across the slippery deck.

Almost at once he heard the man's outcry. Seemingly from no place figures sprang

The Scar let out a groan and jack-knifed into the water.

at him. One of them tried to stop his mad rush, but the Scar charged him and smashed the fellow with a right that dumped him over the rail and into the water.

A belaying pin whirled past the Scar's left ear and smashed against the side of the cabin. In the darkness, he knew that no one could be sure whether the pin had struck him or not and decided to take advantage of it. He let out an agonized groan and before anyone could reach him, jackknifed over the rail into the water as if he had been knocked cold.

He struck the water with a splash and sank immediately. Those on deck would be at the rail, to fish out their pal who was floundering in the water, and to search for him.

THE PURPLE SCAR was an expert swimmer. It was for this sport that Doc Murdock had received one of his four letters at college. He stayed under water now until his lungs ached. Finally forced to emerge, he came up some distance away from the boat. He could see those on deck playing their flashlights on the black water, searching frantically for a sign of him. A couple of them were pulling out their wet pal.

Every sane instinct urged the Scar to beat a swift and hasty retreat, but still that element of his nature which had made him the famous crimefighter he was, lured him toward further risks. Still they were risks that might lead him to the person behind this wholesale robbery and murder. Or at least he could find out what was happening to this stolen food.

Filling his lungs to capacity, he submerged again. Knifing through the water, he went under the boat and came up at the starboard side. The name of the craft was painted directly above him on the prow. *The Gray Gull.*

He had to be careful that the men at the rail did not spot him, for if they did, he knew it would mean quick death. He swam a little farther and grabbed hold of one of the frayed rope bumpers that hung at the side of the boat. He could hear the voices of the men above him, speaking softly but excitedly.

"I guess we won't have to worry about the Purple Scar any more," said one of them.

"You said it," agreed another. "Nothin' but a fish could stay under water that long—and still live to tell about it."

They stood at the rail mumbling for a few moments longer, playing their lights on the water to make sure that the Scar did not appear. Then, apparently satisfied that he had perished, they killed their lights and scattered into the darkness. Some stayed aboard, others climbed back onto the wharf and resumed loading the boat with stolen provisions.

They had to hurry it up, too. It was not safe to stay here too long. A prowling police boat might come along and spot them. Or some of the guards in the yards might mosey over and discover them.

The Scar came out of the water, slipped over the rail and onto the deck. He moved like a shadow through the darkness. There was someone directly ahead of him, near the wheel. A giant of a man.

The Scar crept forward, as silently as he could, but the *squish–squash* of his wet shoes turned the man. The ray of his flashlight washed that dreadfully scarred purple face.

"The Purple Scar!" the man choked. "I thought you were—"

He did not finish. One of his gnarled hands dipped to his waist and out came a saw-buck fishknife. But he never got the chance to use it for the Scar was at him, driving a ponderous right into the face and at the same time clamping a hand over the knife-wrist. A sharp twist of the arm and the knife clattered onto the deck. The Scar kicked it slithering down the deck, as he released the man.

This fellow was not the type to be felled by a single blow. He was plenty tough. He shook his head and charged at the Purple Scar. In the darkness he slipped through the Scar's defense and got his iron hands on the throat of the surgeon.

The Scar knew that if he did not subdue this man in a hurry that the rest of the crew would be down on his neck. So he called on a bit of ju-jutsu. For the Purple Scar was well-versed in this art.

THE NEXT moment the big seaman was brought to his knees on the slimy deck, his right arm pinned behind his back in a painful hold.

"Now, my friend, one peep out of you, and you'll be fish food!" warned the chilling voice of the Purple Scar.

The man nodded, gasping painfully.

"Where does this stuff that you're stealing go?" demanded the Scar.

"I don't know," the man groaned. "We meet a ship about twelve miles out. We're just hired hands. The pay's good and the work ain't too hard. So we don't ask no questions and don't get told nothin'."

"What kind of a ship do you meet?"

"Can't say. Never saw her flag or her name, on account of we only work when it's dark, when no moon's out. And nobody ever talks English."

"What do they speak?"

"Heinie."

"Who's running the show?"

"I don't know."

A slight twist of the arm.

"I swear I don't know!" The man perspired. "The guy who runs the show never goes with us. And nobody ever mentions his name. Like I said, the pay's good so we just do our job and don't get too nosey."

There was a loud scuffle and commotion on the other side of the deck, where it was tied up to the wharf. From the sound, it was evident that the crew had finished their chores and were ready to shove off.

The Scar had no desire to accompany them, even though he would like to know the name of the ship that they were to meet. But that would be taking too much risk. There were more important things to be accomplished on land. Besides, if he found out who was behind this thing, he would soon learn all he wished to know about the mysterious ship.

Doubling his fist, the Purple Scar crashed it down on the back of the head of the seaman whose arm he was holding. Promptly and silently the seaman's taut body collapsed as a man's body does when it receives a sharp blow on the medulla nerve center. A harmless blow—but effective.

The next moment there was a faint splash and the Purple Scar was back in the water, powerful strokes carrying him toward a darkened wharf a short distance away.

Quickly reaching the wharf, he got hold of one flat rung of the wharf ladder, clinging there to regain his depleted strength and breath. His brain was awhirl with thoughts. But at least one or two things had become clear.

Someone in the Landon Company, or at least someone who knew the plant inside and out, was stealing goods and selling them, so that it looked as if the meat might eventually be reaching one of the Axis countries. Possibly it was being taken from this country by one of the devilish Nazi submarines that were infesting the coastal waters.

That was in no sense outside the possibilities. Everyone remembered how the big submarine freighter *Deutschland,* in World War I, loaded up time and again off Baltimore—and got away with it for entirely too long a time. And if the Germans had subs of that type more than twenty years ago, what wouldn't the present day Nazis have now?

ON THE other hand, where did the poison meat angle fit into the picture?

The name of Sam Ziggley seeped into Doc's mind as he completed his climb up the ladder and hurried across the dark, deserted wharf. The mask of the Purple Scar was still hiding his face, but he could feel his own worried frown.

Sam Ziggley—that might be a Teutonic name. Leaving that aside, however, and giving Ziggley another motive than that of treachery to America—well, Ziggley had once worked for Landon. He would know the workings of the plant. It would be to his advantage to steal Landon's goods, besmirch his name, and thus weaken his resistance so that he would eventually be forced to sell his business. The fact that the name of the firm was slightly tarnished would matter little in the long run. With money and time and the announcement that the firm had changed hands, that could easily be overcome.

True, Ziggley could have sold his own products to the Axis powers in the same undercover manner Landon's products were being sold at present. But maybe Ziggley feared to take any such chance on at least landing in jail for the duration. It might suit his purpose better to throw the whole blame on Landon.

The Scar walked alongside the wire fence that enclosed the Landon yards, the way he had to go to find a cab that would take him home. He was thinking that he might have to call the police or the Coast Guard to head off the boat with the stolen goods. But that was not the way he had things mapped out. First of all the guilty party would not be aboard and it would do little good to lock up those seamen who probably had little idea of what it was all about. And stopping the shipment would make the leader doubly cautious, put him on his guard. Better to let the guilty one think he was getting away with it for a while. The old adage—"Enough rope—"

Doc sloshed along the dark, deserted street in his wet clothes, careful to keep close to the high fence in case anyone should happen along and see him. Then suddenly, in the dimness, he glimpsed the faint outline of a parked car.

He slowed his pace, keeping even closer to the fence for fear that someone might be sitting in the car. He came closer, then started to go past, when suddenly he recognized that car. At the same moment he saw that it was empty.

His eyes opened wide with amazement. This was *his* sedan! And that meant that Dale was inside the stockyards!

CHAPTER X

ASPHYXIATED

FROM A long, long distance a voice dribbled into Dale's brain. "Dale! Dale darling! Come out of it!"

She opened her eyes, tried to say something. But she couldn't edge the words past the squeezed sponge-rubber that her throat seemed to have become.

"Snap out of it, Dale! Something's going on upstairs. I've got to leave you and see what it is."

That picked her up better than a bromide could have done.

"Leave me?" she choked out, clinging desperately to Doc's strong right arm. He was bending over her, his eyes anxious. "No! Don't leave me! Not in this awful place!"

He helped her to her feet. Her legs seemed rubbery. She felt his drenched clothing.

"You're all wet!"

He grinned, in spite of their serious situation.

"You're telling me."

A low steady drone came from somewhere. Dale heard it and pressed against Doc's arm with new fear.

"What's—that?"

"I don't know exactly. Sounds like one of the machines in operation upstairs."

"It wasn't going when—when whatever it was grabbed and choked me," Dale managed, conscious now of her sore larynx.

"No, darling," Doc told her. "I have an idea that's why you were choked—to keep you out of the way for a few minutes. I've got to go up and find out what's happening."

"I'm going with you!"

"But—"

There was no arguing Dale out of it. So with Doc's wet arm around her slim waist, his right hand gripping the flashlight he had "lifted" from the seaman on the *Gray Gull*, they went up the stairs to the second floor.

The drone of the great machine was louder here. Doc instantly killed his flashlight and, with Dale, started slowly forward.

He stopped short with sudden alarm as to his nostrils wafted that self-same sickish, burning odor that he had encountered in James Donnelly's library. But this time he knew what it was! A newly-discovered etheric-aromatic vapor which produced instant but at the same time only brief unconsciousness. But it was an unconsciousness that would last long enough for a killer to murder his victims without a struggle, and without leaving a trace that they had first been overcome.

Doc wondered fearfully what new horror had warranted the use of the vapor this time. With a minimum of sound he and Dale groped their way between the mammoth machines that were used to separate and prepare the meats into the various products that the Landon Company put out. There were meat grinders, automatic mixers, chopping machines, slicers.

They were passing the slicing machine, when Doc's toe struck against something soft, unyielding. The short hairs on the back of his neck bristled. He knew what it was before he bent over and touched it.

HE TOLD Dale to turn her face away, as he clicked on his flashlight. A shudder passed through him at what he saw.

There, sprawled out on the floor, lay the body of Donato Cabral—minus his head! At least the head was not joined to the body. It lay several feet away, severed by the huge razor-sharp blade of the giant meat-slicing machine!

After that one first but all-inclusive glance at the horror, Doc Murdock got Dale downstairs as swiftly as he could, and took her home. She was badly shaken up by the ordeal she had just undergone. He fixed her a sedative, saw she was safe and resting comfortably, then left.

He parked his car a couple of blocks from his Swank Street quarters and walked briskly to the alley that led to a back door. He used this entrance when he wished to come and go without being seen, and in his present unsightly condition he had no desire to meet anyone.

From the time he left Dale, his mind had been on one thought. The killer was on the prowl tonight. He had killed Donnelly and Cabral. Who would be his next victim? Roger Landon?

The moment he reached his study, Doc took the phone and called the meat packer's home. There was no answer. Doc's face was lined with worry as he cradled the phone.

Where could Landon be at this time of night? Of course there was still a chance that Landon himself was behind this series of crimes. But somehow Doc could not believe that.

His thought returned to the body of Cabral in the factory. Maybe by this time the decapitated corpse had been discovered by one of the watchmen and Landon had been summoned to the plant?

But suppose the murderer had already visited the meat packer? Or suppose he had called Landon and had duped him into coming to the yards to deal him the same fate as he had meted out to the South American?

Whatever the answer, it was up to the Purple Scar to find it out.

Doc stripped off his wet clothes, washed the muck from his body under a quick needle shower and hastily donned a fresh outfit.

Less than fifteen minutes after he had entered the black alley, he emerged again, looking as far from the plastic surgeon that the city knew as possible. He now wore a neat blue suit with a thin pencil line running through the material. His hair was dyed steel-gray and his features had become hawklike. Another shining example of what could be done with rubber masks. And, as usual, beneath this top mask was the ghastly scarred face of the Purple Scar.

Roger Landon lived in one of the best residential sections of Akelton. His home while modest when compared with James Donnelly's, was still evidence that at one time the meatpacking business had paid handsome profits.

Doc was about to go up the stoop to the front door when the sound of an idling motor came to his ears. His first thought was that Landon must be leaving the garage.

HE STARTED around behind the house via the driveway and had come in sight of the two-car garage when, without warning, a black mass flew out of the darkness at him, knocking him down.

The very suddenness of the attack stunned the Scar for a moment. Then as he started to climb to his knees in the gravel, he glimpsed the outline of a hand coming at him. A gloved hand holding a small cylindric object that he could not quite make out in the dimness. But even in his half-dazed mind, he knew that it contained that etheric-aromatic with which the killer *had* overpowered Donnelly, Cabral and possibly Sandy Phail.

The Scar saw that he could not reach the hand in time to stay it. But he did the next best thing. From his breast pocket, he yanked his handkerchief and covered his nose and mouth.

There was a slight hissing sound and through the handkerchief seeped a faint whiff of the sleep-producing aromatic. The Scar lay back and waited.

The killer drew nearer to him. Through half-opened lids, the Scar could see the faint glint of a blade in an upraised hand.

He did not wait for it to descend. He lashed out with his right foot, caught the killer's wrist and sent the knife whirling into the air.

In a wink the killer leaped erect and darted away. The Scar was to his feet and about to give chase, when he heard the sound of an idling automobile engine. That altered his plans. Much as he wanted to nab the killer, he instinctively knew what that purring motor meant. He had to stop it!

Flashlight in hand, he whirled and raced toward the garage. He could see through the window in the closed doors that both cars were in. The motor of one of them was idling.

He pulled the door open. Thick acrid smoke from the car's exhaust gushed at him, almost stifling him. The Scar knew that this smoke also contained poisonous carbon monoxide.

Through the haze that filled the garage, the Scar saw something slumped across the steering wheel of the car. It was a man, his face resting face downward on the wheel, his arms dangling limp and motionless. By his white hair, the Scar knew it was Roger Landon!

Again covering his mouth and nose with his handkerchief, he leaped into the garage. He tore open the door of the car and dragged the man's inert body out into the driveway.

Kneeling beside the man, he instantly felt for pulse beats, heart action. There was just the faint murmur of life left in him.

Stripping off the meat packer's coat, the Scar tore open his shirt and collar and set to work giving first aid treatment. For one awful moment, he thought that he was too late when the man's heart-beats seemed to fade out. But with dogged determination, the Scar coaxed life back into the man. At last Roger Landon opened his eyes.

The Scar took Landon into the house and called an ambulance. While they waited, the meat packer told the Purple Scar that he had received a call from the factory informing him that the beheaded corpse of Donato Cabral had been discovered there.

THEN, SAID the meat packer, he had dressed at once and hurried to the garage to get his car. He had just got into the front seat when a peculiar vapor tangled with his senses. He remembered trying to fight against it—then his consciousness faded. That's the last thing he knew until revived by the Purple Scar.

"It couldn't have been carbon monoxide from the car," he said. "I hadn't started the engine going, and carbon monoxide, of course, is both colorless and odorless."

It was not difficult for the Scar to figure what that "peculiar vapor" was. He had been dead right in his deductions. The killer had been on the prowl tonight and Roger Landon would have been Victim Number Three if he had not snatched the man from the very jaws of death. And it could have been a death that could easily have passed for an accident or even suicide.

CHAPTER XI

GENTLEMEN PREFER THEM

LANDON WAS now far removed from the arrogant individual Dr. Murdock had met the afternoon before in the man's office. He was humble and totally crushed. This brush with death had left him limp with all the fight gone out of him, and had terrorized him into changing his mind about a lot of things.

"Whoever has been doing these things to me, ruining my firm, stealing my products and now trying to kill me has finally succeeded in his purpose," he murmured lifelessly. "I'll sell the business as soon as I can. I want no more of this nightmare. I'll sell to anyone except Sam Ziggley. If he wants the firm, if he's the one behind these terrible things that have been happening, then let him fight it out with the new owner. I'm selling out!"

The Scar's mind was busy with a new thought. Ordinarily he would have dissuaded Landon against this sudden decision to sell. He would have argued any man out of quitting under fire like this. But he said nothing to the meat packer for a very definite reason. Perhaps this was the one thing that would smoke out the killer!

Certainly, if the firm could be bought, then the killer, after the extremes to which he had gone so far, would make every effort to get hold of it. It would be an interesting game to watch. But in the meantime, the Scar would not stand by idle. He would go on trying to snare the killer.

"Just one thing, Mr. Landon," he said. "In the event that this little 'accident' tonight had worked, who'd have profited most? Your nephew, Walter Faber? He's your only living blood relation, isn't he?"

Landon nodded his head wearily. "I'd have left him a few thousand dollars. But he won't get the bulk of my estate. And I wouldn't have left him the firm."

"He knew that?"

"Yes."

The Scar eyed the meat packer intently.

"Who would have inherited the firm?"

From the couch upon which he was lying, Landon looked up into the hawklike face. Then he dropped his eyes as if a trifle embarrassed by the confession he was about to make.

"Miss Zoe Faine, my secretary," he murmured, his words scarcely audible.

The Scar was about to say, "The blond Venus who hides behind hornrimmed glasses and an unflattering coiffure?" But he said, "The young lady I met in your office?"

"Yes," Landon admitted. "I'm—I'm in love with Miss Faine."

"Does she know she's to inherit the firm?"

"Yes."

Doc tried to conceal the profound surprise that this information caused him, as he asked:

"Suppose anything should have happened to both you and Miss Faine, would the firm then have gone to your nephew?"

"No. To those who have been with the firm for the past twenty years or more. There are only a handful. But each is to receive an amount in proportion to the number of years he's been with me."

DOC RECALLED that when Faber introduced Carl Coyne, the plant manager, he had remarked that Coyne had been with the firm for more than twenty-five years. That would come pretty close to making him the oldest employee of the lot and therefore put him in line for the greater division of the spoils.

The Scar, however, made no mention of this to Landon. For in Landon's present shattered state of mind, he might arouse undue suspicions. But it certainly gave Carl Coyne an excellent reason for wanting to commit these murders. He could get Landon out of the way and later remove Zoe Faine, leaving himself with the controlling interest in the firm.

The ambulance was screeching to a stop outside the door. The Scar knew that the intern would be perfectly capable of taking care of Landon and he had to get away.

"I'm leaving you now," he told the meat packer.

Landon's colorless face was wreathed with bewilderment.

"But why? You saved my life. I want to reward you."

"There's no reward," the Scar tossed back as he started toward the rear door.

"But who are you?"

"The Purple Scar!" And the next moment he had left Roger Landon alone in the room.

Groping his way through the dark driveway, the Scar remembered the knife he had kicked out of the killer's hand. He wondered if the killer had returned for it.

He made a brief search and was rewarded by finding it. When he got to a lighted place where he could examine it, he found it to be a brownhandled weapon with a long, razor-sharp blade. The kind of a knife that butchers use. And on the heel of the handle, in small letters were stamped the words:

ZIGGLEY MEAT PRODUCTS COMPANY

In an all-night drug-store a few blocks from Roger Landon's home, Doc Murdock used a telephone.

"I'd like to speak to Mr. Ziggley," he said, when he got his number. "He's not home.... Where is he?... Yes, this is very important.... Where?.... Did you say the Silver Spider Nightclub?... Thanks."

He pronged the receiver, waited a moment, then dropped another nickel in the slot and called a second number.

"Hello. Is this Mr. Faber?" he asked when a sleepy voice answered. "This is the police.... Your uncle, Roger Landon, met with an accident.... Now take it easy, no need to get excited.... No, he isn't dead.... He's been taken to the City Hospital Mr. Faber, I've got to ask you how long you've been home?... Since ten o'clock? Thank you, sir."

The Silver Spider was café society's Number One hot spot, run by a former socialite, Herman Millingway. The Scar knew Millingway, and knew how to worm his way past the plush rope without even mentioning the name of Dr. Miles Murdock.

Doc climbed up on one of the silver-topped stools at the bar and ordered a Scotch and soda. As he sipped his drink, his eyes roved the place. Almost every table was occupied. The place was filled with glamor lads and lassies slightly in their cups.

THE SCAR recognized a lot of faces that Doc Murdock had made "alterations" on. If the owners of those faces had had any idea that the man with the hawklike features and steel-gray hair was their favorite plastic surgeon, they would have been all over his neck.

Doc was not interested in them now. He was looking for Sam Ziggley, knowing that he would recognize the man at sight. It was Doc's business as a plastic surgeon and as a crime fighter to know what important people in the city looked like. Besides Ziggley's face had adorned the newspapers for a good many weeks during that "meat pumping" incident.

He finally spotted Landon's business rival sitting in one of the booths that lined the far wall of the club. Sam Ziggley was about five feet eleven. He was rather good looking in a racketeer sort of way, and he wore his dark glossy hair bushy over his Dumbo ears. There was a wealth of power in his big, tuxedo-clad shoulders. Power enough to choke a person almost to death—or to drive a knife deep!

There was no one in the booth with Ziggley, which was a break, Doc thought, as he slipped off his stool and sauntered forward. He was about half-way when a girl came out of the powder room at the extreme end of the narrow aisle and started forward.

She was a neat bundle of pulchritude, with curves distributed exquisitely, all well revealed by her lowcut gown of shimmering green satin. Her hair fell to her bare shoulders in curls of spun gold. Her features were out of a Petty ad.

At first Doc thought whimsically that maybe that was where he had seen the girl—smiling up at him out of *College Humor.* But as she came closer, he knew that he had met and spoken to her, and not too long ago, either.

To his utter astonishment the girl stopped directly in front of the booth where Ziggley was sitting. She smiled down at the glossy-haired meat packer and he arose as she took the seat opposite him in the booth.

And then like a thunderbolt it struck Doc. He knew where he had seen this dazzling blond before. She was Zoe Faine, Landon's secretary! The girl who wore those horn-rimmed glasses, that unbecoming hair-do. The girl to whom, Landon had just admitted, he would leave his fortune.

Doc had known that behind the girl's ugly duckling make-up that there was real beauty. But he had not dreamed such a stunning transformation could be possible.

He kept right on walking past the booth, with neither Ziggley nor the girl even bothering to look up at him. At the door he buttonholed

Herman Millingway. He flashed a dummy badge that he used in such emergencies.

"Detective O'Brien—headquarters," he whispered. "There won't be any trouble, if you'll answer a couple of questions."

Millingway was uneasy. With the class of customers to whom he catered, the one thing he did not want was trouble.

"How long has Mr. Ziggley been here?" Doc asked, nodding his gray-thatched head toward the meat packer's booth.

"Not long," Millingway answered. "Half hour maybe."

"The girl come in with him?"

"No. She was waiting almost an hour for him. He must've been late."

Doc frowned. That meant that Ziggley had not been in the club at the time of Landon's attempted murder or the beheading of Donato Cabral.

Had Ziggley believed he had killed the white-haired meat packer, then come here to keep his rendezvous with beautiful Zoe Faine? Were these two in league with each other? It was the perfect set-up for that. Landon's trusted secretary, the girl he loved, supping with his most hated rival, the man he openly accused of committing the crimes.

It stunned Doc to think that a girl so beautiful could be mixed up in a business that was so rotten. Not that Zoe Faine's beauty meant anything to the plastic surgeon. He just happened to be from that school that has a profound respect for women and for beauty. It was always distasteful for him to learn that there was a girl involved in any case on which he was working.

He tried to tell himself that she was not implicated, that she and Ziggley were not working together.

But it was tough, arguing with his eyes.

There was one more person on whom Doc must check this night—Carl Coyne. The man had become a mighty important cog in this wheel of mystery that was revolving around him.

From a phone book, Doc obtained Coyne's address. He recalled hearing the plant manager say that he got "on the job" every morning at five. That meant he should leave home about four.

It was exactly a quarter past four when Doc Murdock, the Purple Scar, using one of his pass-keys, let himself into the plant manager's modest three-room bachelor apartment. He waited until he was sure the place was empty, then snapped on his flash.

One look at the apartment was evidence that Carl Coyne was above the average male in the way of neatness. There was a place for everything and everything in its place. Even the bed was made, which made it a little difficult for the Scar to determine whether Coyne had made it up before he left the rooms, or whether it had not been slept in all night!

Passing into what served as a combination living room and study, the Scar went to the shelves of books that lined one side wall. He always liked to find out what books a man read, for he believed they had a lot to do in revealing a man's character, his subconscious.

One thing was plain—Carl Coyne did not read trash. His shelves were crowded with works by the best authors. Classics.

Then there was a section devoted to books on the meat-packing industry, its management, and all other phases. There was a book on butchery that discussed it from slitting a cow's throat to the dissection of every portion of the animal. There was another section of books pertaining to the development of the mind, books on success—the way to a fuller, richer life.

Still another portion of the book shelves showed such titles as "Freud's Works," "*Maeterlinck,*" "*Mein Kampf*"—not translations, but in the original.

THOSE BOOKS told the Scar many things about Carl Coyne. The man was obviously intelligent, had ambition, a desire to succeed, and—most important—he knew German.

The Scar's mind was back in that cramped, musty room just off the secret passageway that led out of the Landon plant to the river. The men who had held him prisoner had spoken German. The sailor whom he had tackled had said that all transactions when they met the mystery ship at sea were carried out in German, though he had protested that he and his mates were all good Americans, and that even if the mystery ship was manned by men who spoke German that they had all come from South America, which was their home.

Now Coyne—he probably spoke German, too. This whole business was beginning to look like a job for the F.B.I. or Naval Intelligence. But the Scar was determined not to go to them until he could produce all the facts. Still, the ramifications of a vicious scheme to send America's food to the country's enemies was making the Purple Scar see red.

He *would* expose this main criminal, whoever he was, now! The man, and those working with him—and against America—should not get away with it! That would be the Scar's contribution to national safety.

Turning from the book shelves, he walked to the desk. What few papers were atop it were neatly stacked. There was an onyx pen-and-pencil stand with the inscription:

To Carl Coyne, for Twenty-five Years Faithful Service.
From the Landon Meat Products Company.

A French phone and a small calendar completed the articles on the desk.

The Scar thumbed through the papers, but found nothing of importance. He then tackled the drawers. In one of the lower ones he came across a small black bank book. He opened it and read down the list of deposits which had been made as systematically as everything else the man did:

Feb. 15	$229.17
Feb. 20	500.00
Feb. 28	229.17
Mar. 10	500.00
Mar. 15	229.17
Mar. 20	500.00
Mar. 30	229.17
Apr. 10	500.00
Apr. 15	229.17

The Scar closed the little black bank book and placed it back in the drawer where he had found it. There was a calculating look in his eyes as he glanced at the desk calendar.

AT LEAST this portion of the mystery was solved. He knew now that Carl Coyne was responsible for the robberies that had been occurring at the Landon plant. For that little black bank book had told its own story. The plant manager had been making twice his salary these past months, smuggling products out of the plant and selling them to his Fatherland—for the Scar could have no doubt of the man's nationality now.

It was not hard to decipher that those $229.17 entries represented Coyne's salary which was paid twice monthly. The $500.00 deposits were payments he had received for the stolen merchandise. Especially was it easy to figure out since this was April 20th and another shipment of stolen foodstuffs had been smuggled out during the night.

The Scar glanced at the inscription on the pen and pencil stand, again.

Twenty-five Years Faithful Service.

Ironic was not the name for it. But—was Coyne also responsible for the chain of murders? Until the Scar made sure he couldn't clamp down on these other activities, as important as they were. However, when the time came, a clean sweep of Nazis on this side of the world, as well as of the Fifth Columnists who were helping them could be made. No more good American food would be headed for Nazi stomachs from this neck of the woods.

CHAPTER XII

SAUSAGE GRINDER

ON THE dot of seven-thirty the next morning the telephone rang in Dr. Miles Murdock's bedroom. Doc was in the shower, following a fifteen-minute workout in his gym. It seemed that he could do with less sleep than any man since Edison.

Grabbing a large Turkish towel off the rack, he went into the bedroom, drying himself vigorously.

It was Griffin on the phone. The detective-captain asked Doc about the attempted murder of Roger Landon last night and Doc told him what he knew.

"Found anything important on Donato Cabral?" he asked then.

"Have I!" Griffin exclaimed. "Hang onto your seat. To begin with his name wasn't Cabral. It was Pete Mando. He wasn't any more South American than you or me. We found his fingerprints in the files. Used to be a confidence man out on the Coast. Things got too warm for him there, so he shipped to South America, changed his moniker and worked out a couple of new rackets."

Which explained quite conclusively to Doc why "Donato Cabral" had suddenly lost his accent when he had become excited.

"According to a receipt we found amongst his belongings at the hotel," Griffin went on, "he had just made a twenty-five-thousand-dollar down payment on a ranch in the Argentine. There was a balance of a hundred thousand due."

A ranch in the Argentine with a due balance of $100,000, Doc mused after he hung up. The exact amount James Donnelly had withdrawn from the bank the day he was murdered—and that money was still missing!

It was shortly before noon when Doc approached the supervisor's desk at the head of the third floor corridor in the City Hospital. The whitecapped woman smiled and said:

"Oh, hello, Dr. Murdock."

"Hello, Jane," he replied. "How's Roger Landon?"

"Still shaken up."

"Anyone with him?"

"His nephew—Walter Faber."

"Has anyone else been here?"

"Yes—a young lady."

"Blond, with glasses?"

"Yes, his secretary. She was here almost all last night and again early this morning. She's very attentive."

Doc made no comment, but turned and walked down the white-walled corridor to Room 305. He opened the door and went into the room where Roger Landon half sat up in a white bed. His face was tired and his eyes were washed-out.

Walter Faber, seated beside the bed, adjusted his nose glasses. Arising quickly and offering his hand he said with surprise:

"Good morning, Dr. Murdock. What brings you here?"

"I heard what happened to Mr. Landon," Doc said, shaking hands first with Faber, then with the meat packer. "I dropped in to see if I could be of service."

"That's very kind," Landon said dully.

FOR A time they spoke of Landon's condition and the near tragedy that had caused it. Then Doc worked around to the subject that had brought him here.

"I understand you intend selling your firm," he commented.

"Yes, I decided that last night," Landon said, in that same weary, beaten voice of the previous evening. "I'm getting rid of it soon as possible."

"At first I tried to argue Uncle Roger out of it when I came to see him last night," Faber spoke up. "But after talking it over and realizing the danger he's been in, it seems the wisest thing to do."

"Have you a buyer yet?" Doc asked.

"Yes," Landon said, unemotionally. "There were several bids as soon as I made my announcement."

"Ziggley included?" Doc exacted.

Landon's face clouded. "Yes. His was one of the first bids. Most of the others were from smaller firms—and scarcely worthwhile. The best came from a Mr. Luis Fetticairn, a South American rancher."

The mention of South America again brought a frown into Doc's face. Was this mere coincidence?

"Fetticairn's had his eye on the firm for some time," Landon went on. "Made several offers to me in the past. Wants the firm for North American distribution of his stock."

"And you've made up your mind to sell to him?" asked Doc.

"Yes," Landon said. "For half a million dollars."

"I've already cabled him for Uncle Roger," Faber said. "He's leaving South America at once by the first plane. It should take him about a week to get here. Should arrive about next Monday."

"Which means until next Monday you're going to be in a rather dangerous spot," Doc told the meat packer. "Don't forget that more than one person will lose all possible hope of receiving any part of the firm by will, if you sell. Might even lose their jobs, if Fetticairn decides he wants his own men. For the next day or so you'll be safe in here, of course. But after that, I'd advise a police body-guard. I'm seeing Captain Griffin today, so I'll arrange one for you if you'd like."

"You're very kind," Landon said.

Footsteps hurrying along the corridor interrupted. The next moment the door burst open. Carl Coyne, disheveled, with staring eyes, swept into the room. Entirely ignoring Doc Murdock, he glared at Landon and Faber.

"What are you doing here?" Landon demanded. "You're supposed to be working at the plant."

"Working at the plant!" Coyne flung at him heatedly. "For almost thirty years I've worked at the plant. Day in, day out. And now I understand you're selling it—that in a couple of weeks I'll be out of a job!"

"Uncle Roger isn't well," Faber snapped in sudden defense of his relative. "You've no right barging in here."

"Keep your mouth shut!" Coyne snapped menacingly. "Is this fair to me, Roger? Throwing me out of a job after years of faithful service?"

"I had to sell, Carl," Landon said, almost apologetically. "But I promise you—I'll speak to Fetticairn. I'll try to make provisions that you and the other older employees be kept on."

"I don't know why you have to make apologies to people to whom you've paid a salary," Faber said disdainfully.

WITH A snort and with his thin face distorted with rage, Coyne started around the bed to try to get at Faber.

But Doc was between them. He placed his heavy hand on Coyne's shoulder, a shoulder unbelievably muscular.

"I think you had better leave now, Mr. Coyne," Doc advised, turning the plant manager toward the door. "People do and say a lot of things when they're angry that they're sorry for later. Besides, Mr. Landon shouldn't be upset."

Doc glanced back at Landon.

"I'll speak to Captain Griffin about that little matter," he said, then walked out with Carl Coyne.

By the time they reached the street Coyne had quieted down.

"I guess I *was* pretty sore," Coyne said as he walked along the sidewalk with Doc, toward his aged Ford. "But that Faber gets my nanny."

"You don't care much for the gentleman, evidently," Doc prompted.

"Or for his father before him," Coyne supplemented. There was almost a snarl in his voice. "Incompetents, both of them."

"You knew his father?"

Coyne cleared his throat, wheezed asthmatically.

"I worked for him. He was married to Roger Landon's sister. He and Landon went into the meat-packing business together. But it didn't take Landon long to learn his mistake. He bought out John Faber, Walter Faber's father. Then John Faber took to drinking. Told everyone Landon swindled him out of his share of the firm.

"When John Faber died, Landon took his sister and her child into his home. Tried to make something of the boy after his sister passed away. Sent him to college, gave him every opportunity. But the boy was his old man all over again—no good!

"Finally, in disgust, Landon gave him a figurehead job with the firm. Called him superintendent. The job I should have had. To make it worse, I had to take orders from him. And now, on top of all those things, I stand a good chance to lose my job. Can you blame me for losing my temper, Dr. Murdock?"

No, Doc couldn't blame him. But it was not his place to say so. Besides, he was not forgetting that Coyne was behind the robberies of the firm that he was supposed to serve so faithfully. What was worse—much worse—he was a traitor to the country that had taken him in and given him a chance to make a successful living! He was—a Nazi!

After leaving Coyne, Doc called Captain Griffin regarding the bodyguard for Landon. But the detective was not at HQ.

"Charlie Mendolsohn's taken a runout powder with a satchel full of ice," the desk sergeant informed Doc. "The captain's over at Mendolsohn's apartment now."

Doc knew Charlie Mendolsohn fairly well. Tall, dark, debonair, the man was one of Akelton's foremost jewelers.

HIS CURIOSITY piqued, Doc hopped his car and shot over to see Griffin at the jeweler's office-apartment on Broadway.

"Enough things ain't happenin'," Griffin complained when Doc came in. "Now this thing's gotta pop."

"Exactly what happened?" the plastic surgeon inquired.

"The Van Home's pride and joy is getting spliced tonight."

Doc was aware of that. It was in all the papers.

"Well," Griffin continued, "the old man was givin' her the famous Van Home 'Rainbow of Diamonds' as a wedding gift. Worth a cool half a million, even if the ice was chopped up and sold in small pieces. Charlie Mendolsohn's job was to reset these jewels."

That was in the paper also.

"He was to deliver the Rainbow back to Mr. Van Home this morning," Griffin concluded. "But instead he took the jewels and skipped."

Doc frowned his doubt of that.

"Mendolsohn's been a reputable jeweler in this city for a long time," he protested. "It doesn't seem probable that he'd pull a stunt like that and ruin his entire life."

"Half a million frogskins is an awful lot of green," reminded Griffin.

"It still doesn't sound like Charlie Mendolsohn," Doc argued.

He took a few minutes and looked around the apartment. The closets were crowded with the jeweler's clothes. His suit-cases and traveling bags were all in their proper places, empty.

"Doesn't look as if he was planning much of a getaway," Doc commented.

"Maybe all that ice chilled his blood and he figured a powder was the only way to cure it," growled Griffin.

Doc smiled faintly. Then he told Griffin about wanting the body-guard.

"Okay," Griffin said. "If you think it's a good idea."

It was a good idea. But it would have been a better idea if Doc had put a body-guard on somebody else's tail, too. Still he had no way of knowing that until after the thing happened.

It grew out of that scrap in Landon's room at the hospital. Faber and Coyne carried their argument over into the afternoon, when they met again at the plant.

According to eye witnesses, they called each other some sizzling names. Accusations and threats flew around like sparks in a blacksmith's shop.

Some said that Faber went out of his way to rub it into the plant manager that his days were numbered.

And then, as he had in the hospital, Carl Coyne lost control of his temper. He sprang at the younger man and began choking him. Only the intervention of the other workers prevented a savage brawl then and there.

"You'll never be around to see me go out," Coyne was said to have vowed.

Late that night one of the watchmen at the factory heard one of the second floor machines in motion. He followed the sound to the largest of the meat grinders and there made a grisly discovery!

The body of a man had been thrown into the machine and ground and mangled beyond recognition. The police arrived on the scene. Captain Griffin was there, in charge. He, in turn, called Doc Murdock in the hope that there might be enough of the body left to put it together again. But there was not.

CHAPTER XIII

FETTICAIRN

Z OE FAINE came into the plant while the police were trying to untangle the puzzle. She had on her secretarial make-up.

Her face was like a ghost and her eyes behind the prop glasses were furtive and frightened. She screamed and fainted dead away when, after insisting, she viewed the mangled remains in the meat grinder.

Doc carried her into the office and brought her around. Then, since there was nothing more he could do here, he offered to take her home in his car.

It was on this ride home that he asked her several pertinent questions.

"Are you in love with Roger Landon?" was the first inquiry.

She turned her face and looked at him with a sort of confused expression.

"What made you ask me a thing like that, Dr. Murdock?"

"My friend Captain Griffin is trying to solve a mystery. I'd like to help him if I can."

"How could my feelings toward Roger Landon possibly have any bearing on the situation?" the girl asked.

"Perhaps they couldn't. But when you take into consideration that last night someone tried to murder Roger Landon and that you were out with the one man whom Roger Landon refuses to sell his company to, it might mean a great deal."

"What do you mean I was out with a man last night?" Zoe Faine tried to bluff.

Doc smiled, but there was no mirth in his eyes.

"I happen to know you were at the Silver Spider last night with Sam Ziggley."

The girl emitted a gasp. After that Doc had no trouble with his questions.

"Yes," she admitted. "I was out with Sam Ziggley. But I had no part in trying to murder Roger Landon."

"Do you love him?" Doc repeated.

"No. I never made any pretense at loving him."

"He loves you."

"And I've tried to respect that love. He met me when I was in the front line of a musical show. He took me out of the show and told me he wanted me to be his wife. I didn't want that. I didn't want anything else for nothing. He was impressed. He said I was the first person he'd ever met who didn't want something out of him.

"He suggested I become his secretary. I went to school, studied, and the worst anyone can say is that I've tried hard to make good. When I finally came to work in the plant, he thought I'd better wear these drab clothes. He said as a show girl I'd be a little too distracting.

"After I worked there awhile, I found out that the reason he wanted me to be his secretary was that he intended leaving me the plant and wanted me to know the business inside and out. I gave him to understand that if he did leave me the firm, I'd sell it. He said that was up to me."

"What were you doing with Sam Ziggley?" Doc queried.

"Mr. Ziggley's been after me for a long time to try to change Roger Landon's attitude toward him and sell him the firm. But even my influence with him couldn't do that."

DOC MURDOCK nodded, as he drew up before the girl's home. But when he drove away his thoughts again were on that gruesome murder in the meat-packing plant.

Meantime the police chemists had scraped up what fragments of clothing, bits of paper and strands of hair they could find in the giant meat grinder. They took these specimens to the lab at HQ and worked far into the night trying to piece them together.

Finally from the coloring of the hair, the weave of the fabric and the pieced together fragments of the papers that the dead man had been carrying, the body was identified as Walter Faber!

One other bit of evidence was picked up near the scene of this ghastly crime. A small length of gold watch chain which had apparently been broken off during the struggle that preceded Faber's death.

This piece of chain was identified as having belonged to Carl Coyne. Because of the violent verbal battle between Coyne and Faber that afternoon the murder was laid at the plant manager's front door. The dragnet was out for him. But Carl Coyne had disappeared.

The police combed the city for him. They searched his home, his haunts, every place where he might hole-up. But the man could not be found.

Immediately upon learning that the body found in the meat grinder was Faber's, Doc Murdock, assuming another of his disguises, visited the dead superintendent's apartment. He let himself into the rooms with one of his keys and went through Faber's belongings. In a jewelry box in the top drawer of the bureau he found a callstub for a watch that was being repaired. It had been left several days before and was to have been ready today. The jeweler was Charlie Mendolsohn!

Also, Doc discovered several small clumps of dry clay embedded in the carpet. It had been dragged in on someone's shoes. Scraping up a bit of this clay, he found it to be of a peculiar, clingy, reddish-brown texture. Sea bottom clay.

Doc had come in contact with the stuff recently and he knew that it was common to one particular spot near here—the ocean side of Red Point where before war was declared they had been dredging to sink the foundation for the new ten-million-dollar boardwalk.

Immediately Doc called Police Headquarters and asked if any of this red clay had been found in their analysis of the ground-up body. The "no" reply confused him slightly, but he was determined to go on along the same lines.

At ten o'clock the next morning Doc Murdock, wearing the hawklike feature of "Detective O'Brien," drove through the gates of the vast stockyards which bore the legend:

ZIGGLEY MEAT PRODUCTS COMPANY

A couple of minutes later he was entering the reception room. A blond girl at the switchboard looked up at him. Ziggley apparently had a weakness for blonds.

"Is Mr. Ziggley in?" Doc asked.

"He's very busy," the girl replied. "Have you an appointment?"

"No. But I think he'll see me," Doc said. He slapped his hand palm upward on the desk and showed his prop shield.

"Detective O'Brien from Akelton City."

HER EYES widened. She manipulated a plug and spoke into the mouthpiece:

"Detective O'Brien from Akelton to see you, Mr. Ziggley."

She looked up at Doc with a half-grin.

"Go right in, sir."

Doc opened the frosted glass door and went into an office where Sam Ziggley's not unhandsome face stared at him from behind an immense desk on which stacks of papers were piled.

Ziggley frowned.

"You wished to see me?"

"Yes," Doc said briskly. "Someone tried to kill me night before last, at the same time they tried to kill Roger Landon."

Ziggley stiffened. "And why should you come here to see me about that?"

Doc tossed the brown-handled butcher knife he had found at the Landon place onto the desk.

"Ever see that knife before?" he demanded.

Ziggley picked it up, scowled blackly.

"Of course. It came out of our slaughter-house. It has our name stamped on it. How did you get it?"

"That's the knife the murderer tried to use on me," Doc said coldly.

Ziggley's eyes narrowed murderously. "That's a lie! You're trying to frame me."

"If I wanted to frame you, I could very easily drag you into the case," Doc said without raising or lowering his voice. "A lot of people would like to know that you and Zoe Faine were together at the Silver Spider the night the attempt was made on Roger Landon's life, and that you were trying to persuade her to make Landon sell to you. But she told you she couldn't. That's plenty of motive and evidence from where I'm sitting, Mr. Ziggley."

Ziggley seemed to wilt visibly. Beads of perspiration the size of buckshot stood out on his face.

"How did the killer get this knife?" demanded Doc.

"I don't know," Ziggley replied with a hint of nervousness. "They're accessible to anyone who visits the plant. We keep them in the slaughter-house."

"Has anyone in the Landon Company been here during the past few days?"

Ziggley swallowed. "Yes. Three people. Zoe Faine, Walter Faber, and Carl Coyne. Coyne's been dissatisfied because he had to take orders from an incompetent like Landon's nephew. He came to see me about a job. I told him that he'd have a very good job if he could change Landon's opinion of me and get him to sell to me. But I wouldn't take him away from Landon.

"Faber came to sort of butter both sides of his bread. He knew their firm was slipping. So he came to assure me that these accusations his uncle was making about me were in no way his sentiments. He told me that he was my friend—and added that he wished I'd keep him in mind in case anything did happen to the Landon Company. I didn't tell him, of course, but I wouldn't give him a job tending my kennels.

"Zoe Faine came on the morning of the day I took her to the Silver Spider. I sent for her. I wanted to try a sort of goodwill campaign inside Landon's firm. I thought maybe if she and Coyne and Faber went to work on the old man they might convince him I wasn't a bad guy."

"And any one of these three could have got hold of the knife?" Doc asked.

Sam Ziggley nodded an affirmative....

IT HAD been believed that Luis Fetticairn, the purchaser of the Landon Meat Products Company, would arrive from South America in a week or less. But more than a month went by—six weeks, in fact—before he did show up in Akelton City. Doc Murdock chafed at the delay, but there was nothing he could do about it but mark time.

Roger Landon was anxious to get the sale over and done with, also. He had broken considerably during the weeks that had passed since the body in the meat grinder had been identified as that of Walter Faber, his nephew. All he wanted to do now was to take the money the sale of his firm would bring, and settle down to as quiet a life as possible for his remaining years. He had confided to Doc Murdock, whom he believed to be Detective O'Brien, that it was his intention to offer his services to the government as a dollar-a-year man, to donate his experience and knowledge of food products to his country.

The days seemed to drag, but finally Luis Fetticairn did arrive, coming from South America by plane. Doc got his first look at the South American rancher in Landon's office at the meat plant. But not even

Roger Landon knew that the man who was his body-guard was Dr. Murdock.

In ill-fitting clothes and a mask that made him look like the popular conception of a none-too-bright flat-foot, he appeared to be just another detective who had drawn the assignment as Landon's body-guard. For more than a month now, Doc had been on that job, but for all his vigilance he seemed no nearer a solution of the chain of murders than he had been from the start.

One thing, though—no more smuggled meat was leaving the Landon plant to make its way via submarine to any Axis country. Since Coyne's disappearance, there were no more shortages, and the Purple Scar knew the reason for that.

But he still was not laying what evidence he had before the F.B.I. or Naval Intelligence, until he could lay his hands on Coyne—and the killer the Scar was after. Of course, they might be one and the same man, but Doc Murdock was inclined to think otherwise.

Doc had been anxious to meet the South American. Not only because he was the man who was buying Landon's firm, but because no one seemed to know anything about the man. Doc had checked and double-checked on Fetticairn, but had got nowhere. Cablegrams came from him in South America all right, but on the whole he was a man of mystery.

Doc had wondered if it could be possible that Fetticairn was simply an agent for the killer, assigned to buy the Landon Company and later turn it over to the man who had murdered in order to get it into his hands. He had come to no conclusion about that, but at any rate, Doc had made certain that he was present on this all-important occasion when Landon would dispose of his company. For Doc was still fired with the belief that the killer, after so many desperate attempts to get possession of the firm, would not sit by idly and let the company go without one last try.

Doc found Luis Fetticairn to be a tall, wiry man with sort of an olive-colored skin that was drawn tight across his high-cheek-boned face, and narrow black eyes that were inclined to slant. Heavy black hair crowned his head, and a Fu Manchu mustache decorated his lip.

He was a trifle eccentric in dress, wearing sports shoes with business clothes and a bright tie that clashed with his entire ensemble. He explained that he was not in the habit of dressing up—and he looked it. On the great pampas where he spent most of his time, he said, one wore only the garb of the gaucho.

HE WAS fired with enthusiasm for this new world he had discovered.

"People told me what a wonderful countree thees is. But I had no idea! This ees my first trip to the United States and I shall never forget eet!"

Besides Doc Murdock, Roger Landon and Luis Fetticairn, there were two other men in the office. Michael Sneed and William Nottage, Landon's lawyers.

After Landon and the South American talked for a short while, Sneed and Nottage produced the important sales documents that Fetticairn was to read and sign. It was at this point in the proceedings that Doc, standing by the door directly behind Fetticairn, suddenly espied a row of faint crisscross marks on both sides of the South American's long, olive-colored neck.

In the plastic surgeon's eyes was surprise as he dropped his gaze to Fetticairn's shoes and spotted tiny bits of reddish brown clay clinging to the heels. The answer hit Doc like one of Joe Louis's Sunday punches!

He knew now what that clay meant back there in Walter Faber's apartment, how it had come to be there, and why none had showed in the meat-grinding machine.

Without attracting any attention, Doc opened the door and slipped outside. He passed up the phone on Zoe Faine's desk in the reception room, but got on one downstairs and called Captain Griffin.

"Griffin," he rattled off excitedly. "I think we're ready for the final curtain. Send a detail over to Red Point and tell them to search every shack on the island until they find a man who's being held prisoner. Meantime, you hop over here to the Landon plant and wait for me at the front entrance. See that neither Landon or anyone else in the office leaves until I get back."

He gave a couple more brief instructions, then slammed up the receiver and darted out of the building. Once more he was on the trail of murder—but this, he was sure, would be the last link in the long chain!

CHAPTER XIV

CODE TO MURDER

TEN MINUTES later Doc Murdock was letting himself into a small house over on Raynor Street. It was a wooden building with an open porch and big bay windows. There was a sign over the front door bell that read:

DR. I.J. HANLYSON

Dr. Hanlyson was one of Doc Murdock's contemporaries, but one who was none too ethical. Hanlyson made plenty of the green stuff, but he was not too particular how or where it came from.

Some claimed it was Hanlyson who remade gangster Hank Saphire's face so that he could slip out of the country. No one ever proved it, of course, because Hank Saphire was never seen again. But it gave a slant on what people thought of Dr. Hanlyson.

Doc Murdock went through the hallway and into Hanlyson's office. The place appeared deserted and looked as if the tail-end of a cyclone had hit it.

Papers were strewn about the floor in wild disorder. Files and drawers had been pulled out, their contents torn into scraps. Before and after photographs of patients upon whom Hanlyson had performed successful operations were scattered every place.

And then, as Doc took another step into the white-walled room, he caught a glimpse of a pair of rigid legs sticking out from behind the desk. He hurried forward. Sprawled out on the floor was Dr. Hanlyson. Dead! His throat slashed across!

As he stood there and looked down at the murdered plastic surgeon, Dr. Murdock began to assemble the many ends of this case in his mind. Some of the answers he had known for some time. Others he had merely surmised. And Doc was not one to strike until he had all the facts ironed out.

He had seen one case bungled through lack of evidence—the first trial of his brother's murderers, just before the Purple Scar had come into being. To make sure there were no loopholes left for criminals to squirm through he had vowed solemnly that no case on which he worked would ever be lost for that reason.

He took this precious moment to review the answers.

It all started back a lot further than the poisoned meat episode when Mrs. Forbes had been killed and so many of the slum people made ill. It began with greed, an obsession for power and wealth.

The focal points were the Landon Company and that ranch in South America, the ranch on which Donato Cabral had made a $25,000 deposit. The killer wanted that ranch and the company, because with the two of them, it would make him a controlling figure in the meat-packing industry. Perhaps he had visions of becoming the cattle king of the continent, which was not altogether improbable. Not with such a ranch on which to raise cattle and an established company like the Landon Company as an outlet to manufacture and distribute these meats.

But to make the final payment on the ranch and to acquire the company meant the need for money, the kind of money the killer plainly did not have. So he must have gone to James Donnelly, laid his cards on the table and got Donnelly's promise that he would get the money.

BUT JAMES DONNELLY'S promises were not worth the effort it took to make them. After thinking the proposition over, the investment broker apparently thought that it sounded good enough to grab himself. So he doublecrossed the killer and contacted Cabral.

Cabral, a crook to the nth degree, didn't give two hoots who grabbed off the proposition as long as he was cut in on it. And since Donnelly was the guy with the money-bags, Cabral signed on with his team.

The killer must have found out about this doublecross that Cabral and Donnelly were handing him. So he murdered Donnelly and stole the $100,000 with which to make the final payment on the ranch.

Since Cabral was to have left for South America the next morning and since Donnelly did not want his name to appear in the deal, it did not take any great deductive powers for the killer to know that Donnelly would have the cash on him.

As soon as Cabral found out that Donnelly had been killed, he must have made an appointment with the man who had made the original proposition to meet him at the Landon plant. Then Cabral, no doubt, got tough and tried to shake the man down for a piece of the one hundred thousand dollars. So Cabral had been killed.

Then the killer, knowing that Landon would be called to the plant as soon as Cabral's body was discovered, saw his chance to kill Landon. He went to Landon's garage, waited until the meat packer came out and pulled his carbon monoxide stunt, which might easily have passed as either suicide or an unfortunate accident—if the Purple Scar hadn't intervened.

The meat that killed Mrs. Forbes had obviously been poisoned as part of a sabotage plot to ruin Landon and force him into selling the firm. At the same time it would discourage prospective buyers, so that the killer could step in and buy it at his own price. Landon's sudden decision to sell simply speeded up his plans.

Sandy Phail was killed because he knew who poisoned the meat, as Doc and Griffin had first guessed.

Which brought things up to date. The murder of Dr. Hanlyson. Who killed him and why? What had he to do with the chain of murders that began with the poisoned meat?

This could be answered by simple deduction as far as Doc was concerned. The killer, after committing these many murders and at last in a position to reap the reward of his deeds, had to lose his own identity and assume another. He had not only to change his name but his entire appearance—even his face.

So he had gone to Hanlyson. He knew the plastic surgeon was without ethics and would play ball with him. But for that very reason, because he was afraid that later Hanlyson might expose or blackmail him, the killer had today decided to add the plastic surgeon to his list of murders. He also had destroyed all the surgeon's notes and files, so that no record of the operation might be found.

Of course, Doc Murdock by this time had more than a pretty good idea who the killer was. But he wanted more than just an idea before he made his last move. He wanted positive proof.

YES, THE killer had done a thorough job destroying Dr. Hanlyson's records. But there was one thing that it was not likely a layman would know. Plastic surgeons, at least all those with whom Doc Murdock had come in contact, kept code books. The code was one that could be interpreted only by those in the profession.

That book was what Doc Murdock was searching for now in the home of the murdered plastic surgeon. He literally turned the place upside down, but there was no sign of the book. Maybe he had underestimated the killer. Maybe he had found the code book and destroyed it.

Doc stood in the center of the floor and his eyes traveled slowly around the office in one last look. His eyes chanced to settle on Hanlyson's diploma, hanging in a neat white frame on the wall.

"What crimes have been committed by this man under your name and protection," Doc muttered.

Then it came to him! Hanlyson had used this diploma to hide his crimes behind. Why, then, shouldn't he have used it to hide the record of these crimes?

Doc rushed to the picture, yanked it off the wall, turned it over. There, stuck to the back of it, held by strips of adhesive tape, was the book he sought.

Quickly Doc glanced through it. Some of the names it contained amazed him—names that made it read like a police blotter, names that had been lost in the years.

And the fees that Hanlyson had charged for his services made Doc feel like a piker.

Then at last Doc came to the name that he had been sure would be there. He read the details of the operation. Everything fitted his deductions perfectly.

Closing the book and stuffing it in his pocket, he reached for the phone. He called the Akelton airport. When he had obtained the information he asked for, he hung up and promptly left the house of murder.

Captain Griffin was waiting for Doc at the front entrance to the Landon plant. There was another man with Griffin. A short, ruddy-faced man wearing silver-rimmed glasses and with a flat black bag under his arm.

Griffin did not recognize the casual individual who came up to him and asked: "Captain Griffin?"

The square detective twisted with a frown and studied the speaker.

"Yeah," he said. "I'm Captain Griffin."

The eyes of the man who had asked the question flickered, and traveled significantly to the man with the black bag.

"I'm Marty O'Brien," he said. "I called you, Captain, and asked you to meet me here."

The look that came into Griffin's square-shaped face was astonishment with a capital A. It was plain that he wouldn't be surprised in the future if a housefly went past his ear, buzzing: "I'm Dr. Murdock."

"Anyone come out yet?"

Griffin shook his head in a slow negative.

"Nobody. They're all still up in the office."

"Good. Let's go."

Dr. Murdock, alias "Marty O'Brien," Captain Griffin and the man with the black bag went into the building and climbed the stone steps to the second floor.

Zoe Faine was at the desk in the outer office. Doc asked her to come inside for a moment.

ROGER LANDON looked up from behind the desk with mild surprise as the four entered. A bottle of champagne had been opened for the occasion and there were four emptied glasses atop the desk.

When Landon saw Captain Griffin he remarked, "You're just in time to help us celebrate. I've sold the Landon Company to Mr. Fetticairn."

Fetticairn turned quickly, a look of confusion on his tight face at this intrusion.

Doc walked over to the two lawyers.

"May I see the papers that Mr. Fetticairn just signed?" he asked.

The lawyers mumbled something about "highly irregular" but at a word from Landon, Sneed fished the legal documents from his briefcase and handed them to Doc.

Doc swept his eyes over the words.

"Half a million dollars," he said. "A lot of money. The same amount of money a person could get for the sale of a certain Rainbow of Diamonds that's missing."

He pivoted to face Fetticairn.

"A very nice buy, Mr. Fetticairn—even for half a million," Doc said, with heavy irony. "Too bad you're not going to be able to derive any benefit from your bargain."

Fetticairn stiffened. His eyes were defiant.

"What *do* you mean?" he demanded heatedly.

"Yes, what do you mean?" Landon broke in sharply. "Why can't he derive any benefit?"

Doc smiled grimly. "Because Mr. Fetticairn will be too busy keeping a date—with the electric chair!"

CHAPTER XV

OUT OF THE MAZE

MURDER SHOWED in Fetticairn's slanted black eyes. His mouth beneath his droopy black mustache looked mean. "Is this some sort of a joke?" he growled.

"No, Mr. Fetticairn." There was a terrible coldness in Doc's voice. "Murder is hardly a joke."

"Murder?" Roger Landon gasped.

"Yes," Doc said. "This man has quite a string of them to his discredit. Mrs. Forbes, Sandy Phail, Donato Cabral, James Donnelly, Charles Mendolsohn, Dr. Hanlyson the plastic surgeon, and almost *you.*"

"You forgot Walter Faber," Griffin cut in.

Doc shook his head. "I didn't forget Walter Faber because Walter Faber isn't dead. Is he, Mr. Fetticairn?"

"I don't know what you're talking about!" Fetticairn denied angrily.

That black spade was over Doc's right eye, but the twin masks hid it.

"I'm afraid you do know what I'm talking about, Mr. Fetticairn, since you happen to be Walter Faber!"

"The man's mad!" Fetticairn exploded. "Stark mad!"

"You better be able to prove your accusations," Landon said threateningly. "Who are you, anyway?"

In that instant Doc Murdock had the top mask off his face. It was like peeling off the outer coating of skin—to reveal the dreadful face of the Purple Scar!

Fetticairn recoiled at sight of it. Zoe Faine screamed and Landon grabbed at the desk to brace himself.

"The Purple Scar!" he muttered. "The man who saved my life."

"Yes, and I intend to prove my statements," the Scar said in that chilling, tomblike voice that he always assumed in this role. "I had an idea Mr. Fetticairn would be a little reluctant at admitting he was Walter Faber, so I asked Captain Griffin to bring along his best fingerprint expert. Hanlyson could change Walter Faber's face, but there is one thing even the best plastic surgeon can't change—fingerprints." He turned to the man with the black bag. "You'll find Walter Faber's prints right there on Fetticairn was drinking."

"That won't prove I'm Walter Faber," Fetticairn defied. "Suppose you haven't a copy of Faber's prints?"

Doc smiled, twisting the purple mask into a gruesome expression—a corpse smiling.

"But we have Walter Faber's prints," he enlightened. "You seemed to have overlooked the fact that Walter Faber once worked in the slaughter-house of this company, handling meats for public consumption. And the laws of this state require that all persons so employed must have their prints taken and registered before receiving their health permit."

The fingerprint expert had opened his black bag, which contained a full and complete fingerprinting outfit, and was busy dusting the glass.

By the furtive, cornered-animal look on "Luis Fetticairn's" face he knew he was beaten. But like all murderers he was not going to give up without a last desperate fight.

HIS RIGHT hand dipped inside his coat. But the Purple Scar was too quick for him. Across the room in one swift bound, he closed his viselike fingers on Fetticairn's wrist.

"I'm just getting my fountain pen," Fetticairn protested vigorously.

"Yes, I'm aware of that," the Purple Scar said coldly. He jerked the "South American's" hand from his coat. It was gripping a black fountain pen.

"With that particular pen you can do a lot of harm," the Scar accused.

Before Fetticairn's nimble fingers could manipulate the clip on the pen, Doc had it wrenched from his hand. He tossed it to Griffin.

"You'll find that pen contains a liquid called etheric-aramo, the vapor with which Mr. Faber rendered his victims senseless before killing them. Simple to prepare. Anyone with a knowledge of even elementary chemistry could have prepared it. All he needed was the formula and the proper ingredients."

The fingerprint expert looked up, with a small white card from the police files in one hand, in the other a powerful magnifying glass.

"These prints on the champagne glass match identically with those on this card," he announced. "There's no question about it. This man is Walter Faber!"

Faber made one more attempt to break away, but Doc's grip on the man's wrist was like tempered steel.

Doc did not bother to explain how he found out about the fountain pen. But after that scramble he'd had with the killer back in Landon's driveway, he had got to thinking that the cylindrical object he had seen could easily have been a fountain pen.

When things began to point more and more to Faber, Doc recalled those four pens that always adorned Faber's vest and how he had seen Faber first choose one pen to sign the paper that Coyne gave him, then quickly caught himself and took another pen. Doc realized what the first pen must have contained.

No doubt Faber had lingered that night in Landon's driveway to make sure of his uncle's "suicide." Then after the Scar thwarted his plans, Faber must have quickly rushed home to have an alibi ready in case anyone called to question him.

Doc had at first thought it odd that the killer had not picked up his knife. Then he realized it was a deliberate plant. The knife had been left there to point suspicion at Ziggley, who must have been Faber's original choice to frame. But when things had shaped up so that he could more easily pin the murders on Coyne, he had changed victims.

"But why did he do all these things?" Griffin wanted to know. "What was his motive?"

Doc explained as briefly as possible.

"You mean he meant to kill me, his own uncle?" Roger Landon exclaimed with horror.

"I don't believe he ever held much love for you, Mr. Landon," Doc replied.

"Why should I?" Faber interrupted harshly. Then at Landon, fiercely: "You robbed, cheated and killed my father! You sent my mother to her grave years before her time. Then you tried to ease your conscience by taking me into the firm. Sure, I accepted. But not to please you. I had my own ideas. And they might have worked out—but *she* had to come along and mess everything up!"

He glared at Zoe Faine with all the hatred in the world.

"It isn't true that I cheated and killed your father," Landon protested. "He did those things to himself. It was he who made up those lies and broke your mother's heart."

FABER TRIED in vain to get at his uncle.

"But if this is Faber, who was ground up in the meat grinder?" Griffin cut in again.

"Charlie Mendolsohn," the Purple Scar replied. "If you recall, Mendolsohn was the same size and coloring as Faber. Mendolsohn had the Rainbow of Diamonds worth half a million. Faber needed that to grab up Landon's offer to sell. So Mendolsohn fit a double purpose."

He told about the call stub for a watch that he had found in Faber's apartment.

"Which gave Faber an excuse to visit Mendolsohn's store. I presume Faber brought up the subject of the Rainbow of Diamonds, asked to see them. Mendolsohn, believing he could trust a man with Faber's reputation, showed him the diamonds. Faber then must have killed Mendolsohn, stolen the diamonds, broken up the set and sold them. Individually, the stones could easily have been disposed of."

One other thing Doc pointed out was that he had called the airport and checked on Fetticairn's arrival. Fetticairn got off the plane at Akelton City, all right. But he had boarded it just outside Washington, D. C.

It was learned later how Faber managed those cablegrams from South America. He simply got in touch with one of his stooges there, a contact which Cabral had previously made. This stooge received and answered all cablegrams for "Mr. Luis Fetticairn." All this had given Faber a chance to hole-up near Baltimore while his new face was healing.

Griffin got on the phone and called for the wagon to take Faber in. As he dropped the receiver into its cradle, he turned swiftly and then looked straight into the Scar's purplish face.

"That detail you had me send over to Red Point just called in," he announced. "You hit the nail right on the noggin. They found a man in one of the shacks all right. He was being held prisoner by a couple of itchy trigger gents. The boys are bringing him to HQ. Guess who he is."

"Carl Coyne," the Purple Scar answered, and went on to explain how Walter Faber had taken advantage of those two flareups he had had with Carl Coyne. "He grabbed the plant manager and handed him over to a couple of his hirelings to hide out until after this deal was sealed, signed and in the bag. Then Carl Coyne would probably become Number Seven on the murder charge. Another convenient 'suicide.' He wouldn't even have risked handing Coyne over to the F.B.I.—as we shall do, which I will explain later—because he would have feared all that Coyne probably has guessed by now."

Roger Landon, impressed by the Scar's seemingly unlimited information, asked:

"Perhaps you can explain the shortages, too?"

The Scar obliged. He told of the secret tunnel, and of the *Gray Gull* which took the stolen footstuffs to the ship at sea, from which they probably were put aboard a submarine.

"And who was behind all this?" Landon queried. "My nephew?"

"No," the Scar said. "Carl Coyne. He's been peeved at you for a long time. Thought he got a dirty deal when you appointed your nephew superintendent over his head and made him take orders. So he decided to take matters into his own hands and lay aside a little nest egg, at the same time he was serving his *own* country. You may not know it, but Coyne is a naturalized American—born in Germany, and is now one of the most active Nazi Fifth Columnists in this country. You will not even have a chance to press your charge of robbery against him, Mr. Landon—for the F.B.I. will take him in charge as soon as he reaches Police Headquarters."

"The dog!" snapped Landon. "Biting the hand that fed him—and I don't mean myself, but this country where he has prospered."

BUT IT was plain that Roger Landon was hurt at the thought that Carl Coyne should have turned out like this, after the years he had trusted him.

"Just one thing more, Scar," Griffin put in. "You said you knew right away that Faber had had a plastic surgery job done on his face and that you knew exactly what doctor had done it. How?"

Doc nodded. "Fetticairn, or Walter Faber, had a network of tiny crisscross marks on the sides of his neck. Marks where stitches had been recently removed. That was Hanlyson's individual way of finishing off an operation. All successful plastic surgeons do the same, sort of like a signature or a trade-mark. No two are alike. I've had occasion to witness several specimens of Hanlyson's work, so I knew inmediately who had done the job."

A couple of bluecoats came in and took Faber out, still voicing protests and denials.

Landon went around behind the desk and sat down wearily. Zoe Faine stepped beside him and laid a comforting hand on his shoulder. Looking at her, the Scar was thinking of Dale Jordan. Soon he would be going back to Dale, and they could be happy together—until duty and danger called again. As they would.

"What about the firm, Mr. Landon?" asked Lawyer Nottage.

Landon looked up at the lawyer.

"I'm not going to sell," he said firmly.

The girl's hand tightened on his shoulder encouragingly, as if to say that she would be right there with him all the way. "I'm going to try to bring this business back where it used to be, and there is still much I can do for my country."

"Good," said the Purple Scar. "That, you'll find, will be the kind of advertising of superior products that can make a good product sell even better."

Landon smiled and offered his hand. "I thank both of you, you and Captain Griffin. I suppose that sounds rather hollow after all you've done. But I mean it sincerely—and will never forget it."

"You can say that again for me," Zoe Faine said sincerely.

The Purple Scar turned and with his friend, the square detective, started toward the door. "Finish" had been written to another case. But Doc Murdock knew that the end of one case simply meant that soon would begin a new and even more exciting adventure. For so long as crime cast its menacing shadow over law-abiding citizens, so long would the Purple Scar be fighting to blot it out!